RAVE REVIEWS FOR
SEVEN BRIDES:

LOVE TAP

Iris hit Monty in the stomach as hard as she could.

"What did you mean by that?" he grunted in astonishment.

"I don't want you making love to me when it makes you so miserable." Iris jerked the bedroll from her shoulders and struggled to her feet. "My father said you should always put a dumb animal out of its misery."

Monty jumped to his feet. Iris tried to run, but her treacherous legs collapsed under her.

"Monty Randolph, don't you lay a finger on me." Iris dragged herself into a sitting position as he towered over her. "Not after you had the gall to say you didn't like kissing me and hoped you'd soon recover from the desire." She couldn't tell whether he was madder at her or himself.

"I didn't—"

"If I knew how to use that gun of yours, I'd shoot you with it."

The *Seven Brides* series by Leigh Greenwood:
FERN
ROSE

SEVEN BRIDES

IRIS

LEIGH GREENWOOD

LEISURE BOOKS NEW YORK CITY

A LEISURE BOOK®

Published by

Dorchester Publishing Co., Inc.
276 Fifth Avenue
New York, NY 10001

SEVEN BRIDES

Iris

Chapter One

South Texas
  Spring of 1875

He's coming.

Iris Richmond smoothed a wrinkle in her dark blue wool skirt with a nervous hand and pulled the matching jacket more closely around her neck. The chill of the March afternoon caused her to shiver, but she never once considered wrapping herself in the heavy cloak she had left folded on the buckboard seat. Her mother had always said when it came to talking a man into doing anything he didn't want to do, a woman's looks were half the argument. Covering herself up would be like going into a gunfight without a gun.

Iris needed all her weapons today. Never had a decision been so important to her as the one Monty Randolph would make in the next few minutes.

She shifted her seat on the bench next to the corral, decided her first position was better, and shifted back again. She was glad the pecan trees that surrounded the bench hadn't started to bud. Only the heat from the midday sun kept her teeth from chattering.

From where she sat, Iris had an unobstructed view of the nearly 100,000 semiarid acres of brush and grass that formed the heart of the Randolph empire. After four years in St. Louis, it seemed an alien land. Despite the inviting coolness of the creek in summertime as it meandered through Randolph country, its banks lined by towering oaks and pecans, or the comfort of the large house on the hill, it was a harsh land. She wondered why she had cried when she was sent to school. What could she have found to miss in the dust, heat, and thorns that ruined her clothes and made her so uncomfortable?

A brisk wind swept up from the south bringing the scent of cattle and whipping Iris's long, thick red hair about her face. She ran her fingers through it, but the wind kept it in a tangle. She wished she had thought to bring a mirror and a brush.

Stop fidgeting. You're acting like he's a perfect stranger instead of someone you've known half your life.

But she didn't know him, not anymore.

Monty Randolph had been the big, handsome, softhearted cowboy she had fallen in love with at thirteen. He had endured her gushing adoration, her turning up night or day wherever he was, even dancing with her at a party in Austin. He had fussed, shouted, cajoled, even cursed, but he also made sure nothing ever happened to her.

10

But last month she had come home for the first time since going to boarding school to find Monty completely changed. He had taken one look at her, turned pale, and left the room without even a civil response to her smiling greeting. And he hadn't let her get near him since.

She had outgrown her childhood crush, but the shock of his rejection cut more deeply than she would have imagined. Not even Rose could tell her what had caused the change in him.

That's not important as long as he agrees to help you.

Iris didn't know how to beg, the mere thought was abhorrent to her, but she had to do everything she could to convince Monty to help her. It was the only way she could avoid complete ruin. Her mind cast itself back to that grim January morning when she visited the lawyer's office in New Orleans. A shiver that had nothing to do with the March wind caused her teeth to chatter. She had been in shock over her parents' death, but she could remember every word he said.

"The situation is not as hopeful as I had expected."

"How do you mean?" Iris had asked. Her parents had been killed in a steamboat accident while on their way to visit her in St. Louis. The law firm of Finch, Finch & Warburton had been named executors of the estate.

"There were a great number of debts to be settled. Your mother. . . ." His voice trailed off.

"My mother was very extravagant," Iris said for him.

"Unfortunately, she was a good deal more extravagant than your father could afford."

"I don't understand." Her parents had never given her any indication that money wasn't as plentiful as ever.

"A year ago your father borrowed a large sum against the ranch. Unfortunately, he never made any of the payments on the loan. Your mother's jewelry collection, which judging from this inventory would have been extensive enough to pay off the debt, was lost in the accident." His expression turned grave.

"I still own the ranch, don't I?" Iris asked. She felt a hard knot in her stomach. She knew it was nerves, but it wouldn't go away. Instead it seemed to grow with each agonizing minute.

"Unless you can make up the back payments within four months, the bank will repossess the ranch. I don't know if the contents of your home are still intact, but I have reports that your herd is being ravaged by rustlers. I suggest you go home and do what you can to secure your inheritance while there's still something to salvage."

Any intention Iris might have had of turning to her city friends had died unborn. It was as though an announcement of her situation had appeared in the *St. Louis Post Dispatch* with the morning coffee. By evening Iris had become persona non grata in at least ten places where she had been welcome the day before. Swearing she would return to St. Louis as their equal or not at all, Iris shook the dust of that city off her feet.

But the dust of Texas had proven even less hospitable. The contents of the house were safe, but the banker proved obdurate. No words would move him. Either she found the money on time or she would lose the ranch.

All the while rustlers continued to eat away at her herd.

Iris grew desperate. Her entire future depended on that herd. If she sold it, the money would soon be gone and she'd be penniless. If she didn't do something soon, rustlers would take every last cow, and she'd be penniless anyway. And even if she managed to keep the herd, in a month she wouldn't have a ranch to put them on.

In her desperation she thought of Monty.

Now he was coming to meet her, but just by looking at the way he rode so stiffly in the saddle, the fixed expression on his face, the way he slowed his horse to a deliberate walk, she could tell she would have only one chance to convince him to help her.

She also could tell he meant to say no.

She was waiting for him.

Monty Randolph pulled back so hard on Nightmare's mouth the gelding squealed in protest. But in the act of turning away, he changed his mind. This was the third time Iris had attempted to waylay him. If she was anything like her mother, she would only become more determined. He might as well find out what she wanted, tell her no, and get rid of her.

Look at her, wearing a dress that'd be torn to shreds if she walked so much as 50 yards through the brush! Doesn't she know she's back in Texas?

Iris had tied her horse to the hitching post and was resting on a bench George had had built in a grove of young pecan trees transplanted from the creek. At 19 she was an enchanting sight, one guaranteed to make any man's heart beat a little faster. She was beautiful, perfect, with just enough fullness to her lips and roundness to her cheeks to add a definite touch of sensuality.

Her hair would stop people in their tracks and cause them to stare. There couldn't be another woman in the state of Texas with hair of such an overpowering red. The sunlight bouncing off it was enough to cause a stampede. Equally arresting, her eyes were a deep shade of green. There was nothing immodest about the dress she wore, but it clung to her body in a manner that would have caused the matrons of Austin to click their tongues.

Monty vowed to show her nothing but indifference, but his body, his pounding blood belied his intentions. At the sight of her full breasts pushing against the cloth of her bodice, he could feel a heavy, tight sensation beginning low in his groin. His hands ached to reach out and touch their firm softness. Willing his body not to betray the tension that stretched his nerves until they ached, Monty slowed his horse to a walk. He might have to talk to Iris, but he'd be damned if he'd be in a rush to do it.

He was tempted to close his eyes so he wouldn't have to look at her, but that wouldn't have done any good. Her image might as well have been imprinted on the inside of his eyelids. She had grown up to be the spitting image of her mother. And no man, once he had set eyes on Helena Richmond, could forget even the smallest detail of her appearance.

If only Iris still looked like the fresh-faced little girl with the billowing red hair who had followed him all over Guadalupe County. She had been a real nuisance, but she had had an endearing quality about her then. No matter how much her adoration irritated him, he could never stay angry with her. He'd even missed her a little bit when her parents had sent her off to school.

He could still remember the slightly gawky 13 year old in a new riding outfit astride that ridiculous saddle horse her mother had bought her. She was a natural charmer, the kind of cute little girl any man would take a shine to.

But the woman who approached him at the dance last month had nothing in common with that gamin. She was a seductress, and the mere sight of her walking across the room had heated Monty's blood to a boil. He had chosen to escape rather than admit his confusion. He still hadn't sorted out his feelings, and seeing Iris now made him feel as if he was putting his head into a noose.

As he rode toward Iris, he comforted himself with the thought that after today he would never be forced to see her again. He was going to Wyoming, and he didn't plan to come back.

"Afternoon, Monty," Iris said with her most brilliant smile.

A smile that could wreak more havoc among cowhands than anything this side of the Rio Grande. And that included rustlers, bandits, and fighting-mad mossy backs. All she would have to do was flash her deep green eyes or flutter her thick, black eyelashes and there'd be a line of fools as long as from here to the Pecos begging to do something stupid like ride all the way to New Orleans just to buy her a garter belt.

Not that she had done anything as disgraceful as display her legs, but Monty wouldn't put anything past a daughter of Helena Richmond. There wasn't much Helena hadn't done at one time or another.

Of course Monty wouldn't be in that line. At 26 he was too young to get tangled up with some female. When he got as old as George, maybe he'd look about for a wife. Then again, maybe not. Rose was a fine woman, a perfect wife if a fella was in the market for such a thing, but Monty wasn't interested in getting married.

He dismounted. Keeping Nightmare between him and Iris, he tied him to the hitching rail. "What are you doing over this way?" he said. "You get lost on your way to a party?"

She was Helena all over again, wiggling about in that dress as if she had ants in her chemise.

"I've been waiting here for the longest time," Iris said, looking up at him from under half-lowered lashes. "Rose said you were due any minute, but I thought you'd never get back."

"Well, I'm here now. What do you want?"

"You don't have to be in such a rush. Dinner won't be ready for another hour."

"I have work to do," Monty said as he loosened the cinch on Nightmare. "Just because you've got nothing to do all day but get dressed up and ride over here to plague me doesn't mean I'm not busy."

Iris sat bolt upright, her eyes bright with indignation. "Monty Randolph, how dare you say I'm plaguing you, especially after you kept me waiting."

Iris would see it that way. That was Helena all over.

"You've been plaguing me since you were thirteen. And you're going to keep on plaguing me until you tell me what you want. So come on, get it over with."

He looked at her across Nightmare's back. She seemed to be trying to decide what approach to take with him. She ought to know by now she'd have a better chance if she just came right out and said it. But then Helena hadn't taught Iris to be straightforward. She hadn't known how herself.

Iris stood up and moved toward Monty, her body swaying seductively as she walked. "Rose tells me you're taking a herd to Wyoming," she said, being more direct than Monty expected.

"I'm thinking about it." He'd made up his mind to leave the beginning of April, but no sense telling Iris that.

Iris circled Nightmare. "I hear there's a lot of land up there just for the taking."

"The best grazing land I've ever seen," Monty said, unable to remain unenthusiastic about his favorite subject. "There's grass as high as your waist as far as you can see, and more water than Texas ever thought about."

"And Indians?"

"They're well north of Laramie and Cheyenne. I don't plan to worry about them—if I go, that is," Monty hedged, still unwilling to commit himself until he knew what Iris wanted. "Hen and I fought Indians where your father bought his ranch. Beat them, too."

Iris was too close. Monty lifted the saddle from his mount and hoisted it over the corral fence.

"If there's all that land, why hasn't somebody taken it?"

"They will. The minute the government runs the Indians out there'll be a stampede like you've never seen."

"So if a person wanted to get plenty of good grazing land, he ought to go now."

"Yeah. He ought to put a herd together and get up there as fast as he can. Jeff says the army is going after the Indians anytime now. They won't last a year."

He moved past her to place the saddle blanket on the fence. He smoothed out the wrinkles.

"It must be a long and expensive trip."

"About four months and four thousand dollars."

Monty couldn't figure out what Iris wanted. The greenest kid on her crew could have told her everything he had. "Anything else you want to know?" Monty asked as he lowered the bars and hazed Nightmare into the corral. "I got work to do." He slipped the bridle over the horse's ears, and the animal cantered away, kicking up its heels.

"When are you leaving?" Iris asked, following him, her eyelashes fluttering like pillowcases in a March wind. She wanted something, and she was just about to ask for it.

"I didn't say I was leaving."

Her eyelashes stopped dead. "I know you are. Your eyes light up like stars on a summer night when you talk about the grass there. You're the only man I know who can get more excited about a cow than about a woman."

Once again Iris was so close he felt hot under the collar. He didn't want to feel any sympathy for her problems, but she was a damned fine-looking woman. He couldn't remain unaffected. But how did he treat a woman who looked hot enough to melt an icicle in January when he could still remember her in pigtails?

Danged if he knew, except to run like hell before he did something he'd regret.

"I know what to expect from cows," Monty said as he lifted his saddle from the rail. "You can never tell about a woman. Half the time they tell you one thing and mean something entirely different."

"Well, I'll tell you what I mean, and I mean exactly what I say," Iris snapped, her eyes flashing, her skin colored by pique. There was nothing silly or coquettish about her now.

"I don't want to know what you—"

"I'm going to Wyoming, and I want you to take me."

Monty couldn't have been more shocked if she'd said she wanted to marry him and had the preacher waiting inside the house. He dropped the saddle on his foot.

"Dammit to hell, Iris," he cursed as he kicked his saddle in frustration. "You can't go to Wyoming."

"Why not?"

"You've got nobody to take care of you."

"I'd have you to take care of me while I was getting there. I'd take care of myself after that."

"No, you wouldn't," Monty declared. "You might think Texas is full of rustlers and bad men, but that's nothing compared to Wyoming."

"I can't stay here."

"Why?"

Iris hesitated, then averted her eyes. "I can't tell you why. I just can't."

George was right. Something was bad wrong at the Double-D. Iris wasn't acting a thing like her mother now. She was young enough and genuine enough that fear had caused her to forget her teasing ways. Monty felt some of the rigidity leave his body. Maybe Helena's lessons hadn't gone too deep. She was almost like the young girl he used to know—open, guileless, able to slip past his defenses no matter how hard he tried to prevent it.

"If you're short of money, you could sell some steers."

Her gaze met his as pride stiffened every part of her body. "Daddy sold everything he could round up last year. All I have left is breeding stock. If I sell that, I won't have anything at all."

He knew that. Everybody in Guadalupe County did. But she was hiding the real reason. "Maybe you should sell your ranch and head back to St. Louis."

"Never!" Iris flashed her magnificent eyes and moved closer until their bodies were almost touching. "Why won't you take me?" she pleaded.

Just like Helena, Monty thought. If you didn't do what she wanted, she'd wrap you in her spell until you were so crazy you didn't know what you were saying. It took all his willpower, but Monty held his ground. He wasn't going to be used by Iris or any other woman.

"Because I've got too much to do to be playing nursemaid to a female over two thousand miles of wild country. Besides, I can't take two herds. It's too risky. I don't have the horses or men. And after such a long dry spell, there won't be enough grass or water for a herd that size."

"I mean to go to Wyoming."

"Then hire yourself a drover. There are plenty who know the trail."

"I want you."

"Well you can't have me," Monty declared, bending over to pick up his saddle. "I'm going to Wyoming for the family, not anybody else."

"I've already got land. Daddy filed two homesteads on Bear Creek last year."

"Good, but I'm still not taking you. There's no use flattering me or crying and looking hurt or any of those other tricks your mother used on any man who came within range. They won't work."

"Why? Don't you like women?"

Monty flushed. If she knew just how much he did like women! They were an appetite with him, one he appeased as readily and as often as he could. He had a lusty, uncomplicated appreciation of their company and the pleasure to be found in their arms.

But he couldn't do that with Iris. For God's sake, he could remember her as a madcap 12 year old, racing her pony across the countryside without regard for life or limb.

But there was nothing of the child about Iris now. She had the body of a woman, the poise and assurance of a femme fatale who knew she was desired by every man she met. Her effect on him was roughly equivalent to a tree falling on a grizzly's head or the force of a flash flood rushing down a mountain canyon. He felt a nearly overwhelming desire to whisk her off to some secluded spot and not emerge again for at least three days.

Monty's body was tight and full, but he never once considered touching Iris. He mastered his impulses with difficulty.

"I like women just fine, but not on a cattle drive."

"Well, I'm going to Wyoming, Monty Randolph, and you can't stop me."

"I don't mean to try."

Iris looked baffled. Monty figured she couldn't believe he had really refused to take her to Wyoming. He guessed she hadn't been told "no" more than a half-dozen times in her whole life. And probably five of those didn't count.

"This is the most important thing I've ever asked you to do. I've got to go."

21

"Why?" There had to be some reason besides rustlers. If that were all, she'd be over playing her tricks on Hen. "Tell me the truth. All of it."

"I might as well. Everybody will know sooner or later," Iris said. The bitterness in her voice and expression banished all traces of the coquette. "The bank is taking the ranch. In less than two months I won't have anywhere to live."

Chapter Two

Monty hadn't known that, but it didn't surprise him. Everybody knew Helena Richmond spent enough money for three people.

"You can stay with us until you figure something out," Monty offered. "We've got plenty of room."

"I don't want charity, Monty. I don't want your pity either. I just want you to help me get to Wyoming."

Monty's resistance melted. All her life Iris had been the spoiled darling of a foolish father and a selfish mother. He doubted she'd ever stopped to think about where the money came from to support the things she took for granted. Now she was on her own with no one to guide her. He couldn't ignore her when it would be so easy to fix her up with a trustworthy drover.

"Hen and I must know at least a dozen experienced men who'd be glad to head up your drive,"

Monty said. "Give me a couple of weeks, and I promise I'll find you somebody real dependable."

"I'm not putting my herd in the hands of a stranger. It's all I've got in the world. If anything happened to it, I'd be as poor as any cowhand you ever saw."

Monty could understood Iris's feeling desperate. He felt the same way. For different reasons, of course, but that didn't make it any less the same. He'd find her a drover, even if he had to pay the man himself.

"You won't have to depend on a stranger. I'll find you somebody who will work with your own men. You won't even know he's there."

"I want you to take me."

"I've already told you I can't."

"You said you wouldn't," Iris corrected. "You never did say why."

"Yes, I did. You just weren't listening."

Helena all over again. She could never believe she wasn't going to get what she wanted. Well, he wasn't going to tell Iris the rest of his reasons. They were personal, nobody's business but his own.

"My offer to find a drover still stands. Now let me help you into your buckboard. If you don't get home soon, your dinner will be spoiled."

"I can help myself," Iris snapped, twitching her skirt to one side so she could see to place her foot on the narrow metal steps.

The sight of her slim, booted foot nearly caused Monty to forget that if he meant to say no to Iris on one thing, he couldn't very well say yes to another.

"You can unhitch my horse," Iris said as she settled herself in the seat. She took up the reins from him. "And know this, Monty Randolph. I mean to go to Wyoming, and you're going to take me."

With that she backed her horse away from the hitching post, turned it toward the trail, and cracked the whip over its head. It trotted away at a brisk pace, Iris's back stiff with defiance.

Monty stared after her, feeling the mask of indifference slide from his face. So many emotions clamored for primacy. Relief he had survived the interview without letting Iris guess that anything more lay behind his refusal than a dislike of women on the trail and the practical considerations of handling a herd of over 6,000 cows. He couldn't let her see his concern she was gambling at too long odds by moving her ranch to Wyoming. Regret she had outgrown the charming child she used to be only to turn into a duplicate of her mother. Disgust that he wanted her anyway.

Pushing aside a feeling of frustration, Monty headed toward the house George had built for Rose after the McClendons burned their dogtrot. The big house sat on a rise up from the creek, its two stories nearly as tall as the towering pecans that lined the streambed. A huge kitchen, an even larger dining room, three sitting rooms, and several storerooms occupied the lower level. Eight bedrooms filled the upper floor. Rose had told George she didn't mind everybody living in the same house, but she wanted enough room so she could be by herself once in a while.

Monty found Hen sitting on the porch.

"What did Iris want?" Hen asked without bothering to get up.

"Wanted me to take her to Wyoming."

"What'd you tell her?"

"I told her no," Monty answered, surprised Hen even had to ask. "I don't want to baby-sit a female on

25

a trip like that. I mean to get this herd to Wyoming without losing a single head. I'm going to set up a ranching operation even George will envy."

"George is still in your craw, isn't he?"

"You're damned right he is."

"He doesn't mean to be."

"Well, he is. I haven't done one thing since he came home from the war that he hasn't had something to say about. He's always got some suggestion, some idea how to do it just a little better."

"He's usually right."

"Maybe, but I'd think of it myself if I didn't have to worry about him looking over my shoulder all the time. It near 'bout drives me crazy."

"It doesn't bother me."

"Nothing bothers you," Monty said, nettled. "I know we're supposed to be identical, but sometimes I don't understand you at all."

Hen shrugged.

Monty stared out over the greening countryside. It was hard to imagine that he would soon be grazing cows on land barren of the familiar cactus, mesquite, and thorn-filled vines. He had become so accustomed to the harsh country of south Texas he could barely remember the rolling, lush green Virginia hills of his birth. But he remembered the wide open spaces of Wyoming. They spoke to him of freedom, of a future he could shape to fit his own dreams.

"I want my own place where I can be my own boss and make my own decisions," Monty told Hen.

"George is agreeable," his brother replied, as imperturbable as ever. "Now what are you going to do about Iris? She doesn't seem like the kind of woman to give up on something she wants."

"She's not. I told her I'd find her a drover, but I've got a feeling she won't accept one."

"What do you think she'll do?"

"I don't know, but whatever it is, I'm sure I'm not going to like it."

Iris allowed her horse its head. She had more important things to do than guide it along a route it already knew. She had to figure out some way to make Monty Randolph change his mind.

She had used nearly every trick her mother had taught her, and nothing had worked. Monty was attracted to her—she couldn't miss the signs—but he was immune to her blandishments. As she cast her mind backward, she remembered he had always been the one man she couldn't twist around her little finger.

She felt like crying from frustration, but she hadn't cried when that heartless lawyer told her she was practically a pauper. She hadn't cried when she discovered that her position in St. Louis society, along with her friends, had vanished with her fortune. She hadn't cried when that wretched little banker had positively gloated over getting his hands on her ranch. She wasn't about to turn into a blubbering idiot now that she needed all her wits to stave off disaster.

She had to find a way to convince Monty to take her to Wyoming. She had no other choice. She would die before she went back to St. Louis, desperately hoping some man would marry her. She might be a spoiled beauty, but she had few illusions. She knew the list of suitable husbands would shrink dramatically once they discovered she was no longer an heiress.

27

Besides, she wasn't ready to get married. She'd never cared two figs for any man except Monty. And while that had been no more than a young girl's infatuation with a handsome cowboy, no one had yet come along to oust him from her dreams.

At least, not for long.

For a moment she considered accepting his offer to find her a drover but decided against it. She had too much at stake. For 2,000 miles through wild, untamed territory, she would be entrusting everything she had in the world to a stranger. And that included herself.

Helena had warned Iris of what could happen to a woman without protection. She had lived on a ranch long enough to know why women never traveled on trail drives. Under the circumstances, she didn't trust anybody but Monty to protect her and not take advantage of her.

Besides, she liked Monty. He used to complain about her following on his heels all the time, but he included her in pranks that would have caused her mother to lock her in her room had she known. He had treated her like a little sister—a fact that never failed to annoy her, even now—but he had been fun to be with.

But his whole attitude toward her had changed. It was almost as though he was angry at her. And it wasn't because she had asked him to take her to Wyoming. He had looked like a thundercloud the minute he clapped eyes on her at that party. Iris had no idea what had caused this change, but she intended to find out.

In the meantime, she had to get to Wyoming. And she had just this minute figured out how she was going to do it. She slowed the buckboard as she drove into her yard.

"Find Frank and tell him I want to see him," she said to the man who ran out to hold her horse's head.

"He just went inside looking for you."

"There you are," the big foreman said to Iris when he emerged from a house newer and larger than the Randolphs'. "I was wondering where you could have gotten to."

"Tell the crew I want them ready to ride out at dawn tomorrow," Iris said, as she climbed down without waiting for the help her foreman didn't offer.

"What's up?" Frank's alert, gray eyes seemed to narrow.

"We're going on a roundup. We're moving to Wyoming."

The chill of the early April morning caused Rose Randolph to pull the shawl more tightly around her shoulders as she waited in the buggy. Her sister-in-law, Fern, sat next to her, complacently gazing out over the limitless expanse of grass and brush.

The last week's warm weather had turned the prairie into a paradise of wildflowers. Whole meadows had turned blue with thousands upon thousands of bluebonnets. They seemed to stretch as far as she could see. An unseen hand had sprinkled white poppies, red Indian paintbrush, and phlox across the hillsides like floral confetti. Rose's four-year-old twins, anxious not to miss a single bit of the excitement, occupied their time picking a bouquet of gaily colored Mexican hats. The bright sun promised a warm day, a good day to begin a cattle drive.

For weeks, as the men worked their way through the early spring roundup, they had cut out cattle and held them on this grassy prairie between two branches of the creek about a mile from the house. Another crew had captured and broken horses until 2,500 longhorns and more than 100 horses were ready to leave for Wyoming. A thin cloud of dust rose from beneath 10,000 restless feet.

Everything waited for the signal to begin.

"Don't go far from the buggy," Rose Randolph spoke firmly to her daughters. "You could get trampled out there."

"But you let William Henry go," complained Aurelia, who wanted nothing more than to follow her eight-year-old brother into the melee of horses and men.

"Your father let him go," Rose corrected. She tried to ignore the fear that clutched at her throat whenever she saw William Henry astride his cutting pony in the middle of a herd of temperamental longhorns. George was determined he should be brought up like every other boy born on a ranch. Rose agreed in principle, but she knew only too well how dangerous longhorns could be.

"Let them go," Fern whispered in Rose's ear. "There's not a man out there who wouldn't break his neck to make sure nothing happened to them."

Rose looked at Fern. Married less than four years Fern joked that she had come for a long visit so she wouldn't be expecting a third son before Christmas. Rose tried not to feel jealous that she hadn't been able to have a child since the twins.

"I'll let you go when they're ready to leave," Rose relented, speaking to her daughters, "but if I do, you're not to go near those cows."

"They won't be in any more danger than Madison would be," Fern said with an indulgent laugh. "He hasn't been near a cow in ten years, but if he were here, he'd be roistering about with the rest of them, just like he knew what he was doing."

"If it comes to knowing cattle, *you* ought to be out there."

Fern laughed contentedly. "You won't find me chasing cows again. I miss my vest and pants, but wearing a dress is a small price to pay for so much happiness."

Rose marveled at the change in Fern. For a woman who had been afraid of having babies and leaving Kansas, she had become acclimated to Chicago and her role as wife and mother with surprising swiftness. Her two little boys were taking a nap—they were too small to be around the herd—but already three-year-old Madison Jr. had his own pony. Madison had built a house on Lake Michigan with enough land around it to have their own herd if they wanted.

"It'll be awfully quiet around here with everybody gone," Fern said. "Will you miss them?"

"Yes," Rose answered, her gaze searching out the two youngest Randolphs. "But it'll be nice to have George to myself."

Rose watched as Tyler fussed with his chuck wagon, making last-minute adjustments in the pile of 15 bedrolls, going over his list to make sure all the supplies he had ordered were in their proper places, checking to see that the water barrel and toolbox were securely fastened. She could remember when Monty would rather starve than eat Tyler's cooking. Now at 22, and nearly as gaunt as he had been at 13, he had been accepted as the trail cook with no more than halfhearted opposition.

Sixteen-year-old Zac hovered near the corral, ready to throw back the bars and release the ramuda the moment Monty gave the signal. Four years of boarding school had polished his manners and improved his grammar, but Rose knew the old Zac still lurked just beneath the surface.

Monty, clearly anxious to be off, stood with George waiting for Salty to start the herd across the creek. George, unaware of Rose's adoring gaze, was giving Monty some last-minute instructions. The bawling cattle made such a din she had to strain to hear what they were saying.

"If you need any money, don't hesitate to contact Jeff," George said.

"I won't need to contact anybody."

"And if you have any questions—"

"I won't. You've already given me enough instructions for three trail herds."

Rose could tell Monty was having trouble keeping his temper in check.

"It's not like I've never been to Wyoming before," Monty said. He gave up on an unsuccessful attempt to smile.

"I just want to make certain—"

"You have, George, over and over again. What you haven't told me, you've told Hen and Salty."

"Do you think they'll ever be able to live together without getting on each other's nerves?" Fern asked Rose.

"No," Rose said. "They're too much alike. I'll miss Monty—sometimes he can be the most difficult brother of all though he's really terribly sweet—but it's time for him to go out on his own. He probably should have done it two or three years ago."

"Why didn't he?"

"George didn't think he was ready."

"The Mexican affair?"

"That was part of it. Monty's good with cows and the men, but he's too impetuous. He never thinks."

"Hen will be with him."

"That's no help. Hen *does* think, and he does even worse things."

"George will always worry about his brothers," Fern said as she gave her sister-in-law's hand a squeeze. "I'm surprised he hasn't come to Chicago to check on Madison and me."

"He probably would if it weren't so far away," Rose said. They both laughed. "I keep telling him they're all grown men, even Zac, but he still thinks of them as helpless children he has to protect from their awful father."

"Madison won't even mention his father's name," Fern said. "I don't think he even thinks about him anymore."

"I wish George could forget him. It would make it easier on the boys." She looked to where her husband stood with Monty. "They've been talking too long. If they don't leave soon, there'll be trouble."

"Just wire me when you arrive." George glanced at his two youngest brothers. "Let me know when they head for Denver."

"Don't worry," Monty said. "I'll take good care of them."

"I'm sure you will, but it's the first time Zac has been away this long, and Rose is worried that—"

"I still think you ought to let William Henry come." Monty didn't mean it, but he knew it would make George forget any worries he had about Zac.

George's eyes twinkled. "You know if he went, Rose would go, too."

Monty pulled a face. "I'd move to Chicago with Madison before I'd go on a drive with a woman."

Just then the sound of galloping hooves heralded Salty's arrival. "The lead steer has just crossed the creek. It's time to move out."

The noise became deafening. Tyler climbed into the seat of the chuck wagon and cracked the whip over the head of the four sturdy oxen. The wagon started forward with a lurch that set the Dutch ovens clanging like dissonant bells.

Making a mad dash to the buggy to give Rose a hug, Zac nearly stumbled over Juliette and Aurelia, who had at last been released from their confinement. They raced to give Monty and Hen hugs before finding safe purchase in their father's arms.

"Try not to fight with Monty so much," Rose whispered in Zac's ear as she leaned out of the buggy to return his hug. It was hard to believe this young giant was the dirty-faced gamin she had first seen peeping into the kitchen nine years ago.

"I will if he doesn't shout at me," Zac replied and raced away.

"A lost hope," Rose sighed as she turned to Fern. "Monty would shout at God."

"Is there enough water ahead?" Monty asked when Hen rode into camp.

"Yeah," Hen replied, "but the grass is looking thin."

The afternoon sun had sunk behind low hills, turning the air the blue-green color of the distant oak trees. The day's warmth still lingered, but the temperature would drop quickly now the sun had gone down. Dust from thousands of hooves hung in the air so thick you could see and taste it.

The incessant bawling and clicking horns formed a backdrop to any conversation.

Tyler had backed the chuck wagon up to the campfire and thrown open the back to reveal a network of storage chambers. He moved between two Dutch ovens and two fires as he prepared supper for the crew. The smell of coffee, bacon, and hot bread cooking over mesquite fires tantalized Monty's appetite.

"Just as long as there's enough water and grass for us," Monty said. He didn't mean to sound callous, but any drovers following behind him would have to worry for themselves. Besides, he was worried already. Things were going too well.

For ten days everything had gone like clockwork. The herd had taken to the trail without hesitation and had bedded down every night without a single stampede. The hands knew their jobs without his telling them what to do, and the herds that had already passed up the trail hadn't used up all the grass.

Moreover, Tyler hadn't turned sullen, the food had been good and plentiful, Zac hadn't argued with him, and the horses were ready every morning.

"This is almost boring," Monty complained. "Either all hell is going to break loose any minute, or we're going to reach Wyoming after a trip Zac could ramrod."

Hen unsaddled his horse and ran it into the rope corral Zac had set up between some trees and the wheel of the chuck wagon. Hen poured himself a cup of coffee from the pot Tyler kept on the fire.

"I don't think you're going to be all that bored," he said, looking at his brother over the rim of his cup. "In fact, I predict things are going to be right lively sooner than you think."

"What are you up to?" Monty asked. He and his twin had always been close, but he never could tell what Hen was thinking. It was as though Mother Nature had created two entirely different people and made them look exactly alike just for the fun of it.

"I'm not up to anything."

Monty didn't trust Hen. He rarely laughed. When Hen's eyes crinkled with amusement, you'd better watch out. "The last time I saw you look like that, you'd just killed two McClendons and stolen their milk cow. You're up to something. I just know it."

"I'm not up to a thing. Zac!" Hen called to his youngest brother as he rounded the corner of the chuck wagon with an armload of wood. "Saddle a horse for Monty. Make it Nightmare. He's going to want to travel fast."

"I'll do no such thing," Zac said. "If George ever found out I saddled that horse for Monty to ride like a cutting horse, he'd blow his stack."

"I'll ride any damned horse I please, no matter what George says," Monty snapped at Zac, "but I'm not riding Nightmare at a gallop over any prairie." He turned back to Hen. "You must think I'm crazy."

"Naw. I just thought you'd be in a hurry once you learned there was a herd on the trail in front of us."

"I know that. I've been seeing their tracks for two days."

"But you don't know who it belongs to."

"It doesn't matter."

"Not even if it belongs to Iris Richmond, and she's riding with it?"

Monty rose to his feet with a roar that sent half the horses in the ramuda skittering against the ropes.

"Saddle Nightmare!" he shouted at Zac. "I'll strangle that woman, even if I hang for it."

Chapter Three

Iris saw him coming astride his huge, black gelding. Between trees, around thickets, over a carpet of red and yellow flowers, he emerged from a low place in the land where trees grew thicker, where the green was more intense. She could hear the angry squeak of leather, the muffled thud of hooves.

She had been waiting for him. In fact, if she were completely honest with herself, she had been hoping for his arrival. Only the knowledge that Monty would be right behind her had given her the courage to leave home.

Yet she felt a sense of unease settle at the base of her spine. She really didn't want to hear what Monty was going to say. It wouldn't be flattering. Still worse, she had a suspicion she deserved it. Still, she felt a certain degree of satisfaction. She had told him she would go to Wyoming, and he had ignored her. She'd show him.

Iris tamped down her excitement. Her easygoing father had always teased that her red hair and Irish blood gave her a perfect right to her temper, but her temper was nothing compared to Monty's. Even though he was as blond as ash wood and as blue-blooded as old Virginia and South Carolina families could make him, there were almost as many stories about Monty's temper floating around Guadalupe County as there were ranchers willing to slap their brand on a maverick.

She tried to tell herself she didn't really need him—she already had a foreman and a crew—but no man had ever inspired her with the same confidence. He could raise more cain than a wild longhorn bull, and he was probably more dangerous than a lobo wolf, but her father had always said he was the kind of man a girl could depend on.

So Iris settled into a chair under the dappled shade of a cottonwood. A light breeze cooled the blush in her cheeks and caused the leaves overhead to rustle noisily. She considered the more picturesque setting of a fallen log across the sluggish stream but decided it would probably ruin her dress. A year ago she wouldn't have given a moment's thought to such a mundane consideration. But she was a supremely practical creature at heart. Until she got to Wyoming and was able to sell her first crop of steers, she wouldn't have any money to buy new clothes.

In fact, she wasn't sure she had enough money to last that long. That was all the more reason to have Monty hovering reassuringly in the background. Only, from the reckless gallop at which he was riding, he didn't look much like he wanted to hover. It was more likely he would thunder and crash all around her.

* * *

Look at her. Dressed like she's out for a Sunday stroll in some city park. Monty guided his horse around a clump of mesquite. Prickly pear cactus would rip her flowered dress to shreds in minutes, but it was the parasol that caused his anger to boil over. He'd never seen anybody use a parasol out on the Texas prairie, not even Helena. It seemed to sum up the folly of Iris's decision to go on this drive. Yet there she sat like a spider spinning her web.

But webs could be broken, and he was about to show her how. Monty rode Nightmare so close the dirt from under his hooves flew all over Iris's dress.

"What the hell do you mean putting your cows on the trail ahead of mine!" Monty thundered as he threw himself from the saddle. He planted himself in front of Iris as though he were a physical obstacle she must overcome. "I told you to stay home."

"How nice of you to come see how I was getting along," Iris said. Her welcoming smile strained to smother a spurt of irritation as she shook out her dress. "I hope you'll stay for dinner. We're having apple crepes for dessert."

"Crepes!" Monty exclaimed, incredulous. "You're feeding men who've spent sixteen hours in the saddle on apple pancakes?"

"Not just that," Iris said, clearly having a hard time preserving her smile in the face of Monty's rudeness. "I've asked the cook to prepare chicken fricassee, potatoes julienne, and hot rolls."

"You're crazier than an Indian drunk on bad whiskey. I'm surprised they haven't quit. I sure as hell would."

Iris lost her temper. She sat erect, all suggestion of relaxed dalliance gone from her attitude, her inviting smile replaced by an indignant glare. "How dare you speak to me like that!" Her silky voice was rough as new wool. "Just because the men are driving cattle doesn't mean they have to eat like Mexican peasants."

"Men need food that will stick to their ribs, not party food," Monty said scornfully, forgetting the object of his visit in the face of this heresy.

"What's so hard about trailing a herd of cows? I've never been so bored in my life."

"If you'd stop hiding in that fancy wagon of yours, you'd know," Monty said. He recognized the travel wagon Robert Richmond had built for Helena. He was certain Iris traveled ahead with the chuck wagon. There was too much noise, dust, and stench with the herd to suit her.

"I don't *hide* in my wagon," Iris protested. "Frank reports to me every morning and evening. I know everything that goes on."

"You don't know a thing unless you see it with your own eyes."

Without warning, he grabbed Iris's hand and pulled her up from her chair. Caught off balance, she struck him in the face with her parasol, barely missing his eye. Monty touched his fingers to the stinging spot on his cheek. They came away bloody. Hell, the damned thing had broken the skin. Muttering a particularly virulent curse, he wrenched the parasol from Iris's hands and broke it across his knee.

Iris gasped at the red streak her parasol had dug across Monty's cheek. She wanted to apologize, to do something to show how sorry she was, but the violence of his reaction shocked her. She stared dumbfounded at the broken remains of her parasol. No man had ever treated her like that. Just thinking about it made her angry. She cast aside all thoughts of him as a kind and benevolent protector.

He took her by the shoulders and pointed her toward the sunburned plain rather than the cool shade of the creek bottom. "Now maybe you can see," he said. The unrelenting heat had wilted the early spring flowers, leaving only brown seedpods and faded foliage. "Men who ride this land are tough and hard, and they need a boss who's tough and hard."

"You're the one who's crazy," she snapped, pulling away from his grip. "What makes you think you can charge in here telling me what to do, destroying my property, insulting me, trying to—"

"You've no business on this trail. You don't know anything about trailing a herd or handling men. In fact, you don't know anything about cows at all."

"You are the rudest, most insulting, pigheaded man I've ever met," Iris shouted at him. "I have every right to be anywhere I please. I don't have to ask your permission. This is my herd and those men are my crew. I'll thank you to know that under my direction we've had no trouble at all."

"I don't suppose you have, being less than two weeks from home, but you'll find trouble soon enough. There's still time for you to turn back."

"I told you before," Iris said, furious at having to make the humiliating admission once again, "my father lost the ranch. The bank foreclosed today."

"Then let your foreman go on ahead."

"No."

"Then go stay in San Antonio or Austin until next summer. Maybe you can find a husband by then. You surely need somebody to get you under control."

"I have no intention of finding a husband," Iris told him, her green eyes ablaze with fury. "And no one is going to get me under control. I'm not a child, and I won't be treated like one."

"You won't find me trying," Monty said, laughing so heartily Iris wanted to hit him. "I wouldn't mind taking you in hand for a day or two, or a couple of nights," he added with a wink, "but I'm not getting leg shackled."

"I wouldn't marry you if you were the last man on earth," Iris said, determined to ignore Monty's insinuation. "You're nothing but a common cowhand."

But there was nothing common about Monty. He was the most attractive man Iris had ever met. And since she had come back home, just about the most unapproachable.

Monty laughed again. "You'll marry somebody. I don't like to say it—it's liable to make you think more of yourself than you already do—but you're a damned fine-looking woman. Shapely, too. I bet you have men falling over themselves to please you."

She was lovely. That dress might be a silly choice for the plains, but in it her femininity reached out and grabbed him like an eagle grabs its prey. If she had worn it to distract him, she had succeeded. How could he remember he wanted her to turn back when just looking at her made him want to keep on looking at her for a long time? He guessed he hadn't been created capable of ignoring a woman, certainly not one as beautiful as Iris. Even now he longed to reach out and touch her. He could practically feel her in his arms. And that feeling was sure making itself evident in the fit of his pants. If he didn't start thinking about something else he was going to embarrass himself.

"They don't exactly fall over themselves," Iris admitted, modestly, "but men do like to please me."

"I'll bet they do," Monty said, with a chuckle. "You'll snare some poor devil and have him so crazy inside a year he won't know whether to slit his throat or yours."

Iris's tolerant humor vanished. "You are the most obnoxious and rude man in all of Texas."

Monty hadn't meant to make her angry. He was just thinking out loud. Beautiful women always seemed to drive men crazy, maybe just to prove they could.

"I can be anything you like," he said, pulling his thoughts away from the inviting curve of her mouth, "as long as you get those cows out of my way. I'll send some men over to help you get them headed back."

"I'm going to Wyoming," Iris enunciated from between clenched teeth, "and nothing you can do can stop me."

Monty never had much hope Iris would give up the drive. That made him angry, but he couldn't abandon her. Whether he liked to admit it or not, he had a soft spot for her.

He could never see her without remembering the young girl who would go anywhere, dare anything, as long as she was with him. She had jumped a canyon on her cow pony because he'd jumped it on one of his big rawboned geldings. He could still hear her laugh as her pony scrambled frantically to keep from sliding into the 20-foot-deep ravine.

Much to his disgust, for a split second, he actually considered letting her travel with him. She would be safe, and he could stop worrying about her.

But even if her presence didn't upset the crew, it would upset him. It already had. And right now the most important thing in the world was proving to George he had mastered his temper and had learned to think before he acted. So far, being around Iris had caused him to demonstrate just the opposite.

It wouldn't do any good to tell himself to ignore Iris, or to tell her to stay away from him. She didn't take advice any better than he did. He had no choice but to convince her to leave.

Iris didn't trust the look in Monty's eye. She liked it even less when he closed in on her. She was used to anger, even outright rage, but this was pure, predatory hunger. And there was nothing covert or gentlemanly about it. She was used to being in control, but she was no longer in St. Louis or her mother's parlor.

She had positioned her wagon some distance from the campsite so she could have some privacy. Now she was virtually alone in the middle of wild country with a man she couldn't control.

"It's not safe for you to be here and you know it," Monty said. He placed his left palm against the wagon, blocking her retreat.

Iris thought she could detect a hint of menace in his voice. He had drawn so close she could feel his breath. For the first time in her life she felt unsure of herself. "How many times do I have to tell you—"

"Men are under a lot of strain on a drive." Leaning on his left arm, Monty let the fingers of his right hand trail down Iris's arm. "Days and nights in the saddle can impair their judgment."

How could such a simple stroke make her skin so sensitive? This was a dangerous man.

Iris pulled away from his touch. "I-I-I have no intention of encouraging—"

"They need all their concentration just to keep from getting themselves hurt," he said, trailing his fingers along her shoulder and up the side of her neck. "They don't have time to be worrying about a female."

His touch left a trail of fire in its wake. And it seemed to be having a strange effect on her breasts. They felt full and tingly. How could that be? Monty hadn't touched her there.

Iris attempted to move away, but he hemmed her in. She looked into Monty's face. He didn't look like the big, friendly man she had been counting on to help her. He looked like a dangerous man hungry for something only she could give him, something he would have whether she wanted to give it to him or not.

For the first time, Iris felt a little afraid of Monty. This was a side of him she hadn't seen before, an aspect she foolishly hadn't anticipated. She had expected his attitude would change toward her now she had become a woman, but she hadn't calculated the change correctly. She had been planning on a man who was so besotted he would do anything she wanted. What she got was a man who looked willing to take what he wanted. She didn't know how to handle a man like this. And her own body had turned traitor. She couldn't be sure she wanted to handle him.

"I can't have them panting after you like stud bulls," Monty said. "Somebody would get hurt."

"Can't you think of anything but cows?" Iris asked. Monty brushed her question aside.

"You can't put temptation in front of a man day after day without him breaking sooner or later."

46

His fingertips moved across her lips, but it was his elbow brushing her breast that caused Iris's body to go limp. It was as though someone had suddenly removed all her bones. Iris could hardly believe his brief touch could cause such a powerful reaction.

"You don't seem to have any trouble ignoring temptation," Iris said.

"I'm not now."

His fingers caressed her neck once more. "You're probably just pretending to like me so I'll go away and leave you with your cows."

"What I would like has nothing to do with cows," he said, fingering one of the ruffles on her dress, his fingers less than an inch from her bosom. "No man could be with you and think of cows." He put his hand under her chin. "I never saw a cow with eyes as green as yours. Skin as soft and white."

"It won't be when I get sunburned because you broke my parasol." Iris tried to sound sharp, but she sounded breathless. She wasn't thinking of sunburn or parasols. All her attention was on the hardly discernible distance between them. No man had been this close to her, not this way. She had always been the one to decide how close, when, and where. Now there was no doubt Monty was in control.

His touch was driving her crazy. She had never experienced such sensations. She had been held in a man's arms; she had been kissed. Neither experience approached in any way the effect of Monty's fingertips brushing her skin. She felt consumed by the fire, yet each touch seemed to leave her yearning for another. It took all her concentration to maintain her resistance. She wasn't 14 anymore; she refused to swoon at his touch.

"There's no knowing what can happen to a woman surrounded by men," Monty said, his lips tauntingly close. "I won't always be around to protect you."

"You're trying to scare me. You think I'm just a kid trying to show off, but I'm not. I'm a woman." She hoped she sounded calm and unruffled. "You don't have to worry about me."

"It's because you're a woman I do worry about you," Monty said, slipping an arm around her.

Iris didn't know what Monty meant by putting his arm around her—she didn't trust him one bit—but she couldn't summon the will to remove it. She felt engulfed by him. She tried to back away, but it was too late. His other arm slipped around her waist. His lips were so close now that she could almost feel them brush her own.

Monty knew he should back away, that he had proved his point, but he couldn't summon the will to release Iris. From the moment he had first seen her at the party, from the instant he'd realized she had changed from the girl he remembered into this gorgeous woman every man in the room lusted after, he had been losing the battle with his desire to hold her in his arms, to cover her with kisses, to make love to her on a summer night.

He had never let himself get close until he decided to try to frighten her into going back home. Now he had overreached himself. He was the one who couldn't step back.

Iris opened her mouth to tell Monty that being a woman meant she could take care of herself, but his arms tightened around her and his mouth captured hers in a searing kiss.

Iris had never been kissed like this. There was nothing respectful or reverential about the way

Monty's lips ravaged her mouth. There was nothing tender or comforting about the way he held her in his arms. She felt consumed.

For years she had dreamed of being held in his arms, of being kissed with delicious abandon, of being wrapped in the aura of manliness that rode with him like a second skin. The reality left her breathless.

On the verge of surrender.

Iris felt the beginning of panic. She had never meant to let things go this far. Now that they had, she didn't know how to stop.

"You ought to go back to your camp." She managed to say the words, but they lacked conviction. "You don't like me, remember."

"I don't like it when you go chasing after men. Certainly not on a cattle drive. It's too dangerous."

Iris could hardly believe her ears. Anger drove out any feelings of weakness or desire. Wrenching her lips from his, she pushed him away.

"I have never chased after men," she said, her voice shaking. "But if I were ever so desperate for attention I had to tag along with a bunch of cowhands starved for the sight of a female, I still wouldn't have anything to do with you."

Monty's rumbling laugh made her angrier. Wrenching herself from his embrace, Iris dealt him a slap she hoped would cause his ears to ring for hours. In an instant, Monty was transformed from an impetuous lover to a raging bull. His anger frightened Iris so much she dashed behind the chair.

It didn't do any good. Monty jumped the chair in one effortless leap. Iris tried to run around the corner of the wagon, but Monty was upon her before she had gone two steps. She pounded her fists into his chest. But taking cruel advantage of his strength, he captured her arms and held them down by her sides as he forced her body against his.

Humiliation and anger caused tears to come to Iris's eyes. She couldn't believe this was happening to her. Nobody had ever treated her in such a brutal fashion. Yet she realized, with a kind of sick horror, she might have pushed Monty beyond the bounds of control. He was no mannequin she could take off the shelf and put back according to her whim.

Monty watched fascinated as the tears swam in Iris's eyes, then rolled down her cheeks. His astonishment turned to horror when he realized he was hurting her. He jumped back, cursing himself. He hadn't meant to. He had just reacted to her slap.

Monty dropped his hands to his sides. "Go home. You don't belong out here." The edge to his voice was the only indication of the effort it took to rein in his temper.

"Let's get one thing straight right now," Iris barked, trying to think of her anger rather than the attraction between them. "I'm not your responsibility. Neither am I your property. I'm going to Wyoming, and you'll have nothing to say about me, my herd, my men, or anything I do."

She wanted to leave him standing, to stalk away, but she couldn't, not when he looked as though he had received the shock of his life. He had hurt her. He deserved to feel rotten, but it had been her fault as much as his. If she hadn't kept after him to do something he didn't want to do, if she hadn't tried to taunt him, if she hadn't—

"Dammit to hell!" a furious male voice exploded. "What are you doing here?"

Chapter Four

Seconds earlier Iris was so angry with Monty she'd have been glad for anybody to drive him away. But now Frank was here, she was irritated he had intruded.

"We're just having a disagreement. Mr. Randolph thinks I have no right to be on this trail. He has just ordered me to go back home."

"You have no say over the Double-D," Frank said, hostility in every aspect of his attitude. "Now you'll be the one to be ordered back."

Iris had only spoken as she did because she was too angry to think. She hadn't meant to set the two men against each other. Too late she remembered the antagonism that simmered between them.

"My business is with Miss Richmond," Monty said, making no attempt to hide his contempt for Frank, "but it concerns you as well. Turn back while you can. You don't know any more about trailing to Wyoming than she does."

"If Miss Richmond wants to go to Wyoming, then I'm taking her. You and your whole crew can't stop us."

"We won't have to. You'll stop yourselves."

Frank looked so mad that for a moment Iris thought he was going to attack Monty. But that would be crazy. Everybody knew Monty was a brutal fighter. No one talked about it when any of the Randolphs were around, but the story of that fight in Mexico had been told hundreds of times in the year since it happened.

Iris stepped between the two men. "Go back to your camp, Monty."

"Go home while you still can. If you don't die of thirst or lose your herd to rustlers or herd cutters, there're Indians." He glanced at Frank, then back to Iris. "If you have to go, you should let me find a drover who could handle the job." Monty turned and swung into the saddle. "If you do go on," he said, turning to Frank, "you'd better keep out of my way. You do anything to endanger my herd, and I'll cut you in half. You let anything happen to Iris, and I'll cut you into smaller pieces than that." He wheeled his horse and galloped away.

"I'll get a couple of the boys and we'll—"

"Your job is to get this herd to Wyoming," Iris said, stunned by Monty's parting remark. "I'll handle Mr. Randolph."

Monty cursed himself all the way back to camp. He hadn't been on the trail two weeks and already he had trouble with Iris and her foreman. George wouldn't like that one bit. He had always thought Monty was too hasty of judgment, too quick to act.

Monty didn't understand that. Madison had a nasty temper, and nobody seemed to care. Hen's was even worse, but nobody paid him any attention. But let Monty do the slightest thing, and George was on him in a flash.

Monty had always had a hasty temper. He got that from his father. He had always been quick to judge, quick to act. He got that from his father as well.

Damn his pa. The man's shadow still hung over the whole family, lurking in their veins and in the dim recesses of their minds like a poison, seeping into everything they did, everything they thought. Why couldn't Monty be like Salty? He never seemed to be unsettled by anything. He never raised his voice or behaved rashly. George probably wished Salty were his brother rather than Monty.

No, that wasn't fair. No matter what Monty and his brothers did, they could count on George to stand behind them. He might give them a blistering once they got back home, but they never had any doubt George loved them.

Almost too much. The responsibility of trying to be worthy of that kind of fierce love turned even tiny failures into major ones. Which was one of the reasons Monty was going to Wyoming. He had to have some breathing room.

He rode down a slope and over a small stream almost lost in the grass and brush that crowded its banks. The water was so low half the sandy bed was exposed and dry.

But life wasn't going to be easy with Iris Richmond on the trail in front of him. Not when he acted as he had back there.

He didn't know what had gotten into him. He never meant to kiss her, especially not the way he had kissed her.

He emerged from the creek bottom and cantered up a small incline out onto a savannah, where scarce rain had made the grass spotty. He rode through a patch of bluebonnets almost up to Nightmare's belly. A stiff wind, unimpeded by the patches of mesquite and cat's-claw, swept across the open savannah whipping the new grass into undulating waves of pale green. Single weather-beaten live oaks were scattered across the savannah like the struggling soldiers of a defeated army making a slow retreat to the blue-green hills in the distance.

Iris needed a good kissing. She probably never let any of those papier-mache gentlemen in St. Louis do more than give her a chaste peck on the cheek. If she kept sending out invitations, she was going to get a few acceptances.

What about you? If she asked, would you accept?

Monty didn't want to answer that question. Ever since Iris came home, he'd been telling himself he wanted nothing to do with her now that she'd turned into a younger version of Helena.

Well, he was wrong. That kiss, the feel of Iris in his arms, had destroyed any self-control he might have had. Iris was a stunning, vibrant creature, fighting back from a blow that would have crushed a less determined person. It was impossible not to be attracted to her spirit nearly as much as to her body.

Monty didn't kid himself. It was her body that caused him to break his resolution. He hadn't known how strong the attraction was until he held her in his arms, until he kissed her, forced a response from her. Iris was no cold-blooded adventuress like Helena. She was a hot-blooded woman more likely to be ruled by her body than her mind. The mere thought inflamed Monty's senses. It inflamed his body, too.

All the more reason she shouldn't be on the trail. There was no one to protect her. She certainly couldn't count on Frank.

Maybe he would talk to her again.

Monty cursed himself. She wasn't his responsibility. She had told him so.

Maybe she wasn't, but he hadn't been able to stop worrying about her when she was a young girl. And he couldn't now she was a beautiful woman.

He pulled up. A patch of brilliant red poppies caught his eye. He started to dismount and pick some to take to Iris. Women liked little things like that, and he had been right rough on her. But he decided against it. She would be certain he was up to something, and the men would think it was crazy.

It was a shame though. They wouldn't last long in this heat.

She didn't know anything about life. Not real life. Otherwise she wouldn't have made the crazy decision to move to Wyoming. She didn't know a thing about blizzards and 40-degree-below weather. She probably wouldn't survive the winter.

Monty started cussing all over again. He didn't have time to teach her. But he couldn't let her stumble along with nobody but Frank as her guide. He'd probably have to keep his eye on her all the way to Wyoming.

That thought sent his temper nearly out of control, and he rode into camp at a gallop.

Tyler had made camp upstream from the herd on the driest part of the plain. Prickly pear cactus mixed with a low growth of purple sage and mesquite. A grove of stunted oaks offered welcome shade from the sun.

"She absolutely refuses to go back!" he shouted at Zac as he slid from Nightmare. "She wouldn't listen to a word I said."

"If you were shouting at her like you're doing now, maybe she couldn't hear you."

"Don't you start talking like a fool, too," Monty barked.

Zac skipped out of Monty's reach. "Rose says no woman can hear anything when she's being shouted at."

"That's the craziest thing I ever heard."

"I dare you to say that to Rose," Zac challenged, his grin taunting.

Monty opened his mouth to reply, then shut it. He sometimes thought Rose's notions were a bit crazy, but he loved and respected her too much to say so. Besides, if he said a word against her, George would kill him. He didn't mind taking on Iris's entire crew, but he wanted no part of George when he got mad. "Get that ramuda secured for the night."

"They're already in the corral."

"Then help Tyler with dinner."

"That ain't my job." Zac occasionally lapsed into his bad grammar now that neither George nor Rose were present to correct him. "Besides, he's *creating* again. You know how he hates to have anybody around when he's coming up with something he never thought of until thirty minutes ago."

Monty groaned. Visions of the dinner Iris's cook was preparing floated before his eyes. "No more than I hate having to eat what he concocts. Why can't he stick to bacon and beans?"

"Because he considers himself a great cook," Hen said, riding into camp, an antelope across his saddle. "Ever since Rose told him he was better than she was, there's no holding him back."

"Don't let him ruin the antelope," Monty said. "I want it cut into steaks, plain and simple."

"Tyler won't cook plain and simple," Zac said. "He says it's beneath him."

"I'll teach him *beneath him*."

"Sit down and be quiet," Hen said as he dismounted. "And stop letting Iris get under your skin."

"This has nothing to do with Iris."

Hen cast his brother a knowing look, then started to untie the antelope from the saddle.

"Okay, so she got me mad," Monty admitted. "She's the most stubborn female I ever met."

"You mean she didn't fall for the famous Randolph charm."

Monty grinned good-naturedly. "She came closer to poking my eye out with a damned parasol. Can you imagine a woman carrying a parasol and wearing a flowered dress thin enough to see through?"

"That's what Helena would have done." Hen lifted the antelope from the saddle.

"It sure as hell is," Monty replied, irritation welling up again. "That's all she knows, to act just like her ma."

"What else did you expect?"

"I didn't expect anything, but I did think she'd have sense enough to stay in St. Louis."

"Well she didn't, and it's up to you to get her off the trail."

Monty followed Hen to where he tied the antelope to a tree limb well above the ground. "I've done everything I can think of except throw her across my saddle."

"I'm surprised you haven't done that."

Monty ignored his brother's comment. "If you want her off, you go talk to her."

"I don't talk to any woman except Rose. Fork out Brimstone," Hen said, turning to Zac. "I've got some riding to do tonight."

"There's a hundred and twenty-six other horses in that corral," Zac said, as he took Hen's horse. "I'll get any one of the others for you. But if you want that crazy devil, you can get him yourself. I ain't getting myself killed just so you can ride around in the dark on a loco horse."

"Coward."

"Maybe, but I ain't no fool."

"You're not waiting for dinner?" Monty called after Hen as he walked to the corral to saddle Brimstone.

"No. I already cut me out a couple of thick steaks. I'll roast them later."

"Damn!" Monty cursed, knowing Hen's decision to cook for himself meant Tyler was preparing something he considered inedible. "I might as well go eat fricassee with Iris."

Iris got up from her chair and set her plate on the wagon steps. She had only taken a few bites of her fricassee. She hadn't enjoyed it. She had hardly tasted the cup of strong, black coffee. It was bitter, and she threw it away. She was too upset with Monty to be hungry. And too angry at herself.

She had never been so thoroughly handled and kissed by any man. She had never allowed it. But

Monty hadn't asked, and he hadn't paid any attention to her objections. And if she hadn't scampered out of his reach, he might very well have spanked her then and there.

She could see her crew gathered about the chuck wagon about 100 feet away. She felt isolated, left out. She saw them moving about, heard them laughing. She wondered if they knew, if Frank had told them. She wondered if they were laughing at her.

Her cheeks flamed at the thought.

She might as well face it. She hadn't lost her liking for Monty. She didn't understand what fascinated her so—his size, his looks, or his indifference to her. Whatever it was, it was powerful enough to render her stupidly helpless. She hoped she could figure it out soon. Mindless capitulation might be okay for a 13-year-old girl, but it was dangerous for a woman.

Still that had been the most exciting few minutes of her entire life. Even now her body felt electrified by his touch. Her lips felt bruised, her ribs crushed. Her nipples still felt swollen and tingly, and something inside her cried out for more. Her mother would have been very angry. Yet a part of Iris gloried in the electric atmosphere of such volatile physical attraction. Nor did it shrink from the danger of clashing with a man such as Monty. It was excited by the same lack of control that frightened another part of Iris to death.

She had never been out of control. That had been her mother's cardinal rule in life. Run away if you must, but never lose control.

But Iris had lost control, of Monty and of herself. And of Frank.

She spotted Frank at the campfire talking and laughing as though nothing had happened. She didn't understand why he wasn't still brooding over his humiliation. It wasn't like him to forget so quickly. He was hard and vindictive. She wondered if he was planning some kind of retaliation. That made her uncomfortable. She might be furious with Monty, she might want to see him brought down a peg, but she didn't want to see Frank do it.

Iris walked over to the campfire. The sound of the rough grass against her boots sounded unnaturally loud. She waited until Frank got his dinner from the cook. When he sat down, she walked over and sat down next to him.

"Are you certain you can get us to Wyoming?" she asked.

"Of course," Frank answered. "Why do you ask?" He looked at her kind of funny. She didn't like it.

"I guess because Monty's so insistent I go back."

"I don't know what his game is, but I wouldn't trust him. I don't trust any of those Randolphs."

"My father did."

"And your father was losing cows."

"You can't think they had anything to do with that."

"They didn't lose any, did they?"

"No, but—"

"Don't trust them. That's what I say."

Iris couldn't say why Frank's attitude should irritate her so, but she practically had to clamp her mouth shut to stop herself from defending Monty. "Getting to Wyoming is what I'm worried about right now, not the trustworthiness of the Randolphs. But I must say I'd rather not have him on my heels stomping mad."

"Don't let him bother you. He's just upset you didn't follow his advice. All the Randolphs are like that. Think they know best about everything. I'll see he doesn't come around here again."

"I imagine he'll stay with his own men from now on, but I don't want any trouble between our crews," Iris said, suddenly aware she would rather have Monty around than Frank.

"You let one of the boys see him with his hands on you, and there's going to be trouble for sure."

"That was my fault," Iris admitted. "I said something I shouldn't."

"I bet it wasn't undeserved."

"Maybe not, but I shouldn't have said it. It won't happen again."

"I was only meaning to—"

"I don't want any trouble. We might need his help before this drive is over."

"We won't." Frank got up. "It's about time you turned in. The first watch will be going out soon."

Iris resented Frank telling her what to do, but she headed toward her wagon. She hurried along. She was used to well-lighted rooms and illuminated paths in protected gardens. Inky shadows made her uneasy.

The wagon stood out as though it were meant to be the center of attention. It had been her mother's traveling wagon. Her father had had it built to Helena's exacting requirements. Twice as large as an ordinary wagon, it contained a bed on a raised platform with four large drawers underneath, a specially designed wardrobe, and a dressing table. The bed was piled high with pillows in case her mother wanted to relax while traveling, and a comfortable chair was provided for the dressing table. There was also a small table with two chairs for dining. Despite the reassuring luxury, Iris wasn't entirely comfortable until she had lighted the four oil lamps hanging from ribs that supported a particularly thick canvas to protect her from the southern Texas sun. It had seemed only logical to Iris she should bring the wagon for her personal accommodation. It never occurred to her to sleep on the ground or pack her clothes in a bedroll.

Monty dominated Iris's thoughts as she prepared for bed. She couldn't understand why he was so determined she not go to Wyoming. She looked at herself in her mirror. She looked the same as always. The sun had neither faded her hair nor ruined her complexion. Maybe he just didn't like her. He surely didn't like being anywhere near her.

That angered Iris, but it also hurt her feelings. Why should Monty dislike her so? She continued to think of it until she put out the lamps and slipped into bed, but she couldn't come up with an answer.

For a long time she lay there unable to sleep. She wasn't tired, and her mind was weighed down by questions that had no answers, worries which seemed to have no solutions. At least no answers or solutions she liked.

Gradually she became aware of another feeling. Loneliness. It was a cold and empty feeling she had fallen prey to more and more frequently since her parents' deaths. As she struggled to deal with the mountain of debt, the tangled accounts, the shock of discovering the money she had always taken for granted was gone, she also discovered she had no friends, no one she could turn to for advice, no one who made her feel better because she knew they were there.

Nobody except Monty.

But he wasn't her friend anymore. She hadn't known when she decided to put her herd on the trail ahead of him she'd be alienating the only person she might be able to depend on. But she knew it now.

She had to find some way to overcome his anger. She was too tired to think of it tonight, but she'd start on it first thing in the morning. She had to have Monty's help.

Iris was up early. The men were just waking when she reached the chuck wagon. Having slept in their clothes, they only had to put on their hats and boots to be ready to ride. Iris studied them as they ate their breakfast, put up their bedrolls, and bucked the fidgets out of their morning mounts. They all seemed relaxed, joking, and happy, but she couldn't rid herself of the feeling that things weren't going as well as they seemed.

Iris had never paid any real attention to the workings of the ranch. Both her parents had concentrated on her winning a place in St. Louis society, but over the years she had absorbed a great deal of unconscious knowledge about cows. She knew the grass was thin and poor for this time of year. She also noticed there was very little water in some streams. Others were dry. She remembered hearing Monty say they had had a dry winter following a very dry summer.

There had been virtually no spring rains. Even the flowers that usually lasted into May were fading. At first she had been thankful because the hard ground meant easy travel. But now she realized it was more important that the cattle had water to drink.

"Don't worry about it," Frank had said when she mentioned it to him. "There's plenty of water along the trail. There always is, or this trail wouldn't be used by every drover in Texas."

They had found enough water so far, but the worst stretches were still ahead. She remembered her father telling stories of dry springs and empty creeks. She had asked Frank why he didn't send a man forward each day to locate water.

"I know where it is," he told her, visibly irritated she continued to question him. "I know this trail like the back of my hand."

But she couldn't forget that Monty had been as scornful of Frank's knowledge as he had been of her own. Despite Frank's assurances, that bothered her. People said many things about Monty, not all of them nice, but everybody agreed on one thing. Monty was the best cattleman in his part of Texas. When he talked, everybody listened.

Except Frank.

Iris hated feeling ignorant and stupid, so she decided as of this moment to start changing that. She would ride with the herd. That was one thing she could do. Even Monty used to compliment her on her horsemanship. He ought to. He had helped teach her to ride.

Iris returned to her wagon. Minutes later she emerged dressed for riding. She felt a little unsure of herself. It had been years since she had done anything beyond drive a buggy or ride in a carriage. Her dress was old and fitted too tightly, especially around her breasts. The boots pinched and the hat was stiff with age, but she didn't mind. For the first time in weeks she felt like she belonged.

For a moment she was afraid she wouldn't be able to saddle her horse—Helena Richmond's daughter had never been allowed to saddle her own horses or mount unassisted—but she managed with a little help from the cook.

It was a short ride to the herd.

The animals were scattered out over more than 1,000 acres about a mile off the trail, grazing as they walked. They stretched in all directions as far as Iris could see. There seemed to be tens of thousands rather than the 3,700 she had brought. She had a crew of 15, including the foreman, the cook, and the boy in charge of the ramuda, but that didn't seem to be enough men to control a herd this size. A quick calculation told her each of the 12 hands was responsible for more than 300 cows.

Iris couldn't imagine controlling a dozen. Feeling a bit lost, she was relieved when Frank rode up.

"What are you doing out here?" he asked.

"I'm dependent on those cows to keep me from starving, yet I don't know a thing about them. I've got to learn, and I can't do that from my wagon."

"I'm supposed to handle everything for you."

"I want to know as well. About a trail drive, too."

"There's not much to know. We drift the herd north, letting it graze as much as we can along the way."

"And that's all there is to it?"

"That's about it."

Iris felt certain there was more, but the scene before her looked just as Frank said.

"Now you'd better go back to your wagon," Frank said. "This is no place for a woman. You might get hurt."

"How?" she asked, looking out over the pastoral scene. A cow occasionally lowed for its calf, but young steers and heifers ambled contentedly along, eating their way north with complete unconcern. An occasional cloud drifted by, but the sky was clear and the weather unseasonably hot for April. Already the dried brown heads of Mexican hat and Indian paintbrush had begun to mute the brilliant red. There were no signs of other humans—no cabins, no welcoming smoke curling skyward from a chimney. Iris had never felt so alone in her life.

"All kinds of things can happen."

Iris pushed aside the feeling of isolation. "Why are we so far away from the trail? If everybody grazes their herds all the way, why is there a trail up to seventy-five feet wide?"

"We have to go off the trail to find grass," Frank explained. "The later in the season, the farther. There may be as many as a hundred herds going up this trail before summer's end. We graze the herd about two hours in the morning and about two hours in the evening. During the day, we put them on the trail to cover as many miles as possible before we reach the bedding ground and they graze some more."

Iris peppered her foreman with questions for the rest of the day. By the time they came into camp that evening, he was out of temper and her head was so full of new information she could hardly remember most of it. But for the first time she felt a part of what was happening. She was just as ignorant as Monty had said, but she had started to learn. She hoped it wasn't too late.

After she dismounted, her body stiff, every muscle screaming its protest against so many hours in the saddle, she hobbled to the wagon, certain the men snickered behind her back. She would have given anything for a hot bath, but she had to settle for a pan of water heated over a cook fire.

She longed to change her clothes, but she had nothing suitable except a second and even more ill-fitting riding dress. She didn't even want to think about the blisters on her hands, her broken nails, or her windblown hair. It was a good thing Monty couldn't see her now. He probably wouldn't recognize her.

She didn't dare think what her mother would have said. Helena Richmond firmly believed a lady should not only remain as far away from the work of a ranch as possible but she ought to know absolutely nothing about its management.

Iris reminded herself her present dilemma was due to the fact Helena had failed to realize there were limits to the ranch's income, that and her father's frequent absences for months at a time, which encouraged rustlers to help themselves to Double-D stock.

It bothered Iris that so many cows could have been rustled without anyone seeming to know about it. She supposed that, in the trackless miles of brush, it was difficult to know how many cows you had and where they were. Still, the Randolphs found a way. Why hadn't her father?

Probably because he wasn't nearly as interested as Monty. Everybody knew Monty was in the saddle from dawn until dusk. He never seemed to tire.

Iris could still remember the first time she had seen him. Her father had allowed her to watch them brand calves during the spring roundup. Monty had been at the center of the activity all afternoon, a demon of energy, cutting a calf from the herd, lassoing it with unerring accuracy, throwing himself from the saddle to wrestle it to the ground until the red-hot iron had stamped the brand of ownership on its hip. Then he would vault back into the saddle to do it all over again. His was an effortless display of skill and courage, a performance that garnered the unqualified respect of every man present.

By nightfall, Iris was in love. For the next year she had followed him everywhere he went. Nothing Monty said or did penetrated the haze that surrounded her. She was beyond the power of words.

That was when her mother decided to send her to a boarding school in St. Louis. "My daughter is not going to marry a cowboy," Helena had announced, "not even one as rich as James Monroe Randolph." Helena had been so determined to restrict Iris's company she had even forced her husband to banish his son from the ranch. She was afraid his illegitimacy might somehow damage Iris's chances of being accepted in society.

As Iris limped toward the campsite, her boots rubbing against raw spots on the inside of her legs, she let herself remember the weeks of weeping that followed that decision to send her to boarding school. At the time she was convinced she was the most miserable girl on the face of the earth.

She had continued to feel that way until the headmaster's handsome 19-year-old son fell head over heels in love with her. Iris found that at 15 it was impossible to pine too long over a lost love when a terribly ardent one was immediately at hand.

She could still remember the excitement of stolen moments and clandestine meetings until the headmaster sent his son off to Princeton, 1,000 safe miles away.

Iris jerked awake. The earth seemed to be shaking underneath her. It sounded as though every cow in the world was galloping past her wagon as fast as it could run.

A stampede!

Without stopping to remember she knew nothing about stampedes, Iris jumped out of bed and hurried into her clothes. Five minutes later she was in the saddle and galloping after the herd that had disappeared into the night.

Chapter Five

The stars faded as a faint glow showed above the horizon in the dark canopy of night. Moments later the first rays of sunlight, looking like tiny, thin shafts of fire, broke through the trees. They were back in camp, the men exhausted and the cattle milling restlessly. Holding the herd in a tight group kept everyone in the saddle. The cows were tired, but the slightest thing could cause them to stampede again. Two men at a time dismounted to grab a quick breakfast before hurrying back.

Iris didn't eat anything. She had no appetite.

"How many did we lose?" she asked her foreman.

"I don't think we lost any."

But Iris didn't feel reassured. The herd looked smaller. She couldn't say why, she certainly couldn't count that many cows and she didn't have Frank's experience in estimating. Maybe it was only the suggestion that some were lost.

"Count them."

"We can't take the time. Monty's right behind us. After the time we've lost rounding them up, he's going to be breathing down our necks. I'll count them when we cross the next river."

"Won't it be too late to come back for any we lost?"

"Naw. We're only a day away now. It won't be any problem for strays to catch up, if there are any."

Iris didn't know why she should continue to feel they had lost cows. The two hands she had asked earlier had told her the same thing.

The thought flashed into her mind that she wished she could talk to Monty. He would know at a glance if any cows were missing. He would also know if something was wrong. She could remember her father saying Monty could scent trouble before it happened. That was why he was always in the middle of it.

She rode alongside the herd as they spread out from the bedding ground, her mind bombarded by feelings she couldn't understand, by fleeting thoughts she couldn't grasp. Maybe she was too tired to think straight. After all, she had been up most of the night after her first full day in the saddle. She hadn't been able to help, but she now knew that, when longhorns stampeded, no power on earth could stop them. They would run until they got too tired to run anymore.

"You'd better use your wagon today," Frank said, riding up to her. "The herd is still pretty excitable."

Iris had no intention of traveling in her wagon even though her body ached abominably, she was dog tired, and she longed for nothing so much as a hot bath and a soft bed. Something was wrong, and she meant to find out what it was. She also meant to learn enough about trailing a herd to be a help rather than an encumbrance. "Tell the driver to go on without me."

Frank scowled. Iris knew she was making things more difficult by deciding to ride as part of the crew, but Frank and the men would just have to get used to it.

"You'll get tired before noon," Frank warned. "You're not used to spending all day in the saddle"

"If it comes to that, I'm not used to spending all day in a wagon either," Iris answered, rather more sharply than she had intended, "but I mean to stay with the herd. If a calf can do it, so can I."

Frank clearly didn't like her answer, but he turned and rode forward, and Iris continued toward the back of the herd. The air was so thick with dust she slipped her bandanna over her nose. She could literally feel the grit in her eyes and on her skin, but she made up her mind to ignore it. It was part of the job, and she was determined to meet its demands.

She was relieved to see the herd gradually settle down as they moved north. Frank said they could have lost 50 to 75 pounds on that run. She might not know much about cows, but she did know a fat steer sold for more than a skinny one.

Iris reached the drag of the herd. As the last of the stragglers walked by, she couldn't resist looking back. Beyond those hills, across more than 100 miles of brush, thorny vines, cactus, and rocky soil lay her home. A home that didn't belong to her any longer. Even though she had spent the first ten years of her life in Austin and the last four in St. Louis, she thought of the ranch as home. It was where she had grown up. The stifling heat and the long, dry summers, the cactus and the scrub oak were as familiar as the traffic and the heated parlors of St. Louis. Now she was leaving it behind for the unfamiliarity of the cold, barren plains of Wyoming.

A shiver of apprehension knifed though her. She was on her own. She was going alone.

For a moment Iris felt overwhelmed. She was surrounded by difficulties she had never experienced, about which she knew nothing. All that stood between her and destitution was a herd and the money she had hidden in her wagon.

Monty. She whispered his name even as she swore she would never ask his help again. He was a bully and a brute, but he was the only man she trusted. He would defend cowhand or rancher alike. He was just as ready to fight over a single maverick as over 20,000 acres of grazing land. He would—

Iris's thoughts broke off when a young steer appeared on the trail a short distance away.

Monty. It had to be his herd.

Iris felt the muscles in her body tense. He would be enraged to have to stop to allow her herd to get a safe distance ahead. She had better be the one to meet him. If it was Frank, there'd probably be a fight. She couldn't get to Wyoming with her foreman laid up with a broken head.

But as Iris rode forward, she grew puzzled. The steer was coming at a very fast walk. One thing she had learned. You walked your stock at a comfortable pace so they could gain weight.

Was Monty trying to run them down? She knew he was angry at her, but she didn't think he was mad enough to do something like that. If his herd drove into hers, there would be trouble and she wouldn't be able to stop it.

It was Monty. She recognized him the instant he appeared. A half-dozen steers accompanied him. Iris spurred her horse into a gallop. She had to stop him.

"Turn your herd aside!" she called out as soon as she was within shouting distance.

"What the hell are you hollering about?" Monty demanded when he pulled his horse to a halt next to hers.

"We had a stampede last night. That's why we're in your way. If you'd just stop here awhile, it won't take us long to get ahead of you."

"This is not my herd."

"You can't ram us. You—"

The lead steer drew abreast of Iris and her mouth dropped open. The steer bore the Double-D brand. That was her steer. A quick glance told her all the other longhorns belonged to her as well.

She had been right. They had lost cows, hundreds of them if she was any judge.

"Where did you find them?" she finally managed to ask.

"We heard the stampede. I started this way with a couple of the boys to see if you could use any help. We ran into this bunch heading south."

"South?" Iris explained. "But the herd was running somewhere between north and west."

"Somebody stampeded your herd so they could cut it. They took off when they saw me coming, but I recognized one of them. Quince Honeyman." He sounded impatient, irritated at being drawn into her trouble.

"I never heard of him." She expected him to tell her to go home, that she obviously couldn't handle the drive, that she was in his way.

Instead he said, "A swarthy man, half Irish, half Indian. Has a scraggly beard that he uses to try to cover up a bullet burn across his cheek. Have you ever seen him?"

Something inside Iris froze. She had never heard of Quince Honeyman, but she had a distinct feeling she had seen the man Monty described. She felt a strong urge to tell him, but she fought it down. He wouldn't do anything except tell her she should have listened to him and stayed home.

Iris shook her head.

"You don't have to worry about him. I put a bullet through his shoulder. He won't be cutting any herds for a while."

He almost sounded as if he had done it for her, to protect her from any future stampede. But he didn't act like a lover, at least not like any lover Iris had ever been around.

The cows reached the drag, and Iris's crew started feeding them back into the main herd.

"Thank you for bringing them back. Frank didn't think any were missing. He wasn't going to count them until we reached the river."

"That's four days away." Monty sounded incredulous, as if she should have known that. "Quince would have been half the way to Mexico by then."

Iris opened her mouth to contradict him, then shut it again. She didn't know what creek or stream Frank had been talking about, but if Monty said the next river was four days away, it was four days away.

"You need to post extra guards for the next few nights. If you have another stampede before the herd settles down, you could get hurt."

No one could accuse Monty of sweet-talking, but he did have a way about him. He *had* been worried about her. Knowing that made Iris feel better than she had in weeks. Now if she could just get him to take a more active interest. .

"Besides, they might stampede my herd next time."

That was what she got for getting foolishly sentimental about Monty. She should have known he wasn't interested in anything except his cows. He never had been. And while he had made it clear he found her very attractive, he had also made it clear his cows came before everything else. Especially her.

Before Iris could return the hot answer that came to mind, Frank rode up.

"What the hell are you doing here again?" he demanded angrily. "Get your men away from this herd."

"He brought back the cows we lost last night," Iris said, speaking quickly before Monty would reply. "Monty says rustlers stampeded the herd so they could cut it."

"That's the craziest thing I ever heard," Frank snapped, furious.

Iris didn't understand why Frank was so angry. She knew he wasn't pleased to see Monty again, but he'd been laughing last night as if he'd forgotten all about their previous encounter. Obviously he was much angrier than she had suspected.

"Two of my best men were riding herd when it started," Frank said. "They'd have seen anybody trying to sneak up on 'em. It must have been a panther. Maybe a wolf."

Frank forced his horse between Iris and Monty. Maybe he thought he was protecting Iris, but all he did was make Monty furious.

"Either you've been sleeping on the job, or you're trying to cover for your men," Monty shot back.

"Why you yellowbellied son of a—"

Frank never got to finish his sentence. Monty jumped his horse straight into Frank's mount. The big, rawboned gelding ran right over Frank's cow pony. Jumping from the saddle, Monty grabbed Frank as he struggled to his feet and hit him a powerful blow to the neck that sent him to the ground clutching his throat in agony and gasping for breath.

"Next time I won't be so easy on you."

Iris was shocked by the sudden fight. Acting purely on instinct, she jumped down from her horse and pulled the rifle from the boot on Frank's fallen pony.

"Monty Randolph, you stop this very minute, or I'll put a bullet in you."

She had the rifle pointed directly at him, but he didn't jump. He just turned and looked at her as if she had lost her mind.

"You'd better put that away before someone gets hurt," he said, pointing to the rifle.

His complete lack of fear made her furious. She wished she had the courage to fire into the ground between his feet, but she had never fired a rifle and she was afraid she might hurt him.

"It wasn't enough that you refused to help me. It wasn't enough that you've kept my crew nervous as antelopes knowing you and your gunslinging brother are dogging our heels. Now you have to try to kill my foreman."

"You fire that rifle, and you're going to have another stampede," Monty said, pointing to the wide-eyed longhorns watching Iris.

"I hope every one of them runs over you," Iris said. "I would love to see something pound you into the ground."

"It would never happen," Monty said, that irritating grin on his face once more. "I'd be astride Nightmare before you could take a deep breath. With you over my saddle," he added.

Iris's eyes flashed and her nostrils quivered. "No man, but most especially you, Mr. James Monroe Randolph, will ever carry me off over a saddle. I'd shoot you first."

"Not unless you take off the safety first," Monty said, brazenly taking the rifle from her grasp. "Now let's put this away before you hurt yourself."

"The only person I'm going to hurt is you."

"You'd be better advised to look to your foreman. He doesn't look too chipper to me."

"No thanks to you."

"Maybe he'll think next time before he calls me a coward."

Iris was too angry to give any thought to her words. She said the first thing that came to her mind. "Maybe you'll think before you act," she snapped in return. "If you don't, you're liable to beat somebody else to death."

Monty turned white. "I never beat anybody to death."

Iris wished she could have bitten her tongue. In all her life, she'd never seen Monty defenseless, never known he could be hurt. He had seemed beyond the influence of normal human emotions. Yet one thoughtless sentence had stripped him of all the strength and confidence that made him Monty Randolph.

"You should be more concerned about your herd than me," Monty said, recovering some of his color. "And don't worry that I'll disturb you again. Next time I see somebody stealing your cows, I'll write you a letter. It ought to reach you about the time you get to Indian territory."

He talked like the old Monty, but as he mounted his horse, he still looked shaken. Iris's anger evaporated. Frank wasn't really hurt, and he'd brought the beating on himself. But her words had hurt Monty deeply. She'd flung the accusation at him without thinking, having only remembered something someone said. But his reaction told her it was very important. She would have to find out why.

"I do appreciate your bringing my cows back," Iris called after him. "I just don't want you attacking my foreman."

"Then keep him out of my way." Monty dug his heels into his mount's flanks. The gelding bounded away, leaving Iris to marvel at how good Monty looked on horseback. He rode tall in the saddle, his back straight, his broad shoulders thrown back, and his powerful thighs gripping his mount's sides. She could easily remember how his strong hands had held her helpless against the wagon. She watched him until he disappeared. It wasn't difficult to remember why she had had such a terrible crush on him. The man still sent her blood racing and her pulses soaring. He was devastating to look at. It was a shame he was such an impossible person.

But even as Iris watched Frank pick himself up and get his pony back on its feet, she realized she didn't feel any animosity toward Monty. Irritation, yes. Anger, too, but apparently a lot of the teenage crush remained. Unfortunately his avoidance of respectable females was legendary. The only ones he was interested in were floozies and cows.

"Next time Monty shows up, let me handle him," she told Frank. "If you can't talk to him without getting into a fight, you'd better stay out of sight."

"That man gets my goat." Frank dusted himself off, but a grass stain remained on the seat of his pants.

"He gets mine, too, but it won't do you any good for the crew to see you lying in the dust at his feet. We've got a long way to go, and we can't do it unless the crew respects you."

"I've got everything under control," Frank said, looking ugly. "The crew and the herd. Now you should go back to your wagon."

"When do you plan to count the herd?"

Frank's expression darkened.

"I told you, a day from now."

"Monty said the river is four days away."

Iris thought Frank was going to explode. She'd never seen him so angry.

"The Brazos River *is* four or five days away, but Dogleg Creek is just ahead. Why do you want a count? You got your cows back."

"I don't know that. You didn't think we were missing any before. Maybe we still are."

"It'll slow us down even more."

"It doesn't matter. Monty can't be any more angry at us than he is already."

As Iris rode back to her wagon, she realized she didn't want Monty to be angry with her. He was the only person she could really trust. As she got farther and farther away from civilization, that became more and more important. Especially if the rustlers were still after her.

She thought she had left them behind in Guadalupe County, but obviously thieves were still trying to steal her cows. She didn't know if they wanted just a few hundred or if they intended to take the whole herd.

That thought caused her blood to run cold.

Iris racked her brain, but she couldn't remember where she had seen Quince Honeyman. But she must. He could be the key to the men trying to rob her.

For the second time in less than a week, Monty cursed himself as he rode back to his camp, but there was something different this time. They were no longer the good-natured curses of a man momentarily out of temper, or curses of resignation aimed at someone else who had forced him to change his plans.

These were bitter, despairing curses aimed at Monty himself.

One of the conditions George imposed before he agreed to give Monty control of the ranch was that Salty would be his foreman. Monty had no objection. Salty was his first choice. What made him angry was that he knew Salty was here to watch him, to exercise the same kind of control George did. But what made Monty maddest of all was that he deserved it. He had just proved it again.

He pushed aside the memory of that fight in Mexico. He hadn't known Iris knew about it. Her flinging it in his face so unexpectedly had been a terrible shock, but one he needed. He needed something to remind him that he was becoming more like his father every day.

He would have been tempted to strangle anybody who said that, but he was as honest with himself as he was brutally direct with others. He had his father's temper—a cruel, vicious streak of senseless fury that struck with the unexpectedness and speed of a panther. And it was just as deadly.

He could remember when he had first talked to George about Wyoming. He had been so sure George would be as excited as he was. They needed more land. Their herds had grown too large. Wyoming land would mean a shorter distance to the new markets opening up around the mines. It also meant gaining new land for virtually nothing. Monty was the logical choice to head up the new ranch.

But George had said he was immature, too hasty with his judgments, too quick to act to be trusted with such a large operation. George didn't mention it, but the fight in Mexico was fresh in everyone's mind. Monty could remember the anger that had made him shout at his brother until Hen had dragged him away and pushed him in the creek.

After cooling off, and enduring a good talking to from Hen, Rose, and Zac, the presumptuous sprout, he had set himself the task of proving himself matured enough to be entrusted with the new ranch.

He had succeeded for a whole year only to lose his temper twice with Iris's foreman.

But it wasn't Frank. It was Iris.

He rode up to the crest of a ridge and looked back at Iris's herd. The men had them under tight control now, but it wouldn't last long. Lax management and poor control were Frank Cain's hallmarks.

But more than that, Monty didn't trust Frank, and it made him furious to see Iris depending on him. She didn't know a thing about men like Frank. Monty couldn't expect her to, not spoiled and protected as she was. Besides, she was used to having men do anything she wanted. It probably never crossed her mind that a man she knew would actually set out to steal from her.

Maybe he'd send Salty over to talk to her. He'd rather send Hen, but he doubted Hen would go. Come to think of it, Salty wouldn't be a good choice either. He became tongue-tied around beautiful women. Rose was about the only woman who didn't send him scurrying for his horse.

Somebody had to keep an eye on her. They had already tried to steal her herd once, and they would try again. They might not mean to harm her, but you never could tell what would happen when bullets started flying.

She could be killed.

An odd feeling skittered along his nerve endings. Iris was a bother and a worry and too ignorant to be turned loose, but he liked her. He didn't know why, but then he'd been a perverse creature all his life. If he took after his father in one way, he was bound to take after him in others. According to George, their pa had once pursued a woman all the way from Virginia to Charleston.

Monty wasn't going to chase after Iris over three states. He just wanted to make sure nothing happened to her. He might even take her up on her invitation to dinner. Nothing she served could be any worse than what Tyler was dishing up.

Tyler had become a good cook. Monty had to give him that. But when Tyler got through with the food, a man couldn't make out what he was eating. And Monty hated to eat anything when he couldn't tell what it was.

*   *   *

During the remainder of the day, Monty's description of the rustler nagged at Iris's mind. She tried to remember where she had seen the man, but nothing jogged her memory. Once she almost decided to ride over and ask Monty if he could remember anything else, but she decided against it. Considering his mood when he'd left, he was liable to send her back to her own camp tied across her saddle.

In spite of their sharp words, she was touched that Monty would leave his own herd to see if she needed help. He could have let them go or kept them himself. Instead, he had risked being shot at to drive off the rustlers and return the cows.

On the other hand, if Monty had really wanted to be helpful, he could have taken her with him. That would have been easier than chasing after her cows and fighting off rustlers. No rustler would mess with a herd when they knew Monty and Hen were around.

Iris was starved by dinnertime, but a single glance at the plate of bacon and beans the cook handed her caused her to lose her appetite. She had never eaten food like this. Nevertheless, she took the plate. She had to eat something, and she might as well learn to eat what the men ate. She wouldn't be able to dine on French cuisine in Wyoming.

She was so tired she could hardly stand up. But when she found a place to sit down, she discovered her body was too stiff and sore to bend. She walked slowly back to her wagon to work some of the knots out of her muscles.

She had let the cook choose the meal because of what Monty had said. The men seemed to be enjoying it more than anything she had ordered for them. She tasted some beans. Ugh. They were disgusting. She might as well be eating husks. They didn't have any flavor except for the molasses, and she hated molasses.

The salt pork didn't taste too bad, but she refused to touch the bread fried in bacon grease. It made her queasy just to think of putting it in her mouth. At least she had had the good sense to bring some wine. It wasn't a substitute for food, but it would get the taste of molasses out of her mouth.

But she no sooner decided to get the wine from her wagon than she remembered where she had seen Quince Honeyman. He had been talking to one of her crew a day or two before they started up the trail.

The wine and the taste of molasses forgotten, Iris hurried back to the campfire to warn Frank. She thought the cowhand's name was Bill Lovell, but she wasn't sure. She hadn't learned the names of all the crew yet.

Neither Frank nor Bill Lovell were in. She handed the cook her barely touched plate. "Where's Frank?"

"He was headed off in that direction last time I saw him," one hand said, pointing toward where the herd was being bedded down for the night. "But I wouldn't walk that way. You never know what you might step in."

Iris was tempted to return a sharp reply, but the brazen way the boy stared at her caused her to change her mind. If this was how the crew behaved with women, no wonder her mother had kept her distance. She would speak to Frank. She had no intention of being treated like that by men when she was paying their wages.

Night was falling, and Iris felt uneasy leaving the campfire behind. It was difficult for her to overcome a fear that something might be hiding in the shadows. She hadn't often gone out at night in St. Louis, and then never alone. The sight of the humps of cattle, some lying down, some still grazing, didn't reassure her. Her limited experience with longhorns had not led her to trust them. She could remember too many of her father's stories about wild mossy horns being as willing to attack a man on horseback as not.

Iris rounded a clump of brush to see Frank no more than 30 yards off talking to one of the hands. Just as she opened her mouth to call to him, she realized he was talking with Lovell.

She stopped dead in her tracks. Frank wasn't berating Lovell. His voice was lowered. They appeared to be having a private conversation.

A horrible thought occurred to Iris. She staggered backward, around the brush out of their line of vision. Suppose Frank was in league with the rustlers? Suppose he was responsible for the stampede?

It didn't seem possible, but it explained a number of things she hadn't understood, most particularly why the rustlers always seemed to know when and where to attack without being caught.

It could also explain why Frank was so upset when she made up her mind to go to Wyoming. It could explain why he didn't want Monty around, why he was furious when Monty showed up with the missing cattle.

Iris tried to slow her racing thoughts. Frank didn't have to be the informer. His orders weren't a secret. The crew always knew about the plans because they all had a part to play. Lovell could be the sneak. Frank could be telling him something confidential without even realizing he was talking to a double-crosser.

But Iris couldn't be sure. She had to think before she decided what to do.

Turning back toward camp, Iris stumbled over a root. Barely keeping her balance, she walked on, her mind in a whirl. What was she going to do? She still found it hard to believe Frank could be involved with the rustlers. He had been her father's foreman for years. Her father had trusted him. He even left the ranch in his care for months at a time.

That was when the ranch had stopped making money. Up until then not even Helena Richmond's extravagances had exhausted the income.

Still Iris had no proof. She couldn't accuse him without it. Besides, who would take his place? If one of the hands was involved, several others probably were as well, including the insolent cowhand at the campfire. She felt an overwhelming desire to talk to Monty. A brute and insensitive bully he may be, but he'd know what to do.

Iris stumbled over another bit of brush. Just as she was telling herself to pay more attention to where she was going, she heard a plaintive bleat and saw a tiny calf lying almost out of sight beneath the brush. It must have been born since the herd stopped for the night. It looked so tiny and new.

But before a second thought could enter her head, Iris heard a baleful bawling from somewhere behind her and turned to see a wild-eyed longhorn cow bearing down in her direction. She was about to be attacked by the calf's mother. A frantic look around told her there was no place to hide except the lowly bush already sheltering the frightened calf.

Chapter Six

Iris started to run in a stumbling, awkward stride. Her abused muscles refused to work normally. The frightened calf bleated so piteously she hoped the mother would be more concerned about comforting her baby than attacking a perfectly innocent bystander.

A glance over her shoulder told her she was not so lucky. Not only that, but several other longhorns, attracted by the calf's call for help, were converging on the spot as well. Iris knew there was no hope of reaching the camp ahead of the charging cattle. No one seemed to have been alerted by their bellows. Not even the cowhands on herd duty had noticed anything wrong.

Iris stumbled but righted herself and struggled on, her abused muscles shrieking in protest. If she could just reach one of the trees.

Suddenly she heard the thunder of hooves approaching from the direction of the camp. She looked up to see Monty galloping toward her. Flinging herself at him, Iris clung desperately to the arm that swooped down and scooped her up as if she was a featherweight.

"Hold on," Monty shouted, as he wheeled his horse and started toward the camp. "They're mad enough to attack anything living."

There was no time to stop and pull herself up behind Monty. Longhorns could run with the speed of an antelope. Monty galloped away with Iris swinging at his side, her body perilously close to flying hooves, only barely ahead of the flashing horns. They headed straight for the camp, Monty hollering like a painted Indian to warn the cowhands.

The men had run to their horses by the time Monty and Iris burst into camp. Monty's horse jumped the fire. The maddened cow plowed right through it, scattering ashes and bits of flame all around. By the time Monty had slowed his horse and circled back, the hands had gotten between them and the dozen or so longhorns. The angry cow made a couple of lunges at their ponies, but the repeated calls of her frightened calf distracted her, and she soon turned back. With a little encouragement, the other longhorns followed.

"Are you all right?" Monty asked as he lowered Iris to the ground. "I saw you trip and fall."

Monty dropped from the saddle and helped Iris over to the only blanket that hadn't been torn up by the rampaging longhorns. She looked white. She couldn't stand by herself. Monty put his arm around her or she would have collapsed. He wasn't feeling too steady himself. He couldn't remember feeling

Leigh Greenwood

so shaken since that time 12 years ago when Hen arrived just in time to prevent some bandits from hanging him.

Blind luck had caused him to be close enough to save Iris. He had been riding slowly, trying to come up with a good excuse for showing up at her camp so soon after she had thrown him out, as well as trying to work up the courage to apologize for his behavior, when the bleat of the calf caught his attention. If it hadn't, he might never have looked up in time.

He couldn't bear to think of what would have happened to Iris if he hadn't.

"Would you like something to drink?" he asked.

"I'll be fine in a minute," she managed to say. "I'm just feeling a little weak."

"You're lucky you're alive," Monty said, relief causing him to speak sharply. "A couple more jumps and that cow would have had you."

"I know," Iris said, her eyes still wide with fright.

What had she been doing, wandering about in the dark? He had nearly been paralyzed with fear when he looked up and saw that cow bearing down on her.

"Now you know why I kept trying to get you to go back," Monty said. "This is no place for a woman."

Monty cursed himself for letting his irritation show. It didn't matter that she had done something wildly dangerous. She was scared and upset. She needed comfort, not a lecture. She looked as if she would burst out crying at any moment. He hoped she wouldn't. He was no good with crying women.

Taking his courage in his hands, Monty settled down next to Iris and put his arm around her. "It's all over now. You're safe."

With a convulsive sob, Iris threw herself against him. She clutched the front of his shirt with both hands and held on as if she was afraid of being washed away in a flood. Monty, who normally knew by instinct how to handle a woman, felt stiff and uncomfortable. He put his other arm around Iris, relieved her wrenching sob had been a solo effort. She still had a death grip on his shirt, but she had herself under control.

"Thank you for saving my life," she murmured.

"I couldn't do anything else," Monty said, his smile showing. "After all the trouble I went to to rescue you from that butte, I couldn't give up on you now."

Iris smiled in spite of herself. She had climbed an isolated rocky outcropping called the Devil's Tooth because Monty had told her not to. He had had to climb up, fashion a harness out of his rope, and lower her to the ground. He had fallen on the way down. He explained the nasty set of bruises by saying his horse had stumbled.

"You told me longhorns were dangerous," Iris said. "I should have listened."

Iris had finally admitted he was right, but Monty didn't feel very triumphant. He wasn't precisely sure what he did feel beyond confused. But then he shouldn't have expected anything else. Things never went the way they should when Iris was around.

"What the hell was that all about?" the cook demanded as he returned from his hiding place somewhere in the trees down by the creek.

Iris felt Monty withdraw, breaking the fragile thread of intimacy. It was an ephemeral feeling, one almost too slight to notice, but she had noticed it, and she regretted its passing.

"Who is the fool who let Miss Richmond go wandering about on foot?" Monty demanded, getting to his feet and pulling Iris up with him.

"I reckon she let herself."

Iris looked up to see the rude cowhand drop to the ground from a tree used to anchor one corner of the rope corral that held the horses. "She didn't tell nobody what she was going to do."

"And I suppose you couldn't use your eyes for a look see," Monty growled.

Iris could have told the boy that Monty was dangerously angry, but the kid seemed impervious to his danger. He sauntered toward them. "I was eating," he said with the same insolent tone he'd used to Iris.

Monty's fist snaked out and grabbed him by the throat. "You're a sorry, white-livered piece of cow dung," he thundered, shaking the boy like he weighed nothing. "You're fired."

"You can't fire me," the cowhand managed to gasp. "I don't work for you." He tried to retain his devil-may-care attitude, but Monty's reputation as a fighter was well-known. Iris saw the fear in his eyes.

Monty tossed the cowhand from him with all the unconcern of a man tossing away an apple core. "Collect your gear and get out. If you're still here next time I come around, you won't have a choice about how to get to your next stopping place."

The man turned to Iris, but she was still too overcome by her near brush with death and Monty's miraculous rescue to respond. Frank galloped into camp, clearly furious.

"Do you know you nearly caused a stampede?" he bellowed at Monty. "What the hell have you done to our camp?" he demanded as he stared in disbelief at the destruction all around him. "I told you once before to stay away from here. Now I'm telling you for the last time." Frank pulled his rifle from its boot. "Now get out, or I'll see you carried out."

"He tried to fire me," the cowhand said. "He just stomped in here and told me to collect my gear and get out."

Frank raised the rifle and pointed it directly at Monty. "You just don't know when to stop, do you?"

"Go ahead and pull that trigger," Monty said. "But I'll kill you with my bare hands before I die."

Iris could hardly believe what was happening. One moment she was being chased by a dozen longhorns. Seconds later she was nestled securely in Monty's arms. Now, before her unbelieving eyes, Frank and Monty were preparing for a gun battle. Nothing in her world had ever moved with such speed and violence.

Iris struggled to gather her wits. This was her camp, her cattle drive. She should be the one giving the orders. Besides, her ignorance had caused the trouble, pitted Monty and Frank against each other once again. If she wasn't to deserve every brutally unkind, rudely unflattering word Monty had ever said, she had to put a stop to this before someone got hurt.

"Put down that rifle, Frank," she said with all the composure she could command. "I won't have any shooting in my camp."

"I'm just going to rid us of this coyote," Frank answered. His rife didn't move.

"Put that rifle down, or draw your pay and ride out right now."

Iris could hear a new confidence in her voice, an element of authority that had never been there

before. It caused Frank to spin around in the saddle
to look at her.

"I mean it. Put it away or you're fired."

"Do you know what he did?"

"Yes, but you don't. I was the one who nearly
started that stampede. If Monty hadn't ridden up
when he did, you'd be burying my remains." She
gave her men a significant look. They all avoided
meeting her eyes.

"But the camp, firing Crowder?"

"I rode through the camp so your boys could get
those cows off my heels," Monty explained. "That
cow was intent on hooking something, and I didn't
want it to be my horse, especially not while I was
still on him. I fired that no good son of a bitch
because he let Iris go looking for you on foot. Any
fool knows the first rule when working around half-
wild longhorns is never go anywhere on foot."

Only now did Iris remember hearing her father
say the same thing.

"That doesn't give you the right to fire my crew,"
Frank protested. "You—"

"If he hadn't fired him, I would have," Iris said.

That wasn't exactly true. She hadn't been able to
think well enough to make such a decision. But she
had told Crowder where she was going, and she
remembered his insolent reply. She also remembered the look between him and Frank. There was
something there. She didn't know what, but she
intended to find out.

"What are you doing here?" Frank demanded.
"Seems like every time I turn around, you turn
up."

"I brought a couple more steers over. They must
have been hiding in the brush. They joined our herd
last night."

"Well next time send one of your men," Frank said.

Iris faced Monty, ignoring Frank. "I'm grateful for what you did, and I'll be happy to have you drop by anytime you like. Have you had dinner?"

"No. Tyler is experimenting again. I was waiting to see if any of the hands got sick before I ate it."

"You can eat with us. We're having your favorite meal—bacon, beans, and bread fried in bacon grease. At least we were."

Monty hesitated. His eyes cut to Crowder, then to Frank Cain.

"I'm afraid you'll have only me for company," Iris said. "Frank has to get back to the herd, and Mr. Crowder has fifteen minutes to leave camp."

The cowhand glared at Iris, anger in his eyes. He opened his mouth to say something, but a glance at Monty caused him to change his mind. He picked up his saddle and stalked off toward the horses.

"Better make sure he takes his own horse," Monty advised Frank. The foreman cast Monty a hate-filled glance before he stomped off after the young cowhand.

"You shouldn't be out here alone with that man," Monty said, turning back to Iris. "You ought to take the train and meet him in Cheyenne."

Iris dropped her gaze so she wouldn't have to look into Monty's eyes. "He just doesn't like you."

"I don't like him either. More important, I don't trust him."

"Why not? My father did."

"Your father and I didn't always see eye to eye." Monty looked as if he wanted to say more, then apparently thought better of it. "Did that cow leave any grub?" he asked, turning to the cook.

95

"Sure," Bob Jenson replied. "My cook fire was on the other side of the chuck wagon. I had the coffeepot on this one."

"How about some beans? Not too many. I got to leave some room for whatever Tyler's fixing up. I have to admit it usually tastes pretty good. It just looks funny."

Monty accepted a plate and sat down to eat.

Iris's resistance collapsed the minute Monty backed away from criticizing her father. Her feeling of isolation had become more and more oppressive. After the episode with Crowder, she didn't feel there was anybody on her crew she could trust.

"Hell!" Monty exclaimed and set his plate down. "Tyler's food is ruining me."

"What do you mean?" Iris asked.

"Perfectly good beans, and I don't like them," Monty moaned. "I used to like nothing better, unless it was Rose's roast turkey. Now Tyler keeps shoving things at me I don't even want to look at, but I like them better than beans." He spat out a husk. "Sorry, man," he said turning to the cook, "but they just don't taste good anymore."

Iris laughed. "I hate them, too. Let me get you a glass of wine. It'll take the taste out of your mouth."

"No, thank you," Monty said, getting to his feet. "Randolphs don't drink."

"Not at all?"

"Madison will have a brandy once in a while, but the rest of us drink milk."

"But this is wine."

"It's still spirits." Monty handed his plate to the cook. "Besides, you shouldn't bring it on a drive.

It's just about the worst thing you can do for the hands."

"I don't give it to the hands," Iris said, irritated Monty was criticizing her again. "It's for my own personal use."

"That's even worse." Monty picked up his gloves and adjusted his hat. "It's not right for the foreman to be doing something his men can't."

"I'm not the foreman," Iris said, her tone glacial. "I'm the owner."

"Same difference," Monty said, heading for his horse. "You take my advice and pour every bit of it into the creek."

"I'll do no such thing," Iris snapped. "My father paid more than five dollars a bottle for this wine."

"I doubt he would have wasted his money if Helena hadn't been prodding him," Monty said, mounting up. He rode his horse up next to Iris. "You stick close to your wagon and stay away from that herd. You want to do something, ask your cook if it's okay. He seems a sensible man."

"I can make my own decisions without having to ask the cook."

"Yeah, but you'll probably make the wrong ones," Monty replied, not the least bit impressed by her irritation. "If you need anything, just give me a holler. I won't be far behind you."

"I'll have you know, Monty Randolph, I don't holler—not for you or anybody else."

"Try it sometime. It'll take some of the starch out of you."

He rode off and left her standing there, simmering mad. She sensed a grin on Bob Jenson's face, but when she turned he was scraping out Monty's plate.

"I'm going to bed," she announced. "Tell Frank I want to see him first thing in the morning."

But once she was settled in bed, she couldn't decide what to say to him. If she told him of her suspicions, she would only put him on his guard. It wouldn't do any good to face him with an accusation. If he were guilty, he would simply deny it. If he weren't, he might get angry enough to leave.

She wanted to tell Monty, but she didn't know what to say to him any more than she did to Frank. She had no proof, and she didn't want to make a false accusation. It wasn't a crime for two men to talk to each other.

She was beginning to realize there was a great deal she didn't know about managing men. She had underestimated Monty's responsibilities. Getting a herd to Wyoming wasn't nearly as simple as it looked.

Chapter Seven

Monty rode back to his camp, unwelcome thoughts jostling each other in his mind. Something was going on with Iris's crew. She knew it, too. She might not know what it was, but she was uneasy. He could see it in the way she moved closer to him when Frank rode in. He could see it in the way she immediately relaxed when Frank left.

He thought for a moment it might stem from a struggle over who was going to run the drive, but he quickly set that aside. She might be the owner and the most beautiful, desirable women in Texas, but the cowhands weren't likely to listen to her unless Frank told them to. That was obvious in Crowder's attitude.

Besides, Iris didn't look angry. She looked uneasy. Not exactly frightened. She was too spirited, too accustomed to immunity from danger to be frightened, but he could sense the uncertainty.

Monty wished now he had tried harder to capture at least one of the rustlers. It was unlikely all three knew who hired them to stampede the herd, but he would bet his hat Quince Honeyman did. That man had lit out the moment he saw Monty on his trail.

But even if Monty suspected Frank Cain of having something to do with the rustling attempt, he had no proof. He couldn't just go busting in there acting as if he was the boss. He'd already gone over the line in firing Crowder.

He felt the heat of embarrassment flow from under his collar. Wouldn't George love to find out about that? It didn't matter that the kid was a jerk, that he was probably a coward, that he was definitely an insolent whelp. Monty shouldn't have laid hands on him. It was Frank's responsibility to discipline his crew. If Iris hadn't backed him up, Monty could have been in a world of trouble.

His temper again. It didn't seem he could keep it under control. But he didn't know how he could be expected to, not with Iris nearly gored to death and that son of a bitch hiding up a tree. Monty guessed he'd lost his head when he saw that cow heading for Iris. The look of pure terror on her face still caused him to feel weak in the knees. She could have been killed.

She was a mettlesome female and a lot of trouble, but her crew ought to be looking after her. If she had been traveling with him, there wouldn't have been a man in the group who wouldn't have been pumping bullets into the cow before she got within 20 yards of Iris.

Okay, she should have known better than to go anywhere near a longhorn on foot, but a decent cowhand wouldn't have let her go looking for Frank by herself. It was almost as if they hoped something would happen to her.

A chill raced down Monty's spine. The possibilities of accidents or danger on the trail were endless. Once they reached Indian territory, there was no law, no one to know if anything happened to her. It wasn't much better in Kansas and Nebraska. As far as Monty knew, there was nothing in Wyoming. She could disappear, and no one would ever know.

Monty cursed to himself. He'd kill the whole damned crew if anything happened to Iris.

He had to keep an eye on her. Even if he had to manufacture excuses, he was going to visit her camp every day. More often if he didn't like the way things were going. He might even get Hen to take a ride over. They might avoid him, but everybody walked in fear of Hen.

But Monty knew he wouldn't entrust this task to Hen or any other member of his crew. He was going to do it himself.

"There she was, running like a heifer with a panther on its trail," Monty told his brothers as they waited for Tyler to finish cooking dinner, "and that cow right on her heels, her eyes crazy wild. I expected Iris to start screaming any minute, but she took out for the trees instead."

"Seems like a sensible thing to do," Hen replied, rather bored.

"Of course it was," Monty said, irritated his twin seemed so uninterested in his story, "but you can't expect Iris to do the sensible thing. Being brought up as she was, she doesn't know any more than a kitten. I expected her to fall down in a fainting fit."

"It might not be a bad idea. That cow wouldn't attack her if she thought she was dead."

"You ever seen a woman faint? They don't lie quiet. They moan and groan and twist about as if they were dying of the miseries."

"That wouldn't fool a cow."

"Sounds like a fake to me," Zac said.

"Of course it is," Monty said. "Why would a woman faint if she's just going to lie there? A man might get bored and go off somewhere else."

"I wouldn't," said Zac. "I'd carry her inside and bathe her head with cool water."

"And get slapped for your troubles when you got it all over her dress," Monty said. "You've been reading too many books at that school. I told George it would ruin you."

"He won't be fit for anything but living in Chicago with Madison," Hen commented.

"Salty said I've been doing the best job with the horses he's ever seen."

"Anybody can take care of horses," Monty scoffed. "It's handling cows that separates the men from the boys."

"I could handle cows, too, if you'd let me," Zac protested. "George said I could. He said you'd let me before we got to Wyoming." This was the first time Zac had been allowed to leave school to take part in a trail drive, and Monty knew he was anxious to prove himself.

"Stop worrying about cows and eat," Tyler said. "It never tastes as good after it gets cold."

"It had better taste like a turkey," Monty said, getting to his feet.

"It's the herbs and spices," Zac said, anxious to show off some of what he'd learned watching Tyler. "He uses them for flavor."

"Turkey tastes fine when it tastes like turkey," Monty said. "I don't like it full of chopped-up weeds and little bitty seeds." He eyed his plate with dissatisfaction. "Do you always have to drown everything in a lot of goop?"

"That's a sauce," Tyler told him, completely indifferent to his brother's complaints about his cooking. "It adds moisture."

"It looks like you spilled something all over it," Monty complained.

"Sit down and eat," Hen said. "It doesn't look worth a damn, but it sure tastes good."

"Rose never serves anything like this," Monty said, not willing to give up yet.

"That's because she likes to please you," Tyler said, turning to feed the hands, who were lining up with none of Monty's reluctance. "I cook what I want. I don't care if you eat or not."

Tension in the Double-D camp had escalated during the last two days. Iris could almost feel the men watching her.

Having brought her wagon up to the protective ring of the campfire, she now took all her meals with the crew. She also insisted that Frank talk to her before he gave his orders. He still didn't like her riding with the herd, but she made it a point to be in the saddle as soon as breakfast was over. He said it unsettled the men and made the cattle nervous, but she was determined to be at the center of things. Something was going on, and she intended to find out what it was.

In that, she failed, but she did notice one thing. The crew had divided itself into two factions. It was a subtle thing, something she would never have noticed if she hadn't been looking for it. It only happened when the men were free to talk among themselves, eat, or sleep. Six of the cowhands stuck together, talking among themselves, working together as much as possible.

And keeping an eye on her.

Along with the cook, those men were the ones who had been with her father the longest. The other six seemed to gravitate toward Frank, away from her. Seven and seven. The crew was divided evenly. A stalemate. If she had had any doubts that something was afoot, they were gone now.

She was certain Quince Honeyman and his cohorts would be waiting somewhere down the road, but she was not about to let them steal as much as one cow. At first she didn't know what to do about it. Then, just as she was dropping off to sleep the night before, she had an idea. At first it seemed too ridiculous to consider. Too crazy. Too dangerous. But the more she thought about it, the more it seemed to be the perfect solution. She had been thinking about it all day and had come to the conclusion it was her only chance.

She'd do it tonight.

The camp had been quiet for hours. Only the sound of one of the riders singing as he circled the herd disturbed the night. Being careful to make no noise that would wake the men sleeping nearby, Iris carefully climbed down from the wagon and worked her way over to the rope corral that held the ramuda. The horses were quiet. Some were lying down, others slept standing up. The night horses for each rider stood saddled and ready. Moving to the horse farthest from the sleeping men, Iris lifted a saddle to his back. The experience of the last week enabled her to saddle the horse quickly and quietly. Mounted up moments later, she rode out of camp.

The quarter moon provided just enough light for Iris to find her way without being seen, but it seemed to her as if she was riding in total darkness. Her heart thumped painfully in her chest. She hated the dark. This wasn't like walking to her wagon. She'd soon be half a mile from camp with nobody to help her in case there was trouble.

She told herself she had to develop some guts if she was ever going to be independent. She was always depending on Monty to pull her chestnuts out of the fire. It seemed ironic she should need to develop courage so she could depend on Monty more than ever.

Iris had nearly gotten north of the herd when she came upon a second campsite, which some of her hands had set up. Two men sat talking quietly, their night horses tethered in the trees near the creek. Iris knew she wouldn't be able to get around the camp without being seen.

But she had to get north of the herd. Cattle stampeded away from whatever frightened them, and she wanted them to stampede south. She had decided that the only way to protect herself was to stampede her cows into Monty's herd. Then he couldn't protect his herd without protecting hers as well.

She would have to turn back and circle round the herd to the south, and that would take a long time. She had timed everything so she wouldn't run into the riders on night watch. Having to go in the opposite direction messed up her schedule. She saw the first rider before she got back to the cook camp.

Iris pulled into the shadows to wait until he passed.

Two men rode night watch at a time, one on each side. It took 30 to 40 minutes to circle the herd. Toby and Jack were on this watch. They were the slowest because Toby liked to sing sad songs. The hands complained his singing made them feel gloomy, but Frank let him sing what he wanted. The songs apparently made Toby's horse sad, too, because he walked very slowly.

Tonight Toby sang about a senorita whose lover died in a duel. She was forced to marry the man who killed him. Naturally the senorita killed herself instead of submitting to such an awful fate.

Iris shuddered and settled down to wait 20 minutes. By that time, both riders would be the same distance from her. It was important that everybody be as far away as possible. She didn't want anybody to suspect what she was about to do.

Iris didn't enjoy the wait. The silence made her aware of the innumerable night sounds she couldn't identify. She didn't feel any better when she remembered Monty had once told her it was the animals she couldn't hear she ought to worry about. She shivered. After the heat of the day, the night was cold and damp. It wouldn't surprise her if she developed a cold. She didn't need that added to her troubles. Worrying about the herd was enough.

She walked her horse a little to work out some of the fidgets. She could feel the dew and the damp settling into her bones. She wished she had thought to put on a heavier shirt. She'd be lucky if she didn't get pneumonia. She looked at her watch. Ten minutes to go.

But as the time drew nearer, she began to have second thoughts. There was no question in her mind she needed Monty's protection, but this was a cowardly way to go about getting it. It was the kind of devious trick her mother would pull. She ought to face Monty, tell him exactly what she suspected, and ask for his help. Surely he would not continue to refuse helping her.

Maybe he would.

He didn't believe going to Wyoming was her only choice. He didn't believe she had any business on the trail, that she knew anything about cows, or that she could learn. He absolutely didn't understand why she couldn't let her herd out of her sight, and nothing she said had made any difference.

She had to have his help. Since he wouldn't give it voluntarily, she had to get it any way she could.

Her 20 minutes up, Iris moved out.

She rode toward the herd. They were lying down, sleeping. Her horse seemed reluctant to approach too closely, so she let him choose his own path. She was just as happy to keep a safe distance. She doubted she'd ever trust a longhorn again after being chased by that cow.

Damn. Now her conscience was bothering her. She actually felt guilty about what she was doing. She told herself Monty deserved it, that he had brought it on himself by being so stubborn and uncooperative, but she knew she was doing the wrong thing and she couldn't make herself think otherwise.

This was her herd, and it was her responsibility. She had no right to force it on Monty. She had made the decision to set out for Wyoming. She had refused the help he had offered. She had scorned his advice. To force herself on him now that she had run into trouble was unfair. It was worse than that. It was cowardly.

Iris had never before been interested in playing fair. Her mother had taught her to use every situation to her advantage. But Monty lived by a different set of rules. And she was coming to feel it was a better way than she had been taught.

Muttering under her breath, Iris turned her horse back toward the camp. She didn't know where she'd find the courage, and she had no idea what she would say, but she would talk to Monty. If she expected him to get her out of this mess, she at least owed him the courtesy of explaining everything before she dumped it in his lap.

Iris hadn't gone far before she found two big steers blocking her path. They didn't seem angry. Only curious.

"Shoo! Scram!" Iris hissed. "Go back to sleep!" The steers continued to stare at her. A couple of cows close by raised their heads. Looking sleepily at Iris, they got up and came over to investigate.

Iris felt relieved. The cows weren't going to attack her, but they didn't appear ready to go back to bed either. She slapped her hand against her saddle, but her pony wouldn't move. The only effect it had on the cattle was to cause more of them to grow curious enough to investigate. In a few minutes Iris was surrounded by cows.

"Monty said you'd stampede at the slightest noise!" she hissed. "Why won't you move?"

Iris tried everything she could think of, and still the cattle gathered around her. The guard would be coming around again soon.

"You are the most obstinate beasts on the face of the earth," Iris said, trying to force her horse to push his way through the cattle. He refused to budge. All the while it had gotten colder. She could feel her head closing up, and she felt a sneeze coming on.

"Now I've got a cold."

Iris

Aaaaacchooo!

At the same moment Iris sneezed, the bloodcurdling scream of a panther split the night.

In an instant, nearly 4,000 cows were on their feet and heading toward the Circle-7 herd as fast as they could go.

Monty and Hen came off their turn at night duty.

"Fork out Nightmare and stake him near my bed," Monty said to a sleepy Zac, who got up to help put their horses in the corral. "I want a horse I can depend on. I'm so tired I could be halfway to the river before I opened my eyes."

"You'd open them fast enough if Iris was about," Hen grumbled.

Monty ignored his brother and crawled into bed.

"What do you mean?" Zac asked, yawning. "I thought Monty had been trying to get her out of the way."

"That's what I thought too, but he hasn't talked about anybody else all day. If I hear one more word about how tough things must be on a woman like her, I'm going to take my bed and sleep with the cows."

Zac looked at his brother, an unholy gleam in his eyes.

"You can forget what you're thinking," Monty growled at his youngest brother. "You say one word to Tyler or Salty, and I'll strangle you with your own picket rope. I'm not sweet on any female, but it just doesn't seem right that a girl who doesn't know any more than how to bat her eyelashes and pick out a pretty dress should be left in such a pickle."

"If you think Iris Richmond is still a girl, you need glasses," Hen said, dropping to his blankets.

"Monty doesn't need no glasses," Zac said, a sly smile on his lips. "The way he described her to me this morning, he can see real good."

Zac dived into the midst of the ramuda to escape his brother's angry charge.

"I hope they trample you to death," Monty called out as he stalked back to his bed. "I should have known better than to let George talk me into bringing that brat along."

"He's doing just fine," Hen said, turning over and settling under his blanket. "You're just in a foul mood because of Iris."

"I am not," Monty practically shouted. "I've hardly thought about her all day."

"Sure," Hen said.

Monty mumbled several curses under his breath, then added a few more for the smile he knew was curving his twin's lips. He wasn't easy in his mind about Iris. She was worried about something. He had seen it in her eyes. She didn't act right either. Iris had always been more conscious of her looks than anything else. Not now. She'd taken to riding each day. She'd even cut one of her dresses down to make an extra riding outfit. That definitely wasn't like the Iris he knew. Even more shocking, she had cut her nails to keep them from catching. He wouldn't have believed it if he hadn't seen her do it. He'd have guessed she'd have walked to Wyoming before making such a sacrifice

Of course it was Frank, the rat. Monty knew he couldn't sleep easy in his own bed if Frank were his foreman. He couldn't prove the man was a crook, but if ever there was a good man likely to go bad, it was Frank.

Monty flipped on his side. But he couldn't get comfortable. He turned over a couple more times before he settled down.

"You'd better come out of that ramuda," he called to Zac. "I don't want to have to take your trampled remains home to Rose."

"The horses are jumpy," Zac said, ducking under the rope and heading toward his bed. "You seen any tracks around?"

"Nothing bigger than a coyote," Monty said. "You're imagining things."

"I'm not imagining that," Zac said, pointing to the herd. They stood with their ears pricked, all looking north.

Monty raised his head and looked, but the horses continued to stand very still.

"I don't know," Monty said. "Maybe they smell a panther." He put his head back down, but the moment his ear touched the earth he jumped to his feet. "It's a stampede," he shouted. "It's headed this way."

Chapter Eight

To Iris's horror, a mass of cattle 100 feet wide was headed straight toward her. Without waiting for her command, her horse took off at a gallop. It was all she could do to hang on.

Iris told herself not to panic. People survived stampedes all the time—her own men had survived one just a few days earlier—but that thought wasn't the least bit comforting when she looked over her shoulder to see a sea of horns closing in around her. Even as the seemingly endless expanse of cattle engulfed her, a single thought kept pounding in her head.

If Monty were here, he'd know what to do.

But Monty wasn't there. He was at his camp miles away, sound asleep. And even if the stampede did wake him, the chances were he wouldn't be able to find her. If she was going to get out of this mess, she would have to get out by herself. Iris held tight to her horse. If she fell beneath the thousands of hooves behind her, there wouldn't be enough left for Monty or anyone else to find.

Gradually the panic receded enough for her to decide that if she could get ahead of the herd, she could veer off to the side and out of the path of the stampede.

Praying she wouldn't lose her balance, Iris pulled her pony to the left of the steer running directly in front of her and urged him forward with heels and knees. It soon became clear that though her mount was sure of foot, he was barely faster than the cows she wanted him to outrace.

With nail-gnawing slowness, they passed that steer and two others, but just as she came alongside of the lead steer, they breasted a small rise. Before them lay the Circle-7 herd. Her cattle were going to smash right into Monty's herd with her in the lead.

Monty was astride Nightmare and headed out of camp before Hen cleared his blankets. Monty was desperate to head off Iris's herd before it reached his own. If he didn't, the two herds would be so mixed up it would take days to separate them.

Shouting to the rest of the crew as he rode past, Monty gave Nightmare his head. The big gelding had been in more than one stampede. He knew what to do.

Monty's heart sank when he reached the herd. Some of them were on their feet, their heads turned in the direction of the dull thunder of 15,000 hooves as they pounded the dry earth at a gallop. Shouting for the night guards to join him, Monty thundered past. He had the feeling he was too late, but he had to try.

They were much closer than he expected. Just as he reached the foremost cattle in his herd, the Double-D herd burst out of a low place in the plain. He gaped in stunned horror when he realized that the rider at the front of the herd was not a cowhand trying to turn the herd.

The rider was Iris Richmond, and she was fleeing for her life.

In a flash Monty's herd was on its feet and running like the wind. Iris was caught in the middle of a stampede of more than 6,000 cows.

Monty's instinctive reaction was to get to the front of the stampede as quickly as possible and turn the leaders. If he could do that, they would begin to mill, to run in a circle, and the stampede would soon be over. That was what he'd always done before; that was what duty demanded of him now.

Iris would be all right if she just rode along with the herd. She was on a good cow pony. Besides, one of her own men would look after her. His responsibility was to his own herd.

But Monty couldn't ignore Iris. Someone else could turn the herd. They could run all the way back to Austin if they must. He had to rescue Iris.

The cows uttered no sound as they ran. Only the clicking of their horns competed with the thunder of their hooves. Occasionally Monty saw the flash of gunfire as members of the two crews tried to keep the cattle together. They were running on a very broad front. He doubted even gunfire would keep them in a bunch for very long.

Monty had never seen so many cattle in a stampede. It seemed that Iris was miles beyond his reach. Yet digging his heels into Nightmare's flanks, he drove his horse into the mass of running animals.

Nightmare didn't hesitate. He was a big strong horse, two hands bigger than the average cow pony. His thoroughbred blood gave him tremendous speed, but right now Monty hoped he could depend on his Morgan ancestors to help him weave his way through the herd to Iris.

The minutes seemed to crawl by as Monty worked his way through, first dropping behind one animal then sprinting past another. The gunfire increased as the two crews fought desperately to hold the herd together. Monty wished they hadn't been doing such a good job. He could reach Iris more quickly in a less compact herd.

Iris was white-faced when Monty finally drew alongside. She held tightly to the pommel with both hands. Her pony was too small and tired to withstand any more buffeting by the stampeding longhorns.

"Hold on to me," he shouted as he leaned over and wrapped a strong arm around Iris's waist.

Iris kept her grip on the saddle. Monty could see she was too frightened to let go.

"Let go," he shouted. "Your horse could go down any minute."

Iris looked numb with fear. Taking a firm hold with his left hand, Monty leaned over, wrapped his arm around Iris's waist, and bodily lifted her out of the saddle.

· That broke her grip. Iris immediately twisted her body around, threw one leg across the saddle, threw her arms around Monty, and clung to him tighter than ivy to a stone wall.

For a moment Monty thought they might both fall out of the saddle. Iris had knocked the reins out of his hand. But Monty didn't worry about Nightmare. A little pressure with his legs, and the big horse started working his way out of the packed mass of animals. It took all of Monty's strength and concentration to keep his balance while he settled Iris in the saddle.

Iris sat straddling his legs, facing him, clutching him so tightly he could hardly breathe. Nor could he see where he was going. An incredible tangle of red hair blocked his vision.

"Move your head," Monty shouted. "I can't see."

Iris held more tightly, her cheek pressed against his.

Having finally retrieved the reins, Monty put a hand on Iris's head and forced it down on his shoulder. By leaning to the left, he had about half a field of vision—the half he needed to work his way out of the herd.

Iris's horse stayed with the herd.

Monty didn't know how it could be so, but he was almost more aware of Iris's body pressed against him than the dangers of the stampede. He was familiar with everything a cow could do, but he had never ridden a horse with a woman sitting on his lap. Even if Iris hadn't been blocking his field of vision, he'd have had trouble concentrating.

Monty hadn't reached the age of 26 without having a fair amount of contact with women. Yet he couldn't control his reaction to Iris's physical presence any more than he could control the herd.

The gentle rocking motion of his horse caused their bodies to rub against each other. Incredibly, he felt his body tighten. He would never have thought himself so susceptible, but by the time he reached the edge of the herd and turned back toward his camp, he would have been embarrassed to climb out of the saddle.

"You can let go now," he said, his voice thick with tension. "We're out of danger."

Her grip did not loosen.

Neither did the tension in Monty's body lessen. The pressure of her breasts against his chest, the smell of her hair, and the pressure of her buttocks as she sat in his lap combined to bring him dangerously close to losing control.

When they finally reached the camp, he brought his horse to a stop near the campfire and slid from the saddle. Iris came with him in a tangle of limbs.

"It's all right now," Monty said as he tried to pry her arms from around him. But she wouldn't let go, and it seemed only natural for Monty to put his arms around her. She clearly needed comfort. The other men could follow the herd as it disappeared into the night.

Monty didn't have much experience at rescuing women. No one had ever held on to him as though her very life depended on him. It had never been up to him to reassure a woman who was so upset she couldn't stop her body from shaking or loosen the death grip she had on his neck.

He should have hated it, but he didn't. He shouldn't have felt so nervous, but he did. He didn't know what to do, and Rose wasn't around to ask. Nobody was around, and that could be a problem. If one of her cowhands happened to ride up now without knowing what had happened, there would be hell to pay.

Women never came on trail drives, but not because of any danger from cowboys. A cowboy would lay down his life to protect a good woman, and that was exactly what was bothering Monty. He didn't want anybody laying down anything before he had a chance to explain he was only protecting Iris from the cows.

He tried to ease her arms from around him, but they felt like bands of iron. He didn't try too hard. Their being there gave him a good feeling. And his body sure hadn't shown any sign of wanting her to move.

"Are you cold?" Monty asked.

Iris nodded.

"You're shaking like a leaf. Let's get some coffee in you."

Keeping one arm around Iris, Monty walked her to the fire. Firmly unclenching Iris's hands, Monty seated her on a log someone had pulled up next to the fire. He took his blanket and draped it over her shoulders. He poured some coffee in a cup and handed it to her. Iris's hands were so unsteady she spilled half the coffee.

"Here, let me hold it," Monty said.

Monty held the cup while Iris guided it to her mouth. She jerked away when the hot liquid burned her lips, but it seemed to steady her. After a couple of swallows she didn't shake so badly.

"Do you feel better now?" Monty asked. He had gotten himself under control. He stepped back.

Iris nodded.

"You'll be okay here."

"Where are you going?"

"I've got to help with the herd."

"Don't leave me," Iris said, her hands shaking worse than ever.

"You'll be okay. There's nothing to bother you now."

"There's nobody here."

Only now did Monty realize that Zac and Tyler must have gone after the herd, too.

"I've got to go," Monty said. "The herd's my responsibility."

But he didn't move. He might have been able to leave Iris if she had looked sad and forlorn. It was Iris trying to look brave that tore at his heartstrings. But if he stayed, he would forfeit his position of leadership. He'd waited years for this chance.

Monty didn't know what decision he would have made. He was saved the choice when he heard the rumble of hooves. Moments later the ramuda trotted into sight. Tyler and Zac had gone after the horses when they stampeded along with the cows.

"Look after Iris," Monty yelled at Zac as he and Tyler put the rope corral back together. "I'll be back as soon as I can."

"What are you doing here?" Zac demanded of Iris after Monty had galloped off. "What was Monty doing with you?" He might be only 16, but Iris could see he already had a few thoughts of his own, and none of them flattering to her.

"I got caught in the stampede," Iris explained. She waved her hand in the direction of the vanished herd. "My horse is still out there somewhere."

"Are you sure it wasn't something else?" Zac asked, obviously suspicious.

"What do you mean?"

"I thought I'd drop dead of old age before Monty paid more attention to some female than his cows."

"Surely, if you saw a woman in danger, you'd—"

"*I* would," Zac assured her, "especially if she was as pretty as you. But Monty—"

"Monty won't thank you for blabbing to everybody you meet," Tyler warned. He reached into one of the numerous drawers of the chuck wagon and drew out a sack of coffee beans.

"Iris ain't everybody," Zac protested.

"She's not family," Tyler said, measuring three tablespoons of beans into a coffee grinder.

That single sentence made Iris feel more alone than ever before. No, she wasn't family. But these boys were, and that unique tie formed a barrier that kept her an outsider.

Tyler dumped the grounds into a pot and filled it with water from the barrel. "You'd better get some horses ready. They'll be coming in soon for coffee and new mounts. And you'd better check those ropes while you're at it. It'll give you something to do besides run your mouth."

"I know what to do," Zac said, sulkily going about his work.

Tyler set the pot on the fire. "Fresh coffee will be ready in a little while." He walked back to the chuck wagon.

"I know how important this herd is to Monty." Iris spoke to Tyler's back as he worked silently. "But my herd is just as important to me."

Still Tyler didn't speak.

"Monty wanted me to turn them over to a drover, but I couldn't."

"You should have," Tyler said, his voice flat and matter-of-fact. "Monty's got enough to do without having to worry about you."

"He doesn't have to worry about me," Iris said, firing up.

"You're a woman," Tyler said. "A man always has to worry about a woman, even if he doesn't like her."

Tyler's words struck Iris like a surprise dagger thrust out of the night. She had taken it for granted Monty liked her. Everything had depended on it. But Tyler's words made her wonder if she had become so used to being admired she couldn't see Monty didn't feel the same way. Even after he proved immune to her blandishments, she had still assumed he liked her.

But what were his feelings toward her? Did he still think of her as the little girl who followed at his heels? Did he see her as the spoiled daughter of the nearly notorious Helena Richmond? Or did he see her as a young woman who exercised a strong hold over him? Probably something of all three, but that still didn't answer the question.

Did Monty like her, or was his attention merely cowboy chivalry?

Shocked, Iris realized she didn't know.

She realized with an equal feeling of foreboding that whether she got to Wyoming safely depended on whether or not Monty cared enough to keep on taking care of her.

Could chivalry last that long, and if not, what kind of feeling would?

Just as important, how did she feel about Monty? *Really* feel. How would she feel about a man who liked her enough to take care of her for 2,000 miles through wild country? What could she offer him in return? What would he expect?

The unanswered questions buzzed in Iris's head until she felt dizzy. She had set out on this journey determined to use Monty for her benefit. She hadn't thought about what would happen when they reached Wyoming. She'd supposed they would separate, go their different ways, and forget each other.

Now she knew that wasn't possible. At least not for her.

She also knew she hoped it wouldn't be true for Monty.

Iris saw him ride in, tired and windblown, but radiating energy as if he hadn't been in the saddle nearly 24 hours. Just watching him made her feel more alive, as if she wanted to get up and do something. It sounded silly, but just knowing he was near made any danger seem less threatening.

She was just as bad as she had been at 15, following him around thinking the sun rose and set on his shoulders. She was an adult now, supposedly she knew better, but she was doing exactly the same thing. She ought to feel ashamed of herself, but she didn't. She felt relieved.

"Where's Iris?" Monty demanded even before his horse had come to a stop.

"Over there," Zac said, nodding to where Iris rested next to the fire. "You going back out? You want another horse?"

"Not right now," Monty said, tossing the stirrup over the saddle and beginning to loosen the cinch. "I need to talk to Iris. Is she all right?"

"Why shouldn't she be? Tyler's been grumbling worse than if he burned something, but he's been watching out for her."

"She sleeping?"

"Naw. She perks up every time somebody comes in. See, just like I told you." Zac winked at his brother. "I think she's waiting for you."

"Well, you make sure you don't go telling anybody else what you think," Monty said, lifting his saddle from the horse's back. "It's not good for her reputation or your well-being."

"If she was worried about her reputation, she ought to have stayed home," Zac said.

"True," Monty said, "but it's too late for that now." He laid the saddle blanket over the saddle, picked them up, and headed toward the campfire as Zac took an exhausted Nightmare to the corral. Monty dumped his saddle next to Iris.

"You find the herd?" she asked, looking up at him.

"Most of them. Some split off. We'll start looking for them as soon as we get the rest settled."

"Did anybody get hurt?"

"No."

Tyler interrupted their conversation and handed Monty a cup of coffee. Then he headed back to the chuck wagon, where Zac stood spying on Iris and his brother.

"I told you he'd head straight for her," Zac whispered to Tyler as he peered at Monty from around the corner of the chuck wagon. "Hen's going to be fit to bite a bear."

"Then you'd better not say anything unless you want him to bite you," Tyler replied sotto voce.

Zac grinned. "I won't say a word."

"Only way that'll happen is if you're dead by the time he gets back."

Out by the fire, Monty continued questioning Iris. "What caused the stampede?" He sat down next to Iris, the hot coffee cup between his hands, and leaned back against his saddle.

"I don't know," Iris answered. "One minute they were all sleeping, and the next they were running straight toward me."

"What were you doing out of your wagon so late? You didn't ask Frank to put you on night duty, did you?"

For once Iris didn't mind Monty criticizing her behavior. If she could have lived this night over again, she would have never left her wagon.

"I couldn't sleep," she said, telling a partial untruth. "Something is going on in my camp, and I wanted to see if I could find out what it was."

Behind the chuck wagon, Zac continued his running commentary. "I wonder what she was doing out of bed," he whispered. "I'll bet she was trying to sneak over this way to see Monty."

"If you wondered less, you might live longer," Tyler whispered back.

"You should talk to your foreman. That's what you pay him for," Monty told Iris.

"What if I'm afraid my foreman is involved?" Iris hadn't meant to reveal her suspicions to Monty. She probably wouldn't have if the stampede hadn't scared her so badly, but now that she had told him, she felt as if a weight had been lifted off her shoulders. She no longer felt alone.

"What do you mean?"

"I'm not sure. Do you remember that man you said was trying to steal those cows you brought back?"

Monty nodded.

"I saw him talking to Bill Lovell back on the ranch several days before we left. When I finally remembered and went to find Frank, he was talking to Lovell. It wasn't like Frank was mad at him. It was almost like they were talking over something important. Then when Frank tried to convince me to rehire that hand you fired—"

"You mean Crowder?"

Iris nodded. "I was even more unsure after Frank did that."

"Then fire him," Monty said immediately.

"That's just like a man," Iris said, irritably. "You think the answer to everything is a fight or running somebody out of the county. He could very well be innocent. And even if he's not, who am I going to get to do his job?"

"I told you to—"

"If you tell me one more time that I should have stayed home, I'll hit you."

"Well you should have."

The night had stretched Iris's resources to the limit. She had no energy left to control her instinctive reaction. She scrambled to her knees and hit Monty in the stomach as hard as she could.

Chapter Nine

"Did you see that!" Zac hissed from his position behind the chuck wagon. "She hit him, and he didn't do a thing. If one of us had done it, he'd be howling mad."

"Don't you know anything about women?" Tyler asked, disgusted.

"More than you think."

"That still wouldn't be much," his brother replied, being careful to keep out of Monty's sight.

Meanwhile, out by the campfire, Iris was berating Monty. "You have no feelings. You think all you have to do is hand down your judgment and everything will work out the way you want it to. Well it doesn't. Not by a long shot."

Monty drew back, stunned at Iris's accusation. "I do have feelings. Besides, I risked my neck to rescue you from that stampede."

"You're always risking your neck, and nothing ever happens to it. Everything's gone your way for so long you don't understand anybody else."

Iris ignored Monty's strangled protest.

"It's cruel to tell me to go back to a ranch I don't own any longer and let rustlers steal my cattle until I'm as poor as a Mexican." Iris's hands moved as fast as she talked. "Is that want you want to see, Monty Randolph, me so poor I have to beg?"

"What does she mean about being poor?" Zac whispered. "Her pa was as rich as George."

"You keep eavesdropping on people's conversations and you're going to be as dead as that stump," Tyler said.

Monty had never thought such a thing. He couldn't imagine a woman like Iris being reduced to begging, not when half the men in Texas would stumble over themselves to give her just about anything she wanted. Didn't she know what she looked like? Did she have any idea how just being around her affected men? How she affected him?

Hell, he couldn't remember the last time his pants fit right, and if he didn't learn to keep his mind on something other than Iris he was going to lose his own herd.

Today marked a change in their relationship.

Until now he had kept on trying to think of her as the young girl with a crush on him. Tonight's ride had changed all that. Iris was a beautiful, mature, vibrantly alive woman from whom distance seemed impossible. Maybe it was the feel of her body in his lap, leaning against him, rubbing against him intimately, holding him in a tight embrace. He would never be able to think of her as a little girl again. He regretted that in a way. As a girl she had had an innocent, endearing charm he hated to lose. Liking her had been comfortable. No complications, no commitment.

But it was impossible to completely regret the change. This woman had nothing to do with the girl of four summers ago. And neither did his feelings. Her effect on him wasn't convenient—women never were. They always picked the worst time to do anything—but it was exciting. She might irritate him, she might trouble him, but she wouldn't bore him.

"You'll never have to go begging," Monty said, finding his tongue. "You can marry just about any man you want."

"That's just the kind of thing a man like you would say," Iris shot back, her eyes bright, her red hair bouncing as she spoke. "You think all you have to do to take care of a woman is marry her off. Find her a husband and she can't possibly have a care in the world."

"I didn't mean—"

"Well, I'm not property, and I have feelings." Iris pounded her chest with her fist. "Far more feelings than you'll ever have. I'll get married because my husband adores me, not because he's rich."

"He'll adore you all right. One look and every man adores you."

"I mean me, the real me."

"That's what I said," Monty said, uncomprehending. "He'll take one look at you and won't be able to deny you anything."

"You're just like all men," Iris said. "All you see is what you see."

Monty was fast losing the thread of this conversation, but he struggled on. "Men are funny like that. Even the most sensible man, one who can fight and ride with the best, who doesn't mind the cold and the wet, going hungry or being a little uncomfortable. Get him hitched up with a woman and all of a sudden he can't be more than thirty minutes away without having to be reminded what she looks like. Soon after that, he gets to liking a bed and regular meals, baths and clean clothes. Next thing you know he's completely ruined."

"How about you?" Iris asked. "Would you adore some female like that?"

"Hell, no!" Monty replied, appalled at the very idea. "George doesn't even do that, and he's so nutty on Rose he sometimes doesn't even know there's anybody else around."

"A man who really adored his wife would give her anything she wanted."

"Not unless he's crazy. Have you already forgotten how Helena ruined your pa? That woman seemed to spend just to show she could do it. Wasn't a bit of sense in half of what she did."

"And how do you know that?"

"Because Rose said so," Monty replied as though that were enough to clinch any argument.

"If Monty keeps talking like that, she's going to take a gun to him," Tyler whispered to Zac. "The damned fool can't seem to understand a female unless it's a cow."

Zac crowed. "Now you're eavesdropping."

Iris felt like hitting Monty again, only harder. He had no business criticizing her mother, even if what he said was true. It didn't make it any better to realize that everybody from Austin to San Antonio probably thought the same. It might have been easier to endure if she weren't now suffering from the result of her mother's extravagance and her father's inability to refuse her anything she wished.

129

"A man who truly adored me wouldn't criticize my family," Iris said.

"He might not say it to your face," Monty said, "but he'd know it just the same. Besides, it never does to hide something like that. It only gets worse for covering it up."

He always had an answer, usually one she didn't like.

Monty stood up. "It's about time I was getting you back to your camp. I want a word with that foreman of yours."

"No." Iris scrambled to her feet.

"There's no time like now. I want him to know I'm onto his game before we start separating the herds. I already had some doubts of my own."

"I don't care about your doubts," Iris said as she rubbed a sore muscle that threatened to cramp. "You can't tell him, then turn around and leave me with him."

Iris could tell he didn't like what she said, but it made him thoughtful. "If he's guilty, we don't know who might be working with him, or when they might try again. We need to wait, to watch the whole crew before we do anything."

"What do you mean *we*? I—"

"We could keep the herds together," she suggested, before Monty could say anything. "Then you could be responsible for everybody. That way you would have an excuse to watch everything he did, to study the men and find out who you could trust."

Behind the chuck wagon, Zac couldn't believe his ears. "Lord Almighty," he hissed. "Wait until Hen hears about this."

"Why don't you rush off and tell him," Tyler suggested. "No point in keeping the good news to yourself."

"I ain't no fool," Zac said. "There ain't no horse fast enough to outrun a bullet."

Out by the campfire, Iris could see Monty hated the idea and was only waiting for her to be silent before he refused. She rushed ahead. "It'll take days to separate them. And you told me you had to keep to a schedule. Why not wait until you have to stop anyway to cross river? By then you ought to know what to do."

"You're crazy," Monty said, when he could get a word in edgewise. "Nobody in his right mind would try to drive a herd that big. We have more than six thousand cows together."

Iris knew the time had come to be honest with him—and herself. She had tried flirting, she had tried subterfuge, and she had tried bluffing. None of it worked. Now it was time for a little straight talk. It was all she had left.

It was also time she accepted the fact that Monty wasn't one of the besotted men who adored her so much he would do anything she wanted. He was clearly attracted to her, but she had the feeling physical beauty was not all-important for him. He liked it and he appreciated it; he could even fall prey to its lure now and then. But in the end he would set it aside for something else.

Only Iris didn't know what that something else would be. She wondered if Monty did.

"Don't say no just yet," she pleaded. She reached out and put a hand on his arm so he wouldn't walk away. "I can't do this by myself. I thought I could, but I can't. I need your help."

Monty was looking at her as if she had grown a second head. He was already looking after 2,500 cows. It shouldn't be that hard to take care of 3,700 more.

131

Monty removed her hand from his arm. His glance was hard and questioning. "I don't have enough men to manage both herds, and there's nowhere I can get more, at least not experienced trail hands. And that doesn't even touch on finding food and water for such a huge herd."

"I already have a crew."

"I can't watch your cows and Frank, too."

"Frank won't dare try anything with you looking over his shoulder."

She would have thrown herself at Monty's feet if that would have worked, but there was a different formula for this man. Right then she swore to find the key. He ought to be brought down a peg. It would make him more human. He would never find a wife if he treated every woman like a dim-witted cowhand and kept throwing up the perfect Rose as an example. Everyone knew Rose was a paragon. Even Helena had been made to feel the sting of unfavorable comparison.

"It won't be for long," she pleaded. "I wouldn't ask that of you. I know you've got to get your herd to Wyoming without losing a single cow or George will have your head."

Iris hadn't meant to anger Monty. She was merely repeating what she had heard. His eyes grew hard and his eyebrows drew together. His mouth tightened until a muscle in his temple started to twitch.

"This is the family's herd," he said, his temper barely under control, "but I'm ramrodding this drive, and I'm going to be foreman of the ranch. I don't need George's say-so for anything I do."

"I didn't mean to hurt your feelings," Iris said, unsure what she had said to make him so angry. "I just thought that since George runs the ranch—"

"I run the ranch," Monty exploded. "George has some say about it, all of us do, but I run it."

"Doesn't look like she knows any more about men than Monty does about females," Zac observed, drawing back behind the chuck wagon. "She just made him madder than a nest of hornets."

"I don't know what they teach you at that school George is sending you to, but I sure hope he can get his money back," Tyler said, then turned his attention back to the couple by the fire.

As Iris considered her next move, one of Monty's men rode up. "The herd hit a mesquite thicket about a mile from here. They're scattered all to hell," he said.

"Damnation!" Monty cursed. "It'll take us days to find them all. We'd better get at it before the herd cutters and rustlers do. Come along," Monty said to Iris. "One of the first lessons any rancher needs to learn is how to find his cows."

Iris nodded her agreement, but secretly she couldn't regret the stampede or the mesquite thicket. They had been able to do what she couldn't. A leveling thought, but victory for any reason was better than no victory at all.

But she meant to learn more about Monty. She couldn't depend upon stampedes and mesquite to keep him at her side.

As Monty and Iris disappeared over a ridge, Tyler said to Zac, "Instead of dancing about waiting for trouble, you'd better fork out some broncos. I see two hands coming."

"I see them, too, and one of them is Hen."

"Thank goodness he didn't get here five minutes sooner."

* * *

"You might as well set fire to the rest of it," Monty said.

Iris stared at her travel wagon. It had been turned over into the campfire during the stampede. The canvas cover had burned completely. Two of the ribs had almost burned through, and part of the panel on one side was badly charred. Most of her clothes and her bed were ruined, but the furniture could be saved.

Her eyes flew to the panel that contained the secret compartment. There was no damage to that part of the wagon.

"It's got to be fixed," Iris said.

"What for? You should never have brought such a big, clumsy thing in the first place."

"I've got to have some place to sleep and keep my things."

"Sleep on the ground and keep your things in your saddlebags."

"Not my dresses."

"It doesn't look like you have any dresses left," Monty said, holding up a piece of scorched and torn material. "Leastways not anything you'd want to wear."

"You don't sound the least bit sympathetic."

"You shouldn't have brought all that stuff."

"I know. I should have stayed home and waited for poverty to overtake me," she said sarcastically.

"You should have met your herd in Wyoming," Monty said, sounding a little less dictatorial than usual. "Nothing wrong with having dresses in Cheyenne or Laramie."

"I'm surprised you don't expect me to wear buckskins."

"I don't think it would be a good idea for you to go around in pants. Fern used to do it, and it caused no end of trouble. Madison won't let her wear them anywhere but the ranch."

"I wouldn't be caught dead in pants," Iris said, shocked at the idea.

"Good thing. Bound to cause somebody to get shot."

"Whatever for?"

Monty looked at her as if she had suddenly lost any sense she ever possessed. "Wyoming and Colorado are full of miners. They're nothing like cowboys. Don't have any manners at all. They're bound to make some insulting remark, and I'd have to kill one or two of them to keep the rest in line."

Iris stared at him, her mouth open. "You'd do that for me?"

"I wouldn't have any choice. What kind of man would I be if I went around letting miners insult a woman under my protection?"

"I'm not under your protection."

"Yes, you are."

While Monty subjected the wagon to a closer inspection, Iris attempted to digest his remarks.

Monty had never shown the slightest desire to protect her. Still he must have been looking out for her. He was always close at hand whenever she needed him. She didn't want to place too much importance on that—it might be no more than Southern chivalry—but maybe it meant he was at least seeing her as a woman rather than an annoying teenager. She hoped so. It would be nice to know she had finally acquired a little power over Monty Randolph.

"It shouldn't be too hard to fix," Monty said, studying the wagon, "but we can't do it on the trail. We'll have to take it in to Fort Worth. It's a good thing the wheels weren't broken. Your chuck wagon, too." The canvas had been shredded, the tongue broken, and the hinged lid torn off.

"We could send them ahead. Then they'd be ready when we reach town."

Monty looked at her as if he was stunned she could have an idea of her own, particularly one worth considering.

"I don't have anybody to send."

"Surely you can spare one man. It must be easier to handle the cows in one herd than in two."

Monty rolled his eyes. "It's going to be harder, but we'll have to manage somehow. I'll send Lovell. I don't trust him anyway."

"I need to get some things first," Iris said.

"Can't be much of value left."

"Nevertheless, there are a few things. I'd rather you didn't stand here watching me," Iris said when Monty made no move to leave. "Some things are private, even on a cattle drive."

"Damned few," Monty said, striding away.

Maybe, Iris thought to herself, but this was one secret she meant to keep to herself.

Monty returned in time to see Iris pick up her saddlebags and take them over to her horse. She was strapping them to her saddle when he realized what was bothering him. From the way Iris lifted them, the saddlebags had to be quite heavy. He didn't know much about feminine belongings—actually nothing at all—but he didn't know what she could have in that bag unless she was carrying the family silver.

He had heard she'd sold everything, but maybe she'd held a few things back. Maybe she did have a lot of forks and knives in those bags. Or jewels, or something equally extravagant. Maybe she should have turned them over to the bank and was trying to sneak them out of Texas. Not exactly legal, but it must have been very hard to have had so much and suddenly find herself with so little.

Let her keep her silver and baubles, or whatever it was. He couldn't see why she'd want to take anything like that to a cow ranch in Wyoming, but it was none of his business.

The crew knew something was up. They stood watching expectantly while Iris and Frank faced each other some distance away.

"You can't both be in charge," Iris tried to explain to Frank.

"We can separate the herds," Frank said. "Then there wouldn't be any problem."

"We can't, not with everybody out looking for the rest of the herd."

"What'll the men say?" He involuntarily glanced over his shoulder.

"Nothing, if you handle it right. Tell them Monty and I are in joint charge. You can come to me for your orders, if you like, but as long as the herds are together, Monty makes the decisions."

"You're going to regret this."

"I may," Iris said, returning her foreman's stare, "but it had better not be for the reasons you've got in mind just now."

"What do you mean?"

"You hate Monty. I don't know why, and I don't care to know. But I won't have you fighting or working against him. I'm only interested in getting this herd to Wyoming. I'll do it with or without you."

Frank stared at Iris for a moment longer. Then he turned and walked away.

Iris felt her strength seep away until she felt as weak as a kitten. She had dreaded this interview. She had wanted Monty to tell Frank, but she knew she had to do it herself. If she wanted Monty to respect her, if she wanted to be able to run her own ranch, she had to learn to make decisions and do the unpleasant jobs. She had always been protected from the difficult part of life, but now there was no one to shield her. She had to do it herself. It was just one more bit of proof it wasn't easy to be the boss. There were probably other difficulties she hadn't foreseen. Maybe Monty had been right when he said it was too difficult to work two herds together. Maybe, but she needed him.

"We're still short about two hundred head," Salty reported. "Mostly Miss Richmond's cows if my guess is correct."

Monty looked about him. Longhorns covered the plain almost as far as he could see. The men kept them in a loose herd over a couple thousand acres while they grazed. The two herds were hopelessly mixed. It would take at least two days to separate them.

"Well, we can't stay here any longer," Monty said. "We'll have to keep going just to find enough grass to feed them. Hen and I will catch up when we find the rest."

"I'd rather one of you stayed," Salty said. "It would be rather awkward for me giving orders to Miss Richmond's foreman."

"He'll just have to take them," Monty replied impatiently.

"Don't be a fool," Hen said. "Frank won't swallow that kind of insult without causing trouble. Salty can go with you. I'll stay here."

"You'll need Salty," Monty insisted. "You can't handle all this alone."

"You can both stay. I'll go with Monty," Iris volunteered.

"You!"

It was a simple word, but the way Monty said it was a terrible insult.

"I *can* ride. And if you're only half as good as you think you are, you can round up those cows all by yourself."

More than Salty's discreet smile, it was Hen's crack of laughter that sent Monty over the edge.

"Even if I were only half as good as that, I wouldn't want you riding with me."

They stood there, at a stalemate, glaring at each other like prairie dogs arguing over a burrow.

"Well, I'm going anyway," Iris said, looking him straight in the eye. "You don't have any choice. You don't own this land. I can ride anywhere I like."

Monty figured Iris wouldn't be satisfied until she had humiliated him in front of every member of his family. Struggling to keep his temper under control, he headed for his horse. "Then you'd better ride like the devil himself is after you. I'm not waiting for anybody."

With that Monty swung into the saddle and headed off at a gallop.

"Wait for me, you mule-headed skunk," Iris called and swung her horse in behind him.

"Do you think they'll stop fighting long enough to look for the cattle?" Salty asked.

"I'm not sure they'll stop fighting long enough to notice the cattle if they walk up to them," Hen said. "I don't know what it is about that female, but she makes Monty about as mad as a bull in springtime."

"And as restless," Salty muttered under his breath.

Chapter Ten

Monty pulled up and turned in the saddle to wait for Iris. They had been following a small valley carved by a meandering creek as it worked its way east through the low hills that bordered the flat prairie. Tall grass was beginning to give way to sage, and pecan and elm to scrub oaks.

He had to give Iris credit. She was so tired she was about to fall out of the saddle, but she had kept up with him all day and hadn't once complained about the pace. He couldn't help but think better of her, and *that* made him uncomfortable. He didn't want to think better of her. He wanted to be able to dismiss her as a foolish female who thought every problem in life could be solved by batting her eyelashes at some rich man.

He hadn't expected it to be a problem, at least not one that would require his whole concentration. It took every bit of his willpower to keep his mind *off* Iris and *on* the missing cows. As annoying as it was to have her tagging along behind him almost like she did five years ago, she was giving his cows more competition than they could handle.

That surprised him. He'd never had any problem putting women out of his mind when it came time to work. From that day a dozen years ago when he and Hen realized if they couldn't defend the ranch and themselves they would be robbed and murdered, the ranch had been his primary concern. It was the only thing he really loved.

And in a sense, that was why he'd insisted on going to Wyoming. He was the only true cowman in the family, though George was the best businessman. Since the ranch belonged to everybody, George made the final decisions.

Monty was given a near free hand with the ranch, but that wasn't enough. Not anymore. He had to be on his own, somewhere a long way from George's watchful eye. That was why he had chosen Wyoming, and in his mind, getting there without the loss of a single cow would prove he was right. Even though the ranch would still belong to the family, there'd be no one looking over his shoulder. No more worry that his orders would be changed and the whole crew know it. This was his chance to prove himself. That was why he had been so furious with Iris for getting in his way.

That was why he couldn't understand his change of heart.

Even when he was angriest at her, he no longer wanted to strangle her and leave her body for the buzzards. Her body was much too attractive to waste. He had spent the better part of the morning cataloging its attractions. He could now recite the list straight through without missing a single temptation.

He'd spent the afternoon cataloging the reasons she was a plague and a nuisance, why he ought to box her up and ship her back to St. Louis, but he kept forgetting them. Instead he found himself making excuses for her and assuring himself she wouldn't make the same mistakes again.

That frightened him badly. He didn't want to like any woman that much. No telling what she might talk him into doing. He was considering taking her back to camp when they cut a fresh trail.

"These are the missing cows," he said.

"How can you tell?" Iris asked. "These tracks look like all the others we've seen today."

"All the rest turned back. These don't." Monty studied the tracks more closely. "They're heading west at a trot."

"You think they were rustled?"

"Maybe."

"By the same men who tried before?"

"Could be."

"But a panther started the stampede."

"Somebody's been following you. My men kept finding the signs. We'd better get back to camp."

"Why? It'll take hours to reach this point again. That would give them more time to get away. Do you need help?"

"I will if I've got to worry about you. There's bound to be some shooting. You'll just be in the way."

"I'm not going back," Iris declared. "They're my cows, and I intend to get them back." She turned her horse in the direction the cows had taken and started off at a trot.

"Dammit, Iris, you can't just head into a gun-fight," Monty exclaimed as his big gelding came alongside her compact cow pony. "You don't know the first thing about what to do."

"Then teach me. It'll take us hours to catch up with them."

"I always knew females were stubborn," Monty grumbled, "but you take the cake. I can't teach you about guns in a couple of hours."

"Then don't try," Iris said. "I already know how to pull the trigger. That's all that counts, isn't it?"

"Not if you can't hit anything!"

"I'll scare them. You shoot them."

Just like a woman who had never stuck her nose outside a parlor to think going after rustlers was as much fun as a garden party. She'd probably scream and faint when she saw her first blood. Then he'd be in a pickle.

But Monty bowed to the inevitable. Iris was going to stick to him like a burr, and he was going to have to see that nothing happened to her. At the same time he was going to have to get those cows. He didn't know how he was going to accomplish both, but Iris clearly expected him to. He knew George would expect him to. Hell, he expected himself to.

Why had he ever wanted to go to Wyoming? He hadn't gotten near the damned place and already his life was falling apart. With his luck, he was bound to come upon some widow woman with eight or nine kids. If he did, he thought with a tug of satisfaction, he'd let them ride in Iris's wagon.

So they kept on. At dusk he was faced with the prospect of camping overnight with Iris.

"This looks like a good place to stop," Monty said, pointing to a scattering of ash and oak alongside a stream.

"I can keep going," Iris insisted.

"No, you can't. You've been in the saddle more today than in your whole life."

"Not quite that much, but certainly more than I'm used to."

"Besides, the horses are tired."

"That's right. Always think about the horses," Iris said, wondering if it really was the horses he was stopping for rather than herself.

"If you don't, you could die out here," Monty replied.

Iris didn't reply. She didn't intend to try to convince Monty she was more important than a horse. She had already lost to cows. It was a good thing he had left his dogs at home. A third loss to a four-legged animal would destroy what was left of her self-esteem.

Besides, she had a more important worry. She wasn't sure she could dismount. The lower half of her body seemed to be paralyzed.

"You're not going to like this," Monty said. A tangle of vines blocked their approach to the stream until Monty found a narrow game trail. There were no vines or brush under the trees. A thick carpet of leaves covered the ground. "It's not what you're used to."

"Nothing that has happened since Christmas is what I'm used to," Iris said as she followed him into the trees.

"You can get down. I'm going to give the horses a drink."

Iris didn't move.

"I said—"

"I don't think I can. I can't move my legs."

Monty looked at her in surprise, then started to laugh.

"Don't you dare tell me that I ought to have stayed at the ranch," Iris said, "or that I should have gone ahead on the train."

"Here, let me help you," Monty said.

"No. I'll get down by myself." But try as she might, she couldn't move her legs.

"Are you through being stubborn?" Monty asked.

"I guess so. It's either let you help me or spend the night in the saddle.

"Your horse wouldn't like that."

"Neither would I. I say that just in case you happen to be interested in what *I* would like."

"A wise man is always interested—"

"You've never been wise, Monty Randolph, at least not when it comes to me. Now give me your hand and stop trying to convince me you're not wishing me a thousand miles away."

"If I told you what I was thinking—"

"Don't. After what you've said over the last few days, I don't think I have the strength to listen." Iris laughed. "Wouldn't Cynthia Wilburforce love to be here now. She was always jealous of me. She said that I was too sure of myself, that I relied too much on my looks. She said she'd give a thousand dollars to see a man put me in my place. Well, I could use that thousand dollars and Cynthia could use a good laugh." She stopped and looked at Monty. "You wouldn't like Cynthia. She's worse than I am."

"Will you stop going on about somebody I don't know and let me help you down," Monty said. "You can reminisce around the campfire."

"It's not exactly reminiscing," Iris said as she took Monty's hand. "It's more like adding up the strikes against me."

She loved the warm touch of his hand in hers. The heat seemed to radiate throughout her body, leaving tingly trails of fire. Lord, this man was just something else.

But holding Monty's hand wasn't enough. She still couldn't move her legs.

"You're going to have to fall off into my arms," Monty said.

"How do I do that?"

"Just take your feet out of the stirrups and throw yourself in my direction."

Iris couldn't help but appreciate the irony of the situation. Five years ago she had spent days on end trying to figure out how to get into Monty's arms. If she'd only known she just had to ride until the lower half of her body ceased to function.

But falling into Monty's arms because she couldn't do anything else irritated her. If she couldn't get there because he liked her, she'd almost rather he didn't touch her.

Almost. She remembered his touch, so firm, so comforting, so strong. No woman could dislike that. But there was no sense in letting him know she was putty in his hands. She'd make a game of it, act as if it was a lark. That way he'd never know her heart was beating too fast or her breath was shallow. He wouldn't know he affected her at all.

"Monty Randolph," she said, giving him a teasing grin, "you are a sneaky rascal. And I thought you'd been hoping to lose me in a gopher hole all day."

Monty grinned back. "Go ahead and enjoy yourself. You're not going to feel like making jokes once you get down."

"What do you mean?" She didn't trust him not to do something terrible just to get back at her.

"You'll see in a minute."

"I'll see right now, or I'm not getting down from here."

"Your muscles are probably cramped. It's going to hurt when you try to stand up."

"Oh. I thought you were going to do something awful like tease me with one of those big spiders or something."

"I don't play stupid jokes like that."

"How was I to know? Men do all sorts of crazy things."

"I don't. Now come on down if you're coming. I can't stand here all night, or I'll have a cramp, too."

Resigning herself to the inevitable, Iris drew her feet out of the stirrups and threw herself from the saddle. Monty caught her effortlessly.

That circumstance, however, did nothing to relieve Iris's embarrassment at finding herself virtually upside down in Monty's very firm embrace.

Iris hadn't felt this excited since Monty lifted her down from a rock she'd climbed years ago. He held her as though she weighed nothing. She felt helpless and insignificant in his arms. The shooting pains in her legs were hardly strong enough to counterbalance the sensation of being held by powerful muscles or pressed against a heavily muscled chest. She'd never realized it, but Monty was a very big man.

"I'm going to put you down on the ground to see if you can stand," Monty said.

Iris tightened her hold on Monty.

"I'm not going to let go, but you've got to try to stand."

Iris clung desperately to him as she righted herself. An excruciating pain shot through her legs the moment her feet touched the ground. Her arms closed around Monty's neck in a death grip.

"It'll hurt like the bejesus," Monty said, "but it's the only way."

"I don't think I can."

"Lean against me. Put as much weight as you can on one foot. When you can't stand it any longer, change feet."

Iris would rather have stayed right where she was. She wouldn't even have minded if Monty had set her on the ground. But she could tell he would never give in to pain himself. He wouldn't understand why she would either.

For a moment the gilded life of a rich and spoiled St. Louis matron didn't seem so bad. But Iris banished the thought. She was being cowardly. And no Richmond was a coward, not even Helena.

Iris had never felt such pain. It sliced though her body from her calf to her hip. Only a grim determination not to humiliate herself before Monty kept her from crying out. She had insisted she could do anything he could do. Now she would have to show she could live up to her boast.

But when she put the second foot on the ground and experienced the same shattering pain, Iris almost decided her pride wasn't worth the agony. But though Helena hadn't been the best mother in the world, she had bequeathed her daughter a wide streak of toughness and a good dollop of pride. Despite the pain, Iris kept testing one foot after another until she was able to stand. She had to lean heavily on Monty, but she could stand.

"Tell me when you're ready to try to walk," Monty said. "That's going to hurt even more."

For a moment Iris felt like giving up. All that work to be able to stand and the worst was yet to come. "Give me a minute," Iris said, gasping from the pain.

"Take as long as you want."

"I thought you said you couldn't stand around waiting for me," Iris said, twisting around so she could look up at him, a smile on her lips that wanted to grimace instead. "Which do you mean?"

Monty wasn't sure what he did mean. Ever since Iris had landed upside down in his arms, he had been prey to the most alarming desire to turn her right side up and kiss her soundly. Having her lean against him did nothing to make that feeling go away. If fact, it was all he could do not to sweep her up in his arms and kiss away the pain. He had never seen Iris hurt so much. He had never thought she would be so brave.

"It's time to see if you can stand without me holding you up," Monty said. It hurt him to see the pain she suffered, but there was nothing he could do. She had to loosen her muscles before the pain would go away.

For a moment he thought she wouldn't make it. She staggered and her legs went out from under her, but Iris's grim resolve kept her going. She held on to his arm for balance, but she bore her own weight.

He should have known not to bring her. No matter how gutsy, she wasn't up to such a long ride. He shouldn't have let her get him angry. He never could think straight when he was mad.

But temper wasn't the only reason he had let her come along. He liked having her with him. She was trouble, but he'd only spend his time worrying about her if he had left her at camp. That was why he hadn't separated the herds. As long as they were together, he'd have a good reason to bring her to his camp.

"Now try a few steps," Monty coaxed.

"Don't you have any mercy?" she asked.

He would have stopped the pain if he could, but he knew there was no other way. "Believe me, it only gets worse if you wait."

"You'll have to hold me. I can't do it alone."

Monty had never entirely let go. Now he slipped his arm around her. "How's this?" he asked. He nearly lifted her off the ground.

"Not that tight," Iris said. "I'm supposed to walk, not float."

Feeling a little self-conscious, Monty relaxed his hold.

Iris took her first step. "It's not as bad as I expected," she said, pleased with herself. A second and third step caused her to smile. "By tomorrow I ought to be walking as well as a three year old."

"You'll be doing that in a minute," Monty said, a feeling of pride welling up inside him. Iris might be a spoiled beauty who didn't know the first thing about cows or ranching, but by God she had guts. She had a lot to learn, but given half a chance, she'd learn it.

"Your legs will start to tingle in a minute," Monty said.

"They're tingling already."

"That means you're better. You think I ought to let go?"

"No!" Iris said, gripping him even tighter.

"Okay," Monty said, quickly putting his arm securely around her waist. "But if your foreman should suddenly ride over that hill, you're going to have to explain that I'm helping you walk, not attacking you."

"I won't have to," Iris said. "Nobody thinks you want to kiss me."

Monty could hardly believe his ears. Here he had been practically sitting on his hands or riding with his hat in his lap and she thought he didn't want to kiss her.

"Don't play your tricks on me, Iris Richmond. Every man you meet wants to kiss you, and you know it."

"Other men. Not you."

"Can you walk by yourself yet?"

"You don't have to be so anxious to get rid of me," Iris said, trying to force her recalcitrant legs to support her weight.

"Can you stand?" Monty repeated, insistent.

"Yes," Iris answered sharply, balanced on wobbly legs. "As long as I don't move."

"You won't have to," Monty said. He took her in his arms and kissed her soundly.

Iris's legs went out from under her completely. Her breath deserted her as well. For a moment she thought her heart had absconded, too. Then it suddenly started to beat twice as fast as it should.

"What are you doing?" she managed to say, amazement in her voice.

Monty felt a little embarrassed to have let his emotions get the better of him. He had never kissed a woman like that before. He wanted to do it again.

"I was kissing you. I would have thought you would recognize it."

"Of course, I recognize it, but why were you kissing me?"

"Don't play games," Monty said. "You've been trying to get me to kiss you for years."

"So you had to wait until I was practically helpless."

"That's why I made sure you could stand," Monty said. He pulled her back into his arms and kissed her again. His tongue slipped gently between her open lips to explore the warmth of her mouth. The sigh she gave encouraged him to be even more greedy in his plundering.

"I've wanted to do this for days," he said when he finally released her mouth.

"If you went looking for those cows just to get me out here—"

Monty burst out laughing. "I don't need an excuse to protect my herd."

It was a good thing she mentioned cows. In a minute or two she might have started to believe he liked her.

Iris wriggled out of Monty's embrace. "How foolish of me to think I could ever be as important as a few cows. Now let's stop wasting time. You have a camp to set up, and I have to learn how to walk. It looks like somebody's already been here," she said, pointing to the remains of a fire.

For a moment she thought Monty was going to make one of his biting remarks, but he merely leveled a questioning look at her. She squirmed under his scrutiny. She wanted to say something to make him turn away, but she couldn't think of a single word. Then, with the puzzling expression still on his face, he turned to study the ashes. Iris was left feeling unaccountably shaken. She had a suspicion something terribly important had happened and she had missed it.

A little way from the ashes Monty found two places where sleeping men had crushed the leaves. A moment later he found where two horses had waded through the stream.

"They've been here very recently," he said. "They're probably the men who made off with your cattle."

"Do you think they're very far ahead?"

"I don't know. I'll take a look around after dark. Maybe I can spot their campfire."

"What will you do?"

"That depends. Right now let's see about getting a fire going and the coffee on. It's going to be cold tonight."

"We don't have any coffee," Iris pointed out. "And we don't have anything to eat."

"Yes, we do," Monty said, opening up his bedroll and taking out two pots, a cup, a tin plate, and eating utensils. "I never travel without enough food to last a week."

Iris was relieved when Monty left her to build a fire. She needed time to think. His kiss had paralyzed her wits almost as badly as the ride had her muscles.

She didn't know how to interpret his kiss. It sure wasn't anything like those dry pecks on her lips she had had from boys before. She had noticed a gradual softening in his attitude toward her during the day, but she wasn't sure whether it represented a genuine change, whether he was bored and had grabbed the first female he saw, or if he was trying to rile her.

She paused to lean against the trunk of an elm at least three feet in diameter. She had never known walking could be so exhausting.

She hoped it meant he would at least give her a chance to prove she wasn't useless. Riding with him all day had given her a very different idea of what he was really like. Her conception of him had been made up of the impressions of an infatuated 15-year-old girl mixed with stories she'd heard of his terrible temper and his expertise with cows.

Iris heaved herself from against the tree and started walking again.

He wasn't the least bit like the men who used to pursue her. He wasn't tender or thoughtful, yet he did think of her and he did try to be gentle. She found herself thinking about him as a man, not just a way to get her herd to Wyoming. Underneath all that bluster was someone of very strong principles, someone who wasn't afraid or reluctant or shy. A man who acted and asked later.

She wondered what else she might find if she dug deeper. One thing, however, she was certain she wouldn't find. She wouldn't find he was in love with her. She had never seen a more unlover-like man than Monty Randolph.

Annoyed at her preoccupation with him, she returned to the campfire ready to do battle.

"You think you've got the answers to everything, don't you?" she said.

"I pretty much do when it comes to cows. But not about much of anything else."

Iris hadn't expected such a candid response. Monty didn't strike her as a man willing to admit his shortcomings.

"Who says?"

"Everybody. Especially my family."

He had gathered sticks and dry leaves and now had a small fire going. He handed her a small pot. "Here, get some water from the stream while I look for some more wood."

Iris took the pot. "Your family must think very highly of you to let you take a herd off to Wyoming."

"You don't want to get into my family," Monty said. "It's worse than quicksand."

She followed as she searched for wood. "It can't be that bad. George and Madison are married and doing just fine."

"Madison had the good sense to take his wife off to Chicago. As for Rose, well, she's a remarkable woman. She's probably the only reason the rest of us haven't killed each other."

Suddenly Iris wished Monty would talk about *her* with some of the reverence he reserved for Rose. She wondered what a woman had to do to have a man feel that way about her. She wondered if it could ever happen to her.

She could cause men to fight over her, but she knew instinctively Monty's relationship with Rose was different from anything she knew. She could imagine Monty arguing with Rose—he had admitted as much—but she also sensed that he would respect her decision even when he disagreed with it.

That was nothing like the way he treated her when they disagreed.

Monty carried his load of sticks to the fire. She went to get the water. She started to kneel down beside the stream, but she couldn't. She either stood up or fell down. There was no in between.

"Hurry up with that water," Monty called out.

"I can't."

Monty looked up from the fire. "Why?"

"I can't bend down without falling."

His amusement irritated her. He was always laughing when he shouldn't.

"Sorry, I should have known." He got up, took the pot from her, bent down, and filled it with clear water. "Keep walking. You'll be okay soon."

Monty settled the pot on some stones and shoved the tiny fire underneath. Within minutes he had boiling water. He put the coffee in the pan. "Coffee will be ready soon."

"It already smells delicious," Iris said, inhaling the rich smell of the black beans, "but what are we going to do for food?"

"Wait and see. In the meantime, you can see to the horses."

Before she thought, she said, "I don't *see to horses.*"

Chapter Eleven

Why couldn't she learn to think before she spoke? She hadn't meant it that way, but she had never been told to see to the horses. She was used to handing the reins over to someone else without even thinking about it. But that was no reason to have spoken as she did.

Monty raised cold eyes from the pot of brewing coffee he swirled over the flame. "Do you know how to take care of a horse?"

"Not really. I—"

"Can you take them for a drink at the creek?"

"Yes."

"Can you picket them so they can graze?"

"Of course. I—"

"Then do it. I'll see to the rest later."

The cruel way he tossed out his orders made Iris start to refuse, but something in the way he looked at her made her change her mind. She turned away to hide her hurt and confusion.

She untied the horses and led them to the creek.

She couldn't believe how much his coldness hurt. It was as if he had no feeling for her whatsoever, as if she was just a hired hand to be ordered about. But it was the hurt that confused Iris. Anger she expected. The hurt surprised her.

The horses waded into the creek and dropped their muzzles into the sun-warmed water.

She wanted Monty to like her. Not just to think she was beautiful. Not flatter her and comply with her every wish. Not even desire her. Just like her. It didn't seem like much to ask, but remembering his look of cold disdain, it seemed impossible.

She had never felt this way about a man before, and she didn't know what it signified. She did know it made her feel very uneasy, and she had never felt that way either. She had always been confident where men were concerned. She *used* to be confident with Monty, too, but no longer. He mystified her. He was attracted to her and thought she was beautiful, but he didn't like her at all.

Their thirst quenched, the horses lifted dripping muzzles from the stream. Iris led them to the tall grass outside the trees. Even a spoiled rich girl could do that. There was miles of it in every direction.

She didn't know why she continued to take issue with Monty on things about which she knew little or nothing, about which she could be nearly certain he knew a great deal. If she had been going to a party, or sitting down to dinner, or meeting somebody important, she would have known exactly what to do. But it was about time she admitted to herself that out here on this abysmal prairie, Monty knew everything and she knew nothing.

Monty was shaving a piece of dried beef and dropping the chips into a pot of water when she returned to the fire. He stopped long enough to hand her a steaming cup of coffee.

"What are you fixing?" she asked. The coffee was too hot to drink. There was nowhere to set it down, so she held it while it cooled.

"What amounts to beef soup," he said. "I always carry jerky and dried vegetables. It's quick and easy. Of course if you want to fix something—"

"I don't cook."

She could tell at once she had said something wrong. Again.

"Don't cook, or don't know how?"

"B-both," she answered, suddenly aware he was looking at her as if she was some sort of rare and undesirable creature.

"Helena!" he said in disgust. "I should have known it." He shaved the last of the beef and began to stir the mixture.

"What do you mean?" she asked, ready to defend her mother.

"Helena considered cooking beneath her. I should have known she wouldn't allow her daughter to learn."

"You don't have to sneer. There are lots of women who don't know how to cook."

"I don't know any. Rose cooks every meal we eat."

The perfect Rose would. And probably she could clean the house, plant a garden, and butcher and clean half-a-dozen hogs before lunch. Then she'd probably sew her own gown and arrive at the ball looking like Cinderella.

"Not everybody can be like Rose," she said, afraid if she said what she was thinking he'd turn her away from the fire and the delicious-smelling soup. Only now did she remember she hadn't had anything to eat since morning.

"Maybe not, but any woman meaning to settle in Wyoming ought to be able to cook."

"Well, I can't."

"So you said."

"Well," she said finally when he didn't say any more, "you must have something to say. I've never known you to be speechless before."

"You'd better look around for some rich city fella. Nobody else can afford to take up with a woman who can't cook or clean house."

"Why not?"

Monty looked up at her. "A woman's not much help to a man if all he can do is look at her."

Iris stamped her foot and immediately winced in pain. "That's a horrible thing to say."

"Would you marry a man who couldn't earn a living, who couldn't do anything but sit on the porch and whittle?"

"I . . . a man can't . . . That's an absurd question."

Monty returned his attention to his soup. "Everybody's got to carry his weight out here. That includes women."

"Well, I watered the horses and staked them out to graze. I hope that earns me at least a cup of soup."

Monty surprised her by smiling. "Two if you want, one for each horse."

She didn't understand this man. One minute he was telling her she was a useless human being, a drag on the human race; the next he was smiling at her as if he actually liked her. She wished he'd kept scowling. At least then she didn't have any trouble remembering she wanted to bash him over the head. Or pour the coffee over him. But when he smiled, she could hardly keep her legs under her. He was the most handsome man she'd ever seen.

She used to think she preferred men with dark hair and a mustache. They looked so dramatic, so mysterious. But she had changed her mind. Monty's hair was so blond it looked almost white. His eyebrows were invisible, his skin burned the color of dark amber, but there was nothing washed out or subdued about this man. Eyes so blue they stood out like brilliant sapphires glowed with an intensity she found almost unnerving. His mouth smiling, frowning, or clenched in anger telegraphed his moods with the subtlety of a shout.

But it was his body that characterized him most fully.

Standing at least two inches over six feet with shoulders broad enough to fill any doorway, Monty was not a man to be ignored. Years of sixteen-hour days in the saddle roping steers weighing over 1,000 pounds had made his arms and thighs rawhide tough. He did everything with unconscious ease, just like last night when he lifted her out of the saddle with one arm.

He was like the animals he herded—powerful, dangerous, living by his instincts. No matter how many hours he spent under a roof, his natural home was under an open sky on a land without fences.

He was primitive and untamable, and he scared Iris to death.

She took a sip of coffee. "Where is your ranch?" she asked.

"It's in the foothills of the Laramie Mountains on Chugwater Creek."

"Mine's on Bear Creek. Is that anywhere close by?"

"Could be."

A typical Monty response.

"Have you been there?"

"No. Jeff bought it and had the house fixed up and stocked so it would be ready to live in."

Iris doubted there was more than a crude cabin on her land.

"Do you plan to live there?"

"Sure. Sitting in Cheyenne or Laramie is no way to run a ranch. Rustlers will steal you blind. Soup's ready," he said. He lifted the pot from the fire, stirring the soup vigorously. "I only have one cup, and you're using it."

"We can eat out of the pot."

"I only have one spoon."

She didn't understand the way he was looking at her. If it had been anybody but Monty . . . but it was Monty, and he wasn't interested in romancing her.

"It's too hot to eat now anyway," she said. "By the time it cools, I'll be finished with my coffee."

She took a sip. She hadn't expected to be alone with Monty. Now that she was, she was unprepared for the way he was looking at her and for the disturbing feelings that had wormed their way into her consciousness.

"Maybe your wife won't like living on a ranch."

"I don't intend to get married," Monty said. He tasted the soup. It burned him. "I like women well enough," he said, panting to soothe his burned tongue, "but I don't want a wife."

"Why not?"

Iris was tired of feelings she couldn't explain. She didn't want to get married, yet she felt upset that Monty didn't want to either. That didn't make sense, but then not much she had done lately did.

"A wife would get in my way. She'd always be wanting me to do something I didn't want to do. She'd end up trying to change me even though she'd swear she wouldn't."

"Did Rose do that?"

"She sure did." He chuckled. "You should have seen the ruckus she kicked up when she first came. We tried our best to get George to get rid of her."

At least Rose wasn't entirely perfect.

"Of course some men need changing if they're going to make a fit husband," Monty continued. "I'd need a heap of changing before a woman would have me."

"I imagine a woman would need a *heap of changing* before she could live with a man like you," Iris responded dryly, "especially on a cow ranch."

Monty flashed his devastating smile, and Iris felt her belly flutter.

"You got that right. I can't think of a single female who's willing to try. Not that I'm asking. I'm not the marrying kind."

Iris finished her coffee and held out her cup. Monty poured it half full of soup. She swirled it around to cool it, then took a sip. It was surprisingly good. "You might change your mind."

"Rose has been trying for nigh on to ten years. I'm too set in my ways."

"But you didn't fall in love with Rose," Iris pointed out.

"She was a mighty fetching little woman, all spirit and spunk," Monty said, remembering. "But she was crazy about George, and he was just as nutty

164

about her. He'd probably have killed me, or himself, if she'd fallen in love with me."

Another reason to dislike the perfect Rose. Iris was thankful they would soon be separated by more than 1,000 miles. That much virtue in one woman was depressing.

They ate the rest of their meal in silence. Then they took their dishes to the creek, rinsed them, and cleaned them with creek sand. Monty put everything away.

"Now I'm going to show you how to take care of a horse properly," he said.

Iris was furious. She had taken care of those damned horses. Why did Monty think a person's name had to be Randolph before he could do a good job? She told herself to stop being foolish. She ought to be glad he was thorough and competent and checked everything himself. That was the kind of man she needed to get her to Wyoming.

But she was hurt.

She tried not to care what Monty thought of her, but she failed. His good opinion was very important, important enough for her to try to earn it. And if that meant learning about horses, she'd learn. Besides, if she was going to run a ranch, she had to know what to do. Horses represented safety and the means for making more money. She wanted to know her men were taking good care of her property.

She also enjoyed Monty's attention. As long as he was trying to teach her something, he would be paying attention to her. She was afraid if he stayed by the campfire, he would curl up and go to sleep.

It had gotten cold by the time they returned to camp. Iris realized she hadn't brought anything to keep her warm, but she refused to say anything to Monty.

"You'd better get some sleep."

"Aren't you going to look for the rustlers?" She knew he wouldn't take her with him. There was no use asking.

"Later, when they're asleep."

"I'll wait up."

"No, go to sleep. You'll need every bit of your energy tomorrow." He handed her his bedroll. "You can use this."

"No. It's yours."

"Take it."

"No."

"Then we'll share it," Monty said, sitting down next to Iris.

"You can't mean for me to sleep inside your bedroll with you," Iris exclaimed.

Monty draped one end of the bedroll over Iris's shoulders and the other over his own. "No. I mean to talk you into using it yourself."

"Where will you sleep?"

"On the ground. It's dry."

"How will you keep warm?"

"I'm not cold."

Actually Monty felt as if he had a fever. He had been around Iris off and on for years, but he'd never felt like this, not until last night. Now he felt as if a fire raged in his veins. He was surprised she couldn't see steam coming out of his ears. They sat next to each other, their shoulders touching.

He wanted to kiss her again. Only this time he wanted to kiss her because she was the most beautiful woman he'd ever seen. He wanted to kiss her because he'd held himself in check all day and he didn't think he could stand it much longer.

"I don't know how you can be hot," Iris said, shivering and pulling the bedroll more securely around her shoulder. "I never knew nights could be so cold. It's almost May."

"Move a little closer. Body heat will help more than the bedroll."

"What I need is a steer to cuddle up to," Iris said, keeping her distance. "I'd be warm as toast from just half the heat they generated during the stampede."

Iris fingered the edge of the bedroll with nervous fingers. She didn't understand herself. Monty had been rude to her. He had treated her as harshly as he would have treated a man, but she still wanted to be close to him.

"I may not be as warm as a steer, but I'm better looking," Monty said. His voice didn't sound quite as it usually did. "And I don't kick as hard."

"Yes, you do," Iris replied, her own voice unsteady. She couldn't be this close to Monty and not be acutely aware of his presence. It acted on her like a magnet, pulling her even when she didn't want to go. "You give me a verbal kick in the pants every time you open your mouth."

"I'm just trying to protect you."

"It doesn't seem like it."

"You have a way of attracting trouble."

"I suppose that's why you're always around." Iris had to do something with her hands, so she reached over to put a stick on the fire. The bedroll slipped from her shoulders. When Monty put it back, he pulled her over until her body leaned against his.

"I'm around for the same reason all the other men hang around you," Monty said, pulling Iris even tighter against him. "I can't seem to stay away from you."

Iris tried to sit back up. "Do you want to?"

"Yes, dammit, but I can't."

Then he kissed her.

The intensity of Monty's kiss didn't surprise or dismay Iris as it had the first time. She still wasn't accustomed to being kissed so passionately, but she found herself responding to it.

But she resisted an impulse to put her arms around him. She refused to hug a man who did his best to stay away from her and cursed when he failed. She broke away. She felt weak but much warmer.

"You don't sound very happy about it," she managed to say.

"I'm not," Monty said, then kissed her with such vigor, stabbing his tongue in and out of her warm mouth, Iris had trouble recovering her breath.

"I wouldn't want you to put yourself to so much trouble. Maybe you'd rather go look for your cows."

She didn't know about other women, but she didn't like his making love to her against his will. She tried to slip out of his embrace, but he wouldn't release her.

"I'd rather look for cows, rustlers, or Indians," Monty growled, "but I can't keep my mind on anything else when you're around."

The magic fled, taking some of the warmth with it. He was hopeless. She didn't understand how any woman in her right mind could seriously consider liking this man.

"Do you think there's any chance you'll get over this strange malaise?" she asked.

Monty didn't seem to hear the barb in her voice. "I sure as hell hope so. How can a man look himself in the mirror in the morning if he goes around panting after some female like a stud bull?"

The last of the warmth ebbed away, leaving Iris colder than ever. "I hadn't looked at it in quite that light," she said, wondering if Monty was constitutionally incapable of saying anything completely nice to her. "Here, let me see if I can help you."

Iris hit him in the stomach as hard as she could.

"What did you mean by that?" he grunted in astonishment.

"I don't want you making love to me when it makes you so miserable." Iris jerked the bedroll from her shoulders and struggled to her feet. "My father said you should always put a dumb animal out of its misery."

Monty leapt to his feet. Iris tried to run, but her treacherous legs collapsed under her.

"Monty Randolph, don't you lay a finger on me." Iris dragged herself into a sitting position as he towered over her. "Not after you had the gall to say you didn't like kissing me and hoped you'd soon recover from the desire." She couldn't tell whether he was madder at her or himself.

"I didn't—"

"If I knew how to use that gun of yours, I'd shoot you with it."

Monty looked ready to strangle her. Iris didn't know whether to attempt to run or beg for mercy. Before she could make up her mind which to try, Monty burst out laughing.

"You always were a spirited little brat." Then without warning, he bent over and scooped her up. Iris kicked and struggled as hard as her stiff muscles would allow, but it was useless. Monty was much too strong.

"What are you going to do to me?" she asked. She had heard tales of Monty's temper. He was capable of anything, including dumping her in the creek.

"Not what you deserve. And not what I'd like to do."

"What's that?" Iris asked, unsure whether to be hopeful or fearful. It had suddenly become crystal clear that Monty could do anything with her he wished. If his kisses were any indication of the state of his mind, he wanted more than she was willing to give.

"I'm not going to tell you. At least not now. I'm going to set you back down, wrap you up, and make sure you're warm."

Iris wasn't about to surrender herself to this arrogant, rude, thoughtless man who was far too sure of himself, even if he was the most exciting man she had ever met. But she couldn't think when she was near him, she couldn't plan what to say or gauge her actions. She felt helpless, lost, unable to control what happened around her.

"And after that?" Iris asked as Monty settled her back on the ground and draped the bedroll around her shoulders. She didn't like the look in his eyes. She had seen it once in some rough men she passed on the river front in St. Louis. Naked, elemental desire, a force she knew instinctively she couldn't control.

At the same time she felt a strong pull to Monty, one so strong she feared she couldn't resist it. Maybe she didn't *want* to resist.

"I'm going to—"

"Hello, the fire."

They froze. The call caught them by surprise. They weren't expecting anybody, and they hadn't heard anybody ride up.

"Come on in if you're friendly," Monty called out. He reached for his rifle. "Stay off to the side, out of the line of fire," he hissed to Iris.

"Who—"

"I have no idea, but we'll see in a moment. Get out of the light."

Iris had hardly backed away from the fire when a dirty brown horse ridden by a tall, thin man with a Spanish cast to his features emerged from the night. Iris started to back farther away until the man's wide-set eyes and aquiline nose caught her attention. Something about him looked familiar. Then he came into the light.

"Carlos?" she said half to herself, hardly able to believe her eyes. "It's Carlos," she said aloud, turning to Monty. "It's my brother, Carlos."

Chapter Twelve

"Iris?" Carlos asked when his sister stepped forward into the light. "What are you doing here?"

"I'm moving to Wyoming. The bank took the ranch."

"I mean here, with him?" Carlos said, indicating Monty and the isolated campsite.

What had she been doing? What would have happened if Carlos hadn't shown up? Iris hoped the darkness hid the blush she felt burning her cheeks. She was glad neither man knew the thoughts going through her mind.

"We're following some of my cows that got lost in a stampede," Iris answered, determined to act as though nothing had happened. She couldn't bear for Monty to know how close she had come to giving in. "Monty thinks rustlers may have driven them off. He was just going to look for a campfire."

"He can save himself the trouble," Carlos said,

172

turning to Monty with no sign of pleasure. "They're on the other side of the ridge, and the only campfire you'll find is mine."

Iris felt relieved she wouldn't be alone with Monty. She needed time to think about the startling change in her feelings toward him.

"How many did you find?" Monty asked.

"Around two hundred. We found them grazing a few miles to the west. I recognized my father's brand."

"It's been a long time, Carlos," Monty said, eyeing the man. "You've changed."

"You haven't," Carlos replied.

"You know each other?" Iris asked, looking from one man to the other.

"I remember him," Monty said. "He didn't stay around long enough for anybody to get to know him."

Carlos shifted his weight uneasily.

"That was Mama's fault," Iris said. "She wouldn't let him stay at the ranch."

"For once Helena showed some sense."

"No, she didn't," Iris contradicted. "I wanted a big brother when I was growing up."

"I wish I had known," Monty said. "I'd have given you one of mine."

"What are you doing here?" Iris asked Carlos.

"I heard you were heading to Wyoming, so I thought I might lend a hand. Might even stay for a spell."

"You mean you wanted to hitch a free ride," Monty said.

"He's my brother," Iris said, firing up. "He can come with me if he wants."

She had always sympathized with the awkwardness of Carlos's position even though he was 11 years older and she didn't know him very well. It had never bothered her that he was illegitimate—his half-Mexican mother had died when he was a boy—but it had sure bothered Helena.

When Iris turned 14, Helena forced her husband to break off all contact with Carlos. But Iris never forgot him. He was Robert Richmond's son as much as she was his daughter, and it seemed unfair he should be denied a home and the companionship of his family just because their father hadn't married his mother.

But Iris's willingness to welcome him now was more than a wish to recreate a childhood relationship. Her loneliness since her parents' death had been so profound, so terrifying, she snatched at the opportunity to have any family with her. Even though the bond that united them had dwindled to a mere memory, she now felt she was no longer alone. He was her brother. She had somebody to belong to. She knew Monty could do far more for her than Carlos, but she immediately recognized that she wanted very different things from these two men.

"Who's traveling with you?" Monty asked.

"My partner, Joe Reardon," Carlos said. "He's a top hand. He can pull his weight on any crew."

"I'm sure he can," Iris said. She hoped his friend would be everything Carlos said he was.

"If you'll take my advice, you'll let them continue up the trail in their own company," Monty said to Iris.

"I've lost two men. Carlos and his friend can replace them."

"Talk to Frank," Monty said to Carlos. "I have nothing to do with her crew."

At that, Monty turned and walked away from the

camp. Iris ran after him. He jumped the creek. She splashed through it.

"I gave you control of the herd," she said. "I haven't changed my mind. Frank still takes his orders from you."

Monty left the trees and headed toward his horse. Iris had to run to keep up with him. Her legs hurt, but she had to stop him. She couldn't let him leave.

"You can't give me control one minute, then hire two men against my advice the next," Monty said over his shoulder. "Leadership isn't something to hand out and take back whenever you like."

"But Carlos is my brother. I can't turn him away."

Monty stopped and turned around so abruptly Iris ran into him. "You didn't have to hire Reardon as well. What if Carlos shows up with another friend tomorrow? You going to hire him, too?"

"I'm sorry," Iris apologized, backing away from Monty like she'd been burned. "I was just so glad to see Carlos. You can't understand—you've got so many brothers—what it's like to be alone. I don't have anybody but Carlos."

"Surely your parents had family."

"Maybe, but I never saw any of them, so they might as well not be there."

Monty didn't move. He just stared at Iris, his jaw clamped so tight the muscles bulged.

"I promise I won't do it again. I'll consult you on everything. Please?"

Monty could feel himself giving in and hated it. He had put a lot of time and thought into planning this drive. He had studied grass conditions to determine the ideal-size herd. He had talked with a dozen drovers to find the best trail, the optimum-size crew, and how many horses he needed in the ramuda. He had also paid very careful attention to details so he could remember rough crossings and where water was plentiful, scarce, or too alkaline to drink. He had done all this because success was imperative.

Then he found Iris on the trail ahead of him, and he started to make one decision after another that went against his judgment and his instincts, decisions that he knew endangered his chances of success. Even Hen and Salty had started to question him.

Now he was about to do it again. He didn't dislike Carlos, but he had no desire to have him on his crew. Carlos was unsteady, lazy, weak of character. He had spent most of the last five years away from Texas, drifting, getting into minor scrapes. Maybe he was tired of roaming and wanted to settle down, but Monty didn't want to have to pick up the pieces if he was mistaken.

But one look told him Iris felt like she had found a long-lost friend. If eyes could plead, hers were begging this very moment. Even in the dim moonlight, they glistened with moisture, their deep green seemingly bottomless. He couldn't say no to her now any more than he could five years ago.

Monty had never thought about how lonely she might feel—he'd had too much on his mind to go looking for extra things to worry about—but it must feel pretty awful to be alone. He'd often wished he didn't have so many brothers all sticking their noses into his business, but he took their support for granted.

Iris had nobody except Carlos.

"Okay," Monty agreed, ignoring the feeling of impending disaster, "but as soon as we get to the river, we cut the herd and we go our separate ways."

"You don't have to be so anxious to get rid of me."

"Since I came up on your herd, you've had two stampedes and at least one rustling attempt. You think your foreman and half your crew are crooked, and you hire two men straight off the prairie. We aren't even out of Texas."

"You think I'm a fool, don't you?"

He used to, but he couldn't tell her that. "Look, this has nothing to do with you. My job is the herd. Nothing else. I can't explain it, but this is the most important thing I've ever done. I've already lost two days, and I'll lose another when we cut the herd."

"In other words, I'm too much trouble."

Monty looked as though he wished he could bite his tongue. "This herd belongs to the family," he finally said. "I can't be thinking of what I'd like to do."

"But it is your success," Iris said, "and that's what's so important, isn't it?"

"Yes." The admission came reluctantly, pulled from him unwillingly.

"Why?"

"You wouldn't understand."

"Try me."

For a second he was tempted. He wanted her to understand. He didn't like her thinking he was cold and unreasonable. But it wouldn't work. Besides, they would separate in a few days and he might never see her again. What was the point?

"You'd have to understand George and the family and a lot of other things."

"I could try."

"And I could try to understand why you're so

determined to have Carlos, but it wouldn't change anything. Look, I've got to inspect the strays and check out Reardon. I'll be back in half an hour. You ought to be safe for that long."

That was a joke. She'd be more safe with Carlos than with him.

But she was puzzled on another score. She hadn't realized success was so important to Monty. She'd always thought he was successful. Everybody else did, too. Yet there was something inside him driving him away from Texas, away from his family—some need so powerful he was reluctant to take on anything that might get in the way.

She had always thought of Monty as a tall, handsome, cheerful, uncomplicated man, secure in his wealth and success. Yet he had just given her a glimpse of a very different man, one for whom the sweetness of success was still to come.

"That seems to be all the missing cows," Monty said when he returned. "We can head back first thing in the morning."

Iris and Carlos were sitting near the fire. She had been trying to rekindle a feeling of family closeness. She hadn't been successful, but she felt sure she would be soon. Things felt a little odd just now, but she knew she was going to like having a brother around.

Carlos had made more coffee. Iris handed Monty a fresh cup.

"Did you meet Mr. Reardon?" Iris asked.

"Yes. I don't like your friend," Monty said to Carlos. "I don't trust him."

"There's nothing wrong with Joe," Carlos said, firing up in defense of his companion.

"That depends on how you look at it. The way I

see it, he's trouble. You'd better be getting back to your campfire before he decides to take that two hundred head for himself."

For a moment Carlos looked as if he was going to argue with Monty. But he subsided when Iris cast him an imploring glance.

"Why don't you move over to our camp?" Carlos suggested. "We've got a better location. Besides, it'll be easier with three of us watching the herd."

"Four," Monty said. "You forgot Iris."

"I never learned how to—" Iris began.

"No time like the present." Monty gave Carlos a hard look. "I already told Reardon we'd be over as soon as we could collect our stuff."

Iris didn't know what was going on in Monty's mind. She had expected him to refuse to move to Carlos's camp or to allow Carlos and Reardon to spend the night with them. Yet he was packing up without a moment's objection. He must not mind Reardon so much after all.

When they arrived, Iris wondered if Monty hadn't agreed to move so that he could keep an eye on Reardon. The two men obviously disliked each other.

Monty dumped his saddle and bedroll on the ground. "Iris will take the first watch. That way she won't have to wake up once she gets to sleep. I'll follow her, then Carlos. Reardon can take the last shift."

"I don't think Iris ought to take a shift," Carlos said.

"I'm giving the orders, and I say she does."

"Who the hell says so?"

"I'm ramrodding this outfit," Monty said, walking right up to Carlos's face, "Iris's herd and mine. You work for her; you take orders from me. If that doesn't sit well, I can't say I'll be sorry to see the back of you."

Carlos turned to Iris. "Is that so?"

"Yes," Iris said. She wanted to explain, but she decided this wasn't the best time.

Carlos looked from Iris to Monty and back to Iris. "It's a damned strange arrangement."

"I'm sure Iris will explain everything to you tomorrow," Monty said. "In the meantime, I suggest you get some sleep. I like my crew to be alert when they're in the saddle."

Monty spread his bedroll on the ground. He positioned his saddle about six feet to the right.

"Where's Iris going to sleep?" Carlos asked.

"There," Monty said, pointing to the bedroll.

"But that's your bedroll."

"I know, but it's the only one we've got."

"Where are you going to sleep?"

"There," Monty said, pointing to the same bedroll.

Carlos looked about ready to explode. Monty looked madder than a wet hornet, but he could be doing this just to make Carlos angry enough to leave. If he *was*, Iris was going to be furious with him. It was her reputation and her brother's feelings he was treating with so little concern.

"I'm going to sleep in it while your sister's on duty. She can have it during my shift."

"And afterward?"

"I'll use my saddle," Monty said.

Carlos untied his bedroll and spread it out on the opposite side of the campfire from Monty's bedroll.

"She can have mine," he said. "I have a blanket." Carlos untied his blanket and spread it on the ground next to his bedroll.

Monty stared at Carlos for a moment. Then he picked up his bedroll and repositioned it next to Carlos's bedroll. Iris's intended bed was now flanked by two bodyguards, each eyeing the other suspiciously and making no attempt to hide his distrust.

Iris felt a bubble of laughter working its way upward. These two men were fighting over her as if she was a little child unable to take care of herself. It made her heart feel good to see Monty acting like a jealous beau. He wasn't her beau, but he was clearly jealous of Carlos, and that was good enough for the moment.

"It seems like a sensible arrangement," Iris said, stepping between the two men. "Now you'd better show me what I'm supposed to do while I'm on guard duty. Then everybody can get to sleep."

"I'll show you," Carlos offered.

"I'm the boss. I'll show her," Monty stated in a manner that allowed no argument. "Tomorrow you can teach her how to ride herd. Frank didn't."

Iris kept her indignant reply trembling on her lips until she didn't feel like uttering it anymore. As sure as she opened her mouth, she'd say something wrong and look like a silly female complaining because her feelings had been hurt.

She was ignorant. She had to accept that, even though the thought burned in her throat. She *would* learn. And when she did . . . well, Monty Randolph had just better watch out.

"What the hell did you mean by hiring those two, Monty?" Hen demanded the next evening when Monty and the others reached camp. He positively bristled at the sight of Reardon. Salty didn't look any more pleased. "I don't think much of Carlos, but that other one will be trouble."

The three of them sat their horses on the crest of a ridge, where they had a good view of most of the herd. There weren't many places where they could observe more than 6,000 longhorns stretched over nearly two miles along the trail. Monty watched as Iris introduced Carlos and Joe to Frank. The big man didn't seem to like the new recruits any more than Hen and Salty.

"Then he'd better wait until he gets somewhere else," Salty said. "The boys and I don't like trouble."

"Neither do I," Monty said. He trusted Hen's judgment. Hen could recognize trouble on its way in. Monty wished now he'd held out against Reardon, but he didn't know how he could have. Iris was so glad to see Carlos, and Monty had known right away Carlos wouldn't stay without Reardon.

"At least now we can get started cutting the herds," Hen said. "I don't like having Frank around."

Monty had been waiting for this. He knew it was coming and he was prepared. "I think we'll keep the herds together for a little while longer."

Hen and Salty stared at him.

"I don't like leaving Iris alone with that bunch," Monty explained. "Frank's up to something. And I don't trust Carlos not to try to take her for everything she's got. He says he's been following her. I don't think it's all for brotherly love."

"Let her go off on her own. You'll find out soon enough," Hen said.

"I can't do that. Who knows what might happen to her?"

"Then she should have stayed home."

"She should, but it's too late now."

"She could go sit in some hotel until the drive's over."

"She won't do that either."

"Then forget her," Hen snapped. "We don't owe her anything."

"I don't like it either," Salty said, "but Monty's right. We can't go off and leave her if there's any chance something might happen to her."

Hen glared at Monty and Salty. "You're both getting soft," he said. "You mark my words. That woman's nothing but trouble; her brother showing up is only going to make things worse."

"He'll calm down," Salty said as Hen rode away. "He always does."

"I'm not worried about Hen," Monty said. "He's not as mean as he likes to sound. But he's right. There will be trouble. And that does bother me."

Monty stayed away from Iris all the next day. It was easy to do. Keeping track of over 6,000 longhorns and a crew of 30, several of whom he didn't trust, took all the time he had. He spent the entire day working out assignments and coordinating the two crews. In a herd this large, he had to repeatedly check to make sure all the grass and water wasn't gone by the time the stragglers got to it.

Still he kept Iris within his sight most of the time. He was certain Carlos was using her, just hanging around looking for what he could take. He may have gotten a bum deal from Helena—everybody got a bum deal from Helena—but he'd had plenty of opportunity to make something of himself. Instead he'd preferred to float about the country, picking up work when he could, blaming his lack of success on anything but his own lack of motivation and willingness to work.

Monty knew Iris wouldn't believe that. He couldn't explain why she'd taken to Carlos as if he was her salvation. Surely she knew a man with nothing didn't attach himself to a woman for purely chivalrous notions.

He kept telling himself Iris's lack of family made her blind to Carlos's faults, but even that didn't explain her eager acceptance of a brother she hardly knew. But maybe her present situation did. He reminded himself she was caught between a man she didn't trust—her foreman—and one who had done everything in his power to make her think he didn't like her—himself. What could be more natural than for her to reach out to a member of her family.

But understanding her feelings did very little to help him control his temper when he rode into camp and saw Iris and Carlos with their heads together. He felt anger and irritation, and a desire to kick Carlos out into the night.

"You two had better be thinking about getting to sleep," Monty said, coming to the campfire for a cup of coffee.

"We've still got a lot to catch up on," Iris said, but she looked bone tired.

"You've got the rest of your lives to catch up. You've had a full day in the saddle and another one coming up tomorrow. Being tired can be dangerous."

"You don't think I can do it?"

Monty recognized a challenge when he heard one, but surprisingly, he didn't feel like responding to it. "I'm sure you can. It's just that you're not used to it. Now I hate to hurry your brother off, but it's time for him to go on watch." He pointed to the stars. "In fact, you're late."

Carlos jumped up. "I can't be late. It'll make a very poor impression on the boss," he said, trying to sound casual.

"I'm the boss," Iris said. Hearing herself say that surprised her almost as much as the men. "You don't have to work if I say so."

Monty's temper had always had a low flash point, but that remark made him smolder. "Everybody on a drive works," he said. "There's no room for dead weight. My brothers and I expect to work harder than any of our men. All they've got to lose is a hundred dollars in wages. We stand to lose more than fifty thousand dollars in cattle."

He hadn't said it to embarrass her or criticize her. He'd said it because of the favoritism she showed Carlos. If she was to have any success at all in running her own ranch, she had to learn that business decisions were a matter of economics, not emotion. She would never succeed if she let her personal feelings for people determine all her decisions.

And then again maybe he wasn't just trying to give her good advice. Why did it make him so mad to see the way she accepted Carlos without question? Maybe he was jealous. He didn't think so, but he sure sounded like it.

"I mean to work as hard as any man on Iris's crew," Carlos said.

"I didn't mean that the way it sounded," Monty said after Carlos had gone. He didn't like the way Iris looked at him, accusing, angry, even hurt. "I was only trying to tell Carlos he would have to carry his weight."

"Carlos is working for me. It's my place to tell him anything he needs to know."

"As long as you're running your herd with mine, I'll have a say in it," Monty replied. Iris's defending

Carlos, a slacker and a parasite, made his temper rise faster than the blooming stalk of a century plant. He could see Iris trying to control her temper, and he reluctantly did the same. It wouldn't do either of them any good to start fighting over something new.

Besides, he didn't want to fight. He liked talking to Iris, and he couldn't very well do that when they were shouting at each other.

"Come on, let's decide where you're going to sleep."

"Maybe I should sleep with my own men."

She looked to where her crew had laid out their bedrolls on the south side of the chuck wagon. The Circle-7 boys were bedded down to the north, closer to the herd. Monty could tell Iris wasn't anxious to go.

"I think you should sleep next to the chuck wagon. That way Zac and Tyler can keep an eye on you."

"I'm not sure. Won't Frank wonder—"

"Nobody will wonder anything. Besides, we keep the fire going all night. Some of the men like coffee when they're riding herd."

Monty took a couple of blankets out of the chuck wagon and spread them on the ground. Then he opened her bedroll. "You can use your saddle or saddlebags for a pillow."

"The saddlebags," Iris said, clinging to them as if they were her last worldly possessions. He still wanted to know what she had in them that was so important, but he'd been so busy he'd forgotten to ask.

Tyler stomped about, cleaning up from dinner and getting things ready for breakfast in the morning. Twice he almost bumped into Iris. He didn't even look at her.

"You have to ignore Tyler," Monty said. "He has no use for women, especially if he thinks they're going to interfere with his cooking."

"I wouldn't have the nerve after that wonderful dinner," Iris said, but all she got for her compliment was a good view of Tyler's back. And silence.

"He doesn't talk much either," Monty said. "Stutters."

"Tell her any more lies about me, and you'll cook your own breakfast," Tyler growled without the slightest trace of a stammer. He neither turned around nor paused in his work.

"Look out," Zac shouted from the direction of the corral. "Horses coming through."

Iris moved just in time to keep from being stepped on by a prancing paint.

"Maybe I'd better sleep with my men after all," she said.

Monty picked up her bedding and carried it to the other side of the chuck wagon. "That's just Zac," he told Iris. "Rose is the only female he cares about."

"And you expect these two to watch out for me? They're more likely to run over me when they pull out in the morning."

"They're just as rude as the rest of us," Monty said, "but you can trust them with your life."

Iris looked at the two brothers going about their business as though she wasn't even there. "I think I'd rather trust my own brother."

"You mean you'd rather trust a—"

"A what?" Iris asked, her green eyes hard and glittering.

"A virtual stranger," Monty said. "You may not know Zac and Tyler very well, but then we don't know Carlos very well either."

Monty couldn't believe his own ears. He had returned a diplomatic answer. Rose would swear he had a fever.

"You'll soon see Carlos is everything he says he is."

"Yeah," Monty agreed, wondering how much prolonged contact with Iris would affect his own personality. He was already in danger of not recognizing himself. "If you have any washing up to do, you'd better do it tonight. The creek will be cold in the morning, and there'll be men moving about everywhere."

Iris looked around.

"It's just beyond the ramuda."

"Would you go with me? I don't feel comfortable in the dark."

He didn't suppose it would do any good to tell Iris he didn't feel comfortable around her at any time, dark or light. It wouldn't solve anything, and it would let her know she could get to him.

She might not know it yet, but he did. She had been getting at him more and more each day. He ought to be thankful Carlos had found them last night instead of wishing every five minutes the man had found cows in Arizona or Nevada instead. Monty hadn't allowed himself to think about it too much, but no telling what he might have done if Carlos hadn't shown up.

He had clearly lost control. In the past, he'd always kept women and work strictly separate. It had been a matter of convenience as well as necessity. Now Iris had forced him to break that rule. But to consider breaking a more profound rule against getting involved with a woman on the trail was madness. It went against common sense.

He had to get some more distance between them.

Yet he found himself thinking more and more about Iris and less and less about Wyoming. It didn't do any good to keep telling himself it would blow over, that he wouldn't remember her two weeks after she vanished from his life. It mattered now, when he was in the middle of an important drive, when he needed all his effort and concentration to make sure they got to Wyoming safely.

If he let his weakness for a beautiful woman ruin his big chance, he would hate himself for the rest of his life. He'd never forgive Iris either.

Yet he couldn't put her out of his mind. He'd already failed at that. He would have to come up with another solution. But what?

Chapter Thirteen

The moonlight bleached the color out of everything. The bedrolls looked especially white against the dark of the ground. A pair of boots, each with a hat perched atop it, stood next to every bedroll. The heat had caused half the men to toss aside their covers. Two young hands snored like bullfrogs in concert, first one in a medium baritone followed by the other in a tremulous tenor.

Monty carried his bedroll over to where his men were sleeping. But just as he was about to spread it out next to his sleeping twin, he hesitated.

What about Iris?

Tyler and Zac weren't as watchful as he would like, but between the two of them they would see nothing happened to her. Not that he expected anything would happen. There were more than a dozen men within the sound of her voice who would rush to her aid at the first sign of danger.

At least she was away from Frank.

Monty opened his bedroll, folded his blanket for a pillow, and lay down, but it was some time before he could get comfortable. He really didn't like Iris sleeping out. He had pooh-poohed her wagon at first. But now she was in his camp, he didn't feel the same way. It wasn't a good idea to have a woman on a trail drive, but if you had to have one, it wasn't proper for her to be sleeping on the ground with the men.

Monty twisted around, trying to get comfortable. Usually he dropped off as soon as his head hit the pillow. Tonight he could feel every blade of grass underneath him. The ground felt rock hard.

Nothing was going to happen to her. No matter how hungry they might get, no wolves or panthers would enter the camp. If it came to a stampede, she was as safe next to the chuck wagon as she could be anywhere except back home in her own bed. But she didn't have a bed anymore. It, along with the sheets and blankets, and expensive cakes of scented soap for all he knew, belonged to the bank now.

A particular clump of grass wouldn't smash down, and Monty slid his whole bed over about a foot.

He wouldn't mind if they didn't get the Double-D chuck wagon fixed right away. He rather liked having her crew eat at his campfire. It gave him a chance to study her men, make up his mind which ones he trusted and which ones he didn't. But he hoped Lovell would have Iris's wagon fixed by the time they reached Fort Worth. He wouldn't be comfortable until she could bed down in private.

Monty turned over again.

"Take that bedroll and put it where you can keep an eye on her," Hen growled.

"I'm fine just where I am."

"Turning over like a flapjack isn't fine. Either get still or move. The rest of us have to get some sleep."

Monty felt a flush of embarrassment rise from under his collar. He was tempted to argue. He was even more tempted to belt Hen in the mouth, but starting a fight would achieve nothing but further embarrassment. Thankful that the dark hid the flush he was certain now reached his cheeks, Monty stood and grabbed up his bedroll.

"I'm only doing this so I won't bother you."

"Yeah, and Christmas comes in July."

Monty managed to step on his brother as he stalked off. Hen's chuckle made him want to go back and step on him harder.

Iris slept undisturbed. Monty noticed the saddlebags. They were no longer under her head. They had been tossed to the side. They were obviously empty.

He paused, thoughtful. He wondered what could have been in them and where Iris could have hidden it. It was obviously important.

He just hoped it wasn't dangerous.

Now that he'd decided to move his bed, he couldn't decide where to put it. Tyler slept under the chuck wagon, silent as death. Zac slept next to him, a bad spring cold making him wheeze like a fat man. The night horses, some saddled, all staked out and ready, grazed nearby. There really wasn't any place for him to sleep except next to Iris.

His jaw set, Monty spread his bedroll six feet away. He was the boss. He could sleep anywhere he wanted. Besides, it was his job to protect Iris, or any other female who happened to show up, so if anybody was to sleep close by, he was the one.

But once he had laid out his bedroll and crawled in, he was more restless than before. Deciding to sleep next to Iris was one thing. Going to sleep next to her was another.

He had never seen Iris asleep. Hell, he couldn't recall watching any woman sleep. He would have snorted in disgust if anybody had suggested he would be sitting on his bedroll watching Iris just lie there. He felt like a fool, but he couldn't turn away. She seemed nothing like the Iris who flirted with every man she saw or the Iris who flew into a temper when she didn't get what she wanted. She was somebody entirely different, and he felt very drawn to her.

Looking at her now made him think of the year Rose had invited the Richmonds over for Christmas. Helena never did know how to celebrate anything but her own birthday. The idea of giving was foreign to her.

When Rose decided to celebrate, she pulled out all the stops. She decorated virtually every part of the house with crocheted snowflakes, angels, bells, mistletoe Zac gathered from mesquite trees, moss Tyler gathered from live oaks, and branches of leaves that stayed green all year. Ten Christmas stockings filled with apples from Missouri, oranges from Mexico, nuts and chocolate all the way from Europe nearly obliterated the fireplace.

The centerpiece was a cedar tree decorated in a manner Rose had learned from the German immigrants who settled in the vicinity of Austin. It was always the twins' job to find the biggest cedar on the ranch. George strung the popcorn and tied on the candles, after which Rose put on the finishing touch with a porcelain angel she'd inherited from her mother.

From the moment Iris entered the house, her eyes had grown large with wonder. She had gone from one room to the other staring at the decorations, the piles of presents, the food. She became totally caught up in the magic of Christmas. She forgot she was beautiful, spoiled, and adored by everybody. She was like any other 13 year old who unexpectedly discovered something wonderful and new.

Monty had never forgotten the sweet innocence of that day. Not even Helena could spoil the magic of that afternoon. Maybe that was why he hadn't been able to put Iris out of his mind. Maybe he was still looking for that childlike naivete in the woman Iris had become.

He had found it at his campfire.

This was not the temperamental redhead with the flashing green eyes, stunning smile, and a body that could cause him to break into a sweat in a snowstorm. She seemed more an angel of peace and serenity, of quiet and repose.

Everything Iris was not.

Yet Monty felt she could be. At least she was now.

He wanted her to be!

Good Lord, he must have lost his mind to be mooning over Iris in her sleep because she looked like the kind of female who would cause a man to get down on his knees in thanks. Everybody looked innocent and sweet while sleeping. The twins, Aurelia and Juliette, were a perfect example. Monty had never seen two miscreants who could look so innocent and angelic after a day of terrifying the ranch hands and giving Rose another gray hair.

Maybe only pretty females could manage it. It was a dead cinch that if Iris could look this innocent awake no man could stand against her. No man would want to.

Damn, he had no business being attracted to a female, certainly not now. He lay down and turned his back to Iris. He would keep an eye on her, but as soon as she got her wagons back he would separate the herds and send her on her way. He might even let a herd or two pass him so there'd be a buffer between them. Let somebody else catch her cows the next time they stampeded. He didn't want nervous, jumpy, wild-eyed longhorns, gaunt from running every night, by the time he got to Wyoming. He wanted fat, complacent cows willing to drop a calf every spring and work hard to find enough grass so they could feed their babies and have them grow into fine, strong steers for market or heifers ready to give him still more calves.

He wanted the most thriving ranch in Wyoming. He wanted to show George and everybody else he could do it on his own.

"I don't like having anything to do with him," Carlos told Iris a week later. "I especially don't like having to take orders from him."

"Monty and I talk things over every day," Iris said, trying to soothe Carlos's irritation. "It's like I'm giving the orders, too."

They talked as they rode alongside the herd. The cows walked about 12 abreast down a trail which varied from 40 to 75 feet wide. The noise of hooves on hard ground, the clack of horns, and grunts and bellows made it hard to hear. The weather continued unseasonably hot and dry. It wasn't yet noon, but Iris's shirt was damp with perspiration.

195

"Well, it feels like he's giving all of them. I don't like being surrounded by Randolphs. They may fight like dogs among themselves, but they stick together against the rest of the world."

"Tyler doesn't leave that chuck wagon long enough to know if we're in Texas or Mexico," Iris said, responding to her brother with a little less patience than before, "and Zac's nothing but an overgrown boy."

"Baby rattlesnakes are dangerous, and so are baby Randolphs. Don't ever forget that."

"I haven't forgotten a thing about the Randolphs," Iris said, losing patience. "Monty has saved my life twice. Twice he's found cows I lost."

"Joe and I found those last ones."

"Monty would have found them if you hadn't," Iris said, refusing to be sidetracked. "I've caused him nothing but trouble, but he's pulled me out every time. And he gave you a job."

"You gave it to me."

"No. Monty could have refused to let me hire you. He didn't mean to hire you at first, but he changed his mind."

"Why?"

"It doesn't really matter. If you mean to stay, you're going to have to work with him. I want you to stay," Iris said when Carlos began to look mulish. "I want us to become family, too."

"You mean like the Randolphs?" Carlos jerked his thumb in the direction of Tyler, the tone of his voice indicating that he didn't consider the Randolphs a good example.

"Yes, I do. They may be tough on outsiders, but it must be wonderful to know you've got so many people who'd do anything for you no matter how much it cost them."

"That's the Randolphs for sure," Carlos said, though he didn't seem to regard their willingness to stand up for each other in such a positive light. "Any one of them could commit murder and the rest of them would still protect him."

Iris climbed down from her wagon, relieved to be out of its stifling closeness. After sleeping in the open for nearly a week, she had looked forward to the privacy of her own bed, but she had lain awake most of the night. She felt isolated, cut off, suffocated.

She paused and took a deep breath. After the dust, heat, noise, and smell of riding with the herd for 16 hours, the morning air felt marvelously clean and refreshing. The stillness was especially soothing. Sixty-two hundred cows made an awful lot of noise. After a while it got on her nerves. She stretched. It caused her stiff muscles to ache, but it was a delicious ache, and she took her time.

Funny, but she was almost getting to like the early morning, rising before dawn, going to bed after dusk. Just a few months ago she would never have considered getting up before nine o'clock or going to bed before midnight. She looked at her hands and pulled a face. Her skin was rough and chapped, old blisters had turned into calluses, but it was her nails that caused her to wince. She had cut every one down to the quick to keep them from breaking or snagging.

Helena would have entered a convent before she'd have been seen with her hands looking like this.

Iris's clothes looked even worse. A couple of places needed darning badly. She shrugged. There was no help for it. She didn't know how to sew.

She hadn't yet worked up the courage to ask one of the men to teach her, but she probably would. There was no telling what kind of humiliation she would learn to accept before this drive was over.

The sound of bleating calves caught her attention. She had been unable to ignore that sound since the night the cow chased her.

"What's going on?" she asked the cook when she reached the chuck wagon.

"It's just one of the men getting ready to shoot the calves."

"Shoot the calves!" she exclaimed. "What for?"

"We always shoot newborn calves or trade them to a farmer for eggs and vegetables. They can't keep up with the herd."

"Where's he taking them?"

"I don't know. Probably to the other side of some thicket so the noise won't bother the cows."

Iris headed in the direction of the bleating. It sounded like two calves.

"He won't like having you watch," Bob called after her.

But Iris had no intention of watching. Nobody was going to shoot her calves. He might as well take her money and throw it away.

She rounded a dense plum thicket in time to see Billy Cuthbert put a pistol to one calf's head. "Stop!" she shouted, and ran forward. "Don't you ever shoot one of my calves."

"Frank told me to."

"Well, I'm telling you not to. Now take them back to their mothers."

"They'll just die," Billy said. "Their mamas won't stay with them."

"Then we'll carry them."

"How?"

Even as Iris started to say she didn't know, the
answer popped into her head. She didn't like it at
first, but after a moment's thought, she shrugged.
It fitted with all the rest. She might as well accept
that cows were more important than people, especially her.

"You can put them in my wagon."

"Are you crazy?" Billy exclaimed.

Iris laughed. "I must be to voluntarily give up my
wagon to a couple of calves."

"Where are you going to sleep?"

"On the ground. Would you believe I actually
missed it?"

Billy followed her back, mumbling under his
breath. Monty and Salty rode up a few minutes
later while the men were unloading what was left
of the wagon's furnishings.

"What's wrong now?" Monty asked.

"She won't let us shoot these calves," Frank
explained. "She's going to carry them in her wagon
until they get strong enough to keep up."

"I don't see any sense in killing a calf," Iris said.
She felt nervous under Monty's penetrating gaze,
but she felt determined as well. "It's not only waste-
ful; it's cruel."

Monty just stared at her as if he was looking right
through her. Iris didn't want to think of what he
would say when they were alone. She just hoped
he would hold his tongue while the men were
listening.

"I need every cow and calf I have," Iris continued.
"If we shoot two calves a day, that'll be nearly two
hundred by the time we get to Wyoming. That's
two thousand dollars. In three years, it'll be even
more."

"Everybody gets rid of the calves," Frank said.

"And everybody's been stupid," Monty said as he dismounted. "That's the best idea I've heard of since the chuck wagon." He turned to Salty. "Get us one. Buy it from a farmer. Send to Fort Worth if you must, but I want a calf wagon in camp by tonight. Did you really think of that by yourself?" he asked, turning to Iris.

Iris nodded, too stunned to speak. For the first time in her life, she had done something Monty liked, something he thought was good enough to copy. She didn't know whether to collapse from shock or float from elation.

"You can put your calves in my wagon when I get it," Monty said. "No need for you to be pushed out of yours."

"I don't want it anymore. I felt uncomfortable, cooped up."

"That's a change. You used to—"

"I know, but I changed my mind."

Monty gave her an appraising look. "You're full of surprises."

"It surprised me, too. I never thought I'd give up a bed for a bedroll."

"I never thought you'd cut your nails," Monty said.

Iris tried to hide her hands behind her, but Monty grasped one and held it up. He opened her palm.

"You've got calluses," he said.

"So do you."

"They come with the job."

Iris raised her second hand, palm up. "So did these."

"Keep it up. You might turn into a rancher yet."

And with that stunning remark, Monty mounted up and rode off, again leaving Iris staring after him with her mouth open.

* * *

Monty came wide awake. Almost in the same motion he threw aside his blanket. He shoved his feet into his boots, settled his hat on his head, and got to his feet. Dawn was still a good half hour away, but he always felt fully awake the moment he opened his eyes. There was no yawning and stretching and turning over to catch a few more minutes of sleep. He awoke full of energy, anxious to be up and doing.

The morning air was cool and still, the sky a slate gray. The cows rested quietly, a light dew adding a chill to the morning air. The men still slept, but moved restlessly in the last minutes before dawn. One man leaned on his elbow smoking a rolled cigarette. The faint smell of coffee and frying bacon mixed with the smell of tobacco.

Monty loved this time of day. It provided him with a small island of peace and quiet before the activity of the coming day. It was a time for making new plans, for anticipating success, of pleasurable anxiety. The problems of yesterday were forgotten. A new, unspoiled day lay ahead. It was a chance to start over with a clean slate.

The silence in Iris's camp was nearly complete. With the repair of Iris's chuck wagon, she had moved back with her own crew. Monty, saying he needed to be familiar with both groups of men, had started sleeping in Iris's camp on alternate nights.

"Coffee's hot," the cook said, taking time from his work to pour a cup of coffee and hand it to Monty. He was one of seven men on Iris's crew who had accepted Monty's authority.

"Thanks," Monty said, taking the cup. "Anything changed?" he asked, looking at the man over his cup.

201

"Something has, but I don't know what." The cook spoke in a low voice as he went about his work. "Something's up. I can feel it."

"Frank?"

"Can't say. He seems to talk to everybody the same, but some know something and some don't."

"Keep your eyes open," Monty said before moving away.

Monty walked to where Iris slept a short distance away. He hesitated to wake her. He wanted her to come back to his camp. She felt she ought to be with her own men, but she wasn't comfortable at her own campfire. She always stayed close to Carlos or himself.

He also noticed something else. She never let anyone touch her. And that included himself. After all the effort she had made to get him to notice her, he didn't understand that. He first thought that having attained the goal of getting him to take her to Wyoming she had dropped her pretense of interest in him.

Though it hurt Monty's vanity to admit that might be one of the reasons, he knew it wasn't the only one. Something else was troubling Iris. Something he knew nothing about.

It certainly wasn't Carlos. Monty's duties kept him on the move, but it seemed every time he saw Iris, she and Carlos had their heads together. Monty found himself growing irritated that Iris could be so taken in by Carlos, even if he was her half brother.

It wasn't Reardon either. He didn't hang around camp. He disappeared as soon as he finished his meals. Monty didn't know what Reardon was doing here, beyond trying to earn a little money, but he didn't like the man. Reardon wasn't the kind to hang around without a reason, and that reason wasn't likely to be to anybody's advantage but his own. He was dangerous and cruel. Monty could see that in his eyes.

No, despite Reardon, it was something else, and Monty meant to find out what it was.

"Why doesn't he separate the herds?" Carlos asked Iris. They had ridden together most of the day, talking while he did his work.

Nothing happened to ease the monotonous routine of keeping the cows moving. The herd had settled down after the last stampede and adapted to the trail with remarkable complacency. There was very little for Iris to do as the endless miles drifted by except worry about her future and complain about the heat.

"He lost too much time with the stampede," Iris said, "and he doesn't want to take the time just yet. It's been a terribly dry spring, and he wants to get as far north as he can before the real heat of summer sets in."

"Maybe he doesn't want to separate the herds," Carlos said.

"What do you mean?" Iris asked. She hadn't told Carlos of her suspicions about Frank. She didn't feel that comfortable with him yet.

"I don't know, but I never heard of anybody keeping two herds together. They're usually anxious to separate them as soon as possible."

"Why? It ought to be easier to drive one herd than two."

"Easier to steal it that way."

Iris laughed. "I'm not worried about Monty stealing my cows."

"Well, you ought to be. Joe was talking about it last night. Said it looked queer the way Monty was lording it over your men."

Iris decided it was time she took Carlos into her confidence. It didn't make sense to say she wanted them to be a close-knit family, then keep secrets from him. Besides, she was tired of continually having to defend Monty. After what she'd put him through, he didn't deserve to be distrusted.

"It was my idea."

Carlos clearly hadn't expected that.

"To combine the herds and put Monty in charge over Frank," Iris said. "We can't have two leaders and—"

"But to put a stranger in charge of your crew!"

"Monty's no stranger. The Randolphs have been our neighbors since Daddy bought the ranch. Besides, he's already chased off rustlers after one stampede."

"Did you see him?"

"Do what?"

"Chase off rustlers?"

"No, but he told me about it when he brought the cows back."

"He could have made it up to gain your confidence, oil up to you, make you—"

Iris's peal of laugher made several of the cattle eye her uneasily.

"You don't know Monty very well if you think he'd bother to *oil up to me*," Iris said. "He was more likely to tell me I'm nothing but trouble and order me to turn around and go back home."

"Well, you have to admit it got him control of your herd."

"No, it didn't. I had to practically beg."

"Why?"

"Because something is going on, and I don't know what it is," Iris told her brother. "Somebody was rustling back home. No matter what trap we laid or how cleverly we covered our trail, they always found out and struck somewhere else."

"Inside information?"

"It had to be. Then there was the episode of the stampede and rustlers."

"You don't know—"

"Monty described one of the men he drove off. I saw that man talking to Bill Lovell back on the ranch. And since then I've seen Frank and Bill in deep conversation."

"You think Frank is involved?"

"I don't know. That's why I was so glad to see you. Finally I had somebody I could trust."

"If you trust me, take my advice and don't trust Monty too far."

"But why?"

"Those people got too rich too fast to have made their money honestly. There's a rumor floating around that their old man stole an army payroll. I also heard that one of those brothers made a killing by tying up with some fancy lawyers back east. Everybody knows they're crooked as a cow's hind leg."

"I'd trust Monty with my life."

"If you trust him with your herd, that's exactly what you've done."

Carlos spurred his horse to chase down a steer that had broken from the trail, leaving Iris to mull over what he had said. She didn't believe Monty was trying to steal her herd, but Carlos had planted a seed of doubt in her mind.

Why had Monty changed his mind about helping her? It certainly wasn't because he had fallen in love with her. He hadn't been near her all day. While she didn't understand Monty, she did know enough about love-smitten young men to know they didn't studiously ignore the object of their affections.

Iris had asked Carlos and Joe to meet her at the Circle-7 chuck wagon. She had been thinking about asking Carlos to be her foreman, and she wanted Monty to let him work with Salty so he could learn the job. She also wanted him to let Joe work with Carlos. She knew Monty wouldn't like the idea, and she was dreading having to talk to him.

Monty scowled when he saw Iris, Carlos, and Joe together. "I've got some new assignments for you two." He forestalled Iris by speaking before he dismounted. He dropped to the ground and reached for a cup of coffee. He kept his back to them. "Joe will have the drag, Carlos the point. Iris, you'll ride swing with me."

He had put them as far apart as possible.

"I'll have new night-duty assignments at supper. Now you'd better get going. Your partners are waiting."

"I wanted to talk with you about the duty assignments," Iris said, incensed that Monty still wouldn't face them. "I want you to change—"

"I can't change anybody without changing everybody." Monty took a last swallow, tossed the rest of the coffee away, and handed the cup to Tyler. He turned to Carlos and Joe. "What are you two waiting for?"

"Nothing," Carlos said, and the two of them walked off.

Monty turned to Iris. "I'll be back in fifteen minutes. Can you be ready by then?"

"Sure, but—"

"I don't have time now. We'll talk about it later."
Then he walked off, leaving Iris fuming.

"Is he always like that?" she demanded of Tyler.

"No. Usually he's full of jokes and good humor. So much so he sometimes gets on everybody's nerves. He's been too serious this trip."

"You mean he's been mean as a snake," Zac said, bringing up the oxen to be hitched to the chuck wagon.

"It's not like him," Tyler added. He packed away the last of his cooking pots and Dutch ovens in the boot beneath the wagon in preparation for heading out to the next campsite. He took the coffeepot off the fire, poured the remaining coffee in a cup, and set it aside, then stowed the pot in its cubbyhole. He folded the hinged lid over the back of the wagon, secured it with a lock, and prepared to depart for the site Hen would choose for dinner.

"I'm surprised one of you hasn't murdered him," Iris said.

"Might have tried," Zac said, backing the oxen into the traces, "but nobody can beat him."

"Your brother must have the patience of a saint to put up with him."

"Monty argues with George, but he doesn't mouth off to him," Tyler said.

"I can't believe that," Iris said.

"None of us does."

"But Monty would defy God."

"Maybe, but he doesn't defy George."

"I can't believe it. I never in my life saw anybody who was so certain he was always right."

"You don't know George," Zac said, adding his pittance.

"No, I don't," Iris agreed, "but maybe I should."

Leigh Greenwood

"George doesn't pull rank often," Tyler said as he sat down to wait for Hen, "but what he says goes. Monty might puff up like a toad, but he'll take it out on one of us. He wouldn't lay a finger on George."

"Why?" Iris asked, unable to believe Monty respected anybody that much.

"For one thing, George is stronger than he is. For another, Rose wouldn't let him."

"Rose!" Iris squeaked. "She hardly comes up to his chest."

"Rose won't let anybody annoy George," Zac said. "She'd shoot Monty if he tried to fight him."

"Not with a rifle," Tyler explained. "Probably use a shotgun. Monty'd be picking buckshot out of his backside for the better part of a year."

Iris didn't know whether the whole Randolph family, including Rose, was crazy or if she was, but she made up her mind not to allow Monty to make any more remarks about her own family. Helena had been a remarkably selfish woman, her father foolishly indulgent, but at least they were sane.

She was just about to launch into another line of questioning when Hen rode up. He slid from the saddle. Zac left Tyler to finish hitching up the oxen by himself and ran to catch up Hen's horse.

Hen picked up the lukewarm coffee, took a couple of hasty swallows, and tossed the rest away.

"Fill your water barrel before you leave," he said to Tyler. "There's not another decent stream in the next hundred miles."

"Why?" Iris asked.

"No rain," Hen replied, accepting the horse Zac brought to him. "There's not enough water for our herd. There won't be any for them that follow."

"What are we going to do?" Iris asked.

"Go ask Monty," Hen said, his tightly controlled voice letting Iris know how much he disliked having her in their camp. "He's ramrodding this outfit."

Chapter Fourteen

The noonday sun beat down on the prairie with cruel ferocity. A skeleton crew kept the herd grazing north while everyone else gathered in the middle of the grassy expanse. A sluggish breeze barely rippled grass that was becoming brittle and less succulent with each hot, rainless day.

When the last of the men arrived, Monty said to Hen, "Tell us what you found."

Monty seemed like a different person when he was acting like the boss, and Iris didn't like the change. He listened without comment, without emotion, without a single glance in her direction. He seemed totally absorbed by the problem. She didn't want her cattle to die of thirst in the middle of Indian territory, nor did she enjoy being completely ignored.

"Is there at least one stream with enough water for the whole herd?" Monty asked Hen.

"No."

"Can they survive without water?" Iris asked.

"Not for a hundred miles," Frank told her.

"Do the streams have enough water for half our herd?" Monty asked.

"Maybe."

"Enough flow to fill up again in twenty-four hours?"

"Possibly."

"Who cares about the herds following us?" Frank asked.

Monty ignored Frank. "We'll divide the herd and keep them at least a day apart. Two if necessary."

Hen uttered a curse that caused Iris's ears to turn pink, then he stalked off.

"How will that help?" Reardon asked.

"It'll give the creeks time to fill back up by the time the second half of the herd reaches them," Iris said, pleased she understood something about the drive before one of the men.

"If we're lucky," Monty added. "Frank and I will be in charge of the first herd. Salty and Carlos will handle the second. Hen will ride ahead each day to find the places with the most water."

"This will give us time to discuss our plans for the ranch," Carlos said, clearly looking forward to the chance to be with his sister without Monty looking over his shoulder.

"Iris and Reardon go with me," Monty told Carlos.

"Why?" Carlos demanded, his eyes bright with anger.

"Because I've got to look after Iris, and I don't trust Reardon."

"I trust Joe, and I—" Carlos began.

"They go with me anyway," Monty said and turned to go after his brother.

"Don't!" Iris pleaded urgently when Carlos started toward Monty. "He's given you joint responsibility for the herd. You'll do better without me to worry about or Reardon to distract you."

"But—"

"If you want to learn about cows, this is the best chance you're going to get. You won't find better teachers than Monty and Salty." Iris hesitated, then plunged ahead. "I've been meaning to ask if you would like to be my foreman when we get to Wyoming."

"Me? When did you decide that? Why?"

"I've been thinking about it. It seemed logical since we're brother and sister. Would you like it?"

A slow smile lightened Carlos's features. "Yes, I would."

"Good. Now do everything Monty asks. I know he irritates you, but I'm depending on him to teach both of us our jobs."

Iris watched Carlos go off and hoped she had smoothed his feathers, but she hardly had time to see how her words were received. A growing disturbance drew her attention to Hen and Monty. They had moved too far away for her to understand what they were saying, but they were shouting.

She was certain they were shouting about her.

"We ought to cut out our herd and let them worry about their own damned cows," Hen was saying, furious at his brother. "We'd get along just fine by ourselves."

"We can't leave Iris with that crowd."

"*You* can't leave Iris. I can do it in a flash."

"You're a phony, Hen," Monty said, furious. "You're the one who's always acting like some damned goody two shoes around women, watching your manners, mouthing pretty compliments, acting like butter wouldn't melt in your mouth. I'm the one you say is rude and thoughtless."

"That's the way I treat ladies. This is Iris."

Instantaneous rage covered Monty like a blanket. He and his twin had disagreed on many things in their lives, but Monty couldn't remember when he had come so close to wanting to strangle him. He grabbed Hen by the shirtfront and shook him hard.

"I know you don't like Iris, but don't you ever speak about her like that again."

"I'll say anything I like," Hen shot back, unfazed by his brother's threat.

"Not if I break your head first."

"That's you, always threatening to beat someone to a pulp."

"And you're always threatening to kill them."

"I don't threaten," Hen said. "I do it."

"I guess that means I'm not as bloodthirsty as you," Monty said, releasing his brother and pushing him away, "but I am just as stubborn. Iris goes with us until I can talk her into taking the train the rest of the way."

"It had better be soon," Hen said, readjusting his shirt. "She's caused enough trouble already."

Monty wanted to deny the charge, but he realized even though Iris wasn't responsible for their problems, every one of them had started with her.

"You worry about finding enough water," Monty said. "I'll take care of Iris."

"Well you'd better do a damned sight better than you've done so far." With that Hen stalked off, shouting for Zac to bring him a horse from the ramuda.

"Is there more trouble?" Iris asked, coming up to Monty.

"No. Hen was just working off some steam." He looked up at the clear sky. "Pray for rain. At least a thundershower."

The next day dawned hot and still. The rolling hills, covered with thick grass standing still in the dead air, stretched away into the distance. The sun rose in a cloudless sky to pour down its heat on the unresisting land. Birds fluttered energetically to gather their breakfast before the heat of the day became oppressive. Iris could hear mice scratching in the brittle grass as they, too, scurried to eat before the hawks, which floated heavenward, could spy them and join in breakfast.

On a distant knoll, a single prong-horned antelope watched the herd as they left the bed ground and began to graze their way north. A chorus of bellowing cows gathered around the calf wagons as their tiny offspring were gathered up and put inside for the day's drive. The wagons were even more crucial today. Monty intended to cover as much distance as possible.

"Today's drive will be easy," Monty said as he pulled his mount to a halt next to Iris. "It's two or three days from now that'll be tough."

"Are we going to make it?" Iris asked. She had confidence in Monty, but the prospect of losing virtually everything she had scared her badly.

"We'll make it," Monty assured her before he rode away.

Iris couldn't remember when it had been so hot so early in the year. By noon, the sun was beating down on them like Texas in August. It didn't do any good to tell herself that it had been hot for the last few weeks, that she only noticed it now because she was worried about water. Just thinking about it made her feel thirsty.

The day went smoothly. The cattle were in good shape and didn't mind being kept on the trail after dark. They grazed for over an hour, then bedded down for the night.

"We made about twenty-five miles today," Monty announced to the crew. "I want all of you to get as much sleep as you can. No sitting up swapping tales or playing cards. Don't even take time to write a letter. In a couple of days you probably won't be getting any sleep at all."

Monty's warning only served to keep Iris awake long after everyone else had dropped off. For weeks she had lain awake thinking of ways to bring Monty to his knees, worrying he would desert her. Now she worried that even his help might not be enough.

The cattle were sluggish and fretful. Their incessant bellowing and the dust they stirred up had given Iris a terrible headache. Thirsty animals continually tried to break away from the herd and had to be driven back. Iris had used up six ponies already. Some of the men had used up their entire string.

"He's driving them too hard," Frank said to Iris on the third day. "Half of them will be so sore footed they won't be able to make it to the Canadian."

"Monty's hoping there'll be enough water in the Washita. He says they can make it that far."

"Last time I came through, there was quicksand."

"We won't have to worry about it this time," Monty said, coming up behind them. "Not enough water."

"Maybe you should hope there is," Frank said, his voice filled with challenge.

"What I hope won't make any difference," Monty said. "I'm going to see how the other herd is getting along," Monty said, turning to Iris. "If Hen gets back before I return, tell him to wait."

"I don't trust him," Frank said after Monty had ridden away. "I don't think he knows what he's doing."

Iris was tired of Frank's constant litany of complaints against Monty. She knew it stemmed from jealousy, but it was getting harder and harder for her to listen to him and keep her own confidence up. She could almost see the cattle's suffering increase with each passing hour. She figured Monty was doing the best that could be done, but she wondered if that would be enough.

"I'm worried, too," she said to Frank. "Everything I own is out there. What would you do?"

Frank looked startled at the direct challenge. "I'd check out some other route," Frank sputtered, caught off guard.

"Until you have checked out your other route and *know* there's another way to get this herd through alive, I want you to do everything Monty says. Everything!" Iris repeated. "Is that clear?"

"Very clear," Frank said, surprised at the force of her command. "But maybe there's something you haven't thought about. Most of your cattle are in the second herd. If there's water in these creeks, the first herd gets it. *His* cows. Think about that for a while."

Iris turned toward the herd. As her gaze moved from one cow to another, she saw the same brand. The Circle-7. The Randolph brand. Where were her cows? Why weren't they in the first herd? She knew there must be an explanation. Monty wouldn't have divided the herd like that. She would ask him that evening.

The few men lucky enough to be off duty lounged around the fire spinning yarns, playing cards, and smoking. They were a bedraggled bunch. Due to the water shortage they were going without shaving and washing. Several days' accumulation of grit and grime clung to their clothes and in the folds of their skin. Hair that wouldn't be cut for another two months was already over their collars.

They didn't smell too good either.

Hen didn't ride in that evening and Monty didn't return.

"Wonder why Monty didn't come back?" one of the hands wondered aloud.

"Probably wanted to eat at his own chuck wagon," said one boy who obviously hadn't liked that night's supper. "I hear his brother is a wonder."

"He didn't stay away because of the food," the cook said. "That man would eat dried buffalo hide if he had to."

"I agree he had his reasons, but what are they?" the first man asked. "He's been sticking to Miss Richmond like she was a shoe and he was shoe-laces."

"Probably seeing how the other herd is doing," the cook suggested.

"Nah. He trusts that Salty character like his own right hand."

"Well, I don't trust him," the second fella said. "And I don't like him."

"You're just mad because he fired Clem."

"He had no right."

"Maybe, but he done it."

"You boys had better get to your horses," the cook said. "There's not a single cow that's lain down yet."

The herd milled about for another hour before a few of them tried to lie down. But they were kept stirred up by those that continually complained of their thirst.

"We're going to lose control of them soon," Frank predicted. "I knew it would happen."

No one answered Frank. It took every bit of Iris's faith to keep believing Monty would get the herd to water before they perished of thirst. It took everybody else's energy to keep the herd on the bedding ground. Desperate for water, the cows continually tried to go back toward the last water they remembered.

"After today, we'll have to keep them heading north even if we have to rope them," Monty had said before he'd left that morning. "They'll never make it back to the Red River alive."

When Iris finally fell into bed, more tired than she had ever been in her entire life, she couldn't sleep. The noise from the herd constantly reminded her that there was no water, that Monty had not returned.

She knew he hadn't abandoned her. This was his herd. He might leave her, but he wouldn't desert his cows.

"Time to get up. I want to be on the trail by sunup."

Iris fought the sleep that clogged her brain, the exhaustion that made her limbs feel as if they weighed 1,000 pounds each. Monty was back.

"The second herd is in worse condition than this one," Monty explained while Iris slipped on her boots. She had slept in her clothes. There wasn't enough water to wash her face.

"The streams haven't been recovering."

"The herd's frantic with thirst," Iris said.

"Then you know how bad it is with the others. We've got to get this one through and go back before we lose the second herd."

Iris's herd.

"But the Washita?"

"Hen says there's barely enough water to keep this herd going forward. There won't be anything for the second."

The day was hotter than ever. Even though there was only a trickle of water in the Washita, it was almost impossible to force the cattle out of the river and onto the hot, dusty plain. Monty drove the cattle and the crew mercilessly. They reached the Canadian an hour after nightfall. The river was low, but there was plenty of water for the second herd if it could only reach it.

"Put them across tomorrow and hold them until I bring up the second herd," Monty told Frank. Monty shouted for the wrangler to fetch him a fresh mount.

"Where are you going?" Iris asked.

"To the other herd," Monty said. "I'm taking half your crew with me."

"Hell, no," Frank objected.

"Do you need more than six men to hold a herd that wouldn't leave this river if there was a prairie fire coming this way?" Monty asked.

"Well, no," Frank admitted, the steam taken out of his resistance.

"Take everybody you need," Iris said. "Most of my cows are in that herd. I'm coming with you."

Monty started to object, but changed his mind. "Be ready to ride in five minutes."

At first Iris couldn't understand how Monty decided on the men to go with him. Not until they were in the saddle did she realize he had chosen all the men he didn't trust. If Frank were trying to rustle her cattle, he wouldn't have anyone to help.

Iris wondered why she had ever doubted Monty. It would have made everything a lot easier if he had taken the time to explain things to her, but it always turned out he was looking out for her. She was foolish to let her fears, or Carlos and Frank's constant griping, cause her to distrust him. He was the one person who had never failed her.

But she had to ask. She had to know. "Why are so many of my cows in the second herd?"

"You think I did that on purpose?"

"I know you didn't. I just wondered." She wouldn't tell him that Frank had planted the seed of distrust in her mind. She was ashamed to admit it.

"On a drive like this, cows get used to traveling with certain companions," Monty explained. "After a while they work out an order they keep the rest of the way. My lead steer went straight to the front, so my cows lined up behind him. Yours lined up after that."

Once again a fear had proved groundless.

But all her fears weren't removed. Coming face-to-face with the real possibility she could lose the herd made her know the meaning of being defenseless. She had understood the words before. Now she understood their meaning, and it petrified her. Only the herd stood between her and complete helplessness, and the herd itself, no matter what she did, was very vulnerable. There were no guarantees, no safety net for it or for her.

Monty didn't understand. He couldn't. He could lose the entire herd, and it wouldn't change anything. George might shout at him, and his brothers might call him a fool, but they'd stand behind him. He wouldn't be penniless. He would always have a family.

She would have nothing. She didn't fool herself about why Carlos had followed her. They were brother and sister, but they hardly knew each other. They might grow close in the future, but he would never have followed her if she had been penniless.

For her, even more than for Monty, the herd was everything. With it, she was somebody. She had a place, a name, some importance.

Without it. . . . Iris didn't even want to think about that.

The herd was already on its feet when they reached the second camp.

"They haven't slept," Salty reported.

"I'll let them graze as long as the dew's still on the grass," Monty said. "After that, we'll throw them on the trail and drive them as fast and as long as they will go."

"Any water in the Washita?"

"No."

"How far to the Canadian?"

"Sixty miles."

"I don't know if they'll make it."

"They have to. I've brought Lightning. Maybe they'll follow him."

The big line-back steer was coal black with a white stripe down his back and black-and-blue markings below. The jagged white slash that gave him his name ran from his right shoulder halfway down his leg. Iris thought him a fierce-looking beast. Monty treated him like a pet.

"We've got our own lead steer," Carlos said.

"Lightning knows there's water ahead. Your steer doesn't. All he knows is the water we passed."

"If we're going, let's get moving," Hen said.

Carlos looked unhappy at having to work with Monty and Hen. Iris decided Salty must have been giving him enough responsibility to make him feel important. With Monty and Hen around, he amounted to little more than an ordinary hand.

"Be glad they came," Iris said, hoping to bolster Carlos's enthusiasm. "We need every bit of help we can get. It's your future as well as mine, you know."

"At least Joe's here," Carlos said.

Iris didn't like being thought less important than Joe Reardon, but she didn't have time to waste on Carlos's fit of temper. The herd was on its feet, but it didn't want to move.

"Get Lightning started," Monty told Hen.

About a dozen followed the black steer, but it took them more than an hour before the entire herd was on its feet and heading north. It was the most exhausting day Iris had ever endured. The herd fought them every step of the way. Cows, sore of foot and nearly dead of thirst, would drop back with calves that only remained alive because of their mother's milk. Yearlings had to be dragged to their feet. Steers maddened by the heat would suddenly turn and attack the closest rider.

Iris barely escaped being gored by an angry cow. She swore it was the beast who had tried to kill her earlier.

There was no such thing as mealtime. Men ate in the saddle or not at all. The men used up so many horses Iris wondered if the ramuda would last.

An unexpected rainstorm put just enough water in the creek they reached a couple of hours after dark to keep the cattle from rebelling. But that night they refused to bed down at all. All night long they remained on their feet, restless, bawling, crying out their misery.

The men remained in the saddle.

"Get some sleep," Monty ordered Iris just after midnight. "Tomorrow's going to be worse still."

"I can't, not while everybody else is working."

"They're used to it. You'll be no help if I have to spend half the day looking over my shoulder to make sure you haven't fainted."

"Why don't you have a cup of coffee with me?" Salty asked after Monty had ridden away.

"It's too hot for coffee," Iris snapped. "Besides, I don't need you looking after me, too."

"Somebody's got to do it. It won't help a bit if you and Monty spend all your time fighting."

Iris saw why everybody liked Salty so much. He had a way of stating the bald truth so you couldn't deny it, but you couldn't get mad at him for saying it.

"Sometimes he makes me so mad I could spit," Iris fumed as she turned her horse toward the campfire.

"He affects a lot of people that way until they learn it's just his way."

"What? To be rude, brutal, thoughtless, arrogant—"

"I've worked with him for nine years," Salty said. "There's nothing you can tell me about that man I don't already know."

"Then maybe you can tell me if there's any feeling in him at all."

"A lot."

"I'm not speaking of cows," Iris said angrily. "I mean something a human being would recognize."

Salty laughed easily. He seemed to be enjoying himself so much Iris couldn't help but smile as well.

"That sounds like something Rose would have said when she first came. She knows different now."

"Well I don't plan to marry one of his brothers and hang around nine years looking for something to like about him. As soon as I get to Wyoming, I don't plan to see him ever again."

"I thought you were kinda sweet on him."

"Whatever made you think that?" Iris asked, staring at him in surprise.

"The boys have been making bets with each other," Salty said. "They think you just might be the woman to catch him."

"Catch him!" Iris squeaked. "If I caught him, I'd throw him back."

"That's too bad. He sure is sweet on you."

"Sweet on me!" Iris realized she was sounding like an echo, but Salty kept coming up with statements that sent her mind reeling. "I've never been treated so rudely by anyone in my whole life."

"You keep coming back for more, so I guess you don't mind it too much. I know Monty doesn't.

Besides, he's not acting right. I've never seen him so jumpy or cross. It's a sure sign."

This time Iris was too stunned to echo. She just sat looking at Salty, her brain in a whirl.

Salty helped her dismount when they reached camp. He handed her a cup of coffee. He took just two swallows from his own cup before he tossed the rest out.

"You stay here for a little while," he said as he handed the cup back to Tyler. "I'd better look in on the boys. You never can tell when one of them might take a notion to go to sleep in the saddle."

Chapter Fifteen

Iris nodded absently. She had more important things to think about than cowboys falling out of their saddles from fatigue. She wasn't sweet on Monty. She couldn't be. He wasn't waiting around for her to come rushing to him. He had done his best to avoid her.

But at the moment Iris wasn't capable of dealing with Monty's feelings. Her own had caught her completely by surprise.

She *was* sweet on Monty. She had been since the moment she set eyes on him at that party. That was why she had walked across the room to invite him to dance. It had had nothing to do with her schoolgirl crush. It was a woman's reaction to seeing a man she found so attractive she had ignored the teachings of a lifetime. Maybe that was why her body felt so strange whenever he was around. Did all women feel this way when they were with the men they cared about?

Lord, Iris thought to herself, this couldn't be true. Surely she couldn't *want* to fall in love with Monty. He might be everything she most wanted in a man, but he was also everything she most disliked. No woman in her right mind would want to fall in love with a man who represented her worst nightmare.

And she was in her right mind. She had thought all this out. She was here because she had no other choice. She had chosen Monty because he was the best person to get her to Wyoming. She had kept after him because she didn't trust him not to vanish over the next hill if she didn't.

True, she had let him kiss her and liked it, but that didn't mean anything. Other men had kissed her and she had liked it, too, but that didn't mean she was in love with them or was sweet on them. Still, she had to admit Monty had a way of kissing her that drove all the other kisses out of her mind.

She wouldn't let that upset her plans. She was a sensible, pragmatic woman. She knew what she wanted, and she knew how to go after it. She was going to let Monty get her to Wyoming. She was even going to let him help her set up her ranch, help her run it if he would. But as soon as she got back on her feet, she intended to head back to St. Louis. She had a few scores to settle there.

After that?

She'd probably get married. She wanted a family. Being on her own was frightening. She was going to surround herself with people who could never desert her. She was going to *belong*.

Long ago she had decided exactly the kind of husband she wanted. She ran through the familiar list in her head only to find it no longer satisfied her. Money was still important, as was social standing and a large home with a staff of servants. It went without saying her husband would absolutely adore her.

But she wanted more than that. He had to be someone she could depend on to take care of her. There were more dangers in this world than poverty, and she wanted a man who could keep them all at bay. She wanted a husband she could respect, one she could talk with, one who had the answers to questions. He still had to adore her, but he must have a mind of his own.

He had to be just a little exciting. Maybe even a little rough around the edges. She never wanted to go on a trail drive again, but she had to admit St. Louis would seem rather tame after this.

He had to be sure of himself with her. Even a little aggressive. She didn't mean to let him gain the upper hand, but she would become bored if she always knew what to expect. If a man waited for permission before he took what he wanted, giving in lost half of its appeal. After all, if she wasn't worth a determined pursuit, if his desire for her didn't drive him at least a little bit beyond the limits of control, he couldn't love her very much, could he?

Merciful heavens! You've just described Monty. You want to marry Monty!

If Iris hadn't already been seated, she would have collapsed. She *couldn't* be in love with Monty. It must be the exhaustion of 18-hour days in the saddle. The worry of losing her herd. Maybe the heat and the dust and the noise and the smell had driven her temporarily insane.

That must be it. She wasn't herself. She was too tired to know what she felt. She wouldn't feel this way once she reached Wyoming. She probably wouldn't feel this way tomorrow.

She had to get some rest. Then tomorrow, or when they finally reached the river and she could stop worrying that her entire herd would die of thirst, she would figure out why she had ever done such a crazy thing as think she wanted to marry Monty Randolph.

Breakfast was a steady stream of haggard men—their eyes sunk into deep sockets in their heads, their gait a shambling walk—staggering in for a few bites of food and a few swallows of coffee before stumbling back again.

Iris felt almost as bad as they looked. She was so exhausted she had passed the point of feeling tired. She didn't feel anything at all. She had spent half the night pacing around the campfire, wrestling with her feelings for Monty, unable to come to any acceptable, comprehensible conclusion.

Unable to face the thought of food, Iris had saddled up and ridden out only to be greeted with the news that the herd refused to leave the bedding ground.

"They're trying to turn back to the last water they remember," Carlos said, "but it's too far. They won't make it."

Too exhausted to fight off panic, Iris rode on, desperately looking for Monty.

"He can't get them going," Carlos called after her. "You're going to lose the whole damned herd."

Iris didn't stop to answer. She had to find Monty. He would know what to do. He had to. Already men and horses were exhausted with the effort of controlling the cows determined to turn back to the only water they remembered.

Iris reached the front of the herd to find a dozen men sitting their horses, waiting. Monty was nowhere in sight.

"What's happening?" she asked Salty.

"They won't follow Lightning."

Iris watched the miserable animals mill about in confusion over several hundred acres, bellowing their pain and their thirst.

"Monty's afraid they'll go blind."

"Go blind?" Iris repeated. "Why?"

"From thirst. I know it doesn't make sense, but if it happens, nothing will stop them from turning back to the last water they remember."

Iris felt herself losing her battle with panic.

Salty lifted his eyes toward the horizon. "It's going to rain, but it won't get here soon enough."

Iris didn't ask how he could look at a perfectly clear sky and predict rain. But if it wasn't going to come soon enough, it didn't matter if he was right or wrong.

"Where's Monty?" she asked.

Salty turned back toward camp and pointed. "There."

Iris turned to see Monty coming toward them with both calf wagons bouncing along behind him.

"Everybody get a rope on a calf," Monty called out as he jumped down from his saddle. He immediately began lifting calves to the ground. Each time he set one down, a cowboy would come up, drop a rope over the frightened animal's head, and lead it off in the direction of the Canadian River.

"I thought you said those calves couldn't keep up," Iris said, completely confused.

"Even a newborn calf can walk faster than a herd that's not moving at all," Monty said, not pausing as he set another calf on the ground. "Their mothers won't follow Lightning, but maybe they'll follow their own calves, especially if they're bawling. And so will any other longhorn within hearing distance."

Iris remembered the night more than a dozen cows had hurried to help the mother of the calf she stumbled over. She shuddered.

"This may be the only way to get them to water."

Hen was setting calves down from the second wagon. Within minutes they had a dozen bawling calves heading north at the ends of ropes. But their cries were drowned out by the din of more than 3,000 full-grown cows bellowing their distress.

The herd didn't move.

Monty and Hen continued setting calves on the ground until there were more than two dozen on foot. There were more calves than men, so the extras were tied to the backs of the two wagons. When the wagons started forward, the calves started to bleat.

Still the herd didn't move.

"Spread out," Monty directed. "Move through the herd."

Nobody moved.

"Why aren't they doing what he said?" Iris asked the man driving the wagon.

"It's too dangerous," he explained. "If those longhorns go crazy, and they're not far from it now, a man in the middle of a herd would be practically helpless."

Iris turned back toward the herd. Still no one moved.

"It's too late," the wagon driver said. "They've already started to turn." Iris followed the direction of his gaze to where a pair of cows had walked through the cordon of cowboys and started south. "They'll die, every one of them."

Iris stared helplessly at those two cows. It seemed impossible that her entire future could be destroyed by anything as absurd as two cows walking in the wrong direction. Without stopping to realize what she was doing, Iris spurred her horse forward. She didn't know what she was going to do, but she couldn't let them turn the herd. Anybody could stop two cows.

Doing exactly what she'd seen the men do so many times, Iris hazed the two cows back into the herd. But her elation was short-lived. More cows turned.

Even as Iris turned to drive them back, she saw Monty untie a calf from the wagon and lead it into the middle of the herd. Iris forgot what she was doing, giving her pony its head to do what it had been trained to do. As she watched, her heart in her throat, Monty led the loudly protesting calf deeper and deeper into the milling mass of cattle.

Farther and farther from safety.

Iris sat paralyzed. These were her cows. Monty was risking his life to save her cows. Suddenly the enormity of what she had done in forcing him to take on the burden of her herd was overwhelming. He hadn't wanted to do this. He had tried every way he knew to stop her, but she wouldn't listen. She might as well have been the one forcing him to thread his way through a mass of thirst-maddened, half-wild cows.

If anything happened to him, it would be her fault.

With a muffled cry, Iris forgot all about the cows trying to turn south. She forgot about the danger.

She forgot about everything except Monty.

Galloping her pony to the closest calf wagon, Iris leaned out of the saddle and untied one of the calves. Then she led her protesting calf into the midst of the herd.

Toward Monty.

Tall, slim animals of powerful muscle and bone surrounded her. Their massive horns, spanning as much as six feet, terrified her. All ended in sharp points capable of disemboweling a pony or goring her to death with a single twist of the head.

Iris resolutely turned her attention to Monty. If she was going to die, she'd just as soon it be a surprise. Besides, Monty had seen her coming. He stood still.

He was waiting for her.

All of a sudden, from more than a dozen different directions, cowboys began leading calves into the midst of the herd. But Iris was only vaguely aware she and Monty were no longer alone. He had turned now, angling over to meet her, leading his calf north.

His gaze had locked on her. He rode forward, but he looked only at her. Without looking away from Monty, Iris angled her horse north.

A movement behind Monty broke Iris's gaze. A cow was following him. Now three cows followed. Iris felt an upsurge of hope. She looked behind her. Several cows followed, their heads low, their bellowing unremitting, but they followed. Looking around she noticed small pockets of movement forming around the calves. Like ever expanding ripples, the pockets grew larger and larger until they began to merge with each other.

The herd was moving. They were headed toward water.

Iris didn't know where her body found the energy, but she didn't feel tired anymore. Monty's idea, and his courage to do what no one else dared do, had saved the herd. She had helped because she had found the courage to follow.

Iris couldn't imagine what had come over her, how she had managed to find the nerve to do what these hardened men had not dared. She wasn't courageous. She wasn't foolhardy either. It was totally unlike her and contrary to everything her mother had taught her about survival.

If it's dangerous, there's always some fool you can get to do it for you.

Then, as though it had been there all along just waiting for her to discover it, Iris knew how. And why.

She followed Monty because she loved him. She couldn't do anything else.

The rain reached them in midafternoon. One minute the sky was a brilliant blue. Half an hour later rain pelted the ground with the force of hail. The cattle didn't have to wait until they reached the Canadian. They broke their thirst in the shallow pools that collected in the hundreds of tiny depressions across the prairie. Even after the calves were once again restored to the safety of the calf wagons, the herd moved steadily north, pausing only to take sips from the shallow pools as they passed.

"They wouldn't drink their fill right now even if they stood in water up to their bellies," Monty explained to Iris. "They'll continue to take just a few swallows until their bodies have recovered."

Iris and Monty rode side by side, rain soaking their clothes, pouring down their faces, their rain slickers forgotten. He hoped the men were too busy with their work to watch Iris. She rode completely unaware that her rain-soaked clothes were plastered to her body, leaving little to the imagination.

Her shirt molded itself to her shoulders and the curve of her breasts. Monty found his own pulse quickening when he realized he could see the shape and color of her nipples. Her skirt clung to her hips and thighs with equal definition, but the thickness of the material kept it from turning transparent.

Monty untied his slicker from behind his saddle. "Here, let me help you put this on," he said, pulling up his horse.

"Why? I'm already soaked."

"I know, but I don't want everybody else to know."

Iris looked down at her clothes, blushed, then smiled as Monty draped the slicker over her shoulders. It felt good. She hadn't realized the rain was so cold. "Even a woman like me hopes a man thinks of something more than her body," she said.

"I do, but not when I'm riding next to you drenched to the skin."

Monty figured he would never understand women. As soon as you mentioned they were pretty, every one of them insisted they wanted to be loved for themselves, not their beauty. But the minute you forgot to mention their eyes, lips, hair, or their new dress, you were in hot water. It didn't make sense. Eyes looked greener in a pretty face. A dress looked better on a shapely body. It all looked better if the woman was kind, intelligent, and trustworthy.

Iris was proving to be even more of a woman than he had expected. Her leading that calf into the herd had forced him to see her in a whole different way. He still could feel the shock and fear that had nearly paralyzed his mind when he looked up to see her. A hundred different thoughts had exploded into his brain simultaneously: that she was a stunning creature and he didn't know how he had kept away from her so long; that she was crazy to risk her life for a few cows; that he'd never seen any woman look more noble, more determined, more fearless; that she looked absolutely scared to death; that both of them could be ground into nothingness under 1,000 different hooves; that there was nothing of the parasitic Helena in this glorious woman; that Iris had followed him where no one else had, not even his twin brother; that there couldn't be a more desirable woman in the world.

She continued to surprise him. She might stumble, but she managed to rise to every occasion. She made mistakes, but she didn't repeat them. She was turning into a woman he admired.

He had become much more interested in her than he'd expected. And that was dangerous. This was more than he could handle. He ought to send her away before he lost the last of his control, but it was too late. She might leave, but he wouldn't send her.

He couldn't.

Monty decided to drive the herd on to the Canadian even though it meant driving at night. It was still raining when they arrived.

"We've got to get them across," he said. "If this rain keeps up, the river may be too high to cross tomorrow."

The exhausted men grumbled. Frank and his crew grumbled loudest of all when they had to leave the dry comfort of a tent they had set up on a knoll. But Monty got the entire herd across and settled on high ground before he allowed anyone to rest.

"We'll stay here a couple of days to let the cattle recover," Monty announced that evening.

After the men turned to their work, Monty's eyes searched the group until he found Iris standing a little off to the side. She seemed to be staring into the horizon. The rain had halted momentarily and a cold breeze swept down from the north. Monty picked up a blanket from the chuck wagon. Iris didn't move until he draped it over her shoulders.

"This will keep the wind off you."

"I'm not cold," she said.

"You should be."

"Nothing else is as it should be."

Monty had never seen Iris in a mood like this. He felt as if only part of her was aware of him. A tiny part. The rest was somewhere far away.

All day long he had been wanting to talk to her. It had been a struggle to hold back until he could find a moment when they could be alone.

But now that he had that moment, he didn't know what to say. This wasn't the Iris he knew, the defiant redhead ready to give him back word for word. She looked upset, confused, unhappy.

She ought to be euphoric. Not only had the herd come through in fine shape, but she had been partly responsible for that success. It would be a long time before she could handle a ranch on her own, but she had the nerve, the brains, and the ability. She lacked only the experience.

"That was a brave thing you did out there today."

She spoke without turning toward him. "I was scared to death."

Monty smiled. "I guess you were. But you did it, and that's what counts."

"Were you frightened?"

"Nah. I—"

She spun to face him, her face intense with the emotions that held her in their coils. "Tell me the truth. Were you frightened?"

"No. I knew I was taking a chance—you always take a chance when you work with longhorns. They're born crazy and get worse, but I knew I could get out if there was trouble."

Iris's expression didn't relax. "I didn't. I thought I would get killed, but I went in anyway."

"Why?"

"Don't ask stupid questions."

"I'm not. I don't know why you did it."

"How could I not?" Iris said. "I was the one who decided to make this trip, who talked you into keeping our herds together, who practically forced you into being responsible for me. How could I stand aside and see you trampled?"

Monty laughed softly. "If I'd gotten trapped, the boys would have started shooting."

"But I didn't know that," Iris said, her voice rising. "I was petrified you would be killed. I could just see them running over you, stepping on your—" She shuddered, unable to continue.

Monty realized she was badly upset. He took her by the shoulders and turned her until she faced him. "And you still came after me."

"I couldn't do anything else." Her voice was a thread, a whisper.

Monty drew her to him until her stiff body touched his. He slipped his arms around her and drew her close. With a convulsive movement, Iris put her arms around Monty and held him as tight as she could.

"I was never so scared in my life," she said. All the tension that had gripped her since that morning, the agonies of the mind that had held her in their thrall as well, fell away to unleash a sense of relief so overwhelming it brought tears to her eyes.

"I just kept looking at you. The whole time crazy thoughts kept running through my mind. Something kept saying over and over again, 'Monty won't let them hurt you.'" She laughed unsteadily. "That was stupid. You were in even more danger than I was."

Monty experienced the oddest feeling. It wasn't like anything he knew. He felt more peculiar than he ever had in his life. His arms tightened around Iris, and his groin tightened. At least he recognized that feeling. It made him feel good to feel her softness against him. It made him feel good to have her come to him for comfort. It made him feel even better to know he could give it.

"I think you've learned part of the secret of courage."

"What is that?" she asked, her voice muffled by his chest.

"You've got to be crazy. At least a little bit."

She laughed. "And what is the secret of the rest?"

"One part belief that what's happening can't really be happening. One part believing danger might happen to somebody else but not you. One part certainty that if it does, somebody will show up to pull you out before it's too late. One part being scared to death and swearing that if you ever do get out you'll never do anything so stupid again."

Iris chuckled. "That doesn't sound very brave to me."

"There is one more part."

"What's that?"

"Blind stupidity that keeps you from realizing you're in mortal danger. Or knowing and not caring. George says I'm like that."

Iris raised her head from Monty's chest and smiled up into his eyes. "Thanks. I feel better." She started to pull away, but he wouldn't let her go.

"Why did you really do it?"

Iris dropped her eyes. "I've already told you."

"I don't believe you."

Iris looked up, smiling again. "You never do. You must think I'm the most persistent liar in the world."

"I don't. I never—"

"And you question my every motive. No, you go farther than that. You're certain I tell you one thing but have something quite different in mind. You can't deny it, Monty, not if there's an ounce of truth in you."

Monty was appalled to realize every word she said was true. But he didn't feel that way. So what if she had wheedled and flirted to get him to do something against his will? He didn't hold that against her. She was a woman. They did that sort of thing. Helena had been a master at it.

But he didn't think she was a liar. Really, he didn't.

"I don't know what I said—George says that I never do, that I just start talking and never pay attention to myself—but I didn't mean that," Monty said. "And if I did," he continued, forced by his basic honesty to confess all his sins, "I don't now."

"Why? I'm the same person I was when you told me to go back home."

"Maybe, but you're not the person I thought you were."

"And who was that?"

"I thought you were just like your mother."

Monty felt Iris stiffen in his arms and pull away.

"I'm in no mood to stand here and listen to you insult my mother. Thanks for what you did today. I always knew you were the only man who could get me to Wyoming. Now I'm going to bed. I've never been so tired in my life."

Monty was tired, too, but he wasn't sleepy. There was a great deal Iris hadn't told him. There were things he hadn't told her either.

Monty was gone when Iris awoke next day. Relieved, she swallowed a quick breakfast and walked over to her chuck wagon to talk to Frank and Carlos. After that she went for a short ride.

The ride didn't solve anything. She came back to the Randolph camp just as much in love with Monty as the night before, just as confused as to what she was going to do about it.

She slid from the saddle and looked up, expecting Zac to hurry up to take her horse, unsaddle it, and put it in the ramuda. But Zac didn't move.

"Aren't you going to take my horse?" she asked, a little surprised at this attitude.

"No."

"You took it yesterday."

"You rode our horse yesterday. That one belongs to your ramuda," he said, pointing to where a second rope corral held the Double-D horses. "If I was to take it, somebody might say I was trying to steal it."

"Suppose you take it over for me."

"I'd have to run all the way there and back," Zac objected. "If I'm not here when the men come in, Monty will have my head."

241

"If you're not here, they can put them up themselves," Tyler said from where he was fixing dinner. "I expect they know how."

"It ain't your head Monty's going to break," Zac said.

"He won't break yours either. You run faster than he does."

Zac grinned. "Yeah, but Monty's a great one for sneaking up on you when you least expect it."

"I'll tell him you did it just for me," Iris cajoled. Zac looked her over as though he were trying to decide if her importance to his brother was strong enough to make it worth the trouble.

"You don't look like you think my influence is worth much," Iris said, amused as well as nonplussed by Zac's weighing her up as though she were a commodity to be bought and haggled over.

"You never can tell about Monty. He doesn't like girls a whole lot."

"Maybe he just hasn't found one he likes enough."

"Naw, he likes them all for a day or two, but he gets tired of them after that. Says he likes cows better. You get tired of a cow, you can sell it or eat it. You get tired of a woman, and you near 'bout got to leave the country."

"Take the lady's horse," Tyler said.

"You ain't my boss," Zac said, eyeing Tyler uneasily. "George said I didn't have to listen to anybody but Monty and Hen. And Salty."

"If you don't take that lady's horse, I'm going to cut the corral rope and light a fire under that broom-tailed sorrel."

"I'll be chasing horses for the next two days," Zac said, shocked by Tyler's treachery.

"A whole lot easier to take the lady's horse."

Zac glared at Iris. He flung a clod into the earth and uttered a few curses Iris felt certain he hadn't learned from George. Then he grabbed the reins from Iris, flung himself into the saddle, and spurred the tired animal into a gallop.

"The boy talks too much," Tyler said, handing Iris a cup of hot coffee. "I keep telling George he ought to beat him regular."

"And George doesn't?" Iris asked, bemused at this glimpse into the Randolph family.

"Zac's no fool. He does everything George tells him just like he enjoyed doing it. It's just the rest of us that want to kill him. He particularly likes to bait Monty. Going to get him a broken head one of these days."

Iris couldn't believe Tyler really meant what he said. But then she'd never had a family. She didn't know if it was possible to love your brother and want to break his head at the same time.

But she enjoyed these small and as yet infrequent signs that she was gradually being accepted by the Randolphs. She had to admit she felt more comfortable with the Circle-7 crew than she did with her own men.

Frank seemed to be growing more and more distant. Carlos just looked grave. Not a day passed that he didn't urge Iris to cut her herd and move away from Monty.

Iris ambled over to sit in the sparse shade of a small, twisted oak. She sorted through her options once again without coming up with anything new. As long as she distrusted Frank, she had no one she could depend on except the Randolphs. Tension among her crew was so thick she could almost see it, but she knew Frank wouldn't try anything as long as Monty and Hen were in charge of the herd.

As long as she stayed with Monty, she was safe. Who would protect her if she left?

Carlos would try, but he was only one man. Joe Reardon was his friend, but Iris didn't think Joe would take a risk unless he could see an advantage to himself. She had no reason to distrust him, none to dislike him, but she did distrust him and she did dislike him. She was used to men staring at her, but she could never accustom herself to being stared at by Joe Reardon. It was completely different.

There was none of the worshipful admiration she had come to expect from the youthful cowhands, none of the mature appreciation she received from older men. There was something almost cynical, something that recognized and took stock of the value of her beauty. But there was also something that seemed to hold it cheap, to think of it as a commodity to be used and cast aside when it lost its appeal.

Iris had never been treated as a commodity, and the feeling was unpleasant. It was worse than Monty's rudeness.

Zac came running around the corner of the chuck wagon so out of breath he could hardly speak.

"All hell's—going to—break—loose," he gasped. "Monty's—just fired—your whole—crew!"

Chapter Sixteen

The coffee cup fell from Iris's nerveless hand. "You must be mistaken," she said, certain Zac had misunderstood. "Not even Monty would do a thing like that."

"He would if he thought he should," Tyler said, looking into Iris's eyes for the first time she could remember. "Monty never lets good sense get in his way."

"But why would he fire my crew?"

"No use asking me," Tyler said, turning back to his work. "Tell Zac to fetch you a horse. Then get yourself over there and ask him yourself."

But Zac hadn't waited for Iris. He had thrown himself bareback on the first horse he reached and galloped back to the camp. By the time Iris saddled her horse and reached her own camp, the fireworks were just about over.

Monty stood squarely in the center of the camp. Hen and Salty were close by, but Iris could tell Monty had done this on his own authority.

"What happened?" Iris asked. "Zac said you fired my crew."

"Only some of them," Monty said.

"Who? Why?"

"He accused me of trying to steal from you," Frank said. He jerked his bedroll out of the chuck wagon and threw it on the ground next to his saddle. "He said he wanted us out of camp within the hour." He walked to where the wrangler was bringing up his horse. "He ain't even giving us time to eat."

"And you did this without consulting me?" Iris said, turning to Monty. She was confused and surprised. And angry. She had no doubt Monty had a reason for what he had done, but she couldn't believe he would take such a momentous step without consulting her. They were her men. He couldn't fire them.

"If you're going to do something, you might as well do it right away," Monty said, not taking his eyes off the men gathering their gear.

"Are we missing any cattle?" Iris asked.

"No," Frank said. "Not a single one."

"Then how—"

"I saw him talking to Quince Honeyman," Monty said.

Iris's gaze whipped around to Frank.

"A man's got a right to talk to anybody he wants," Frank said angrily.

"I don't trust anybody who consorts with thieves."

"Who said Quince is a thief?" Carlos demanded.

"I said it," Monty said, turning on Iris's brother. "Anybody but you see him?"

Iris

"If a man's thieving, he's thieving whether one man sees him or a hundred."

"I don't think Carlos wants to take your word," Joe said. He said it in a flat voice, but Iris couldn't help but feel he was trying to cause trouble. That angered her. She was only keeping him on because of Carlos.

"He doesn't have to take my word for this or anything else if he doesn't want to," Monty answered. "The trail out of here is the same for him as anybody else."

"You can't fire Carlos," Iris said, turning on Monty. She hadn't thought he included Carlos with the men he distrusted. The fear that she might lose her only family made her reckless. "You can't fire anybody unless I say so."

"Maybe you two would like to take a walk down to the river," Salty suggested. "There might be a few things you want to talk about before we finish up here."

Iris opened her mouth to refuse. She wanted Carlos to know how she felt about him. Being alone with Monty put her at the mercy of his more forceful personality. But she had overreached herself this time, and she knew it. Besides, after saddling Monty with the responsibility for her herd, she owed him that much.

She nodded her agreement. Whatever their disagreements, they shouldn't be discussed in front of the men.

She didn't know how she was going to argue with a man over hiring and firing when the overriding question in her mind was whether he'd ever kissed another woman the way he'd kissed her. She couldn't find the energy to worry about Frank's future when her own prospects for happiness had been reduced to rubble. She didn't know how she could carry on a logical argument when just being around Monty deprived her of rational thought.

She couldn't concentrate on business when her heart was crying out for love that she was afraid Monty didn't have to give.

Neither spoke until they were screened by a thick tangle of vines and bushy growth that made the river unapproachable along much of its length. They both spoke at once.

"Why did you—"

"I would have told you—"

"You first," Iris said.

"I've known for some time Quince was following us," Monty said. "I've just been waiting to see who his contact would be."

"Why didn't you tell me? I'm not arguing about Quince or Frank, but it's my herd, my foreman. I ought to know. You've made me look like a fool by firing everybody without telling me. I'm tempted to tell them all to stay."

She hadn't meant to say that. Her temper had caused her to sound as if she was issuing a challenge. Now that she had, she was too stubborn to take it back. She pulled at a bush limb to hide her nervousness.

"You can if you like."

He looked impatient with the whole conversation, but he controlled his temper.

"What would you do?" She began plucking leaves from the limb one by one.

"Cut the herds and let you go on ahead like we were at first."

"Knowing Frank, or somebody else, is trying to steal my herd?"

"If I'm going to be responsible for your herd, I give the orders. When that doesn't suit, let me know."

"You know I can't do that."

"Yes, you can. All you have to do is—"

She released the stripped limb. It snapped back with a thwack. "Dammit, Monty, I can't leave. You know it, and I know it. I said you could give the orders, but the least you could do is tell me what you're going to do with my crew. I don't want to hear it from Zac."

"That wasn't fair," Monty admitted. "It's just that I'm used to doing things without asking."

"Is that why George gets mad at you?"

Iris didn't know why she asked that question, but when Monty's brows drew together and his hands balled into fists, she wished she hadn't.

"George doesn't get mad. He just disapproves. He's disappointed that my ungovernable temper and lack of judgment cause me to jeopardize the family's position. He wonders if I will ever be mature enough to think of the consequences before I act." Monty spoke as if he was reciting a litany he had heard many times.

She had always wondered what was wrong between George and Monty, but she had wandered onto treacherous ground. She retreated quickly.

"If you fire all those men, we'll have too many cows and too few hands. What are you going to do?" She selected a second limb and began stripping it of leaves.

Some of the rigidity left Monty. "Hire more as soon as I get the chance. Get along as best we can until then. My men will be able to do more work now they're not watching yours. Besides, I've kept the six hands who were with your father before

Frank became his foreman."

"Plus Carlos and Joe."

Monty looked stubborn. "I don't trust them, especially Joe."

"I don't trust Joe either, but Carlos is the only relative I have in the world. Right now I feel like he's the only friend I have as well. And don't look like I've just hurt your feelings," Iris said irritably. "You've been most generous with your criticism of my conduct, motives, ability to think, just about every aspect of my character. Carlos is the only man in the entire group who doesn't treat me like an idiot."

"He's out for what he can get from you."

"He's got a right. He's my father's son." Iris broke the limb off the bush and began to skin off the bark.

"You can give him everything you've got if you like, but I mean to see he doesn't take it."

"I haven't made up my mind to give him anything, but he is my brother. How would it look if I let you fire him? How would he feel?"

"I don't care how he feels."

"You wouldn't fire your brothers."

"The hell I wouldn't! The minute one of them starts slacking off, I'll send him back to the ranch, and they know it. Randolphs are expected to work harder than anybody else."

"Well, you're a family," Iris said, groping for another argument. "You know you love each other despite what happens on one cattle drive. Carlos doesn't know that. Nobody ever wanted him. If I fire him now, he probably won't ever come back."

"I don't want him back."

"You've got to let him stay."

"He won't if I ride him every hour of the day, give him the worst jobs, and cuss him out no matter what he does."

Iris got so mad she slashed the bush with her stripped twig. She could put up with Monty knowing more than she did about everything, with his always having an answer, but she wouldn't put up with him being a brute and a bully, especially when it meant he was driving off the only family she had.

"You do that, and I swear I'll make your life hell from here to Wyoming. I'll stampede your herd every night. They'll be so skinny you won't be able to see them unless they turn sideways."

Much to Iris's amazement, Monty's furious look vanished and he broke out laughing. "You're a little tiger when you're riled," he said. "Okay, Carlos can stay, but Joe has to leave."

"Joe, too. Carlos won't stay without him."

Monty's good humor vanished as quickly as it appeared. Maybe George had the authority to tell him what to do when it came to the ranch, but she would bet her last cent no woman did, not even the perfect Rose.

"There's no point in exchanging one thief for another."

"You don't know he's a thief. He hasn't stolen anything." Iris broke the limb in half. Then into smaller pieces.

"I know his type."

"That's still no reason to fire him. George has given you a chance. Why can't you do the same for Carlos and Joe?"

For a moment she was afraid she had made a mistake in mentioning George again. But though Monty looked furious enough to chew his way through a six-inch tree trunk, he controlled his temper.

"Okay," Monty said. "You're wrong, but I guess that's fair enough. Besides, I need the hands. But they've both got to answer to me. The first time one of them goes behind my back, he gets his marching orders. They've also got to accept I'm the only one giving orders. I won't have Carlos expecting special treatment because he's your brother."

"That seems fair."

"They can't work together," Monty added. "I don't care if they've been inseparable since the cradle."

"They won't like that."

"I don't like having them here. Hen likes it even less."

"What about me?" Iris asked. Iris tossed away the broken limb. "Do I have to take orders and acknowledge your supreme control and work when and where you tell me?"

"I wasn't talking about you."

"Then let's talk about me now. I want to know exactly where I stand. If I'm going to be treated like a hired hand in my own crew, I want to know."

"You going to sabotage me if I don't tell you?"

"I don't know. Maybe I'll slip jimsonweed into Tyler's coffee and take over the cooking."

"I thought you said you couldn't cook."

"I can't. You wouldn't have a single hand left after the first evening." Iris moved to a tangle of grape vines wound around the trunk of a dead tree.

"Okay," Monty said, his smile once again banishing his thundercloud expression. "I promise to consult you before I make a decision. Mind you, I've never done it before, so I'm liable to forget more often than not, but I'll try."

"I've never been ignored," Iris responded, experiencing a foolishly giddy feeling at his smile, "but I'll promise to try not to get so upset."

"Helena always did."

"I know my mother's behavior wasn't always what it should have been," Iris said, some of her good humor seeping away, "but I'd appreciate it if you'd stop criticizing her at every turn. You wouldn't like it if I did the same with your parents." Iris plucked a green grape and tossed it into the river.

"You're welcome to say what you please about Pa," Monty said. "No matter what you say, you're bound to be wide of the mark."

"You know what I mean," Iris said, irritated Monty always seemed to have an answer for everything.

"Okay, I'll lay off Helena. Now let's get back. I want Frank and his men as far away as possible before they make camp. That's why I'm not offering to feed them. I'm hoping that'll make them keep riding until they get out of Indian territory."

"You think they might come back?" She found a bird's nest, but it was empty.

"I think they might try to stampede the herd to get even," Monty said. "It would punish me and give them a chance to cut out a few cows for themselves."

"You don't think they would—"

"I certainly do. Hen and I don't mean to go to bed tonight. If the herd does stampede, you stay with Tyler. Salty and the boys will take care of the cows. Hen and I will be out looking for whoever caused it."

It seemed to Iris that every time she thought she was beginning to learn what to do, something else cropped up to make her realize how ill prepared she was to undertake this trip. In frustration she pitched green grapes at Monty.

He ignored her, heading back to camp at a brisk pace.

"Carlos, you and Joe come here a minute," Monty said when he reached camp. "The rest of you, finish collecting your gear."

Monty turned and walked back the way he had come without waiting to see whether the men followed. Iris felt an urge to hang back and let Monty handle it by himself, but she knew she couldn't. She had forced him to do something he didn't want to do. She had to make sure Carlos and Joe wouldn't cause trouble.

"I ain't doing that," Joe said when the terms had been explained to him. "I'm no thief, and you ain't treating me like one."

"Monty doesn't think you're a thief," Iris said, trying to make the conditions sound more palatable. "You'll know that once you've worked together for a while."

"These are the terms," Monty said, not making any effort to placate the two men. "They're the only ones I'm offering."

For a moment Iris thought Carlos was going to leave with Frank.

"I'll stay," he said at last. "I've been trying to get Iris to cut out on you, but she won't. Now that you fired her crew I can't leave her with nobody but you to look after her."

"I don't want either of you here," Monty said with equal candor, "but Iris seems to think you have as much right to be here as she does. As long as she feels like that, I'll try to go along with you."

"Did you really say that, Iris?" Carlos asked, clearly surprised.

"Of course I did. I always thought Dad ought to have left you something. I've been thinking that—"

"You can talk about that later," Monty interrupted. "Are you staying or not?"

Carlos turned to Joe.

"Okay," Joe said, "but the first time anybody starts acting like I stole something, there's going to be trouble."

"Don't start anything you don't plan to finish," Monty said.

He said it quietly, almost as if it were unimportant, but Iris could see Carlos and Reardon stiffen. Joe had tossed out a threat and Monty had accepted his challenge. Iris knew that could mean trouble.

"Get back to the herd." Monty dismissed Joe and Carlos and turned to Iris. "You might as well get the bank draft ready."

"What do you mean?" Iris asked. He had caught her by surprise.

"You've got to give them a draft on your bank. They'll never leave without one."

She didn't have a bank. Every cent she possessed was in the form of 162 gold pieces strapped around her waist in a money belt.

"Could you do it for me and let me pay you later?"

"No. I'd have to use the family's money."

She really hadn't expected him to agree, but his blunt refusal surprised and hurt her. If he had to refuse her, why couldn't he at least try to sound sorry about it?

"You can pay them, can't you?" Monty asked when Iris didn't answer.

Leigh Greenwood

"What would happen if I couldn't?"

Monty looked as though he'd never been asked such a stupefying question. "They'd be justified in taking every head of cattle you owned."

"Oh," Iris said, her worst fears confirmed. "Well, I have the money, but there's a slight problem."

"There's always a *slight* problem with you. Why can't you do things like everybody else?"

"Because I'm a woman," Iris flashed back, "and you men won't let me."

"You can't blame it on me. Seems about all I do is let you do whatever you want."

Iris felt a pang of guilt at the trouble she had caused, but she didn't have time to worry about Monty just now.

"Could we go back down to the river?"

"What do you want to do that for?"

"I'll tell you when we get there."

"Okay, but it had better not take long."

"You need to bring your horse. I'll get mine."

Monty looked at her as if she'd lost her mind. "You hoping to talk me into running away?"

"Be serious. Will you bring your horse?"

"Oh, hell, why not?"

"Okay," Monty said when they were well away from the camp. "What now?"

"I don't have a bank account."

Monty looked at her as if a roof had just caved in on him.

"I didn't trust them, not after what that miserable banker did to me. Besides, he said he wouldn't be surprised if there were other people who'd come demanding payment for debts we didn't yet know about."

"What has this got to do with—"

"You couldn't expect me to leave my money with a man like that," Iris exclaimed. "How did I know he wouldn't give it away to anybody who asked? He'd have been happy to see me reduced to begging."

"So what did you do?"

"I hid it."

"Great. But the bush you buried it under is five hundred miles away. You need it here, not in south Texas."

"I didn't bury it, and it's not in south Texas."

Suspicion sharpened Monty's expression. Why did he do this? He didn't even know what she was going to tell him and he was ready to tell her she was wrong. She didn't suppose she'd ever earn his approval. She wondered if he realized that he treated her far worse than George had ever treated him.

Probably not. She was a woman. He would never see the parallel.

"There's a secret panel in the wagon. Mother used it to hide her jewelry."

Monty looked thunderstruck. "So when you said you wanted to be private—"

"I removed the money from the secret panel."

"And put it in your saddlebags. That's why you wanted me to bring your horse."

"It's not there now," Iris confessed. "But I wanted everybody to think it was."

"Either I've been working too hard, or I'm having a sunstroke," Monty said. "I don't understand a thing you're saying."

"The money's in a belt around my waist," Iris confessed at last, "but I didn't want anybody to know that."

"You mean you've been riding over two hundred miles of wilderness carrying a fortune around your middle?"

"It's far from a fortune," Iris said. "I barely have three thousand dollars."

Monty looked dumbfounded. "Don't you realize some of those men I just fired would kill you and throw your body in the river for three hundred dollars? If they knew you had three thousand dollars, I wouldn't have time to worry about cows for protecting you."

"I didn't have any other choice."

"You did, but that's beside the point now. What do you want me to do?"

"I want to give you the money, and you pay the men."

"Then everybody will think I'm carrying a fortune and come gunning for me."

"Everybody knows you're rich. They won't think anything of it."

"They will, but I don't think six weeks' wages is going to arouse too much curiosity. Certainly not as much as knowing you've got nearly ten times that much. Give it to me. I'll take care of it until you can put it in a bank."

Monty held out his hand. Involuntarily, Iris took a step back.

"I want to keep it."

Monty reacted as though she had slapped him. "Don't you trust me?"

"Of course I do. I've trusted you with everything I own, including my life."

"But you don't trust me with your money."

"It isn't that. I don't know if I can explain it."

"Try." It was a command, not a request.

Iris hadn't known until just now she couldn't rest easy if she handed over her money. How could she possibly explain it to Monty so he wouldn't feel hurt or angry?

"The herd and this money are all I have in the world. I can't tell you how it terrifies me to know I could lose them both quite easily. If I weren't so tired after being in the saddle all day, I don't think I could sleep for worrying about it. I can't let either of them out of my sight. That's why I couldn't send the herd off with some drover I'd never seen before. That's why I can't hand my money over to anybody, even you."

"So you're going to let everybody think I have the money so I can be in danger."

"I seem to be doing that a lot, don't I?"

"Yes."

"Will you do it?" She didn't know how she got the nerve to ask, but she did. She couldn't think of anything else.

"I might as well," Monty said, heaving a sigh. "After this trip, George is going to think I have no common sense. If he ever finds out about this, he'll be certain of it. Count it out. I hope you don't have big bills."

"It's in gold."

Monty actually groaned. "Nobody carries gold. You might as well put a gun to your head."

"Nobody knows about it."

"They will."

"How?"

"I don't know, but somehow they always find out. Never mind. It's too late to do anything about it now. Count out the money, and let's get back."

Having Monty glare at her made it hard for Iris to remember her sums. She made a mistake. That got her so upset she made another.

"Here, let me do it," Monty said.

"No, it's my money, and I'll count it. But it would be easier if you'd go watch the river or something. You make me nervous glaring at me like that."

It only took her a few moments once Monty had turned his back.

"I still think you ought to let me keep it for you," Monty said as he put the gold pieces into his saddlebags. "At least divide it up. That way you can't lose it all at once."

"That way I can't watch it all at once."

"All right, you might as well do it your way. You're going to anyway."

Carlos and Joe should have returned to work, but Carlos waited to make sure that Monty didn't bully Iris. He stood discreetly to one side drinking coffee. Joe rolled a cigarette.

"I never saw anybody pay off in gold," Joe Reardon whispered to Carlos as they watched Monty count out the gold pieces to Frank and the other fired cowhands.

"Why not? The Randolphs are so rich they can do anything they please."

"But doesn't it strike you funny," Joe said, "bringing gold on a trip like this? Even for the Randolphs."

"No. Why should it?"

"Well, for one thing, nobody does it. They pay off in town at the bank, or they have somebody bring the money out when the drive's over." Joe struck a match on the side of his pants, lit up, and took a drag.

"What are you getting at?" Carlos asked.

Joe exhaled smoke through his nostrils. "I just remembered that rumor about old man Randolph stealing a Union payroll during the war. There was quite a flap about it at one time. Some old coot even attacked the ranch and dug up half the yard, but it died down when there was no flood of gold pieces around south Texas."

"If they had that gold, and I don't believe they did, there's hundreds of ways they could have got rid of it."

"Sure there are, but maybe they didn't. Maybe they were content to keep it, just spending a little bit here and there."

"What are you getting at?"

"There ain't no banks where we're going. Maybe they thought it would be easier to bring gold."

"God, I hate the smell of that tobacco. Can't you smoke something else?"

Joe ignored him. "They'd need enough to run the ranch for years. They could have a fortune with them. The old man was supposed to have stolen half a million."

"Even if they got two and a half million, they ain't going to give you any of it for the asking."

"No, but that Monty fella is getting rather sweet on your sister. Suppose he was to want to marry her and we was to say we wouldn't hand her over unless he gave us a couple of saddlebags of those shiny gold pieces."

"I don't want Iris to marry him. She's going to make me her foreman. She might even make me a partner in the ranch."

"Don't be a fool," Joe hissed. "You could buy a dozen ranches with the gold he must have. Then we wouldn't have to live on no ranch. We could live anywhere we wanted, pay somebody else to ride out in the snow when it's below zero."

"I don't like it."

Joe blew a smoke ring. "You ain't in love with her yourself, are you?"

"Of course not, but—"

"Then there ain't no buts."

"What if he don't want to marry her?"

"Then you can be her foreman, and I can marry her."

Carlos shook his head. "I don't like that either."

"Would you rather I tell her what you was doing these last years? You think Randolph is going to keep us on once he knows you're a wanted man?"

"You'd rat on me?"

"I'd never do that unless it was for your own good," Reardon said, "and passing up this kind of chance ain't for your own good."

"You think she'll agree to marry you?"

"If Monty don't want her, I don't plan to ask her. Either way I don't plan to spend the rest of my life looking at the wrong end of a cow. Agreed?"

"Since you got me over a barrel, I'll think about it, but I don't like it. After her being so nice, it ain't right. Now put the cigarette out. If you start a grass fire, Monty'll get rid of us for sure."

Joe took another drag off his cigarette. He didn't like the change in Carlos. Damn that woman. She seemed to be able to twist just about every man she met around her little finger. It was a good thing Joe was different. The thought of being married to her was enough to make a man's mouth water, but if he could trade her for gold, he would. He could buy dozens of beautiful women with a half-million dollars.

He ground his cigarette out under his heel and headed for his horse.

Chapter Seventeen

Frank and his men disappeared after receiving their money. No one tried to stampede the herd that night or any other. The days merged into one another, each long, hot, and exhausting, but each a steady march toward the high plains of Wyoming. The weather continued dry, but rain to the west kept the creeks and rivers flowing with enough water to provide for the entire herd.

Timbered hills gave way to vast expanses of prairie. Periodic fires kept the plains free of trees except for an occasional grove along a river or a meandering stream. Zac filled the skin slung under the chuck wagon with a mixture of wood and buffalo chips, but there weren't many of the latter to be found after the great slaughter of the buffalo during the previous three years.

Dips and folds in the land could have hidden rustlers, herds of buffalo, or the entire city of St.

Louis, but they never did. An occasional antelope gave some variety to their steady diet of pork, but the sameness of their food challenged even Tyler's powers of invention.

One day Monty took Iris to a high point where she could count six separate herds following in the distance. More than 600,000 longhorns had come up the trail four years earlier, enough to form an unbroken line from Abilene, Kansas, to Brownsville, Texas.

But the dullness of routine was shattered one afternoon when they topped a rise and found themselves face-to-face with more than 50 Comanches, mostly women and old men on foot.

"Let me do the talking," Monty hissed. "Everybody go about your business. Salty, watch for Hen. I don't want any guns."

"I'm going with you," Iris said.

"Stay here. It's too dangerous."

"It's my herd, too."

Iris hardly knew why she insisted upon accompanying Monty. She was more frightened than she had been the day she led the calf into the milling herd, but she had to go. She had to know what was happening to her herd.

And to Monty.

One man, obviously the chief of the band, rode forward and held up a hand as if to command them to stop. The cattle, still grazing forward, veered off to the right. The hands followed, keeping them close together.

The chief apparently didn't speak English because he started making signs with his hands. When Monty addressed him in Spanish, he turned back to his band and signed for two young bucks to ride forward to translate.

"They're Apaches," Monty whispered to her. "No doubt renegades. What does the chief want?" Monty asked the braves, who spoke in heavy guttural Spanish.

After the question had been properly interpreted to the chief, he dropped his blanket from his shoulders and dismounted. He was a fine specimen of a man standing fully six feet and perfectly proportioned even though well past middle life. He looked every inch a chief. Even though Iris didn't know sign language, she could guess the meaning of some of his gestures.

He wanted beef. He claimed all the country in sight as the hunting grounds of the Comanche. He said the white men were intruders. He said the great slaughter of the buffalo by the white hide hunters had left his people poor and hungry. He had always counseled peace, but his band numbered only squaws and old men because the younger men had deserted him for other chiefs who advocated war. He offered to allow them to pass through his country for 20 beeves.

"Dismount," Monty said to Iris. "This is going to take a while."

Monty dismounted and lay down in the grass. Iris had never seen him do that. Not knowing what else to do, she did the same. The Apache translators seated themselves in their own fashion.

"It's no use being in a hurry with these people," Monty explained. "Unless you're willing to waste as much time as they are, they'll beat you every time."

Showing no desire to hasten matters, Monty plucked a grass stem and began to chew on it. After listening patiently to the chief, he launched into a long, rambling conversation, avoiding all reference to the demand for beef. He asked how far it was to Fort Sill and Fort Elliot. He asked how many days it would take the cavalry to reach them. He then talked about the numerous times Indians had stolen cattle and said the white man's chief in Washington was very unhappy with the Indians. He said cattlemen had asked the government to send soldiers to protect them from Indians demanding cattle for the privilege of passing through the territory.

He then said he didn't owe them anything.

The chief invited Monty and Iris to come to their village to see his people.

The invitation caught Iris by surprise. She didn't want to leave the protection of the trail crew, but she did want to see if the chief spoke the truth. Besides, the old men and women didn't seem very dangerous. At least not as long as Monty was with her.

"Let's give them some of our supplies," Iris suggested to Monty.

"That's a good idea." Monty called Salty and told him Iris wanted to take the Indians some food. Salty didn't look as though he liked the idea, but he soon came back with the food.

Iris felt brave enough while the crew was close by, but when the Indians closed in on either side of her and the men disappeared into the distance, she found herself wishing she had stayed behind.

The Indians had made camp where a stream valley widened into a broad flood plain with ample groves of cottonwoods and willow clumps providing space and shade and water and wood. Leaves on the cottonwood rustled continually, their whitish-gray, furrowed trunks larger than a man could reach around. The gray soil near the camp was covered with sparse vegetation, but up on the plain, there was plenty of grass for the poor, overworked ponies. The tepees, hide-covered cones, were set up in a large circle; the plain tan color of the buffalo hides was blackened at the top from smoke. Emaciated dogs searched between the tepees for discarded bones.

Iris had never seen misery equal to what she found in the Indian village. Women and children stopped their tasks to watch them ride in, the women's faces lined by years of hard work and too little food and rest, the children gaunt and unnaturally quiet. With arrogant indifference, the Apaches dropped the bags of food on the ground. Within minutes every scrap had been taken.

Iris wished she could have brought more.

The procession stopped before the largest tepee in the camp. It had been decorated with geometrical designs, religious symbols, and pictures commemorating a warrior's deeds.

"This is the chief's tepee," Monty whispered.

"What is he going to do?" Iris whispered back.

"Invite us inside to talk some more."

"How long will it take?"

"I don't know."

Iris didn't want to get down or go into the tepee, but Monty dismounted without hesitation. She followed rather than wait outside alone. The chief looked uncertain when Iris started toward the tepee, but Monty told him through the translators that half the cows belonged to Iris. If he wanted beef, he would have to talk with her as well.

At this point Iris would have been willing to give him 20 cows just to get back to the herd and as far away from this village as possible.

The dim light inside the tepee made everything surreal. By the time the chief had completed the interminable ritual of lighting a pipe and passing

267

it around, Iris would have given him 30 cows. She hesitated when Monty passed the pipe to her, but having forced herself into the midst of this exclusively male ritual, she knew she had to take the pipe. Taking great care, Iris inhaled a small amount. The smoke of strong tobacco mixed with aromatic herbs bit into her lungs. Only the greatest effort kept her from coughing.

Monty smiled his approval. Iris felt dizzy with success. By the time she had breathed the smoke-filled air inside the tent during another hour of ambling deliberations, she was genuinely dizzy.

But an even bigger ordeal lay ahead. Women entered the tent bearing bowls and trays of food. She and Monty were expected to stay for dinner.

Monty might complain he didn't recognize anything Tyler fixed, but he didn't hesitate at a single dish even though most of them seemed to be made of the same indistinguishable mush. Iris did recognize a stew made with wild peas and prairie turnips and seasoned with the faint taste of some kind of meat. She ate some small chunks of meat and hoped Monty wouldn't tell her later it was rattlesnake. She refused a dish of what had to be grasshoppers. A mush of pumpkin and wild berries wasn't bad. She actually enjoyed the peeled sweet thistle stalks offered last, probably more because they signaled the end of the meal than because they tasted faintly like bananas.

She knew the Indians had deprived themselves to provide this feast, so she ate just enough to be polite. She hoped they would give the leftovers to the children. Remembering the children's gaunt faces, she would gladly have given them the whole meal.

"We've been invited to stay the night," Monty said.

"Invited?"

"It's something of a command."

"Where will we stay?"

"They'll show us."

The aimless talk continued. As Monty translated less and less, Iris's mind wandered from the question at hand. The thought she would be separated from Monty nearly petrified her. It had never occurred to her, when she'd insisted upon accompanying Monty, that they would leave the herd or that, when they arrived at the Indian village, they wouldn't return after a little more talk. The discovery that she was expected—no, required—to spend the night caused a band of fear to wrap itself tightly around her chest.

The longer they talked, the tighter the band became. By the time the chief signaled the end of the talks for the evening, Iris could hardly breathe. She reached out for Monty and gripped his hand as though it were a lifeline. The chief, noticing, muttered something to one of his braves. The man motioned for Iris and Monty to follow him. He led them to a tepee nearly as large and fancifully decorated as the one they had just left. The man spoke to Monty and turned to leave. Monty, obviously surprised by what the man said, answered in rapid Spanish.

Iris wished she could understand them, but Helena had refused to allow Iris to learn a language she considered suitable only for servants.

Monty tried to argue with the Apache translator, but the man turned away. Iris grabbed Monty's arm when he started after the man.

"What's wrong?" she asked.

"The chief means for us to sleep in the same tepee. He thinks you're my woman."

Iris had never experienced anything like the shock that practically lifted her off her feet. Her entire body was invaded by a delicious excitement that had nothing to do with her present dilemma. She couldn't understand why she should be feeling anxious anticipation rather than fear and trembling, but she was sure of one thing. Monty must stay. He must not leave her alone.

"There's plenty of room for two people," she said, glancing around the tepee. "It's very large."

"This has nothing to do with space. I can't sleep in there alone with you. You'd be ruined."

At the moment, Iris's fear of being left alone overrode any fear about her reputation. "You can't leave me. Not here. I'll follow you if you try."

"They won't hurt you," Monty assured her. "We're their guests. It would violate their honor."

"Maybe, but I don't intend to find out. You've got to stay. No one will ever know."

"I'll talk to the chief." But when Monty attempted to return to the chief's tent, the Apaches blocked his path. Monty's body tensed as he prepared to force his way though the barrier.

"Don't," Iris called. She grasped Monty's sleeve and pulled him back. "They won't let you. They may get mad if you try."

Realizing the futility of trying to appeal to the chief, Monty said, "I'll sleep outside."

"It's going to rain." It had already begun to sprinkle.

"I've got my slicker."

"Don't be so stubborn. There's plenty of room inside for both of us."

When Monty didn't move, Iris took him by the hand and pulled him toward the tepee. One brave smiled and nudged his companion, but Iris was not deterred. Her mind had leapfrogged all her doubts. No matter what, she wanted Monty at her side.

"This is a mistake," Monty said, still rooted to the spot.

"Maybe, but we can't talk about it now."

"We've got to. If I go in there, I don't know if I can come out again."

"I don't want you to."

Monty stared at her. "Do you know what you're saying?"

"Yes." She pulled again, and this time Monty took a step forward.

"Maybe we—"

"We'll talk inside."

Iris's legs felt so weak, her belly fluttered so nervously, she nearly stumbled when she stooped to enter the tent. Light coming through the smoke flap and from the coals of a small fire relieved the darkness of the interior, but she could barely make out a bed of buffalo robes at the back of the tepee.

One bed.

Until now Iris hadn't considered how loving Monty would affect her. There had seemed little point. Now she realized in one flash of discovery that she wanted to make love to him. Her body was crying out her need to be held by him, to feel the incredible pressure of his lips on hers, the joy of being held close to his heart.

She didn't know if he wanted to make love to her. If he did, she didn't know if he would let himself.

Monty halted just inside the door and looked around the interior of the tepee. He chuckled, but it seemed strained. "I bet you've never slept on a buffalo robe before."

"No. I never ate whatever we had for dinner either, but I survived it."

"They're close to starving. They served us the best they had."

"Will they let us go in the morning?"

"Yes. The chief is just hoping to get as many cows as possible."

"How many are you going to give him?"

"Two."

"But they're so hungry."

"They'll only eat everything now and be hungry again."

"What are you going to do?"

"I've got another deal."

"What is it?"

"I'll tell you tomorrow."

Iris knew they were talking around the one thing that occupied both their minds. She eyed the buffalo robe out of the corner of her eye.

Monty also eyed the bed uneasily. Iris was desperate to know what he was thinking, but he looked so tense she didn't dare ask. She didn't think she could stand to know he didn't want her.

"I don't know if I can stay here and not touch you," Monty finally said. "I wouldn't have succeeded that night at the creek if Carlos hadn't found us."

The hard pressure of Iris's fear gave way to the supple tension of excitement. Monty did want her. He wanted her so much he didn't think he could control himself. Iris felt a growing tautness. She felt the same way. She didn't know how to tell him she wanted him to touch her without making him think she was like the women he was used to. She could sense that while he might welcome such a revelation now, he would reject her for it later.

"I trust you," Iris said.

"You shouldn't."

"You wouldn't hurt me."

"No."

Iris walked over to the robe and knelt down on it. "Then I'm not afraid."

She didn't know if he understood. Even though she searched his face, it was too dark in the tepee to catch any nuance of expression.

"Are you sure?"

"Yes."

Monty lowered himself next to Iris. He had tried to keep his distance. If she had acted upset or cowered in the corner or simply tried to keep as far away from him as possible he could have controlled himself. At least he would have tried. But her calm acceptance of their intimacy, her virtual invitation, swept away any desire to resist. For months he had been tortured by dreams of making love to Iris.

Now his whole body trembled with excitement. He was tight again just with the thought of her.

He wondered what Helena had told Iris about men. Clearly Iris hadn't listened to all her mother's advice. He didn't know why Iris wanted him, but there was nothing manipulative in her now.

She simply wanted him.

And he wanted her. God, how he wanted her. He reached out and caressed her cheek with the back of his hand. She didn't pull away. She didn't strike his hand down.

She didn't move at all.

She felt so soft. She looked so thin, almost gaunt, in the shadows as the light played on the planes of her face. Helena had combined medium height with an erotic plumpness. Iris's height and athletic slimness was nearly the opposite of her mother's indolent allure. Where Helena gave the appearance of inviting an excess of pleasure, Iris made him feel keenly alive, lean, and hungry for more.

"Are you frightened?" he asked. She sat so still. Silent. She hardly seemed to breathe.

"No." Her voice was a bare thread.

"Do you want me to stop?"

She shook her head.

Monty didn't think he could.

Her skin felt so warm and soft. He couldn't remember being so aware of a woman's skin before, not that he would attempt to compare Iris to any female he had known. It was gradually dawning on him that Iris was unlike any woman he had ever known.

Iris moistened her dry lips. Her stomach seemed to shoot up into her throat, find her heart already there, then plummet back down with a jolt. The force and rapidity of her pulse made her feel unwell, yet she had never felt more intensely alive.

The man she loved was about to make love to her.

She ignored the fact Monty might not love her. She had spent years unaware she loved him. Maybe the same thing had happened to him. Everybody said Monty was too taken up with his cows to have any time left for a woman. He spent his life in the saddle. In fact, she was the only female he'd been interested in for more than a night or two. He was her first and only love. Maybe she was his as well.

But she had no time to wonder whether she might be right, not when a very real Monty sat next to her, his hand on her throat, his lips brushing her lips. His touch, his presence must mean more than a moment of physical need. Otherwise why would he have struggled so hard to resist? If she waited a little while, maybe she would know.

She could almost see Monty holding himself back. She could sense the tension in the air as if it were a tangible force, feel it as his control wore thin. There had to be a release. Iris waited for it. She could feel it coming even before she heard the sharp intake of breath as he grabbed her and swept her into a fierce embrace.

Something inside Iris escaped its bonds. She felt free, untrammeled. There was no question, no doubt, no feeling that she ought to do something else. Everything felt right. Completely so. Fragments of her mother's advice floated unbidden through her mind only to be discarded. She wanted no mentor hovering in the background telling her how to reduce a man to helplessness.

She was the one who had been rendered powerless, and she gloried in the freedom to kiss Monty back without attempting to calculate the effect of her seductiveness on him, to return his embrace without worrying about whether she was giving up too much or too little. She rejoiced in being able to think only of how happy it made her to know Monty wanted her.

"I shouldn't have let you leave camp," Monty whispered against the side of her neck.

"You couldn't stop me."

"I can't stop myself either," Monty replied. His lips forced her mouth open, and Iris shivered with shock and delight when she felt his warm tongue dart into her mouth with the hunger of a bee plundering a flower for nectar. No man had ever dared such a thing with her.

Monty wasn't like other men. For no other man in the world would she have forsaken the safety of the drive to follow him into a Comanche village, to eat their food, to spend the night in their midst. Only Monty could instill such a feeling of safety within her. Only with Monty did she want to make love. She had never wanted a man to touch her until now. She had always set definite limits. She would let Monty do anything he wanted.

Only for Monty would she take such a risk.

She was taking a risk now. She knew it. She understood the consequences.

"You're so very beautiful." Monty murmured.

"You can't see me. I could be as pitiful as one of those women outside and you wouldn't know."

"I would know," Monty assured her. "A man always knows."

But did he know a woman could be beautiful on the inside as well? Did he see what she was like? Did he know anything of her dreams?

No, but she knew very little of them herself. Until the boat accident, she had accepted her mother's counsel without question. After that, her decisions had been determined by the need to survive. Only gradually had she come to realize she wanted things that had nothing to do with either of those paths.

Monty had taught her how to be herself, had helped her uncover something new each day. Right now he was teaching her that her body was subject to much more powerful urges than she had ever imagined possible. She wouldn't have broken away from Monty and crawled out of the tent if someone had offered her all the money her father had lost. She wouldn't have gotten on her horse and ridden back to camp if they had promised her the largest ranch in Wyoming.

Her place was here, in Monty's arms. If her mind didn't know it, her body did.

Monty's hand moved from her shoulder to cup her breast. Even through her shirt and chemise, the impact nearly lifted Iris off the ground. Her body went rigid; her breath stilled in her throat.

No one had ever touched her body. No one had dared. She had no way of anticipating the excitement that coursed through her with the speed of lightning. Neither was she prepared for the nearly irresistible urge to explore every part of Monty's body.

Nice women didn't do that, did they?

The question was destined to be forgotten before it was answered. Monty's impatient hand delved into the front of her blouse. The feel of his hand on her hot, sensitive breast drove everything else from her mind.

Gentlemen didn't do this, did they?

Obviously Monty did. He also unbuttoned her blouse, slipped her chemise from her shoulders, and covered her feverish skin with kisses. Iris felt she ought to do something, say something, make some response, but his onslaught so surprised and overwhelmed her she was unable to do more than moan with happiness. The waves of pleasure teased her senses like ripples in a pool threatening to drown her in their blissful depths.

Dazed, numb, and yet more alive then ever before, Iris found nothing prepared her for the feeling of Monty's lips on her breasts. She was certain her body did leave the ground. Monty took unfair advantage of her momentary helplessness to remove the remainder of her garments.

Iris lay naked in the arms of a man.

But not even the shock of that realization had the power to penetrate the veil of sensual delight that wrapped Iris in its cocoon. As Monty continued to tease and tantalize her body, the feelings that had seemed to be everywhere and nowhere at once started to coalesce. First they seemed to flame in her nipples as Monty teased and tasted her with his tongue.

But even before her breasts became so sensitive that she could hardly lie still under his assault without crying out, the center of heat had begun to move lower in her body. The slow-moving vortex of warmth centered itself in her belly and started to grow in strength and intensity. Iris could hardly think of anyone or anything else, only the burning, tingling, yearning that would not be satisfied.

Until Monty's hand moved between her thighs.

Iris gasped in surprise when his fingers entered her body. She flinched in defense, closing, withdrawing. But the need now spreading to every part of her slowly relaxed her muscles, allowing her to open herself to him.

It was almost like an unwinding. She could feel the muscles release their grip, feel the tension flow from her limbs. She could feel herself relax, sinking into the buffalo skin, loosening until she offered no resistance to his assault.

But at the very moment she felt as though she might dissolve completely, Monty touched the nub of her existence, sending shock waves throughout her entire body. Monty pressed his advantage until Iris's whole body felt like a coiling spring.

"This may hurt a little at first," Monty warned as he moved over her.

But Iris was beyond worrying about a small discomfort. Her whole body was undergoing an experience at once overpowering and profoundly different. Her body tensed slightly as Monty entered her, but she offered no resistance. Monty hovered at her threshold, teasing, tantalizing, until Iris was frantic for release.

"Please," she groaned, then wrapped herself around him.

Almost at once he filled her. Immediately Iris felt a sharp pain, and she tensed again. She was too full. It would hurt. She didn't like it.

"It won't hurt anymore," Monty whispered. "It won't ever hurt again."

Monty moved inside her, slowly, rhythmically. There was a rapidly diminishing pain, a feeling of fullness. In its place Iris felt a new sensation, one that invited her to move with Monty, that drove her to meet him and then fall away before rushing forward again. Their movement gradually quickened, and Iris felt as though her entire body ached for release. Her arms, her legs, everything twitched and tingled and moved in a frantic effort to relieve this absolutely marvelous ache that flowed into every part of her body and kept her suspended somewhere between slight discomfort and the most marvelous feeling she'd ever experienced.

Iris pulled Monty closer, kissed him with a fervor fired and stoked to great heat by his attentions to her fevered body. Her tongue plunged into his mouth, seeking the answer as to why he plunged into her body.

The answer wasn't long in coming.

Iris felt Monty's body grow taut, heard his breath become short and harsh. Before she could wonder at its cause, a circular band of aching, pulsating need exploded from deep inside her body and rolled from one end to the other. Gasping from its intensity, Iris felt it begin again and again. She felt exhausted. She felt powerful. She clung to Monty as though he were life itself.

Monty began to buck uncontrollably in her arms and Iris felt the heat of his release flow inside her. It only made her need grow even more urgent. She strained against Monty, but he seemed incapable of movement. Iris felt the moment slipping away from her. So close, yet it was slipping away. "No." It was a harsh, guttural sound. "Don't stop."

He started moving again.

Almost immediately the feeling flooded Iris's body once more. Gasping, straining, and fighting, it pulled Iris into its core and flung her beyond the realm of ordinary feeling. Her own body became as rigid as Monty's had been. Muscles tensed until she was sure she would break into tiny pieces.

Then everything shattered and she felt the sweet ache of release streaming through her body, flooding her with a delicious sense of fulfillment, washing away the tension until she felt unable to so much as lift her arm.

She felt exhausted, drained, replete. And yet so aware of the wonderful, strong arms that held her close against his warm, damp chest.

Iris couldn't sleep. Monty's soft breathing made her feel warm and safe, but it didn't make her sleepy. If fact, his presence kept her so keyed up she wondered if she would ever sleep again.

She wondered if he felt as changed as she did. No, it wasn't his first time. He hadn't experienced the double shock of making love for the very first time with the one person he loved above all others. There couldn't be anything else like it.

She hoped Monty felt at least a little bit like that.

She smiled to herself. She had always taken it for granted that making love to her would have a profound effect on the man she gave herself to for the first time. It had never occurred to her that the event would change her even more completely. She felt transformed, reborn, recreated. Nothing of the old Iris Richmond remained. She wondered if Monty had felt anything like the way she did. She hoped so, but she couldn't sleep. Why could he?

She told herself she couldn't sleep because she was so deeply in love she might never feel sleepy again as long as she was next to Monty. She told herself she couldn't sleep because the impact of making love to Monty was much greater than anything she'd ever anticipated. She told herself she couldn't sleep because she was too happy to waste these precious hours unconscious.

Why could Monty sleep?

She refused to believe it was because the last hour meant so little to him. She'd know tomorrow. He would tell her.

Chapter Eighteen

Monty had dressed and gone by the time Iris woke. Her initial feeling of well-being changed to panic. She dressed quickly. She had to find Monty. She didn't feel safe without him.

She experienced a fleeting regret that the magic of their first night together hadn't lasted any longer. It should have had its conclusion in a completely different set of emotions. They should have waked to the new day in each other's arms, new souls changed forever. But she couldn't worry about that when she was alone in a Comanche village. Right now nothing mattered except finding Monty.

She found him barely a dozen feet from the tepee entrance, talking to the Apache interpreters. The feeling of relief was so profound it made it difficult for her to stand without leaning on something. She should have known he wouldn't leave her. If he didn't trust her with

Frank, he certainly wouldn't trust her with Indians.

Iris liked knowing that. She had never felt uncared for when her parents were alive, but somehow their attention didn't have the same impact as Monty's. With them she had always felt safe, provided for. Now she felt guarded, valued. She couldn't state the difference any better than that, but she could feel it. And she liked the feeling.

Monty came toward her as soon as he spotted her.

"Get ready. We're going back to camp. They've agreed to let us pass for two beeves now and three later."

"Do we have to eat with the chief again?"

"No," Monty said, his broad smile assuring her everything was going to work out just fine. "You can wait until we get back. I'm sure Tyler will be happy to whip up something unrecognizable."

Iris felt inordinately relieved to know they were going back to camp without further delay. "You shouldn't complain about Tyler. He's a very fine cook."

"Then let him open a restaurant. I just want some decent fried bacon."

Iris decided Monty would be very much at home in Wyoming. At least until civilization arrived. She also decided she wished the half-dozen young braves who seemed to have materialized from nowhere to follow at their heels would find something else to do. Surely there was at least one buffalo that hadn't been killed. If nothing else, they could clean up the campsite. If they didn't, they'd have to move in a matter of days.

Leigh Greenwood

Iris endured one more visit with the chief, one more long exchange in Spanish. She made a silent vow to learn the language if she ever went back to live in south Texas. She hated the feeling of being left out.

Iris's uneasiness increased when eight Indians mounted their ponies and prepared to leave with them. "Why do they need so many people to bring back two cows?" Iris asked, glancing back at the line of braves following them out of the village.

"Only two are coming to take back the cows," Monty said. "I hired the other six to help us until we reach Dodge."

Iris could hardly believe her ears. "You hired Indians? Comanches?"

Monty laughed. She didn't know what the man found so funny about salting his camp with Comanches, but she was coming to realize Monty laughed at all kinds of unsuitable times.

"I need the hands. I can't replace Frank and the others until we reach Dodge. Besides, as long as we've got Comanches with us, I don't think other Indians will be too anxious to attack us or demand cows. I think Frank is still around somewhere. I'm hoping the sight of six Comanches prowling around the camp will make him think twice before trying to run off any of our cows."

Iris was sure Monty was right, but she doubted the crew would be very enthusiastic about working with Comanches. However, she intended to leave that to Monty. He was always asking her to let him take care of things. Well, this was one problem she had no intention of trying to take off his hands.

"There's something else."

Monty was acting strange, as if he didn't want to say whatever it was. Iris was surprised. His most devastating observations hadn't caused him a moment's hesitation. She wondered if he was going to say something nice, and the novelty of it had thrown him off stride.

"I'm going to have to keep away from you for a bit. This may seem a little unusual . . . after last night . . . but I don't want to do anything that might start the men talking."

He wouldn't look at her. She couldn't remember having seen him so uncomfortable.

"I wasn't expecting you to do anything different."

That was a lie. She expected everything to be different, the sun, the moon, the entire universe. She felt recreated, as though nothing of the old Iris remained. She didn't see things the same way and she didn't feel the same way. It was as though she'd been living in a dream all her life and had just now woken up to reality. For her, the whole world had been transformed. It obviously hadn't been for Monty.

"I know. It's just this is rather awkward on a cattle drive." He looked at her. "I wouldn't do anything to hurt your reputation."

Iris didn't think she had much reputation left. She would have cast the rest of it aside for Monty. But he wasn't ready to do that for her. Maybe he never would be.

"What did you bring back all these Indians for?" Zac asked the minute Iris and Monty rode into camp.

"To help out until we get to Dodge," Monty said. "Salty, help these men cut out that lame steer. That sore-footed cow, too. I doubt she'd make it to Wyoming anyway."

All Tyler said was, "They'll have to do their own cooking."

And that was the end of it. Some of the men looked a little put out, but nobody protested.

Iris decided she didn't understand cowboys.

There was no one in the noon camp when Hen rode in. "Where's Monty?" he asked as he dismounted and turned his mount over to Zac.

"Checking the crossing," Zac said, pointing to where a short distance away Monty's horse splashed through the swift water of a shallow stream.

Hen walked toward his brother. They met at the far end of the remuda. "How much did it cost you?" Hen asked as Monty jumped from the saddle.

"Two cows and the wages of six braves until we're well out of Indian territory," Monty replied.

Hen's gaze narrowed as he took a hard look at his twin's broad grin. "You damned fool!" he cursed furiously. "Why did you have to sleep with her?"

Hen's unexpected and explosive outburst wiped the smile from Monty's face. "What makes you think I—"

"Don't waste your time lying to me," Hen hissed. "Save that for the men. You let one of them guess what you've done, and there'll be hell to pay."

Monty felt his temper fire like a Chinese rocket. "Just because we stayed overnight—"

"You'd think after all your carping about showing George you'd stopped acting like an idiot every chance you got you could have managed to last one night without climbing into bed with the one female in all the world capable of wreaking enough havoc to ruin this drive. Why didn't you grab yourself a squaw? It couldn't have caused more trouble."

Monty knew Hen didn't like Iris—Hen didn't like any woman except Rose—but he had never expected this kind of outburst. It shocked him, but it also infuriated him that Hen would be so unfair. Maybe Iris wasn't perfect, but she was pretty damned good, especially considering she had Helena for a mother.

It also angered him he could be so transparent. He never knew what was going on in Hen's mind. "I tried not to," Monty said, making no attempt to deny Hen's accusation.

"Damn! I'd rather you said you had made up your mind to seduce her the first chance you got. At least I could believe you'd started to grow up. But you're just as much a fool as ever."

Monty could feel his anger starting to get out of control. "Just because you're a cold-blooded devil doesn't mean the rest of us can live like eunuchs."

"Go find yourself a whore if your itch needs scratching, but stay away from women like Iris."

Anger churned in Monty's gut like boiling water. He could feel the muscles in his arms jumping, tensing, just wanting to hit something. He turned and stalked away, but Hen followed.

"You spent a year trying to convince George to start this ranch. I backed you. Jeff claimed the homestead, built and stocked the cabin. Zac left school early. We spent months planning this drive, and you're ready to jeopardize it all just because you can't control the itch in your pants."

"Lay off," Monty warned. "Being my twin doesn't give you the right to say anything you damned well please."

"I can call you a jackass if I want," Hen shot back. "I'd say it even if you weren't my brother."

287

"I'm warning you—" Monty could feel blind anger rolling over him, consuming his reason, drowning his resistance. He tried to push it back, but it washed over him like the incoming tide.

"You don't frighten me," Hen taunted him. "I've whipped your ass before. And if you keep on letting your britches rule your head, I'll do it again."

Monty charged his brother with all the ferocity of an angry bull. Hen squared up to his attack, and the two of them went down in a tangle of arms and legs, the air filled with their curses.

"Monty and Hen are fighting!" Zac shouted to Tyler as he dashed up to the chuck wagon.

"They're always fighting," Tyler replied.

"They mean it this time. It's about Iris." Zac yanked the top off the water barrel, scooped up a bucket of water, and slammed the top back in place. "Come on," he called as he ran off again. "Hurry, before they kill each other."

Apparently ignoring his brother, Tyler walked over to the fire and stuck his finger into a pot of beans. Satisfied with the temperature, he picked up the pot and followed Zac.

"They wouldn't stop no matter what I say," Zac said and threw the bucket of water over his brothers.

They didn't even pause in their struggle.

"You need something that won't run off," Tyler said as he hoisted his pot of beans aloft. He began to pour the thick, sticky mass over the fighters in one continuous, hot stream.

The violence of the curses from both men scorched the air, but they stopped fighting.

"I'll cook you in one of your own pots!" Monty shouted.

"Not if I get to him first," Hen threatened.

Tyler returned to his fire with an unhurried tread.

"As for you—" Monty shouted, turning on Zac.

But Zac, having a lively appreciation for keeping his own skin whole and in an unbruised condition, was well on his way back to camp, his tread as hurried as he could make it.

"This is all your fault, yours and that stupid woman," Hen blazed as he scraped gobs of sticky beans from his shirt and flung them away with a flick of his wrist.

"Don't call Iris stupid," Monty barked. Using his index finger, he removed a blob from his cheek. He tasted it and found it to his liking.

"You won't have to worry about me calling her anything to you ever again."

"Yes, I do. You may not talk much, but you're never quiet about things you don't like."

"It won't matter if I'm not here for you to hear it."

Monty froze. "You're leaving?" It had never occurred to him Hen would desert him. They had fought over one thing or another ever since he could remember, but they had been each other's shadow all their lives.

Monty's words seemed to strike Hen with an equal impact.

"No. I told George I'd help you get this herd to Wyoming, and I won't go back on my word."

"Don't bother," Monty replied, deeply hurt that Hen's loyalty to George should be greater than to his own twin. "I can get them there without you."

"I'm staying."

"Suit yourself, you stubborn son of a bitch. But you make sure you stick to your job. I can take care of the rest."

"You'd better," Hen retorted, "or I'm going to beat the hell out of you again."

Monty was still so angry it took him a moment to master the impulse to attack Hen all over again. *Why not?* he said to himself. *Everybody already thinks you're nothing but a hotheaded fool. You could save everybody a lot of trouble by proving it.*

But Monty didn't want to fight Hen. He didn't want to fight anybody. He just wanted to get rid of the empty feeling inside, this horrible feeling of failure that rode him like a demon every time he failed to live up to George's expectations.

He had never needed his father's approval; he had despised the old bastard too much to care what he thought, but it was different with George. George would have sacrificed his own success if it would have helped Monty.

That made it worse, but it was Rose who made it awful. It tore her up to see George upset over his brothers. Monty could still remember the time she had looked at him with tears in her eyes, tears for George, tears for him. Hell, it made him feel so bad he wanted to go out and shoot himself.

Would it ever be any different?

But as Monty's temper cooled, he admitted to himself he wouldn't have gotten so angry if Hen hadn't said exactly what he'd been saying to himself. He knew Iris was causing him to do one thing after another he shouldn't, but he couldn't seem to help himself. Where Iris was concerned he didn't seem to be able to think clearly.

And since he'd made love to her, everything would probably become more difficult. Usually a night of lovemaking filled him with energy, made him anxious to get back to the ranch, to the herd, to his work. It temporarily freed him of his need of women.

He didn't feel free of Iris. He had not exhausted his fascination with her. If anything it had actually increased.

Even now the memory of last night was so strong it was almost as if he were living it again. The feel of her skin against his own was more vivid than the smell of the warm beans or their heavy thickness as they dried on his clothes.

But there was more to it than that. He didn't think of her only when his body needed to be eased. He never had. She had always been somebody special, first when she was a love-struck teenager following him about, then when she turned into a stunning woman trying to cajole him into taking her to Wyoming. He had always wanted her to be safe, comfortable, and happy, even though he hadn't wanted to be personally responsible for her.

That had changed. Now he found himself thinking about her before he thought of his cows. That in itself was ominous. He had stopped thinking she was like her mother. Monty had when he first saw her at Christmas—she had looked so much like Helena she could have been her double—but he had had plenty of time to realize Iris was very different.

She had certainly tried to talk him into doing something he didn't want to do, something that wasn't in his best interest because it benefitted her. But she had done it because she was badly frightened, not because she was greedy or cruel.

She was also honest. She had stopped trying to charm or flatter him into doing what she wanted. Now if she wanted something, she asked for it. She might get angry if she didn't get it, but she didn't sulk and she didn't connive.

Monty realized in addition to liking Iris, to being strongly affected by her physical beauty, to being concerned with her well-being, he was starting to admire her. She was a very different woman from what he had expected, and he found himself comparing her to Rose and Fern. He found himself thinking of being with her for the rest of his life.

The logical extension of that thought startled Monty so much he almost called for his horse so he could start separating the herds right then and there. He had been around George and Madison enough to know this wasn't mere lust at work. There was something else going on, something that took hold of a man and wouldn't let go no matter what he did.

Monty wasn't ready for that. He wasn't ready to think beyond getting to Wyoming and winning his own private battle with George. Once he'd done that, maybe he'd think about his future. But not now.

But he knew no matter how upset he might be now, he'd forget his resolution the minute he saw Iris. She had looked even lovelier this morning than she had last night. At first it had only irritated him to see the looks the men gave her when she walked up to the campfire. Now, after last night, it upset him. He didn't want the crew looking at Iris like that. He knew what was in their minds—it had been on his—and he didn't like it.

But he couldn't do anything about it. He couldn't hide her in her wagon. He couldn't force her to travel with the chuck wagon, not after he'd practically forced her to ride with the herd so she could learn how to manage cows. He couldn't send her to a hotel at night. There was nothing but Indian tepees for hundreds of miles in any direction. He couldn't tell the men not to look at her without making himself into a bigger fool than he was already.

Hell, there was no end to the consequences of letting Iris come on this trip. If he'd known when he came upon her on the trail what he knew now, he'd have carried her back, even if she'd kicked and screamed. But he couldn't do that now. He would have to look after her all the way to Wyoming.

Monty cursed. She'd gotten what she wanted, only he was doing it of his own accord now. He wouldn't back off even if she asked him to. Hen was right. He couldn't think straight when he was around Iris.

He had to begin keeping his distance, as much because of Hen as for himself. Hen was his closest friend in the world. Nothing had ever come between them. They had been each other's conscience, guardian, companion. Hell, Hen had risked his own life to save him that day the rustlers were about to hang him. Monty could almost feel the rope tightening around his neck.

Monty had to make certain the men acted respectfully. Firing Crowder had sent the message that he wouldn't tolerate insolence, but it wouldn't be a bad idea if the men just stayed away altogether. It would be safer for everybody. A few well-placed words would take care of that.

Now all he had to do was figure out what excuse to give Iris.

Iris was hurt and confused. She was also mad. She had expected Monty to be distant, but she hadn't expected him to practically ignore her.

For days she had ridden next to the bawling herd, clouds of dust coating her body with dirt, noise assaulting her ears until she felt as if her brains were scrambled. Her body ached from hours in the saddle trying to hold on while her trailwise pony took out after an errant cow and drove it back into the herd. Her legs felt bowed, she had calluses in places she wouldn't mention in mixed company much less expose, and the ceaseless wind had chapped her lips and given her split ends. And to top it all off, she was tanned as brown as an Indian. Not once had Monty commented on how hard she had worked or how much she had improved. He had hardly spoken to her at all.

The sight of her wagon pulled into the shade by the stream made her think wistfully of her bed, but it was an exercise in frustration. Five cows had dropped calves during the night, all of them hers. She knew it was to her advantage to save every calf she could. Monty's, too, but now he acted as if it was nothing special. It irritated her that he should take her sacrifice for granted so quickly. All he had said was, "Your clothes are going to get wrinkled in that bedroll." Fortunately Tyler had room for her trunk in the chuck wagon, or she might have turned the gun on Monty instead of the calves.

Now he had her working like a cowhand; the pampered daughter of a rich rancher was doing the same work as unlettered boys who got paid 30 dollars a month. She used to spend more than that on a dress she might wear only once. She thought of the meager hoard of coins hidden once again in the secret compartment in her wagon. It would be a long time before she could spend that kind of money on a dress, even one she planned to wear over and over again.

But as Iris took the reins from Zac and climbed into the saddle, she knew it wasn't the work, the money, or the loss of her wagon that had put her into a state. As usual, it was Monty.

Eight weeks on the trail had given her a very different picture of the man she had first swooned over five years ago. But even though she knew Monty had only slightly more subtlety and sensitivity than a buffalo bull, she had expected their night together to revolutionize their relationship. It had changed her life forever.

But Monty went about his work like always. Except that now he seemed to look right through her.

She didn't understand. For the last three days he'd hardly spoken to her. Not once had they eaten a meal in the companionable silence she used to enjoy so much. At first she thought he was avoiding her, but he was always close by. He seemed to have surrounded her with a ring of protection so hostile none of the men came near her. It was almost as though he was angry at her. She knew he was still upset about Hen, but she had no idea why he was angry at the men.

Iris overheard Zac talking to Tyler.

"Nothing's ever kept them mad at each other this long before," Zac had said after Hen and Monty had sat through breakfast without speaking to each other. "They've hardly said a word to each other all week."

Tyler had cast a brief glance at Iris, but his expression was blank, and he said nothing.

"Even when they're fighting, they're usually thick as thieves. Get one mad and you got them both to deal with. Which ain't fair," Zac said, apparently remembering some past injustice. "I can watch out for one of them, but nobody can keep his eyes on both of them. Especially Hen. He can move like an Indian. You can usually hear Monty coming a mile off."

"If you watched your tongue, you wouldn't always have to be looking over your shoulder," Tyler added.

"Well, if Monty didn't have a temper like a wounded panther, I wouldn't have to worry either way."

Zac had gone away to dismantle his rope corral and prepare to drive the remuda along with the cattle to the noon resting place.

No one had to tell Iris that she was the difficulty that had come between Hen and Monty. She could see it in the strained way Monty acted toward her. It leapt out from Hen's behavior. She doubted a leper could feel any more shunned.

Yet Monty must still be concerned about her. He rarely let her out of his sight. He organized the jobs so she would be with him. She slept near the Randolph chuck wagon, with Monty, Tyler, and Zac forming a ring of protection around her. Iris began to feel like a prisoner too valuable to be let out of sight yet not worthy of friendship.

Iris couldn't understand these contradictory feelings. If she liked somebody, she liked him no matter what. It didn't make sense to like somebody and hate him at the same time. But it obviously made sense to Monty, and she was getting the worst of both sides.

She couldn't stand it any longer. She had to talk to Monty. Every time she thought of making love to him, of the hopes she had built on that night, it made her sick at heart. Nothing would change her conviction that Monty cared for her, but there was something going on inside him that she didn't know about. It somehow affected her, and it stood in the way of her happiness. Iris knew what she needed to be happy. It wasn't the herd; it wasn't enough money to go back to St. Louis. It wasn't even an adoring husband who would do everything in his power to please her.

It was Monty. Irascible, cantankerous, temperamental, handsome, charming, dependable Monty.

Nothing else.

Having made her decision, Iris felt much better. Her anxiety to talk to Monty made the afternoon pass slowly. Thus she was irritated to ride into camp and find nearly every cowhand in the outfit gathered around the chuck wagon. The presence of so many people would make it nearly impossible to talk to Monty alone. She had to have privacy. She thought Tyler might be cooking a favorite meal tonight, but she could detect no cooking aromas. She rode straight to the rope corral. Zac was nowhere to be seen. She dismounted, tied her horse to a bush, and headed toward the campsite. As she looked up, a movement in the gathering of men enabled her to see what was causing all the commotion.

A young woman stood talking to Monty.

Chapter Nineteen

Iris found herself hurrying forward. Where could the woman have come from? What was she doing here? It hadn't occurred to Iris until this very moment, but she ached for female companionship. Her sense of isolation had been made all the more acute by Monty's behavior of late. She hoped the woman wasn't just a visitor. She hoped she would stay with them for a while.

"My name is Iris Richmond," Iris announced as the men fell back to let her pass. "I hope you're not in any trouble."

"She was attacked by Indians," Zac said.

"Indians!" Iris exclaimed.

"I'm Betty Crane. It was Comanches," the woman said in a soft Southern accent. "They killed my husband, took everything we had, and left me to die."

Iris's gaze flew to Monty. They had spent the night in a Comanche village. How could the Indians

298

have treated them so well and killed this woman's husband?

"There are many different bands of Comanches," Monty explained. "Some of them still hope to drive the white man out of their lands."

Iris remembered the chief saying he had lost many young braves to the warrior chiefs. She wondered if any of the sons of the women who had prepared their food had helped kill this woman's husband.

"I'm so glad you found us," Iris said, trying to drive the fearful images from her head. "You don't have to be afraid anymore."

"I feel safe already," Betty said, looking at Monty. "Mr. Randolph has most kindly offered to take me as far as Cheyenne."

"It won't be any trouble at all," Monty assured her.

Iris couldn't prevent the slight rigidity that made her smile less spontaneous. Their situations were not at all alike, but it hurt to think Monty had been so quick to take Betty under his protection when he was still trying to find a way to get rid of her. Nor could she believe the deference Monty accorded Betty. It was almost as if he was talking to his mother or an aunt.

"Were you able to save anything at all?" Iris asked, wondering why Monty should treat this woman so differently from the way he treated her.

"Nothing," Betty said. "They went through the wagon and took everything they thought they might be able to use. Then they piled everything else back inside and set the wagon on fire. They even took the mules. I imagine they're eating them now."

Iris had never cared for mules; they were ugly and often uncooperative. But she didn't think even the most rebellious mule deserved to be eaten.

Then she remembered the terrible hunger of the Indian women and children. They would eat anything just to stay alive.

"Mrs. Crane wants to go to Dodge," Monty told Iris.

"Please call me Betty. I'll look for work there," she told Iris. "After this, I have no desire to live outside a town."

"I don't blame you," Iris said. "If that had happened to me, I probably wouldn't stop running until I reached the Mississippi." She drew Betty Crane to a place by the fire. "You must be starved. You'll feel better as soon as you get some hot food inside you. Tyler is a marvelous cook."

"Thank you, but I can't sit down and do nothing."

"Yes, you can. After walking so far, your feet must be killing you."

"We don't have anything for you to sit on, ma'am," Monty said. "We sold all of Iris's chairs in Fort Worth, but the boys will find you a log. There's bound to be something along the creek we can use."

"I don't want to be a bother," Betty Crane said.

She had hardly gotten the words out of her mouth before half the men took off toward the creek. Almost immediately Iris could hear them rampaging through the brush, calling back and forth to compare their finds.

"It's not a bother, ma'am," Monty said. "We'll be happy to take care of you."

Monty fell silent. He obviously had something more to say, but he seemed reluctant to continue. Iris found that amazing. He'd never been the least reluctant to say anything to her.

"I don't mean to distress you, ma'am, but I need to know where you were when you were attacked. I want to bury your husband."

"I wouldn't dream of letting you do that," Betty said, fear leaping into her eyes. "They might still be around."

"Marauding Indians generally keep on the move. But just in case, we'll take a couple of our own Comanches. I don't think they'll bother us."

If Iris had been asked to characterize herself, she probably wouldn't have used the word selfless, even though she did believe she was generous, kind, and willing to put herself out for anyone in need. Under no circumstances would she have called herself a jealous woman. There had never been any reason. All her life she had been the center of attention.

But as Iris watched Monty fuss with the log the boys dragged up until he was satisfied it was comfortable, dry, and free of hordes of biting ants, as she listened to him painstakingly describe features of the surrounding countryside until he found one Betty remembered, she felt the demon of jealousy worming its way into her heart. It was so unexpected, so unfamiliar, she didn't even recognize it until one thought ran through her mind like a refrain.

Why didn't Monty treat her like this?

That evening Monty didn't disappear to check on the other herd. He didn't seem the least bit shy about eating his dinner next to Mrs. Crane or about being seen talking to her. He was his most charming, and that was very charming indeed.

When Mrs. Crane got up to refill Monty's plate and bring him some fresh coffee, Iris bit her lip. It had never occurred to her to ask Monty if she could bring him a second helping or freshen his coffee. He had done that for her, several times, and she had accepted it as natural. Now she realized it wasn't. Helena had trained her servants to wait on her and Iris hand and foot. Without realizing it, Iris had grown up expecting everyone to do the same.

As Betty Crane moved from one man to another, refilling plates and coffee cups, thanking each of the men who had searched for the log, assuring the rest she would do her best to see her presence didn't make their work any harder, Iris realized she was looking at a very different kind of woman, one whose relationship to men had nothing to do with money, beauty, or social standing.

Betty would never be considered beautiful. She might be considered nice looking when she got some sleep, had a bath, washed her hair, and put on a nice dress, but she was a rather plain woman. She probably wasn't much older than Iris, but her ordeal had left deep lines in her face that food and rest would only partially erase. There was nothing seductive about her. She was short, flat chested, straight of lines, yet she moved with a quiet grace. The soft gentleness in her voice was almost a caress.

I'm a Southern woman, too. But Iris knew there was a difference between them, a difference the men had sensed immediately. No one had ever offered to find a log for her to sit on. Why?

These thoughts fled when Monty came over and dropped down next to Iris. Her heart beat faster. She told herself to act calm, even to act cool toward him. She wasn't going to let him know she had noticed his absence. She certainly didn't want him to know she had been thinking of him nearly every waking moment.

But she couldn't entirely control her reaction. The body that Monty dropped so casually at her feet was enough to make her temperature soar ten degrees. He simply had no idea how attractive he was. Just thinking of the power of his long legs made her body start to tingle. The arms and shoulders that could throw a full-grown steer to the ground could crush her without being aware of the effort.

But it was his attitude of absolute confidence in himself that had the greatest effect on Iris. If a woman had Monty at her beck and call, she'd have the world at her feet.

"You're going to have to lend Mrs. Crane some of your dresses," Monty said in a low voice. "The one she's wearing is about to fall off. It'll never last until we reach Dodge."

The first sentence he'd said to her in days that wasn't about cows, and it concerned another woman. The stab of disappointment hurt as much as a real pain. But Iris shoved her disappointment aside. Right now they had to help Betty. "She's nowhere near my size."

"I imagine she can cut a dress down to fit," Monty said. "She seems a very capable woman. I'll give her my blanket to sleep on, but I don't know what I can find for a pillow."

Iris bit back a retort. She felt real sympathy for Betty Crane. She knew enough of being alone in the world, of having lost family, to know how she must feel. But she couldn't rid herself of this demon of jealousy. Monty had never worried about finding a pillow for her.

Monty got to his feet. "I hate to leave, but I've got to check on the other herd. You can take care of her for an hour or so, can't you? I'll be back to see if you've got everything settled."

He left. Just like that. After making love to her and then not speaking to her for nearly a week, he walked off into the night, his only concern for some dumb cows and a woman he'd never seen before.

Tears stung Iris's eyes. She had never felt so miserable, so worthless, in all her life. Not only did Monty expect her to be kind to Betty and take care of her—Iris, a woman who'd never even had to take care of herself—he expected her to give Betty some of her clothes, let her cut them up.

But Iris knew it wasn't the clothes and it wasn't Betty. It was Monty. It was always Monty. He worried about Betty Crane's threadbare dress, but he didn't see that Iris's self-esteem was in tatters. He was concerned about providing a warm, comfortable bed for Betty, but he didn't see that Iris was miserable. He meant to risk his life to bury Betty's husband, but he couldn't see that Iris's love was dying of starvation.

As far as Iris could tell, he didn't see her at all.

Betty returned to her seat next to Iris. "I don't want to impose on you," she said, "but I was wondering if you could—"

"I don't have many dresses," Iris said, hoping she could use the smoke from the campfire as an excuse for the tears in her eyes, "but you're welcome to anything you think you can make fit."

"It isn't that," Betty said. "You've provided me with food and protection. I don't need anything else. I was just wondering what I could do to help. I don't want to get in the way, but I feel I ought to do something. I can't ride, or I'd offer to help with the cows."

At least this was something Iris could do. "That won't be necessary," she said. "In fact, the men would prefer it. They'd like to keep me safe in camp, too, but I have to be doing something."

"I'm afraid I'm not very comfortable with this country," Betty admitted. "It's so terribly cruel. I only agreed to go to Texas because David wanted to. I agreed to go to Kansas for the same reason."

"What will you do now?" Iris asked.

"I don't know. I have no place to go."

Iris's heart went out to Betty. It was mean and petty to be jealous of this woman. She deserved every bit of kindness she and Monty could give her.

"You can stay with us as long as you like," Iris said, getting to her feet. Betty rose, too. "If you like, you can go to Wyoming with me. I'm starting a ranch there, and I've been dreading living alone."

"Surely you're not going to attempt to live through those winters by yourself."

"I meant female companionship. My brother will be my foreman. Men are very helpful, but they fall short when it comes to companionship."

"I know," Betty said. "David did his best to provide for me. Poor man, he really wasn't very good at it, but he never realized I wanted his companionship more than anything money could buy."

Neither does Monty, Iris thought. He doesn't realize anything at all.

"Now let's see about finding you somewhere to sleep."

Monty sat his horse on a rise. The panorama of the herd as it stretched over miles of virgin land untouched by any sign of human habitation thrilled his blood. Not even Texas could offer such an unbroken vista.

In two days they would leave Indian territory, and the threat of Indian attack. The dangerous part of the trip was behind them. The rest would be a monotonous trek across Kansas and Nebraska until they reached Wyoming. It was time to bring the two halves of the herd back together. Grass and water were plentiful, and it would be easier to handle.

But it wasn't long before Monty's thoughts turned to Iris. His avoidance of her had been successful as far as the men were concerned, but it had only intensified his feelings. Betty's arrival brought them into even sharper focus.

He felt great sympathy for Betty's plight. She was a gracious woman in need, and it would never have occurred to him not to do everything in his power to help her, just as it wouldn't have occurred to him not to risk an encounter with Indians in order to bury her husband. He would have expected the same of anyone else for himself or his wife. That was the way he had been raised.

But the shocking revelation came when he compared Betty to Iris. He hadn't meant to, but it was inevitable. They were so different. Betty appeared to be everything a sensible man looked for in a wife. Calm, capable, cheerful about any work she had to do, attractive enough to make a man look forward to their nights together.

Iris was everything a sensible man avoided. She was temperamental, too proud to take advice, incapable of performing even the most basic domestic duties, and so beautiful that it was difficult for him to keep his wits about himself.

He had convinced himself that her total unsuitability for life in Wyoming made the thought that kept popping into his head entirely out of the realm of possibility. He might have a bad habit of acting first and thinking later, but he'd never been so lost to common sense as to consider marrying a woman so ill equipped to dealing with the life of a rancher's wife. Yet that was the thought that kept forcing its way out of the mental junk pile into which he repeatedly tossed it.

Monty had never wanted to be anything but a rancher. That was all he really knew. He'd go crazy in a city. Even a small town. He loved the freedom of the plains, the open spaces, the need to pit himself and his skills against the forces of Nature. He was a physical man who loved a physical life.

Iris was just the opposite. She rode with the herd and slept on the ground because he had practically forced her to. She was going to Wyoming because she didn't have any other choice. She knew precious little about cows and apparently even less about keeping a house. The man who married Iris would have to employ a full staff of servants.

The man who married her would also have to move to the city.

But seeing Betty Crane had brought home to Monty that all this didn't change his feelings. He was still crazy about Iris.

Did he love her?

He didn't know. He had never liked any woman enough to ask himself that question. He had spent years wanting to get away from George, but now he wished he could talk to him. George was crazy about Rose. Sometimes Monty thought he was too crazy about her, but somehow George never lost his grip. It seemed his love for Rose meshed perfectly with what he wanted to do with his life.

He wondered about Madison. Fern had been able to make the switch from living on a small ranch in Kansas to running a mansion in Chicago. Maybe Iris could change, too.

But this was the reverse, from comfort to hardship.

Monty cursed and dug his heels into his horse's sides until he fell into a slow gallop. He had spent a week arguing with himself without finding any answers. He had made up his mind to stay away from Iris until they reached Dodge. There he would find her a drover, separate the herds, and let her move on without him. It would be agony to let her go, but he'd been suffering agonies all week long. A final break couldn't be worse than this prolonged torture.

But Betty's arrival had forced him to confront his feelings for Iris, and their intensity surprised him.

Talking to her tonight, being next to her, had destroyed all his resolutions, overset all his carefully thought-out decisions. It made no difference that Iris was a hazard and a liability. He was crazy about her.

He kicked his horse into a hard gallop. He had to reach the second camp quickly. If he thought about Iris any longer, he'd do something desperate.

Betty Crane had made doughnuts. The chuck wagon had stayed in the same place all day while the second herd was being brought up. Iris figured that was the only way Betty could have had time to do so much cooking. She didn't know how Betty managed it over a campfire. She didn't know how Betty had talked Tyler into letting her use his equipment, but there they were, plates and plates of golden-brown doughnuts. There probably wasn't a single food in all the world that cowboys liked half as much.

They nearly went crazy.

"You shouldn't have told us until later," Monty said, stuffing two doughnuts into his mouth. Iris would have sworn there wasn't enough room for one. "Everybody will ruin their dinner."

"I didn't make that many," Betty said, moving the plate out of Monty's reach. "I only made two for everybody."

"I'm the foreman of two crews. I deserve double rations," Monty said.

Betty laughed, then handed him the plate. "I bet you got into a lot of trouble when you were a kid."

"He still gets into a lot," Zac said, snatching an extra doughnut for himself. "He only gets away with it because he's so big and mean." He danced out of Monty's reach.

"He's very kind to let me travel with him," Betty said. "It can't be easy to worry about all those cows and a woman as well."

"It's not that much trouble," Monty said.

Iris's palms itched to slap that silly grin off his face. To think of the things he'd said to her! She hoped he choked on that blasted doughnut.

But there were more signs of Betty's industry to come. Somehow she had coaxed a cow to give milk. Then she'd rummaged around in the brush along the creek until she'd found a nest full of eggs. Having somehow managed to separate the butter from the milk, she had baked a cake. She had made a kind of preserves with fruit and raisins, which she spread between the layers. The men raved over it.

She had also found time to bathe, wash her hair, and cut one of Iris's dresses down to fit her. She looked rather pretty. All during dinner she refilled plates and handed the coffeepot around. Iris had never felt so much like a useless barnacle. She felt as if she had come face-to-face with another perfect-Rose type.

But Iris couldn't blame the men for fawning. Betty already knew half their names, had something to say to each one, and managed to smile and look as if she wasn't doing anything special.

"I have to do something to pay them back for all the extra trouble I'm causing," Betty explained to Iris later. "I don't have any money, but I know how men like something sweet."

Betty's explanation just made Iris feel worse. She hadn't thought of thanking anybody for the trouble she caused them, especially Monty. She'd been far more trouble than Betty Crane ever thought of being.

It wouldn't have done any good if you had. What can you do except bat your eyelashes, wiggle your hips, and look pretty?

Iris had never felt so miserable. How could she have expected Monty or anyone else to fall in love with her? There was nothing about her to love. She'd always thought of herself in terms of money, position, and beauty. As long as she had them, people would love her. And they had. Until she lost the first two.

She had thought her looks would save her, but it was clear that even though Monty was powerfully attracted to her, her looks weren't going to cause him to fall in love with her. As for Hen, well, she didn't even want to think about what Hen thought about her.

Then Betty Crane had showed up—plain, ordinary Betty Crane with nothing more than the clothes on her back—and everybody had started falling over themselves to please her.

Well, Iris had learned a hard, bitter lesson, one she had begun to suspect some time ago. She didn't want to become the kind of woman her mother had wanted her to be. She didn't want to spend her life trying to dazzle men and keep them on a string, to wheedle and cajole and tease until they gave her jewels and clothes and everything else she desired. She didn't want people following at her heels because of her looks.

She wanted to be like Betty. She wanted people to like her for herself. But what was there about her to like? She didn't know how to approach men. She expected them to pursue her. She had been taught to think of them as adversaries in a game of cat and mouse, never as companions. She expected them to take care of her, yet she had never prepared food, set it out, or cleared away afterward. She'd never done anything for anybody but herself.

Iris sighed. How had she managed to live 19 years and learn only part of what it meant to be a woman? Now was a good time to start on the other part, and Betty was the best possible teacher.

"I sure hate having to put up with Randolph, but it's nice to be with you again."

Iris looked up to find Carlos smiling down at her. He dropped down next to her.

"I'm plum wore out. Joe says he's the same."

"I imagine you're glad to see him again."

"Yeah. I got along with that Salty character okay—he's a straight shooter—but it's always nice to get back to friends."

Friends. Iris realized she didn't have any, not any she could count on. The only person she felt she could depend on was Monty, and she'd had to force him into a position where he couldn't do anything else.

"When did she turn up?" Carlos asked, pointing at Betty. "She looks a little fancy for out here."

"That's one of my dresses. Indians killed her husband and took everything she had."

"Poor thing," Carlos said, looking sympathetically at Betty. "She seems to be holding up right fair. Where's she going?"

"Dodge, maybe. I'm not sure."

"She cooks a mean doughnut. The boys will be sorry to see the last of her."

Iris wondered if anybody would be sorry to see the last of her. She wondered if anybody would even notice. She'd been so preoccupied with Monty and her own problems she hadn't noticed it before, but she moved about as though she were in a separate world from the rest of the men. The Randolphs talked to her, except for Hen, but everybody else acted as if she wasn't even there.

Iris watched the grins and cheerful kidding that seemed to spring up wherever Betty went and experienced a new kind of hopelessness. She couldn't do that. Nobody was glad to see her; nobody looked forward to talking to her; nobody seemed happier because she was there.

Nobody except Carlos.

Suddenly Iris made up her mind. She got to her feet. "Come with me. I want to talk with you about something." As soon as they had gotten far enough away so they wouldn't be overheard, Iris turned to her brother. "Have you thought about what I said the other day?"

"Huh?"

"About being my foreman?"

"Yes. I'd like that."

"Good. I'm going to give you half the ranch as well."

Chapter Twenty

"Do you know what you're saying?"

"Of course I do. I'm going to give you half the ranch. You deserve it as much as I do."

"But you don't know a thing about me. I might be a terrible foreman. I might try to kidnap you and take the whole ranch."

Iris laughed. "You can't be a worse rancher than I am. Besides, if I get married, I might *give* you the whole thing."

Of course she didn't mean that, but right now the idea of being relieved of the burden of worrying about the herd had a strong appeal.

"I think I'd like to settle down," Carlos said. "Being footloose isn't as much fun as you'd think."

"I can't imagine it would be any fun at all," Iris said. "Never knowing where you were going to sleep or what you were going to eat. Not to mention not having a roof over your head."

"Not much for the roaming life, are you?"

"None at all. If I ever get done with this horrible drive, I'm going to buy myself a big house, hire a cook and housekeeper, and go shopping for new clothes." She pulled at her riding outfit. It was dusty and worn with overuse. "I'm never going to wear this horrible thing again."

"You can say that. You're rich."

"No, I'm not. Daddy was nearly broke. Everything I have is in front of me. Why else do you think I'm here? That's why I'm counting on you to help me. Besides, half of it is rightfully yours."

"The will left everything to you."

"That doesn't matter. You're just as much Daddy's child as I am."

"It's mighty kind of you to make me your foreman. You don't have to do any more."

"Yes, I do."

"Have you said anything to anybody else?"

"No. Why?"

"Give yourself time to think about it a little more. You might be getting married before long, and your husband probably won't want you giving away your inheritance to a half-breed Mexican bastard."

"Don't ever call yourself that again," Iris said, angrily. "You're Carlos Richmond. Your mother was my father's first wife. She died when you were five."

"You know that's not true."

"It doesn't matter. That's what I'll tell people. Now if I'm ever going to get back in the saddle, I'd better get to bed. There are times when I wish I'd taken Monty's advice."

"What was that?"

"Take the train and meet you in Cheyenne."

"Why didn't you?"

"Insanity, and a determination not to let these cows out of my sight." She looked out over the herd.

For as far as she could see, dark shapes dotted the landscape. The whites and pale yellows of their coats were still visible, but the thousands of dark shades and patterns had begun to merge into one mass. Most moved about slowly, grazing as they went. Some of the calves, their hunger satisfied now that they had been released from the wagon, gamboled about, carefree and unconcerned. Here and there a cow or steer had lain down, tired from the day's long walk, stomach full of the rich grass.

Three cowboys were on patrol, but Iris could see only one, the singer of some doleful lament. Though the song didn't seem to bother the cows, its mournful quality grated on her nerves. Fortunately the singer was moving away from her. Maybe she would be asleep before he returned.

"I wonder if anybody would care what happened to me if I didn't have a herd," Iris muttered, half to herself.

Somebody will always care for a beautiful woman like you.

She could just hear Monty saying it. Yes, maybe somebody would, but that somebody wouldn't be Monty. And if he did, he wouldn't care for her the way everybody seemed to care about Betty.

Iris thought of her big house, servants, parties, and clothes. All during this trip she had kept her spirits up by promising herself she would go back to St. Louis one day, that she would have more of everything than the people who had turned their backs on her. Only now she didn't want to. Her life there seemed as alien to her now as living with cows would have seemed a year ago.

She actually liked some aspects of trail life. She still got tired, but her body had ceased to ache so much at night or be so stiff in the morning. She liked being outside, being up and active. She felt more energetic, more alive. She liked the open spaces as much as she feared the loneliness.

She'd never expected to be a frontier wife, but right now she'd trade everything she had been looking forward to for a ranch house and Monty.

And a cook. He'd leave her if he had to eat her cooking.

Twenty feet away, behind a sprawling thicket of thorn-covered vines, Monty let his muscles relax. Completing Nature's call, a process that had been interrupted when Iris and Carlos paused close by, he buttoned up his pants, his forehead creased in thought.

He couldn't get over the shock of hearing Iris say she planned to give Carlos half of her inheritance. He had always known she was capable of generosity, but this reached into the realm of sacrifice. It represented an outright gift of more than 80,000 dollars and a loss of 15,000 dollars in future income. It meant a serious reduction in Iris's future standard of living. Clearly, this wasn't the same Iris who began the trip little more than two months ago.

Iris had been changing right before his eyes, but he had been too busy assuming she was like her mother and attributing selfish motives to everything she did to put it all together. Along with that discovery came the more disquieting thought that maybe he had never known Iris at all. Maybe he had been so busy *assuming* and *taking for granted* he simply hadn't seen the truth from the beginning.

But that didn't explain why a woman who would give half of everything she owned to an illegitimate half brother who had no legal claim on her would want to go back to the empty life she'd led in St. Louis. It didn't explain what a woman who would risk her life to make a 2,000-mile drive over the prairie to carve out a ranch in the Wyoming wilderness could find to interest her in parties and dress shops. It didn't explain why a woman of Iris's courage and character would be satisfied to become a social butterfly.

So what was the truth about Iris? She had begun to study how to be a rancher, but he doubted she would succeed in the brutal wilderness of Wyoming without a man to help her. Maybe that was why she had given Carlos half her ranch. But if that had been her only reason, she could have just hired him to be her foreman.

Monty told himself he was wasting his time wondering about Iris. In the end she intended to get as far away from Wyoming as possible. What he should do was stay as far away from Iris as possible. He should do everything in his power to forget the feel of her warm skin as he kissed the hollow of her neck. He should wipe from his memory the fragrance that clung to her when she had just bathed in one of the streams they crossed. He should refuse to remember the enchantment in her smile or the laughter in her eyes, the fire in her hair, the gleam in her eye. He should forget the feel of her softness when he held her in his arms, the sweetness of her kiss.

Most of all, he should forget the feeling of contentment he'd felt after they'd made love. He ought to be able to do that. He had put women out of his mind before. But he couldn't escape the feeling that this time was different.

In the days that followed, Iris tried to believe Monty still liked her. She reminded herself time and time again he had warned he wouldn't do anything to jeopardize her reputation with the men. But she started to wish Monty was more bedazzled and less discreet. She didn't care if everybody knew she loved him. She didn't care if the men knew they had made love.

But Monty cared. He continued to be so thoroughly out of temper, even Tyler began casting him questioning glances.

Betty was preparing a turkey when Iris came into camp. Iris didn't know how to lay a fire. She had no idea how to even begin to clean and cook the large bird. She ought to ask Betty to teach her, but that would have to wait.

"Do I seem snobbish to you?" she asked.

"Of course not," Betty replied. She paused in her work, surprised. "Whatever would make you ask that?"

"Well, none of the men come near me."

"I'm sure you're imagining things," Betty said, resuming her task.

"I'm not. I've known it for a long time. It just seems that it's gotten worse lately. If I speak to them, they mumble something and run away like they're afraid."

Zac came hurrying up and dumped a load of firewood at Betty's feet. "They are. Monty'd be on their hide if they didn't keep moving." He turned to Betty. "I'll sure be glad when we let you off at Dodge," he said, completely unconscious of the rudeness of his remark. "We've been using twice the firewood since you got here."

"Sorry to make extra work, but Monty's been so good to me. Cooking his favorite dishes is the least I can do."

"Well, he ate Tyler's cooking before you came, and he didn't die from it."

"But he does love turkey, and it takes a lot of wood to cook a turkey."

Monty had acted as if he'd found a gold mine when he shot that turkey. Tyler had taken one look and said he was fixing braised beef medallions from a steer that had broken its leg and had to be shot. If Monty wanted a gamy turkey, he'd have to cook it himself. Naturally Betty volunteered to cook it for him. Iris tried not to be jealous, but she didn't succeed.

"What did you mean about Monty?" Iris asked Zac.

"He doesn't want any of the men hanging around you. If they so much as speak to you, he glares like a bull about to charge. Why do you think he's always going around like he's got a sore tooth? Usually he laughs so much he gets on George's nerves. He kids Rose so much she locked him out of the house once for a whole week."

That remark raised Iris's spirits for one whole day, but when she had the leisure to study Monty's expression, she didn't find it so forbidding. In fact, it didn't look any different from normal. As far as she could remember, he always went around looking like a thundercloud.

Except when he was around Betty. Then he was all smiles and compliments.

It hurt. There was nothing Iris could do to explain

it away. She found herself wishing, along with Zac, they would reach Dodge soon.

Iris had made up her mind to talk to Monty. She had Zac fetch her horse before she'd finished her breakfast. The minute Monty climbed into the saddle and headed for the herd, Iris rode after him.

"I want to talk to you," she called out over the sound of pounding hooves. She practically had to ride her horse into his to get him to slow down and speak to her.

"What about?" Monty kept his horse at a trot.

"Carlos."

"Wait until tonight. I'm busy right now."

Monty kicked his horse into a canter, but Iris stayed at his side.

"I don't want to wait until tonight. I don't want anybody to overhear us."

"I really don't have time to—"

"Maybe I ought to ask Betty to talk to you for me."

Monty jerked his horse round until he faced Iris. The startled animal threw up his head and half reared in protest. Monty opened his mouth to make a stinging retort, but Iris's beauty hit him like a sledgehammer. He saw her every day. He should be used to it by now. But every now and then it caught him unawares, and he felt as if he was seeing her for the first time.

Surely no one had ever had such deep green eyes. Only once, when gentle spring rains had covered the plains shoulder deep in lush grass, had he seen anything to equal the richness of their color. Just before evening, in the distance where the gently undulating sea of grass rose to meet the blue horizon, the color had been so intense, so deep and true, he would always remember it—and its promise of renewed life.

That same promise was somehow inherent in Iris. He didn't understand it. It wasn't in what she did. It was something imbedded in her character, something that clung so tenaciously to life that everybody around her could feel it. Not even the fiery contrast of her flaming hair nor the sharp edge of her temper could overshadow the feeling that everything about her was too exciting to miss.

Maybe that was what drew him back to her every time he tried to break away.

"What does this have to do with Mrs. Crane?"

"Nothing, but you always seem to have time to talk to her."

"She doesn't stop me in the middle of my work."

"That's because she doesn't have to chase you down on horseback just to get you to listen to her for five minutes," Iris shot back.

Monty thought of the many times he had longed to talk to Iris, to simply sit next to her, the times he had practically had to put on blinders to keep from staring at her. If she ever learned how he nearly lost control every time he saw her, how easy it would be for her to make him do just about anything she wanted, his life wouldn't be worth a dried buffalo chip.

"I thought you wanted to talk about Carlos."

"I do. I want to know how he did with Salty."

"He hardly knows enough to keep out of his own way."

Iris made an obvious attempt to control her temper. "Salty told me he did very well."

"He was being kind."

"He'd know a whole lot more if you'd *be kind* enough to teach him what to do."

Monty stared at her as if she'd lost her mind. "Do I look like a school marm to you?"

"No, but—"

"Or do you think I just decided to come on this trip so I could do your bidding?"

"No, but—"

"From the minute you set foot in Texas, you've had a list of things you wanted me to do. You wanted me to round up your herd, take you to Wyoming, protect you from Frank, find your lost cows, fix your wagon, save you from a stampede—"

"I never asked you to do that."

"—save your cattle from Indians. Now you want me to teach your brother how to manage a herd."

"He's going to be my foreman when we get to Wyoming," Iris explained. "I'm going to give him half my herd."

"I know, and I think you're crazy."

"You know!" Iris repeated, stunned.

"I overheard you tell him a few nights ago."

Iris swelled with indignation. "You can't spare five minutes to talk to me, but you can sneak around eavesdropping on my conversations?"

"I didn't do any such thing. You caught me . . . uh . . . I was just . . . I had to go to the bushes," Monty confessed. "You were talking close by. I couldn't leave without you knowing."

"So you stayed hidden and listened to every word."

"Would you rather I had come running out hitching up my pants?"

She was glad he hadn't, but that didn't make her any happier he'd heard everything she said.

"You ought to think about this some more," Monty advised. "If I were you, I'd send Carlos on his way."

"You're not me."

"Then hire yourself an experienced foreman, and let him teach Carlos what to do."

"All I want you to do is let him ride with you. You don't have to spend a lot of time telling him things. He can figure it out by watching you."

Monty pulled up. "This conversation is going to take a while, isn't it?"

"If you insist upon being so stubborn."

"I'm only trying to be realistic," Monty said, turning toward a single oak that grew in the dip between two ridges, "but I don't expect you to see that."

"Naturally," Iris said, turning her horse to follow him. "Women never do."

"Running a ranch isn't simple."

"It can't be that hard. Any fool who buys himself a few cows can call himself a rancher."

"Any fool who buys himself a boat can call himself a ship's captain," Monty responded, his temper flaring, "but I imagine you'd expect a little more of him before you set sail on his ship."

Iris had let her temper betray her into saying something she hadn't meant. Now Monty was angry. Very angry.

"All I want you to do is help Carlos learn about cows," Iris said as they halted in the shade of the oak. "It might not take much work."

"It will."

"Well, I'll make a trade with you," Iris snapped, her temper glowing just as hot as Monty's. "I'll take care of Mrs. Crane. You can use the extra time to teach Carlos."

Monty's gaze narrowed. "Is this about Carlos or about Betty?"

"Carlos. But you wouldn't have to worry about *Mrs. Crane* anyway. Just about every man on the crew is falling over himself to take care of her."

"You're jealous," Monty said, the light of unholy glee in his eyes. "You've got more wealth and beauty than that poor woman will ever have, yet you're jealous of her."

Iris dismounted and looked at Monty across the saddle. "I have a great deal more than *wealth and beauty*, but it certainly doesn't seem to have much of an impact."

"What do you mean by that?" Monty demanded. He dismounted between the two horses.

Iris hadn't meant to say anything, but her hurt and anger had been festering for days. She tried to hold it back, but she couldn't.

"I mean that ever since that night in the Comanche camp, you have done just about everything you could outside of abandoning the herd and going back to Texas to avoid spending so much as five minutes with me. If I'd known it was going to upset you so much, I'd have asked to sleep in the chief's tepee."

"I should have slept outside."

"Well, you didn't."

"No."

"And?"

"And what?"

"That's what I was going to ask you."

"I warned you I couldn't stay in that tent and calmly go to sleep, not with you only a few feet away."

"But you can walk into camp with me only a *few feet away* and not even notice I'm there."

"I told you I couldn't make any promises."

"I'm not asking you to make promises." She had prayed he would, but she was realistic enough to know it wasn't likely now. "I just want us to be like we were before. I enjoyed eating dinner with you, talking to you about the day's work. I like you, Monty. I enjoyed being with you."

That was such a perversion of the truth as to make it practically a lie, but it was as close as she could come without telling him she loved him. She couldn't admit that just yet, not when he seemed to have no feeling for her beyond an uncontrollable physical appetite.

"That night was a mistake," Monty said, his voice tight, his gaze sliding past hers.

Iris didn't think anybody had ever said anything that hurt her so much. After giving Monty a part of herself she could never give anyone else, he was rejecting her. Iris felt a terrible constriction in her chest, as if her heart was being crushed and she couldn't breathe.

Nothing had ever affected her like this. A year ago she might have been surprised and hurt at his rejection, but she would have been far too angry to feel the pain. She would have been determined to show him how utterly indifferent she was to him. Rather than sit about thinking of ways to get him back, she would have worked out at least a dozen schemes to make him regret what he'd done.

Instead she'd spent hours, *days*, thinking of what she had done wrong, wondering how she might have done things differently, wondering if she could find a way to rekindle his interest in her.

Well, she wouldn't beg. Her pride and self-respect were in tatters, but she had some small portion left. Still she couldn't prevent the tears from welling in her eyes, nor the teardrops from running down her face.

She looked away. "I didn't realize my presence had become objectionable. I didn't mean. . . . But it's too late now. What's done is done. I'll move back to my camp. But I would appreciate it if you'd let Carlos—"

Monty dropped the reins and came around her horse. He took Iris by the shoulders and spun her around to face him. Iris didn't possess the strength to stop him, but she lowered her face so he wouldn't see her tears.

"It was a mistake to think I could spend a night in your arms and not want to do it again and again," Monty said. "I was a fool to think the memory wouldn't torture me every hour of the day."

Iris couldn't find the will to resist when Monty kissed her. She knew she should. She was only torturing herself by giving in to the need to be in his arms once more, to feel the heat of his desire warm her all the way to her soul. She told herself there was no comfort in his arms, that his strength was an illusion. But her perfidious heart overruled her mind, and she melted into his embrace.

Being in Monty's arms seemed to recreate the magic of the evening in the tepee. Once again Iris experienced the bliss of knowing Monty desired her, of sensing his longing for her in every fiber of her being. Once again she recalled the happiness she felt when she believed his love was for more than a night. Once again she remembered in vivid detail what it meant to be loved by a man like Monty.

Iris felt her willpower eroding quickly. If she didn't back away now, she never would. She would lose all power to think for herself.

Marshaling her dwindling resources, she pulled out of Monty's embrace. "You don't seem tortured to me," she said, turning her face to one side. "I've never seen you act so charming as you are with Betty."

Monty tried to take her in his arms once more, but she moved away.

"You are jealous of Betty," he said.

"No," Iris said, turning her head away to keep from having to look at him. "I'm just hurt that you seem to enjoy her company so much more than mine."

She couldn't tell him it hurt to see him treat the other woman with a kind of deference, kindness, and thoughtfulness he had never shown to her. With Betty's situation being so much worse than her own, it sounded selfish and petty.

"I told you I couldn't make any promises."

"And I told you I'm not asking for any."

"Then what are you asking for?"

For him to love her as much as she loved him. For him to want to spend every minute of every day with her. For him to think her the most precious human being in the history of the world. But he had already told her that was impossible. So what was left? Her dignity. It was a poor substitute, but it was all she had left. Iris forced herself to look Monty in the eye.

"I want you to treat me like you do Betty."

"I don't understand."

"Every day I get up at dawn and eat my breakfast squatting on the ground. Then I spend the day in a saddle riding herd, chasing runaways, helping the herd ford one river or stream after another. Every night I drag into camp too tired to care whether I eat anything at all. I even take an occasional turn on night watch, but I still feel like a burden. Betty walks into camp and in five minutes there's not a man on two legs who wouldn't break his back to look after her. Why?"

Monty looked uncomfortable. "You're different."

"I know. I'm rich and beautiful, remember, and she's poor and alone. But everybody treats me like it's the other way around."

"Men don't know what to do with a woman like you. Not ordinary men," Monty said, looking as if he didn't know quite what to say. "You've got too much of everything. It scares them off. They understand Betty. She's one of them."

Iris didn't know if she was crazy or if Monty was. She'd never heard such a silly excuse in her life. "Don't you mean *us*?"

"No, I don't. I stayed away from you because I needed to think, and I can't do it when I'm around you. I never could. Not even when you were a freckle-faced sprite who dogged my heels like a mongrel pup."

"I never did," Iris said, suddenly feeling a warm flush all over.

"You were the talk of the county." He smiled. Not his wide, flashing grin, just a lopsided, reluctant, halfhearted, almost shy grin. Iris found it totally endearing.

"Did you figure anything out?" she asked.

"Yeah."

"What?"

"We're no good for each other."

A cold chill flushed away the warmth of his smile.

"Do you mind explaining that?"

"We don't want the same things."

"How do you know what I want? You never asked."

"I heard you tell Carlos you wanted houses and clothes and servants."

She wanted to tell him that she hadn't meant it, but she doubted he'd believe her. "You shouldn't believe everything you hear."

"You want that night in the tepee to mean something, too."

"Didn't it?"

"You're a beautiful woman, Iris. A man can't help wanting to make love to you, but that doesn't mean—" Monty seemed to grope for words.

"That it means any more to you than a roll in the hay."

"That's not what I was going to say."

"But it's what you meant. You have no plans to turn your back on all the other females in the world, get married, settle down, and raise a family."

The look of horror on Monty's face was more eloquent than words.

Iris drew herself up. Her pride wouldn't let Monty see he had broken her heart. "Well, I want someone who's willing to do more than come looking for me when he's in the mood. You just teach Carlos how to manage a ranch, and I promise I won't expect anything of you ever again."

Iris jumped on her horse and galloped away.

Monty started after her, but stopped. If he followed, it would be the same as saying he wanted her to share his future. He didn't want to give her up, but he wasn't prepared to keep her on those terms.

His heart ached for the pain she must be suffering, but it would be better if she believed he cared less than he did. He would not give her false hope. He wouldn't lie to her.

But wasn't he lying to himself?

*   *   *

Betty was cooking prairie chicken and dumplings when Iris stumbled into camp. Iris stared, unable to believe her eyes.

"Monty kept complaining he never had anything normal to eat," Betty explained. "Tyler is a wonderful cook, but Monty likes plain food best."

"She had me crawling through those trees on my hands and knees," Zac complained indignantly. "You ever try to catch a prairie chicken by throwing a rain slicker over it?" He rolled up his sleeves to show Iris the scratches he had gotten in the brush. "I hope Monty chokes."

"You can have some, too," Betty said. "There's plenty."

"You ain't never seen Monty eat when he likes what he's eating," Zac said. "He'll take the pot and eat until it's empty. There won't be no seconds."

Iris hated the horde of uncharitable feelings that thronged her heart, but at that moment she would have given half her herd to have Betty Crane back on the prairie walking toward some other trail crew.

Would she ever be as good as this woman?

Betty was always thinking of others, always helping somebody, doing something special, little things that only a woman would think of. A woman who had been trained to be a wife and housekeeper, not a woman who had been trained to be a social ornament.

Betty didn't know how to be an ornament. Iris hadn't known how to be anything else.

But she was learning. She'd show Monty Randolph she was more than a spoiled, rich woman concerned only with beauty, wealth, and adoration. She'd been taught to live that way, but she didn't want to. She hadn't for a long time. But she'd never fully understood the difference until Betty arrived.

She should be thankful she had learned the lesson so soon. Instead she found it hard to accept that Betty Crane had to be the instrument of her learning.

Iris had ridden the entire length of the herd looking for Carlos. She pulled up when she found Joe working drag.

"Have you seen Carlos?" she asked, nearly choking on the dust. "I can't find him anywhere." Joe didn't seem to mind the dirt and the stench of riding with the tail of the herd. Iris hated it.

"He rode out with Monty midmorning. Monty said that if he was going to be your foreman he needed to know how to scout a trail."

Iris's mouth fell open. She couldn't understand what had caused Monty to work with Carlos after he had told her he wouldn't.

"You look surprised," Joe said. "Monty said it was your idea. You wanted Carlos to learn how to manage a herd."

Iris had overheard quite a few pithy curses during the drive. She tried out a couple and found them rather satisfying. She aired out every curse she could remember and a few she made up.

Joe laughed at her. "I thought you liked Monty. I thought he was the closest thing on earth to your savior."

"Don't be sacrilegious," Iris snapped. "I used to think Monty was a gentleman, but I know better now."

"Good. I hated to see you looking at him with cow eyes."

"I *never* looked at him with cow eyes," Iris said

furiously. "As a matter of fact, I can't stand him. And if it comes to that, I can't stand cows and ranches and dust and this continual bawling and stench." Why should she try? It wouldn't make Monty love her. He had taken her honor, and now he wanted to move on.

"Wait until you try to survive a Wyoming winter."

"I'm not at all sure I'm going to," Iris said.

"What do you mean?" Joe asked, the sneer wiped off his face, his expression suddenly intent.

Iris was too busy trying to think of what she could do to irritate Monty the most to take much notice of the change in Joe.

"I have a good mind to leave the drive at Dodge and let Carlos take the herd to Wyoming. He could even run the ranch while I go back to St. Louis. Or Chicago. Maybe even New York."

"What for?"

"To find the richest, most handsome, most ferocious husband in the world. Then come back here and show Monty Randolph he's not nearly half the man he thinks he is."

Iris smiled with satisfaction. The more she thought about the idea, the more it pleased her to think of Monty being beaten at his own game.

"I don't think that's such a good idea," Joe said.

"I think it's a wonderful idea," Iris contradicted. "All those fancy, rich Eastern men want a woman who's just as fancy."

"I may not be rich," Iris admitted, "but I'm just as respectable as any of them."

"It wouldn't make any difference if you was rich as John Jacob Astor. Ain't one of those snooty men going to marry a bastard."

"What are you talking about?" Iris asked. Joe's

remark made so little sense she wondered if she had heard him correctly.

"You're a bastard," Joe said, too clearly for Iris to doubt her hearing. "Your ma ran off with a two-bit clerk in a dry-goods store. He threw her out after a month. Robert Richmond married her just to keep her decent."

Iris's entire body went numb, as though she had ceased being able to feel anything.

"That's not true," she managed to say.

"Sure it is. Ask Monty if you don't believe me."

"Monty knows!"

"Sure. All the Randolphs know."

Chapter Twenty-one

Iris wanted to die.

She thought of some of the things she had done, some of the things she had said, and hoped she would never have to meet anyone she knew ever again. Most especially she hoped she would never have to come face-to-face with Monty.

"I don't understand. Surely my f-father"—She couldn't help stumbling over the word—"wouldn't have told anybody."

"Your old man showed up trying to put the squeeze on Richmond. Said he'd tell everybody in Austin and San Antonio if Richmond didn't pay him twenty thousand dollars. Helena nearly had a fit, but Monty got rid of him for her. Nobody could understand why though, not when she'd been making a play for George."

"I don't believe you," Iris cried. Each disclosure felt like a physical blow, one coming right after the other until she reeled from the impact. "You're lying to me. Why? What do you want?"

None of these things could be true. They were too horrible.

"You ever hear about that fight Monty had in Mexico, the one where he killed the fella?"

Oh, God! Monty had killed her father to keep him from telling the world she was his bastard daughter! And she had spent the past two months accusing him of every petty misdeed she could think of. And after he had risked his life to protect her reputation.

Iris felt sick with shame.

What must Monty think of her? She couldn't look like anything except a spoiled, shallow female willing to do just about anything to get what she wanted. She had told him she wanted a husband so besotted he would do anything she asked. He had overheard her tell Carlos she wanted houses, clothes, and parties—all the things a stupid, foolish woman would prize over honesty, dependability, and courage. She had convicted herself with her own words.

And that night in the tepee! She had wanted Monty to make love to her. She had virtually asked him to. She cringed at the memory. Looking at the situation as Monty must see it, she could see how he might think she would do anything, no matter how disgraceful, to get whatever she wanted. Her mother and father had. Why should anybody expect anything different from her?

With a groan, Iris turned and galloped away. She didn't stop until she reached the scattered cottonwoods and brush that grew along the creek. Flinging herself from her horse, she staggered blindly among the trees. She leaned against a small cottonwood and was violently sick.

Her whole life seemed to come crashing down before her eyes. She was a sham, a fake, as common as any drunk or vagrant she had ever looked down on. She wasn't as good as the illiterate Mexican servants her mother had despised. Not only was she a bastard child, she was the daughter of a blackmailer.

And Monty had known all along.

Another wave of nausea shook her body. In the depths of such misery as she had never known, Iris didn't know how she would ever be able to face him again.

When at last the convulsions no longer wrenched her body, Iris stood up. Her horse had disappeared. She headed toward camp, but the sight of Betty and Tyler moving about making preparations for dinner filled her with horror. She couldn't go back there. If people had avoided her before, they would shun her now. Stumbling as she ran, Iris hurried to the remuda. Blindly she caught up a horse and started to saddle him.

"You can't ride John Henry," Zac called out. "That's one of Monty's horses." Zac bumped his head as he jumped up from where he had been dozing under the chuck wagon. He erupted with a stream of curses.

Iris backed away from the horse as if she expected it to attack her. She caught up a zebra dun. It was too ugly and small to belong to any of the Randolphs. Taking a firm hold of the mane, she pulled herself on to his back. Turning the horse toward the rope, Iris kicked it in the ribs. The horse shot forward, jumped the low-slung rope, and headed toward the open prairie at a gallop.

"Come back here!" Zac shouted.

"Where is Iris going?" Betty Crane asked.

"I don't know," Zac said, "but I tried to stop her. You've got to tell Monty I tried to stop her."

"Why?"

"He'll skin me alive for letting her go off like that. He's crazy in love with her."

"I didn't realize that," Betty said.

"Neither does Monty," Tyler said, looking after Iris, his usually expressionless face furrowed with worry. "And neither does Iris."

Monty was feeling good. They were only two days out of Dodge. The hardest part of the journey was over. He had paid off the Comanches and sent them back to their people with enough beef to get them through the winter. Because of Dodge's reputation as a lawless town, he was planning to pass about ten miles to the west, so he had sent Hen and Salty ahead to hire some new hands and buy enough supplies to take them to Ogalalla.

But that wasn't the real reason he was feeling so good.

His indecision was past. He had decided he had been stupid to stay away from Iris. That was no way to solve anything. He had a feeling he might be in love with her. While the idea scared him practically to death, it excited him as well. He didn't know what he wanted out of life, but he knew he wanted it to include Iris. He couldn't wait to tell her.

"She didn't say where she was going?" Monty asked. He had been surprised to find Iris away from camp. He had warned her over and over again of the danger of going anywhere alone.

· "Nope," Zac replied, being careful to keep a safe distance between himself and his brother.

"That's not like her."

"I can't help that. She just threw herself on that zebra dun and lit out of here like a panther was after her."

"Do you have any idea where she was going?" Monty asked, turning to Betty Crane.

"No. She appeared to be upset about something, but she didn't say anything to me."

"Do you know?" Monty asked Tyler.

"It wasn't Hen," Tyler said. "He wouldn't do that."

"I know." No matter what Hen said to Monty about Iris, he would never utter a word to anybody else.

"There might be Indians out there," Betty asked, obviously worried. "I came from that direction."

"We've left Indian territory. How long has she been gone?"

"Not long," Zac said.

"About half an hour," Tyler corrected.

Monty looked uneasy. "If she doesn't show up by noon, I'll have to go after her."

Everybody stared at him.

"You can't go," Zac said, looking at Monty like he was crazy. "There's nobody to be in charge except you."

"Well we can't just leave her out there," Monty said. "Knowing Iris, if she headed for Dodge, she'd end up in Indian territory."

"I imagine she'll turn up soon," Tyler said. "She might have a poor sense of direction, but she's a right sensible girl."

"You better see somebody about eyeglasses the minute we get to Denver," Zac told Tyler.

"I don't need glasses," Tyler said.

"You do if you're thinking Iris looks like a sensible girl."

Monty made no attempt to hide his ill temper. He paced back and forth between the campfire and the remuda. Every minute or so he would erupt with a string of curses, break, smash, or throw something, then start pacing more furiously than ever. Tyler ignored him. Betty watched him with trepidation. Zac kept as far away from him as possible. No one spoke to him.

He was in a quandary for which he could find no satisfactory answer. He had to go after Iris. But if he did, he would have to abandon his responsibility for the herd. There was no possible way he could do both.

He couldn't wait long enough to send someone to Dodge to bring Hen and Salty back. There was no one else with any experience heading up a drive. At this moment he would even have welcomed Frank back.

That just shows how desperate you are. Hen said you'd ruin yourself over this woman. Why don't you send somebody else? Why not Carlos?

But he couldn't remain in camp not knowing what might be happening. It could be several days before anybody found her.

What could have made her run away? Iris had a volatile temper, but she didn't do stupid things. She knew how dangerous it was out there. All the more reason for Monty to worry. Whatever was wrong was serious.

Which brought him back to his initial problem. He had to go after her now, but he couldn't do so without leaving the herd virtually unattended. Monty uttered another string of curses and walked a little faster.

Then he stopped in his tracks. There was no decision to be made. He had known from the beginning he was going after Iris, so why was he wasting his time over a decision that was already made when he ought to be thinking about what to do next?

Monty felt a great weight fall away. Then he remembered something he once heard Rose say and felt even better. *Any man can do a good job when the answers are easy. It's how he does when there are none but hard decisions that measures him.* Well, this was a hard decision, probably the hardest of his life, but he'd made the only decision he could. If he could live with it, everybody else would have to as well.

Feeling like his old self again, Monty set off to tell Tyler that he had been promoted from cook to drover.

"But I don't want to be in charge," Tyler protested. "I came along to cook, not ramrod this drive."

"Let me," Zac pleaded. "I can do it."

"Carlos will help you," Monty said, ignoring Zac. "According to Iris, about a quarter of the herd will soon be his."

Several gazes turned to Carlos, new interest and curiosity in them. Tyler ignored Carlos and gave his brother a hard look. "You've got no business doing this, and you know it."

"Carlos ought to be in charge," Joe said.

"This is a Randolph drive," Monty said, leveling Joe with a steady, unnerving gaze. "And nobody ramrods a Randolph drive but a Randolph."

"Even if he's the cook?" Betty looked skeptical.

Monty turned to Betty. "Don't let Tyler fool you. He may look like a monk, but he's tough as shoe leather."

"What about me?" Zac asked.

"You're as hardheaded as a dried oak stump, but you might turn out okay yet. You got that food ready?" Monty asked, turning back to Tyler. His brother handed him the bulging saddlebags. "What did you pack?"

"Beans and bacon," Tyler said. "Even you can cook that."

"I'd better hope so," Monty said, with a quick grin. "Iris sure can't."

"Are you sure you can't wait until Hen and Salty get back?"

"Even if I sent someone now, it would be past midnight before Hen could get back. I can't leave Iris alone out there at night."

"You could send one of the men," Betty suggested.

"I ought to be the one going after her," Carlos said. "She's my sister."

"Yeah, he ought to go," Joe agreed. "I can handle the herd for him."

Monty faced the two men. Much to his own surprise, he didn't experience the wave of anger that usually swept over him when his actions were questioned. Neither did he feel his usual irritation that Iris had saddled him with two men he neither respected nor trusted. He had found himself faced with a difficult situation. He had thought it through and made the only decision he could make. Everyone else would just have to accept it.

"I'm going after Iris, and Tyler's in charge here. Anyone who doesn't like that arrangement had better saddle up and ride out ahead of me. That okay with you, Carlos?"

"I guess, but I don't like it."

Monty didn't waste time on Joe. "I'll hold you responsible for your friend," he told Carlos as he swung into the saddle. He was riding Nightmare. "I don't know when I'll get back. Hen and Salty ought to be back by tomorrow afternoon. If I'm lucky, I'll be back before them."

"What if you don't find her?" Betty asked.

Monty hadn't let himself think of that question. It was a possibility he couldn't accept. "I'll keep looking until I do."

Monty hadn't been gone five minutes when he heard a horse galloping hard behind him. He turned to see Carlos coming toward him. Puzzled, he pulled up and waited.

"I found out why Iris ran away," Carlos said as soon as he pulled alongside Monty.

"Why didn't you tell me before?" Monty asked, irritated Carlos should have waited so long.

"I didn't know then."

"Know what?"

"Joe told Iris about her father. Her *real* father."

Anger swept over Monty with the speed of the north wind, but it wasn't a hot anger. It was cold and deadly. He resisted the temptation to ride back and beat Joe Reardon until he begged for mercy. He had to find Iris. In her state she might do anything.

"Thanks," Monty said. "Now you'd better get back. I know Reardon is your friend, but you can tell him that if he's still around when I get back, he'll answer to me for this."

"Joe didn't mean—"

"You can also tell him I don't intend to accept his reasons, no matter what they are."

Monty turned and rode off, a new urgency riding with him. He didn't know all the crazy ideas Helena had tried to teach Iris, but he would have bet his herd she had drummed into Iris's head the importance of family and birth and position in society. Learning she was the bastard daughter of a common clerk could make Iris desperate enough to do just about anything.

Monty found her a half an hour after dusk. She was riding along the crest of a ridge, silhouetted against the sky, perfectly visible to anyone within miles, friend, outlaw, or Indian.

Since Monty had spent the whole afternoon worrying about her, his nerves were stretched taut, his stomach balled in a hard knot. He had endured eight horrible hours of imagining nearly every awful thing that could happen to her, from a rattlesnake bite to being thrown from her horse. His relief was nearly physical. So was the rush of anger that she should have done anything so incredibly dangerous.

Iris seemed to be retracing her path through the grass. She was concentrating so hard she didn't see him coming until he was about 50 yards away. When she turned, she seemed not to recognize him for a moment. Then with a cry, she drove her horse down the rise and across the prairie.

Damn! What did she mean by running from him? Didn't she know he had come to help? Nightmare's long, powerful strides ate up the distance between them with incredible swiftness.

"Go away! Leave me alone!" Iris cried when Monty came alongside.

Monty reached out and grasped her horse's bridle. He brought them both to such an abrupt stop that Iris nearly fell off. She fought to wrench the reins out of his hand. When Monty proved too strong, she slid off her horse and started running through the waist-high grass. Riding after her, Monty came alongside her and bent low from the saddle. Slipping his arms around her waist, he lifted her off the ground.

"Put me down and go away! I don't want to talk to you!" Iris kicked and hit him with her fists, but she couldn't break his hold on her.

"Stop it, dammit!" Monty grunted, his teeth clenched from the physical effort of holding her off the ground. With a mighty heave of powerful muscles, he hoisted Iris into the saddle before him. "We're going to talk, but I can't very well do it with you dashing across the hillside."

"You can't want to have anything to say to the bastard daughter of a blackmailer," Iris sobbed. Her struggles ceased and she collapsed against his chest. "Randolphs don't associate with people like that."

"That just shows how little you know about me," Monty said. His arms tightened around Iris. "I like beautiful redheads no matter what."

"You can't like me. Not knowing who my father was."

Monty made a noise that sounded like a cross between a snort of contempt and an embittered laugh. "My father turned vicious when he got drunk, gambled away the family fortune, seduced I don't know how many women, killed at least one man in a duel, and is rumored to have stolen a half-million-dollar payroll during the war. Compared to him, your father was up to no more than Sunday-afternoon pranks."

"Did he really kill somebody?" Iris asked, her tears momentarily stopped.

"He seduced his best friend's sister, then forced a duel on him."

"But you're not illegitimate."

"I would rather be the bastard son of an honest cowhand than the spawn of that son of a bitch. Where do you think I get my hellish temper, or Hen his readiness to kill? That man's foul blood is in us all."

Iris desperately wanted to believe Monty, but what about the rest? "That wasn't all Joe told me."

Monty pulled Nightmare to a halt. "What else did he say?"

"It was about my mother. And George."

Monty sighed as though he knew he was getting into more trouble by talking than by keeping quiet. "I guess you'll have to know sooner or later."

"Then it's true."

"I don't know. Depends on what Joe told you."

"That my mother made a play for George. That you killed my father."

Monty started back toward Iris's horse, which was grazing 100 yards away. "Damn! The bastard didn't leave anything out, did he?"

Oh, God, it was true! She had hoped it wasn't. All day she'd tried to think of some reason Joe would have lied to her. But he hadn't. Monty's reaction proved it.

Monty sighed again. "A couple of years ago, I sort of developed a crush on Helena," he began. "Not that there was anything unusual in that. Practically every man who set eyes on Helena fell in love with on her the spot."

Iris had a sick feeling in the pit of her stomach. How could she love a man who'd been in love with her mother? "Did you fall in love with her?"

"Good God, no!" Monty exclaimed, startled.

Iris experienced an enormous feeling of relief. She had never expected she would be the only woman Monty had ever loved, but she couldn't have stood it if the other woman had been her mother.

"But Helena pursued me. She asked me all kinds of questions about the ranch and George and Rose. Fool that I was, I didn't see what she was after."

"What was that?"

"Helena knew long before everybody else that your father was getting short of money. She was looking for her next husband, and she had set her sights on George."

Iris felt her face flame with mortification. Marrying Robert Richmond to give her child a name was one thing. Attempting to break up a happy marriage so she could marry a rich man was quite another.

Iris's horse had his head buried in the tall grass when they came up to him. Monty hooted, and the startled animal threw up his head. Monty caught hold of the reins. He tied them to the saddle and continued on.

"Rose has always wanted a house full of children, so she was delighted a couple years ago when she found she was expecting a baby. But right from the first everything seemed to go wrong. She was sick a lot. The baby came too early and died. Rose had a very difficult time getting over it. Took her nearly a year. She never was as pretty as Helena, but she was real worn down for quite some time. I guess Helena thought George would be easy prey, what with Rose so sick and peaked looking."

Iris wondered if there was anything else her parents had done that would make her feel still more worthless and misbegotten.

"Helena used to come over to the house pretending to be worried about Rose, but she was really making up to George. It didn't do her any good.

George never could see anybody but Rose, but Helena said some things that hurt Rose. I came in one day and found her crying. I was so all-fired mad I could have singed the hair off Helena's head. I went to her house and told her if she ever said anything else to make Rose cry I was going to tell Robert what she was doing.

"I was fool enough to think she would be embarrassed at being caught and that would be the end of it. The words were hardly out of my mouth when she started screaming like she was being attacked by Apaches. The whole household came running. She told Robert I had tried to make love to her, right there in the front parlor, mind you, and the poor fool believed her. He marched me out of the house at the end of a shotgun. Told me if I ever came back he'd fill me full of buckshot."

"What happened then?"

"Nothing. I never went back and Rose got better."

"What about my father?"

Monty regarded Iris uneasily. "I never knew your father. When I ran into him in Mexico, he was just a stranger trying to pick a fight. I shouldn't have hit him so hard, but he said some terrible things about George and Rose. I left Mexico two days later. That same day he was killed in a knife fight. Helena liked to tell people I was so crazy in love with her I had killed him for her. Some people still believe it."

Iris cringed at the memory of having once accused Monty of killing a man in a fight. It seemed that everything she ever said to him had taken on a new and unsuspectedly cruel meaning.

"Now I understand why you disliked me for such a long time."

"I never disliked you." Monty's reserve fell away. He was once again a man eager to convince a woman of his feelings for her.

"Then why did you walk out on me that night at the party?"

The uneasiness came back. His gaze slid away from direct contact. "I was afraid you'd be like your mother. You looked so much like her."

Iris looked at him with a blank stare.

"The only Iris I knew was a tomboy who followed me about getting in the way all the time. I couldn't identify her with the femme fatale I saw that evening."

Now it was Iris who couldn't look Monty in the eye. Both her parents had tried to hurt him, and she had tried to take advantage of him, yet he was still looking after her, still worried about her. He had even left his herd to come find her. What had she done except be trouble from the first day to the last?

"Any more questions?"

Iris shook her head.

Monty relaxed. "Then I want you to forget all of this," he said. "It's over and done with."

"How can I? My father tried to kill you, and my mother tried to break up your brother's marriage. You ought to hate me."

"It didn't take me long to find out you aren't anything like your parents. Each time you've been faced with a problem, you've done something Helena would never do."

If she could just be sure he wasn't saying all this just to make her feel better. She had never given Monty any credit for kindness—he'd always been so rough on her—but she did now. She now saw that he had been nothing but kindness from the start. She had been too self-absorbed to see it.

*Nothing has changed. You're still thinking of no
one but yourself, and he's still having to neglect his
responsibilities to look after you.*

"You ought to go away and leave me to go to
Wyoming by myself," Iris said. "I've been nothing
but trouble."

"I thought you wanted to go back to St. Louis."

That startled Iris. She hadn't thought of St. Louis
in so long she could hardly remember having sworn
to go back.

"I used to. I wanted to show them I was every
bit as good as they were." She thought of Anna
and Jane, Lloyd, Tom, and Calvin—all the people
whose good opinion she had considered essential nine months ago. They wouldn't approve of
her being on this drive; they especially wouldn't
approve of her being alone with Monty. Yet she
wouldn't change one thing she had done if she
could. "I don't feel that way anymore. I realized
right after you overheard me talking to Carlos I
didn't want to go back. It's just as well. No one in
St. Louis would speak to me once they found out
who my father really was."

"It doesn't matter."

"Yes, it does."

"It doesn't matter to me."

Iris really wanted to believe him, but Monty had
never lived in towns or cities. He didn't know the
power of society or the importance of what other
people thought of you. And he had no idea that
other people's opinions could be based entirely on
the nature of a person's birth.

He had no idea that being born a bastard
was only a little less terrible than being a
whore.

"Maybe not now when you're hundreds of miles from anywhere," Iris said, "but your family wouldn't think that way. And you wouldn't either, not if it concerned your wife or children."

"You've got a lot to learn about the Randolphs," Monty said, "one thing in particular."

They were descending into a hollow between two ridges. Iris saw the beginning of bushy growth a short distance away. A little farther on a ribbon of trees in the bottom of the hollow betokened the presence of a stream. Monty evidently intended to make camp here for the night rather than attempt to return to the herd.

She had been wondering what he meant to do. She had found retracing her steps nearly impossible even in the light. Now that it was dark, she couldn't imagine how he could find his way back to camp. Everything looked the same to her.

"We don't care what other people think," Monty was saying. "George married Rose even though her father fought for the Yankees and we all wanted him to get rid of her. Madison married Fern even though he knew he wouldn't be able to go back to Boston."

"And you?"

"I've been telling people to go to hell ever since I was old enough to say the words."

The shadows deepened as they traveled deeper and deeper into the vale between the ridges. Salmon and bluish purple streaked the sky above, but the fading light didn't reach them. They seemed to be sinking into a greenish-gray haze that hovered a few feet above the deep grass. She could make out the faint sound of water from a spring trickling over gravel and among the clumps of grass to grow into a stream. An occasional bird chattered, disturbed on its roost. Even in the still air of the early evening, the cottonwoods rustled noisily.

Iris leaned into the curve of Monty's arm. He thought he didn't care, but he would. Sooner or later he would have to care. It would be nice if they could ignore the world. It felt good to be in his arms. For the first time since they'd made love she felt safe.

He wanted to give her support, confidence in herself, but she knew it was only temporary. Sooner or later it would be taken away. Not even Monty could protect her from the world.

"What did Betty say when she found out?"

"She doesn't know. Nobody does."

"But how did you find out?"

"Carlos told me after I left the camp."

"But if you didn't know, why did you come?"

Monty looked at her in surprise. "I couldn't leave you out here. It's dangerous."

"I didn't see anything but miles and miles of grass."

They had reached the bottom of the ravine. A small grove of trees had sprung up on a sandy bottom where two springs came together to form a small pool. A small stream flowed out the far side. The air was cool under the trees. After the heat of the plains above, Iris shivered. Monty jumped down from Nightmare. Iris allowed herself to slide into the saddle while he tethered her horse.

"You didn't answer my question."

Monty turned to help her dismount. She looked down into his eyes and wondered why it had taken her so long to realize she loved this man. All those years she had spent flirting with schoolboys, being spoiled by men of address and means, she had never been in danger of falling in love with any of them because she had never forgotten Monty. Next to him, the rest just couldn't measure up. They might be better looking or richer—all of them were more adept at the art of courtship—but not one of them could make her feel so safe and secure. She had never looked to them when she had a problem or worried about her future. It had always been Monty.

Now they were sequestered in this cool glen, miles from anyone, alone, safe from the world, and Monty stood looking up at her with eyes that seemed to brim with love. She didn't care if he never answered her question. If she could just stay here forever, nestled in the comfort and safety of his arms, she promised she would never ask for anything more.

But she knew it was impossible. The world would find them and drive her away. She no longer had a future. It had been taken away. No matter how much he loved her, the gulf between them would remain. She was grateful for the comfort and assurance, but it didn't change anything. She wasn't good enough for him. Sooner or later he would say good-bye.

Monty held up his arms to help her down. Pushing aside a desire to throw herself in his arms and cry her heart out, Iris slid out of the saddle and into Monty's waiting arms.

"I came for several reasons," Monty said, making no move to put her down. "I guess the most important is that I love you."

Chapter Twenty-two

Iris couldn't believe her ears. Nor could she believe the way she felt. For weeks she had longed for Monty to say those words. She had believed they would make everything in the universe fall into place. Yet the moment he looked into her eyes as though he really loved her, the moment the hope she had so carefully controlled broke its bonds and soared aloft, her heart sank.

He couldn't love her. Nobody could love her now.

"Did you hear what I said?" Monty asked. "I said I loved you."

"I heard."

Monty looked nonplussed. "I expected more of a reaction than that. But I guess you can't go to blushing and swooning when you don't love me. I won't say an—"

"But I do love you," Iris hastened to assure him. He looked so hurt and confused, as if he'd finally figured out how to do the right thing and couldn't understand why it hadn't worked. "I've been in love with you for years."

"Why didn't you tell me?"

"Because you were too busy trying to send me back to Texas."

Monty had the grace to look abashed. Briefly. Then his wolfish grin broke out again.

"I didn't really mean it."

"You sure convinced me."

Iris tried to twist in his arms so she could look him in the face, but it was hard to stare down such a brazen creature as Monty under the best of circumstances. It was impossible when she was being held tightly in his arms.

"Can I convince you I've changed my mind?" Monty asked.

More than anything in the world Iris wanted to believe Monty. She told herself if he loved her enough, nothing else would matter. They could hide in the wilds of Wyoming and never come out again.

Some nagging inner voice tried to tell her she was making a foolish mistake, but Iris wouldn't listen. It wasn't what she wanted to hear. She wanted to believe Monty loved her. She needed to believe it.

"You could try."

Monty let her slip from his arms, her body sliding intimately across his, until her feet touched the ground. Once she was balanced on her own feet, he released her, took her face in his hands, and gently covered her mouth with kisses.

"This is for the times I wanted to kiss you but didn't because I thought I shouldn't."

"When did you decide it was all right?" she asked, her lips barely parting from his long enough to form the words. She placed her hands on his, holding them to her face, thrilled by his touch, happily yielding to their strength.

"This morning after I left you."

"But we'd been fighting."

"I think best when I fight."

Iris decided she would never understand Monty. But as long as he would hold her and tell her he loved her, nothing else was important.

He held her face in his hands and kissed her with all the hunger of a man who's been denied far too long. His lips covered her mouth. Iris wanted to laugh aloud when he kissed her eyes and the tip of her nose. He forced her lips apart and his tongue invaded her mouth, electrifying Iris's entire being. Her tongue joined with his in a sinuous dance of joining.

"Women don't like to fight," Iris said, pulling his hands down to her waist and slipping into the circle of his arms. "We like to be pampered and cared for. It's hard to feel loved when you're being shouted at."

"I'll never shout at you again," Monty vowed. "I promise to whisper everything in your ear."

Iris doubted she'd understand a word if he insisted upon blowing in her ear. Even before the tingling sensation had subsided, she felt the warmth of his tongue as it traced the outline of her ear. She melted inside.

"Do you promise never to tell me to go back to Texas?" Iris asked. She meant to say *send me away*, but he was kissing the back of her neck. It made it hard for her to think.

"I promise to make you forget where you are."

It wouldn't be hard as long as she was with him. Even now she could hardly remember she was in the middle of the western Kansas prairie hidden in a grove of cottonwood trees at the bottom of a ravine. She was in Monty's arms, his aroused body pressed tightly against her own, his lips devouring the sweetness of her neck and shoulders. There wasn't room in her mind for anything else.

The pressure of her breasts against his chest caused her nipples to become achingly sensitive. Even as Monty's hands caressed her back, massaged the skin between her shoulders, and pulled her close to him, she felt the lines of pleasure begin to reach out from her breasts to the rest of her body. They seemed to regroup at the spot in her abdomen where Monty's arousal threatened to burn a brand in her sensitive skin.

The flow reversed when Monty unbuttoned her shirt, reached inside her chemise, and covered her breast with his callused hand. Iris gasped at the shock; at the same time she leaned against him hoping to intensify the feeling. Keeping their lips locked in a series of passionate kisses, Monty managed to loosen her shirt enough to slip it over her shoulder. He untied the top of her chemise and laid bare her breasts.

Iris's knees nearly buckled under her when his lips touched an achingly sensitive nipple. Pulling himself away, Monty untied his blanket from the saddle and spread it on the ground. As Monty laved her breast with his hot, insistent tongue, Iris sank, helpless, to the ground.

Iris put her hands around Monty's neck and pressed him against her. She couldn't seem to get enough of his touch. She wanted to be covered by him, to be engulfed by his body, to be absorbed into his being until she was no longer Iris Richmond but a permanent part of Monty Randolph. Maybe then she could believe he loved her, believe all the terrible things in her past didn't matter now, would never matter again.

She pulled him up until his lips captured her mouth. Her frantic fingers hurried to unbutton his shirt. She gloried in the feel of the powerful muscles that rippled so easily under his smooth, warm skin. She pressed her breasts against the roughness of his chest until she felt absorbed.

She offered no resistance when Monty sought to remove the rest of her clothes. She couldn't wait to lie next to him, their bodies entwined, her whole being free to belong to him.

She thought she had remembered every sensation, every feeling, every second of that night in the tepee. But as Monty's lips once again tasted one aching nipple and his fingertips teased a second, and his other hand moved down her body until it found the nub of her desire, Iris felt as if she had never experienced anything like this in her whole life. Her entire body seemed to become a mass of erotic sensation, feelings bombarded feelings until every sinew was stretched so tight Iris felt she would snap in two.

But even as Iris thought herself incapable of feeling more, Monty's hungry mouth moved down her body until he found her very core. Iris rose off the ground with a cry as old as the coupling of man and woman, her body arching against him in a surge of feeling so intensely wonderful she thought she would never be able to feel anything again. Wave after wave swept her body and she felt as though her life were gushing out of her on a floodtide.

But even as the waves began to recede, Monty wouldn't let her rest. With hand and mouth and tongue he plundered her body, searching out her pleasure spots, rekindling the fever inside her until she felt she would be consumed by it. When he at last moved between her legs, Iris threw herself at him, desperate for release.

But Monty wasn't nearly so impatient. With maddening deliberation, he continued to stoke the tension within her. Iris wrapped her legs around his body, attempting to force him to release her from this prolonged agony, but she was helpless against Monty's strength. He continued to torture her body until she felt herself growing weak. She seemed to be losing her hold on Monty. Everything seemed less clear, less solid.

Then just as she feared she would pass out, Iris felt the tension break like a wall of water, a torrent gushing and streaming and flowing from her.

She was only dimly aware of the heat of Monty's seed spilling inside her as she slipped into a quiet oblivion.

Monty stood up. "I think it's time to get going."

They had finished a supper of beans and bacon that Monty had cooked. He took her plate down to the stream and washed it along with his own.

"Going where?"

"Back to camp."

"But we'll be in the saddle practically all night. Wouldn't it be better to sleep here and leave early in the morning?" She didn't want to give him up to his responsibilities, at least not for a few hours yet.

"Hen and Salty are in Dodge, so I had to leave Tyler in charge. I won't be able to sleep for worrying about what could happen while I'm gone."

Iris let Monty lift her into the saddle, but she felt her spirits sink. She tried not to feel rejected, but she couldn't escape the fear she had used up her allotted time and was being set aside while Monty took care of his next duty. He couldn't like her as much as he said. She couldn't be very important to him if he couldn't forget his cows for just one night.

Iris knew something was wrong long before they reached the campsite. "There's been a stampede," Monty said when they found a swath of torn-up ground.

"Do you think it's our herd?" Iris asked. Even her inexperienced eye had no trouble seeing the trampled grass in the moonlight.

"It has to be. There's not another one this size in this part of Kansas."

As they followed the path of the stampede, it became increasingly clear it couldn't have been any other herd. Monty kicked Nightmare into a gallop. He had put his saddle on the zebra dun for Iris, but she couldn't keep up with him. Rather than leave her behind, Monty took hold of the bridle and practically dragged the zebra dun into camp.

It was not yet dawn, but everyone was saddling up. Much to her surprise the camp looked exactly as they had left it.

"It was Frank," Tyler said. "They weren't interested in attacking us. They just wanted the herd."

"Why didn't you go after him?" Monty asked.

"There weren't enough of us," Tyler replied. "I sent Zac to Dodge for Hen and Salty."

"We were just getting ready to leave when you rode up," Hen said. He looked up from folding his bedroll. He pointed to the trail. "We won't have any trouble following them."

"Anybody hurt?" Monty asked.

"Young Danny Clover," Hen told him, his expression as clear an accusation as any words could have been.

"How badly?"

"He's dead. He was on night duty. They strangled him so he couldn't sound the alarm."

Monty didn't have to say a word for Iris to know he held himself responsible for the boy's death. Neither did Hen have to say anything for her to know he agreed with Monty.

But she knew who was really responsible. She was. Monty would never have left the herd if she hadn't taken out over the prairie like a silly idiot. If Monty hadn't followed her, he might somehow have prevented the attack. He might have saved the boy.

"When did it happen?" Monty asked.

"About midnight," Tyler said.

"Then they've only got six hours on us. We ought to catch them tonight. Everybody mount your fastest horse. We ride out in fifteen minutes."

"I'm going with you," Tyler said.

"Me, too," Zac said. "You can't stop me," he said when Monty showed signs of refusing. "I'll follow you if you try."

"Okay, but if you don't follow orders, I'll tie you across your horse and leave you until somebody has time to bring you back."

"I'm coming, too," Iris said, dismounting quickly. She had remained in the saddle, too absorbed by the conflict of emotions around her to realize she would be left behind if she didn't get moving.

"No," Monty said.

Iris looked up quickly. Not even when he was most angry at her had Monty used that tone of voice. He wasn't angry now. He merely spoke to her as if she was a hand, somebody who could be dealt with by a curt order.

"I want you and Betty to go to Dodge," he said. "You'll be safe there until we get back."

Monty strode off to choose a horse from the remuda. Iris ran after him.

"It's my herd. I have a right to go."

"Right has nothing to do with it," he yelled back at her as he entered the corral. "It's what's best for everyone. You shouldn't have been on this drive in the first place. I should have taken you to Rose that very first day. I won't make that mistake again."

The words were like a knife, cutting her heart right out of her chest. "What do you mean *you won't make that mistake again?*" She felt as if she was talking to a stranger, a man who looked like Monty but didn't act like him at all. He certainly didn't act like the man who had held her in his arms last night.

Monty chose his mount, slipped a bridle over his head, and led him out of the corral.

"It's too dangerous out here for someone as inexperienced as you. I won't make a worse mistake by taking you on an even more dangerous trip. You keep doing things without remembering you're not in St. Louis anymore. If we had been in Indian territory when you ran away, you might be dead by now." Iris started to object, but Monty silenced her with a quick kiss. "I don't have time to explain right now. Go on to Dodge, and we'll talk when I get back."

He picked out a blanket and saddle.

"We'll talk now if I have to follow you all the way across Kansas."

Monty whipped around. Iris fell back from the blaze of anger that flashed at her from his eyes.

"Yesterday you were in danger. There was never any question that I would go after you. But you're safe now, and it's time I put my other obligations first."

Iris had come first all her life. She tried to believe Monty, but it was hard for her to believe he could love her without putting her above everything else. But it wasn't just being placed second. She was being ignored, left out, and she didn't know how to sit back and wait.

"So you're sending me away."

Monty finished tightening the cinch on the saddle, slipped an arm around Iris, and started to join the other men.

"I didn't mean it like that," he said. "It's just that right now the most important thing is to get the herd back and find out who killed Danny. This is a responsibility I accepted when I took this job. I can't ignore it just because I'd rather do something else."

"I'm not asking you to ignore it. I'm just asking to go along. I want to catch Frank as much as you do. Besides, this can't be any more dangerous than going to the Comanche village."

"I was a fool to let you do that. This time you're going to stay put."

Iris felt if Monty left her now he would never come back. Maybe it was irrational, but her belief in his love was too fragile to withstand being sent away. In desperation, she reached out to bring him back to her. "And if I don't?" Why was she always challenging him? It was as though she had to prove a point she had ceased to care about a long time ago.

Monty stiffened, stopped, and turned around to face her. There was something severe and uncompromising about his expression. It was not anger or irritation, just cold decision.

"We're going into a gunfight. I've already lost one man. I don't mean to lose another. I can't make the best decisions for my men if I'm worried to death about you."

"You don't have to worry about me. I can take care of myself."

Monty's temper snapped. "You can't. You never have. I don't know why you can't understand that sometimes what we want has to take a backseat to our responsibilities. Rose always does."

Monty turned to leave, but she pulled him around. "I have no doubt your perfect Rose understands everything," Iris retorted, hurt and angry. "But all I can see is you spending your whole life doing what George wants you to do, always worried about responsibilities. What about what you want? Do you even know what that is?"

"That's not important now," Monty answered impatiently.

"Of course it's important," Iris said, lowering her voice so the men couldn't hear her. "Do you think I want to get married knowing you're going to spend the rest of your life trying to satisfy George's every whim?"

Monty looked as if he'd been hit in the face with something wet and cold. "Who said anything about marriage?" He practically yelled the question.

Iris was mortified. All motion around them ceased. She could practically feel the eyes watching them, hear the ears listening.

"You said you loved me," she said in a barely audible whisper, glancing significantly over

363

her shoulder at the waiting crew. "I naturally assumed—"

"I just figured that out last night," Monty hissed. "I haven't had time to think about anything else yet."

Iris died a little bit inside. "You don't want to marry me?"

"I didn't say that. But even if I don't want to get married, it doesn't mean I can't love you."

It was because she was a bastard. That had to be the reason. How else could a man love a woman and not want to marry her?

The men mounted up. Monty tried to take Iris by the hands, but she pushed him away.

"You don't want someone to love. You just want someone who'll do what you want, who won't make demands on you when it's inconvenient."

"If that were the case, I wouldn't love you at all. You haven't done a single thing I've asked, and everything you've done has been damned inconvenient."

He didn't understand. She didn't want to stand in the way of his work. She understood his dedication to the herd, his family, the crew, his job. She'd seen it every day for months. She didn't even mind his efforts to please George all that much. She didn't like it, but she accepted it.

She wanted to be with him. She *needed* to be with him. As long as she was with him, as long as she could still believe he loved her, she could stand anything.

"If you plan on catching up with Frank by tonight, you'd better come on," Hen yelled. The men waited, keeping their distance.

"Iris, I've got to go! Wait for me in Dodge. We'll talk about it then."

He had shouted at her, then dismissed her. In front of everybody, he'd shouted at her as if she was a servant, as if her opinion didn't matter, as if he didn't have time to worry about what she wanted. She followed him to where he joined the others. She watched as he mounted up, issuing commands all the while.

Then she saw it. The four Randolph brothers, all in a row, closing ranks to face the world.

Then she understood.

She would never come first with Monty. Either his family or his work was more important; she didn't know which, but it didn't matter. Whatever the order, she came behind both of them. If she even came that close.

He hadn't even kissed her. He didn't have a tender word of good-bye. He had shouted at her, told her to go to Dodge, said love didn't have anything to do with his ordering her to stay behind.

The tender bud of hope that had been born of their night of love withered and died in the harsh glare of reality. Again she saw the four Randolph men lined up facing her, a phalanx she could never penetrate. For them it was family, duty, and cows. Everything else came after that.

"Go find your cows," she said, putting on a brave face. "But be careful. Frank hates you."

She wouldn't let him see how much he had hurt her. She wouldn't let him know how much she needed him.

"We'll have to hurry if we hope to make Dodge before night," Betty said.

Iris nodded, but there was nothing in Dodge for her. Everything she wanted had just left astride a leggy gray gelding named John Henry.

* * *

"What are you going to do?" Iris asked Betty.

The trip into Dodge had taken longer than Iris expected. As they approached the town, dusk was not far away. Iris looked forward to getting out of the saddle, taking off the heavy money belt that held her gold, and soaking in a hot bath. Riding almost 15 miles a day at a leisurely walk was nothing compared with the more than 30 miles she had ridden this day.

"I'll probably see if I can get a job cooking or washing."

Iris might not know much about keeping house, but she knew cooking and washing was very hard work, the kind done by women who had no other choice.

"Don't you have any family?"

"Yes, but they don't have the money to pay my way back home." Betty was quiet for a moment. "Besides, I'm not certain I want to go back. My husband and I had a difficult life, but I have become accustomed to a certain amount of freedom. I fear I would find it impossible to endure the restrictions of my home."

"You could marry again."

"I imagine I would have to."

"But you don't want to?"

"I married my husband because I had to marry somebody. When I marry a second time, I hope I will be able to choose a man I like. One who has some consideration for what I want."

That struck close to home. Monty might like her a great deal—Iris had decided that regardless of what he thought he couldn't love her—but he didn't respect her. He didn't think anything of her intelligence or her ability. Even if he didn't care about her birth—and Iris had decided he was mistaken about that as well—he didn't care about her as a person.

Monty didn't love her, didn't respect her, didn't have a lot of concern for what she wanted. Any way she looked at it, Iris had nothing now, no promise of anything in the future.

He used me, and I let him.

But she had used him, too.

It was over, done, gone. It had never worked from the very first. It was time to put it all behind her and start again.

She might not be good enough to marry a Randolph, and she certainly wasn't as useful as the perfect Rose, but she was too good to be used and then cast aside. But what could she do? Where could she go? She couldn't go back to St. Louis, and things weren't going to be any better anywhere else.

She would go to Wyoming and learn to run her own ranch. Monty had said she didn't know anything about ranching and cows. Well, she would show him. He wasn't the only person who could figure out what to do with cows. Carlos would help her. He wouldn't look down on her. They were two of a kind.

"Would you consider cooking and washing for me?" Iris asked Betty.

"Surely there'll be someone in the hotel to do that."

"I mean in Wyoming. I'm going to start my ranch. I'm also going to learn how to cook at least one dish. Maybe it'll only be chicken and dumplings, but they'll be the best chicken and dumplings in Wyoming."

"Then you're not going to wait for Monty in Dodge?"

Iris shook her head. She couldn't spend another month in the same camp with Monty. She couldn't bear to come face-to-face with her dashed hopes every day. Monty would get her herd safely to Wyoming. If she'd learned one thing, she'd learned that. The only danger to him or the herd had come because of her.

Betty appeared to be giving her proposal some serious thought.

"I can't promise to pay you very much," Iris said. "I won't have much money until I sell my first calf crop. In fact, we might be reduced to eating bear meat by then." Her stomach heaved at the thought.. "I don't even know what kind of house I have to live in."

"How will you get a crew?"

"Carlos will take care of that. He's going to be my foreman."

"I like Carlos, but I can't say I like having Joe Reardon around."

"What's wrong with Joe?"

"I don't know anything against him, but I don't trust him. Besides, Monty distrusts him, and Monty has good instincts about men."

The thought of Monty was like a stab of pain. She guessed it would never be easy, but she had to put him out of her mind and she had to start now.

"What Monty thinks doesn't matter. I don't expect we'll be seeing him again."

"Are you sure you want to do this?" Betty asked. "It won't be an easy life."

"I'm quite sure I *don't* want to do it, but I have no choice. All I possess is that herd and some land along a creek."

"You could get married. A woman as beautiful as you must know dozens of men who would jump at the chance to marry you."

"That's what everybody says, but it hasn't worked out like that. You would think this red hair would be good for something besides giving me a bad temper. And the things I've been told about my eyes would turn the head of even the most sensible female."

"And your skin, your figure, and the fact that you're the most beautiful woman I've ever seen," Betty added.

Monty had never praised her hair and eyes. She couldn't remember that he had mentioned them more than once or twice. Maybe he didn't find them attractive. Anyway, he didn't find them attractive enough to keep her with him.

Iris pushed away the unwelcome thought. It was too late. From now on she was determined to think of nothing but her cows. She was determined to show Monty she could be just as single-minded as he could.

"You would think it would all add up to something," Iris said. She could feel the tears welling up to the surface. "My mother was absolutely certain I would marry some rich man who would give me everything my heart could desire."

What had Monty wanted to give her? Not marriage, not a family and the security she so desperately wanted. Maybe it was the fault of her red hair. Men didn't think of her as the wife and mother type, just someone to enjoy as long as the attachment lasted.

"Only she forgot to tell me that I had to be very careful, that some girls have foolish hearts. But I guess Mama never thought I'd be stupid enough to fall in love with the one man in all the world who wouldn't care a snap of his fingers for all my charms."

"Monty?"

"Yes, a man who likes cows better than he likes women. Isn't that funny? I used to own enough fancy dresses to outfit half of Dodge, but he never even noticed me until I'd worn this riding outfit threadbare."

"He does care. He went after you even though he was worried about the herd."

"I know, and I wish he hadn't. For one night I thought he really loved me." Iris didn't like the look of disapproval Betty gave her. "But now I know he doesn't care."

"I can't believe that."

"Not the way I want to be cared for," Iris said. "I used to think I wanted all those things my mother told me to want. I guess I'm not very much like her. One lousy trip across this terrible prairie and all I want is Monty. But not on his terms."

The buildings of Dodge had grown closer. Iris gathered herself and squared her shoulders as though she were about to face some great task.

"Now I'm through feeling sorry for myself. That spoiled little girl Monty despised so much doesn't exist any longer. Will you come with me?"

Betty paused only a moment. "Yes."

"Thank goodness," Iris said. "I don't know that I would have had the courage to go alone."

But she would have gone if she'd had to walk all the way by herself. She hadn't given up. She'd never give up. Monty Randolph belonged to her. He was the only one who did not know it. She had a month to learn how to convince him, and she didn't mean to waste her time.

Chapter Twenty-three

Monty lagged behind the others. He wasn't anxious to reach camp.

He should have been feeling on top of the world. Everything had gone just as he planned. They had caught up with Frank and his men about an hour after midnight that first day. Thanks to the deadly accuracy of Hen's guns and Monty's plan of attack, it had taken less than five minutes to recapture the herd. The only casualties this time were to the rustlers. They buried Quince Honeyman and Clem Crowder on the prairie. Monty would take Frank and Bill Lovell to the sheriff in Dodge.

But the closer he came to camp, the closer he came to Dodge and the decision he didn't want to make, a decision he had fought against the whole time he had been gone.

He had decided he and Iris couldn't possibly have any future together. He would divide the herd as soon as they got back and let Iris and Carlos go on to Wyoming alone. He would follow later with the Circle-7 herd.

He had also decided he and Iris should never see each other again.

"Where's Iris?" Monty asked even before his feet hit the ground.

"She and Mrs. Crane left for Dodge just like you wanted," Bud Reins, the man Monty had left in camp with the chuck wagon, told him.

Instead of returning to the original camp after he recaptured the herd, Monty had grazed the herd in a slow arc north. Zac had been dispatched to bring the chuck wagon to the rendezvous spot. They were now about 20 miles north of Dodge.

Monty had been gone six days.

"Good," Monty said, a weight off his shoulders. He'd been worried the whole time that Iris might follow him. Or maybe get lost again. He was relieved she had shown some sense for once.

"Salty, I want the men to separate Iris's herd from ours while I'm in Dodge. I'm sure she'll want to be on her way as soon as she can."

Monty knew his orders were a surprise. He hadn't told anyone of his decision. He hadn't wanted them asking questions or arguing with him. He didn't even want them to know what he was thinking. It had been painful enough as it was. To have been under the intense scrutiny of his brothers for six days would have been intolerable.

But six days had been more than enough time for him to decide he and Iris were no good for each other. The moment he started thinking of marriage, he knew it would never work. She wasn't the kind of wife he needed, and he wasn't the kind of husband she wanted. It wouldn't matter whether they were locked up together on a Wyoming ranch or in a St. Louis mansion; one of them would be miserable. They would come to hate each other before a year was out.

He hadn't wanted to give up Iris. He still didn't. Every time he argued to his conclusion, he would start all over again, hoping he would come to a different result the next time. But it was always the same. They had nothing in common except an uncertain temper and a stubborn streak a mile wide. He was as unsuited to be a husband and father as she was a wife and mother.

But deciding to give up Iris had been the hardest decision he had ever made. When he sent her to Dodge, he had some hazy notion about them staying together somehow. But a few days away from the aphrodisiac of her presence, and he knew that was impossible. It had also given him time to realize he loved her too much to let their relationship come to such a painful end. If it had to end, better it should end now.

"You mean to let her go on alone?" Hen asked.

Monty hadn't heard him come up. "Yes. The worst part of the trip is over. She can hire extra men in Dodge, and Carlos can handle her herd the rest of the way."

He would worry about her every minute, but he had to do it now. Postponing it wouldn't change anything. It would just make it harder.

"Especially with you right behind."

"I won't be right behind. I'm not going with you."

Now Hen really looked surprised.

"Somebody up here always has cows for sale. I'm going to buy a herd and start my own ranch."

"What about the Circle-7 ranch?"

"There's plenty of open range near the Circle-7. I'll be close enough to run both ranches. But as soon as I get things running smoothly, George is going to have to hire himself another foreman."

Hen smiled, pleased. "So the monkey is off your back at last."

Monty looked a little self-conscious. "I guess you could say that. Anyway, Iris helped me realize I couldn't go on letting George, or anybody else, arrange my life for me." Monty's expression turned bleak. "I was busy telling her that Randolphs didn't care what anybody thought when it hit me I was the only one who did. But as soon as I realized that, I realized I really didn't care. I got this herd here despite more trouble than a man ought to have. It doesn't matter whether I brought it on myself or not. I handled it."

"What about Iris?"

"What about her?"

"You're in love with her."

"I know."

"So when are you going to ask her to marry you?"

"I'm not. It wouldn't work."

"You're wrong."

"Dammit to hell, Hen, make up your mind! First you fall into a rage because you think I'm paying too much attention to her. Now you say I'm making a mistake by not marrying her. You don't make any sense."

Hen's expression never changed. "I didn't like her at first: I thought she was silly and self-centered. She's changed. But even if she hadn't, it wouldn't make any difference. You love her, and you're not going to change your mind. Common sense has never worked with you. I don't expect it will now."

A half grin was the best Monty could do. "Well, it had better work because I'm doing this as much for her as for me."

"You going to tell her?"

"When I take Frank and Bill into Dodge."

He'd be willing to let them go free if it would have postponed the trip to Dodge or changed its purpose. Never had he wanted to see anyone so badly as he wanted to see Iris. He would have given Nightmare to have one more day with her.

"When can I expect to see you at the ranch?"

"I don't know. I'll let you know."

"You're serious about this, aren't you?"

"Absolutely, even if George hates it."

"He'll like it," Hen said. "He'll be surprised, but he'll like it."

"What do you mean you never had anybody named Iris Richmond in the hotel?" Monty demanded of the clerk at the Dodge House. "She came to Dodge six days ago. This is the only hotel in town. She had to put up here."

The man spun his book around. "Look for yourself. There ain't been no ladies here by that name."

"If she'd been here under any name, you'd remember her. There were two of them, a stunning redhead with dark green eyes and a rather plain female with light brown hair."

"Maybe you ought to talk to Sheriff Bassett. Maybe he'll know something."

Monty didn't understand. Iris's name wasn't in the book. She hadn't been here. He had expected to find her waiting for him, very angry, possibly so furious she wouldn't speak to him, but waiting. It made him feel a little better to know Betty was with her, but Iris had no place to go. Where could she have gone?

"I got two horses and a letter for you," the sheriff told Monty. "Don't know nothing else except those women left town on the first train. Took 'em down to the depot myself. Can't have decent women wandering around Dodge, especially not one like that redhead. I get enough trouble from Texas cowboys like you." He reached inside a drawer in his desk. "Here's your letter. Your horses are at Ham Bell's livery."

Monty was too stunned to move. He couldn't believe Iris had left him without a word. It wasn't right. It didn't make sense. She couldn't have gone. He still had things he wanted to say to her.

She had left him!

The words screeched in his brain like a demonic yell. He was so mad he wanted to smash something. He wanted to hurt somebody as much as he hurt. And he did hurt. Worse than ever before.

He felt horribly frustrated. He was used to confronting his opponents, fighting for what he wanted. Hard physical contact, brutal and punishing, was a purifying process in itself. But there was no one to fight, nothing but this terrible emptiness, this gnawing pain. The awful knowledge that something he wanted desperately had been taken from him.

Monty held out his hand for the letter, but he didn't open it. He just stared at it. Iris must have been really anxious to shake the dust of Kansas from her boots. Or anxious to avoid seeing him again.

He longed to tear the letter into a million tiny pieces.

"Is everything all right?" the sheriff asked.

"Yeah," Monty replied absently. "I'm just surprised. That's all."

"I'd be more than surprised. I'd be disappointed as hell if I was expecting that little lady to be waiting for me. Though where you managed to find her between here and Texas I'd love to know."

The sheriff's words brought Monty up short. Was he so obvious, was the shock so great, his response so vivid, that a perfect stranger could practically read his mind? Pride, a commodity all the Randolphs had in great abundance, enabled him to pull himself together. What he felt was private, not to be shared with anyone.

Not even his brothers.

"She came with us," Monty said.

"Got any more like her?"

"No. She's the only one."

Monty took his letter outside. He didn't want to read it with anybody watching. He didn't want to read it at all, but he had to sooner or later. Putting it off wouldn't make it any better.

Dear Monty,

I've decided to take your advice and go the rest of the way by train. I realize now I should have listened to you in the beginning.

Thank you for taking such good care of me. Betty is going with me, so you don't have to worry about either one of us. At last you'll be free to give all your attention to your cows.

I won't forget what you told me that night on the prairie, but I guess I always knew we were too different. You were right not to think of marriage. It wouldn't have worked. You're a very sweet man in spite of yourself, and I hope you find someone who can love you and make you happy. I know you will wish me the same.

                              Iris Richmond

Monty crushed the letter in his hand. He had never thought it was possible to feel so miserable without being sick. His feeling this way was all the more inexplicable since he had come to Dodge to tell Iris the very same thing.

Then why did he feel as if his heart had been cut out?

Because he had been looking forward to seeing her again. He had been hoping that he was wrong, that something would change. No matter how hard he had tried to convince himself, he really hadn't been ready to give her up.

Now she had done it for him.

The enormity of his feeling of loss surprised him. He couldn't imagine not seeing Iris again. For months his days had started and ended with Iris. Thinking about her, worrying about her, loving her had become as much a part of him as being a Randolph. He didn't know how he could give her up without losing some essential part of himself.

Maybe he already had. Maybe people never forgot their first love, no matter how foolish and impractical. He didn't think he could. He would always carry her in his heart. And if the way he felt now was any sample of the way he would feel in the future, there would be no room left over for anyone else.

She was headed to Wyoming with Betty. She was safe. At least he didn't have to worry about her. Not yet.

Monty's hand unclenched. He smoothed the letter and put it into his shirt pocket. Then he headed toward the livery stable. It was time to get his horses. It was time to leave town.

He wished he could leave his memories behind half as easily.

But this wasn't the end. He wouldn't leave it here. Right now he had a herd to buy and a ranch to start, a new life to begin, but after that he meant to find Iris. She might have made the same mistake he did in thinking it was over, but she was wrong.

They were both wrong.

"All I really want to do is learn to cook a turkey," Iris said, "even if Monty isn't here to eat it."

"You'll have to wait until we get a proper stove," Betty insisted. "Besides, there aren't any turkeys in Wyoming."

Iris's first glance at the cabin, which had been built to serve as the ranch headquarters, had left her gaping in dismay. It was a crude log house, half in the ground, with only one window, and a large bearskin for a door. Nothing inside had been finished. The dirt floor would turn wet in winter and spring, and the mound of skins was unlike any bed she had ever occupied. There was nothing on the ceiling to prevent dust from floating down over everything in the cabin. She had seen adobe huts in Texas she'd rather live in. If Betty hadn't been with her, Iris knew she would have turned around and left.

Carlos and Joe could lay a floor, but she would need to buy a stove and decent beds. Iris knew she must jealously guard each coin as it left her purse. She would wait until she sold the remuda before she bought anything for the cabin.

Betty fixed their meals in a pot on the potbellied stove in the cabin or over an open pit in the ground. She insisted Iris practice cooking both ways.

Leigh Greenwood

They had been at the ranch for a month now, and Iris had spent every day trying to turn herself into the kind of wife Monty wanted. She and Betty had cleaned and scrubbed and decorated until the miserable hovel had started to look like a home. She had learned to cook at least three whole meals. It wasn't much, but it was a beginning. And she had also ridden over every inch of her land until she knew it like the back of her hand.

Each day seemed to bring something new to further demonstrate to Iris how her life had changed, but she started to take pride in her accomplishments. She studied grass and streams, looked for water holes and hay meadows, and decided on a new site for the future ranch buildings. She still had a lot to learn, but she was no longer the silly female who had set out to capture Monty Randolph with a smile and fluttering eyelashes.

She had hoped the hard work would help her think less about Monty, but it hadn't. She still couldn't remember him without pain. She didn't think she ever would. Betty had told her it would get better with time, but for once Betty was wrong. It only got worse. Everything she did seemed to remind her of Monty. She had given up trying to keep from saying or thinking his name. But every time she mentioned it, it only made the pain of his absence hurt more deeply.

It had been terribly difficult to leave Dodge without seeing him one more time. She wondered what had happened when he got her letter. She had spent hours imagining him leaving the herd to come after her. After a week she knew he hadn't. She pictured him on the trail, counting off the miles as they brought him closer to her.

She refused to imagine him forgetting her.

She had almost worked herself to a fever pitch by the time she saw the first cow on the horizon one sunny September afternoon.

"They're here," she shouted to Betty. Iris was astride her horse and 100 yards away by the time Betty emerged from the cabin.

The first person she saw was Carlos, who rode proudly at the head of the column. It made her feel very good to know she had given him half her inheritance. He had become a different man. A good man.

"Welcome home," she said, smiling broadly when she was within hearing distance.

Carlos looked surprised to see her. "I didn't expect to see you here."

"Where did you think I had gone?"

"I didn't know. Hen said nobody knew."

"What did Monty think?"

"I have no idea," Carlos replied. "I haven't seen him since he went into Dodge."

"Where is he?"

"I don't know. Hen cut the herd and sent us off ahead. We hired some new hands, and I haven't seen a Randolph since. I can't tell you how happy that makes me."

"But what happened to Monty? Where did he go?"

"Hen said he left to buy a herd. I don't know. Can't say I care."

Iris felt caught between surging hope and nagging dread. Where had Monty gone? Would he come back? Would he want her when he did?

"The men will eat duck," Betty said to Iris, "especially if we give them plenty of biscuits and gravy."

Iris wished she could work up as much enthusiasm for cleaning the duck as for cooking it. She was glad to hand it over to Betty when she heard someone ride up.

Her heart no longer beat faster when she saw a stranger. The Circle-7 herd had arrived a month ago, and still no one had heard a word from Monty. Iris tried to keep believing he would come for her, but each passing day made it harder not to give in to the fear that he was gone and would never come back.

"It's a woman," Iris said, staring in amazement as an elegant woman dressed in men's clothes climbed down from the saddle. She rode astride and was clearly able to dismount without assistance. The woman was no stranger to horses, though Iris would have sworn everything about her spoke of considerable wealth. Iris felt ashamed to open the door.

"Good morning," she said, stepping outside.

"Good morning," the visitor replied. "I hope I haven't come at an inconvenient time."

"No. We were just thinking about what to fix for supper. I'm Iris Richmond. I'm the owner of the Double-D ranch."

The woman hesitated a moment. "My name is Fern Randolph."

Iris froze. "Monty's—"

"Monty's sister-in-law. I married his brother Madison."

Iris felt embarrassed. Madison was very rich. Fern lived in huge mansions in Chicago and Denver. Her cabin must look like a cow shed to a woman used to a house full of servants. But Iris couldn't turn her away. As embarrassed as she was, she wanted to know what had happened to Monty. She had forced herself to stay away from the Circle-7. But now that Fern was here, she wasn't going to let her get away until she had gathered every scrap of information she could about Monty.

"I'm afraid this isn't much of a cabin. Maybe you'd prefer to sit outside."

"It looks a lot like the house I grew up in," Fern said, coming toward the cabin without hesitation. "A tornado destroyed it. I think I knew Madison really loved me when he bought a house, cut it into quarters, had it carried out to the farm, and set it up for me."

"You grew up on a farm?" Iris asked. She really didn't know anything about Fern.

"In Kansas. I did the cooking, cleaning and washing, and I took care of the beef herd until Madison decided I was badly overworked and whisked me off to Chicago to scare me half to death with a huge house and six servants."

So it was possible. If Fern had done it, Iris could, too.

"Come right in," Iris said. "I've got a thousand questions, and you're the person to answer them."

They started out talking over coffee. Then they moved outside. Finally they took a ride.

"You've got some excellent land here," Fern said as they headed back to the ranch. "You ought to do very well."

"I would if I knew as much as you."

"You'll learn." Fern laughed suddenly. "Isn't it odd? I would have given my eyeteeth for someone like you to talk to when I first went to Chicago. Madison knew he couldn't take me to Boston. He wanted to try, but I wouldn't let him. Now here I am teaching you how to live like I did for so long."

"Do you ever miss it?"

"Often. Not enough to give up Madison and the boys, but I miss the open spaces and the freedom from dresses. I think my pants are the thing I miss most."

"I was afraid to ask."

"I used to wear pants all the time. Refused to wear a dress. I only put one on to win Madison. I keep wearing them to keep him."

"Not all decisions are that easy."

"Oh, it wasn't easy, though it may seem so now. I imagine it was just as hard as your decision."

"I didn't have any choice. This ranch was all I had."

"I wasn't referring to the ranch. I was referring to your decision to give up Monty. You obviously still love him."

"I—How can you tell?"

"You've used his name at least a hundred times this afternoon. Whenever I talk about him, your face becomes terribly intense, like you don't want to miss a single word. But I guess this ranch is the most obvious proof. You're trying to turn yourself into something you've never been because you think it's what Monty wants."

"Isn't it?"

"If you really want to know the answer to that question, you'll have to ask him."

"How can I? No one knows where he is."

"Would you ask him, if he were here?"

"No."

"Why not? He loves you as much as you love him."

A spasm of pain twisted Iris's features. He couldn't. He wasn't here. "You wouldn't say that if you'd heard him when he sent me off to Dodge."

"Maybe he didn't understand his feelings very well then."

"Maybe not, but I did. I had caused him no end of trouble and he wanted me out of his life."

"Why do you think I came here today?"

"I've been wondering that."

"Because Monty asked me to come. He wanted to know how you were getting along."

"Why didn't he come himself?"

"The letter you left discouraged him just as effectively as his words discouraged you. Now he's trying to do the same thing you're doing."

"What?"

"Turn himself into the kind of husband he thinks you want."

"I've been here for two months, and I haven't even heard from him once. He can't have thought of me very much."

Fern smiled. "Let me show you something."

They were approaching the ranch house. Fern led Iris to a dip sheltered from view by a ring of huge boulders. On the other side Iris discovered a wagon. Inside she found a coal-and-wood-burning cast-iron stove, two beds with thick mattresses, several quilts, a table and she couldn't tell how many chairs, a chest, a wardrobe, a pantry, a coffee grinder, and sacks of flour, sugar, coffee, and bacon. Just about everything she had been planning to buy with the money she got from selling the remuda.

"Monty wanted to make sure you had enough supplies for winter. He said you were worried about money."

Iris's vision misted over. Monty had been thinking of her. He still loved her. He had to, or he would never have sent all this. But did he love her enough to marry her?

"Monty didn't pick out all this. He—"

"I bought it, but he gave me a list of what you would need."

Fern paused, waiting for Iris to respond. Iris didn't say a word. She couldn't. She didn't know where to begin.

"It would be nice if you thanked him," Fern said.

"I'll write him a letter. You can take it to him."

"In person."

"I can't go to the Circle-7. Hen hates me. I don't think Tyler or Zac like me very much either."

Iris knew her objections were irrational, but she couldn't think clearly. For two months she had waited for this moment, worked toward it, prayed for it. But now that it was here, she was petrified. Her whole life hung in the balance. If Monty rejected her again, it would be final. Forever. She didn't know if she was ready to take that chance.

"Hen's gone," Fern told her. "No one seems to know quite where. Tyler left for New York to learn more about cooking. And Zac is on his way back to school after spending a couple of weeks with us in Denver. However, Madison is there."

"I couldn't—Monty wouldn't want—You just don't understand," Iris finished lamely.

"Monty won't be there either."

Monty had left Wyoming! Iris didn't understand why he had sent the wagon. He couldn't still love her.

"When did he go back to Texas?"

"He didn't. After you left him in Dodge, he bought a herd and started looking for a ranch of his own."

"What!"

"According to Hen, who has never learned to express himself in a manner that takes into account other people's feelings, bringing you to Wyoming put Monty through such hell he figured handling two ranches would be a snap. So he bought a herd and established his own ranch to the north of the Circle-7. According to Hen, he was determined to show you he wasn't living under George's thumb anymore."

Hen's remarks left Iris unscathed. Nothing anybody said could matter now. Suddenly all her hopes were fully alive again.

"I've got to see Monty."

"I was hoping you'd say that. Be at the Circle-7 tomorrow morning as early as you can. I'll take you to see him."

Iris's heart beat wildly. She felt so light-headed she couldn't think. Monty wanted to marry her. He must. There could be no other explanation for the wagon and the ranch. She wanted to go right now, even though she knew it was impossible. She didn't know how she could wait until tomorrow.

"I'll be there by nine o'clock," she said.

"Good. Now I'd better be getting back. There is one disadvantage in marrying into the Randolph clan. Every one of them thinks he has the right to worry about you."

Iris couldn't see that as a disadvantage. After having no one worry about her for weeks, she thought it would be absolutely wonderful.

"I don't like it," Carlos said. "We've been getting along fine without those Randolphs. I can't see any reason to start up with them again."

"I can't accept all those things without at least thanking him," Iris said.

"Send it all back. Now that you got the money for selling the horses, we don't need it." Joe had sold the remuda to one of the big ranches owned by rich men from back east. He had gotten more than 1,000 dollars for it.

"You'll never take the wagon back to Mr. Randolph, go to Cheyenne and buy all the things he already bought, and get back here before the snow sets in," Betty said. "You may think it's all right to sleep on a pile of skins or cook over a hole in the ground, but you won't come winter when you get nothing but soup cooked on that potbellied stove."

"I don't mind soup."

"Well, I do," Joe said. "I don't see no reason why she shouldn't be civil to her neighbors."

Carlos knew what prompted Joe's remark. He hadn't made any progress on his plan to marry Iris. She not only made it clear she wasn't interested in him; she kept her distance. Carlos knew she didn't trust Joe. He wondered if he could. Clearly Joe hadn't forgotten his plan to ransom Iris for some of the Randolph gold.

It was hard to forget about 20,000 or 30,000 dollars, but if the Randolphs did have all that gold, they wouldn't be diddled out of it so easily. They had never had a reputation for being fools. Neither had they had a reputation for being suckers.

The Randolphs defended their own. If Joe hadn't understood that before, he certainly should have after they hunted down those rustlers. Staring into the ice-cold blue eyes of those twins would be enough to put the fear of God into anybody. Murder had flared from Hen's eyes as clearly as cold-blooded purpose rode in Monty's. Joe hadn't wondered when Tyler so readily exchanged his cooking spoon for a gun. Neither did it surprise him when that crazy kid, Zac, suddenly turned into a man with a grim purpose. One look at the four of them and Joe knew the rustlers didn't have a chance.

"Okay, go if you must, but I'm coming with you."

"I'm going alone. This has nothing to do with you."

Carlos opened his mouth to object.

"Leave her to go by herself," Joe said as he gripped Carlos by the arm and spun him around. "We can't afford to waste a whole day if we're going to get our work done before winter."

There had been snow flurries at the higher elevations already. The first winter snow could come at any time. They had to cut as much hay as possible. The cows hadn't yet learned how to forage through a Wyoming winter.

Carlos jerked his arms out of Joe's grasp. "You be home tonight, or I'm coming after you," he said to Iris before turning and stomping out the door.

"He'll settle down," Joe assured her. "He's just jealous. He thinks you don't have as much faith in him as you do that Monty fella."

"I think Carlos is doing a fine job," Iris said, "and I've told him several times."

"I know, but he still needs time to build up his confidence."

"He'll have it," Iris said dryly. "Years and years of it."

The same thought coursed through Carlos's mind as he walked to the bunkhouse. He looked forward to those years. He liked having a ranch of his own, even if he didn't yet legally own a single cow. He liked working for himself. He looked forward to the chance to become a solid, respectable citizen. But the look in Joe's eye told him Joe hadn't given up his plan to ransom Iris. In fact, the anger told him he would fight Carlos to keep that chance alive.

Carlos looked around him. The ranch was barely worth the name. The house was barely a cabin. The cracks in the bunkhouse still had to be filled with mud, and they had just one corral. But he was surrounded by endless grass watered by runoff from mountains rising in the west. It would be a fine ranch in five or ten years, something a man, and his sister, could be proud of.

Carlos decided then and there he wasn't going to let Joe kidnap Iris. He didn't want her to marry Monty, but if that was what she wanted, well, it was her business. After all she had done for him, he couldn't repay her kindness by getting in the way of her happiness. Neither could he let Joe extort money from the Randolphs even if they were rich enough to pay. Iris had given Carlos the best chance he was ever going to have to make something of himself. He wasn't going to ruin it by letting Joe pull a stupid stunt like this.

Only he didn't know what to do. Now that he stopped to think of it, he realized Joe was a hard, cruel man. He didn't know if Joe had any real loyalty to anybody but himself. As far as he could remember, Joe had always looked at everything as a chance to get something for himself. There was no gratitude for what he got.

Joe would not be easy to stop.

Chapter Twenty-four

Iris felt a pang of jealousy when she saw the Circle-7 ranch buildings. The bunkhouse had been put together with logs and mortar, but the house had been constructed of wooden planks probably brought in from Laramie. The shingle roof wouldn't spread a layer of dust over everything in the house, and the several windows were real glass. A trail of smoke from a metal flue told Iris the cook prepared the meals on a stove just like the one Monty had sent her.

A man stepped out on the porch as Iris rode up. "Good morning," he said. "You must be Iris Richmond."

Iris was speechless with shock. Fern hadn't told her George Randolph would be at the ranch. She wasn't prepared to face the man who was the cause of so many of Monty's problems; nor was she prepared for the wave of anger she felt toward

George. He must have come to check up on Monty. She would have a few things to say to him before she left.

She was also surprised he didn't remember her. She guessed it showed that, without pretty dresses and someone to fix her hair, she wasn't anything special to look at. Not exactly what she wanted to hear when she was going to see Monty for the first time in two months.

"I'm surprised to see you here," she said. "Did you bring Rose?"

The man laughed easily. "I've always known I looked a lot like George, but I still can't get used to being mistaken for him. I'm Madison Randolph. My wife called on you yesterday. Come on in. Would you like some coffee? It's damned cold out this morning."

Iris was greatly relieved. The thought of facing George and his perfect wife scared her to death.

"Is Fern ready?" Iris asked, trying to conceal her impatience. "I promised my brother I'd be back before nightfall."

"I think we can do that, but unfortunately Fern won't be able to go with you."

"Why?" Iris held back the rising panic. After waiting so long, after working up her courage and building up her hopes, she had to go today. She didn't think she could stand to wait any longer.

"I'll let her tell you."

Iris found Fern reclining on a real bed in a real bedroom. "I'm pregnant again," Fern confessed, looking at her husband rather than Iris. "I was trying to keep it from Madison as long as I could, but I had an attack of morning sickness over breakfast."

"And I ordered her to bed."

"I was hoping to have a few more days of freedom, but as long as this monster of selfishness is determined to keep me producing sons, I have to spend my time resting and pretending I like it."

"If I would let her, my wife would ride until the Women's League for Decency forcibly removed her from the saddle."

"Unfortunately he's an old-fashioned brute who believes in tyrannizing women, especially his wife."

From the way Fern gazed adoringly at her husband, Iris could tell she had no real objection to his tyranny. Iris thought she wouldn't mind it either. It certainly beat riding out on a cold morning searching for cows that didn't want to be found and that would object to whatever she wanted them to do as a matter of principle.

"Enough about me," Fern said. "Can't you see Iris is anxious to see Monty?"

Iris hoped her anxiety didn't show that clearly, but she was afraid it did.

"I'll be fine," Fern assured her husband. "Salty has promised to check on me. I've been through this before, remember?"

"I know, but—"

Fern turned to Iris. "This man thinks leaving me for the afternoon when we're on a ranch is worse than leaving me for weeks when he goes east on business."

Madison's grin was perfectly free of self-blame. It seemed that unshakable self-confidence was a Randolph family trait.

"Promise you'll stay in bed," Madison said.

"I'll stay inside. I'll go crazy if I stay in bed."

It made Iris jealous to see the way Madison pampered his wife. If Monty would just do that with her.

"So you had to go and fall in love with Monty," Madison said when they were in the saddle.

"Y-yes," Iris replied, not prepared for such a direct question.

"I don't know whatever possessed you to fall for such a pigheaded loudmouth, but at least he's got good taste. You're a lovely young woman."

Iris appreciated Madison's compliment, but she was angry at his criticism of Monty. "He's none of those things. I nearly drove him crazy, and he never lost his temper. Well, not too many times."

Madison laughed. "I'm his brother, remember, and I know his vile temper. Defend him by all means, but do it to someone else."

Iris felt sorry for Monty. "Doesn't anybody in your family like him?"

Madison looked a little surprised by the question. "We admire his good qualities. He's a hard worker, dependable, unquestionably the best cowman in the family."

"But don't you like him? George doesn't, and Hen got so mad at him he hardly spoke to him most of the way."

"There's something you'd better understand if you're thinking about marrying Monty," Madison said, his expression a bit paternal. "We're a difficult family. I suppose we love each other, but we fight each other almost as hard as we fight outsiders."

"I don't understand that."

"Fern says we're all crazy—I think that about sums up Rose's opinion, too—but that's the way things work. Anyway, Monty's just as cold-blooded as the rest of us."

Now Iris understood part of why Monty had such a difficult time giving of himself. It must be awful if the act of loving your own family also made you vulnerable to attack. She supposed it was better to be loved like that than in the self-indulgent way her parents had loved her, but Iris was glad she hadn't been raised a Randolph. Her parents' love had made her feel warm and secure. Loving in Monty's family was like trying to love a rattlesnake. No matter how much you loved it, you didn't dare get too close for fear of its deadly embrace.

She didn't know if Fern was right about Monty loving her—she must be, mustn't she, or he wouldn't have sent all that stuff? Iris would show him love didn't have to hurt. She would show him she knew how to give, not just take. There was so much she wanted to show him—if he would just give her the chance.

Monty kept telling himself it wasn't yet time to see Iris.

He had promised himself he would own his own ranch before he asked her to marry him. He had land and a herd now, but nothing else. He had set his hands to work building a bunkhouse, but he slept in a tent because his ranch house was still a pile of lumber. He didn't even have a corral. He staked his horses out to graze and hobbled them at night. He felt like a squatter in the middle of a vast open plain.

Several times he started to saddle Nightmare for a ride to the Circle-7, but each time he stopped himself. He had promised to set up and manage the ranch, and he meant to keep his promise. But every time he went to the Circle-7, he had to fight this terrible temptation to go see Iris. It would be easier if he stayed where he was. Besides, Salty was more than capable of handling the ranch by himself.

Monty had made a commitment to George for one year, and he meant to see it through. That meant he wouldn't be able to spend more than a couple of days a week at his own place, but that was okay. He'd get by.

But he didn't mean to wait that long to see Iris. He'd only reached his ranch site three days ago, and already he was so anxious to see her he could hardly keep his mind on his work. But he couldn't ask her to marry him when he had no home to bring her to.

He couldn't decide what kind of house he wanted to build. Everything depended on whether Iris had changed her mind about him. After spending months making her believe he wanted nothing to do with her kind of woman, he figured it would take more than a wagonload of furniture to make her believe he wanted to marry her.

Monty had a tough hide, but he balked at the thought of conducting such a campaign under Betty's and Carlos's scrutiny. Probably Joe's as well. That man seemed to be Carlos's shadow.

But he couldn't wait too long. Once that wagon rolled up to Iris's door, she would know he was in Wyoming. If he didn't go see her soon, she'd believe he didn't love her.

But was it too soon?

He could kick himself for spilling his guts to Fern when he'd seen her in Cheyenne. He guessed he'd just kept it locked up too long. Fern had come around when he wasn't expecting her, asking questions, knowing too much. Next thing he knew he was saying everything he had been unable to say since the day he rode into Dodge and found Iris gone.

But if he had to tell someone, he was glad it was Fern. He would hate having one of his brothers know he was acting so simpleminded over a woman. He still had Iris's letter. He tortured himself by rereading it at least once a day.

No matter what he tried to do, his thoughts kept coming back to Iris. Talking to Fern had let down his resistance. Now he couldn't shore it up again.

He had to see Iris or go crazy.

Monty gave up the battle. He snatched up his saddle and headed for Nightmare. He was going to see Iris. Come hell or high water, Betty or Carlos, he was going to find out if there was a chance she could ever love him.

At the very moment Monty was preparing to visit Iris, she topped a windswept rise 100 yards away and spotted him. Unsure of herself, she pulled her horse to a halt.

"If you think I'm going to wait here with my teeth chattering from the cold while you work up the courage to talk to him, you're mistaken," Madison said. He slapped Iris's horse on the rump. "Get going."

The animal leapt forward, Iris struggling to regain her balance. The sound of her approaching horse caused Monty to look up. He stared for a moment in disbelief. Then he dropped the saddle and started forward at a run.

Iris dug her heels into her horse's side. She had no more doubts now. They came together in a melee of flashing hooves and flying stones. Without waiting for him to say a word, Iris threw herself from the saddle and into his arms.

"I bet your mama never taught you to do that," Monty said.

"She taught me to go after what I wanted, and I want you."

"Even if I'm a stubborn cuss who can never think of the right thing to say?"

"Even then. If Madison can change enough for a nice lady like Fern to enjoy being married to him, you can, too."

"We're not alike," Monty warned. "Madison has brains and ambition. Someday he'll be richer than all of us put together. All I want is to run a few cows, ride a good horse, and love a pretty woman."

"And come home to food you can recognize."

"That, too," Monty said laughing. He hugged Iris close. "Be serious now. I've got to know if you think you can put up with me. I love you, but I'm rough and thoughtless and full of temper. I guess I was just made ornery."

"I'll take my chances."

"Have you two made up your minds what you're going to do yet?" Madison asked as he pulled up next to them. He had caught Iris's horse. "I don't mean to stay out in this weather."

"Madison's gotten so used to living inside a big house he doesn't like the outdoors," Monty said, taking hold of Iris's horse's bridle.

"I never did, not even when it was Texas and it was hot as hell." He tossed Iris's horse's reins to Monty. "I'm going back to check on Fern. I wouldn't put it past her to try for one more ride while I'm gone. You've got one hour to hash out everything between you. If you're not back at the house by then, I'll send Salty after you. I'm not leaving Fern again today."

"I can't believe he's as tough as everybody says he is," Iris said as they watched Madison ride off. "He hasn't talked about anything but Fern all morning."

"Maybe he uses business as an antidote for all that sugar he lavishes on his family." Monty tied Iris's horse to the hitching post.

"I'll never treat you like Madison and George treat Fern and Rose. I think the world of Rose, but she scares me half to death. I couldn't be comfortable around Fern because I could never be certain she couldn't ride and rope better than I can."

Iris pulled his arm from around her. "So you can love me because you know you're better at everything than I am."

Monty pulled her back into his arms and kissed her with satisfying thoroughness. "I like you just the way you are. I know I get mad at you now and again, but I wouldn't marry anybody I didn't like well enough to yell at."

"You really do love me?"

"I love you more than I ever thought possible."

"And you don't care about my horrible parents?"

"I never did."

"Prove it."

Monty looked as though he wasn't quite certain of her meaning.

"We've got a whole hour," Iris said.

Monty didn't need a second invitation. Sweeping Iris into his arms, he carried her into his tent. Their lovemaking was hard and urgent. There would be time for slow loving in the years to come. Right now they could only yield to their urgent need of each other.

"Are you sure you want to marry me?" Iris asked as she nestled in his embrace. "I'm still a loss as a rancher's wife."

"Of course I do. Why do you ask?"

"After what you said when you sent me off to Dodge, I wasn't sure."

"I suppose I deserve that, but I had a lot of things to work out right then. I couldn't handle everything at once."

"Did you work them out?"

"Mostly. I guess I'll always be sensitive to what George wants. He's been more of a father to me than Pa ever was. But I can live without his approval. I'd rather not, but I can. Madison always has."

"And Hen?"

"Hen's different."

Iris felt her stomach tighten.

"Hen's the one who told me I was a fool to let you get away."

Iris twisted around in Monty's embrace until she could see his face. "But Hen hates me."

"No, he doesn't. He got angry because he thought I was letting you talk me into doing all the wrong things, but he doesn't hate you. He told me if I was fool enough to let you get away, I could find myself another twin."

"I don't understand your family," Iris said, settling back against the warmth of Monty's large, comforting presence. "I don't think anybody could."

"Nobody understands Hen. It's like he's two different people and you never know which one you're talking to."

"Why did you decide to start your own ranch? I don't want to come between you and your family."

"You made me realize I need something I can truly call my own, something I don't have to answer to anybody for."

"You can run my ranch."

"Carlos is your foreman."

"I know, but he'd work for you."

"A more important question is, can you be happy as a rancher's wife?"

"I can't say I'll be delirious if I never see a city again, but I won't mind it. I'm starting to feel at home here. I like the space and the peace. I don't even mind the work. I also like not having to pretend to be somebody I'm not. I never realized until this drive that I'm not at all what my mother hoped I'd be. She'd probably be very disappointed in me." She looked unhappy for only a moment before she delighted Monty with an enchantingly smug smile. "Besides, Betty is teaching me to cook."

"You? Cook?"

Iris punched him. "Okay, so I'm not very good at it, certainly not as good as Tyler, but I can eat it. And you can look at it and tell what it is."

"No sauces, huh?"

"Betty doesn't know any sauces."

"Good."

There was a short pause. "When did you know you wanted to marry me?" Iris asked.

Monty drew Iris close. "When I got to Dodge and found you gone. I suppose I already wanted to, but I was too worried about a lot of other things to figure it out. But when you left me, all I could think about was finding you. I knew right then none of the other things mattered unless I had you."

Iris felt a knot in her heart loosen. She had found a haven in Monty's love. She had come home. She was safe.

"Tell me what you plan to do with the ranch," Iris said, snuggling close. "Do you plan to live here or at the Circle-7?"

"That depends on you."

"How?"

"We can live at your ranch, the Circle-7, or my ranch. Take your pick."

"Do you have a house?"

"No. I was waiting to make sure you'd marry me."

"Then we'll live at the Circle-7 until you do. I don't think you'd call what I've been living in a house either."

"I want you to move in right away. Now. Today."

"I can't leave Carlos."

"Yes, you can. You certainly should leave Joe Reardon."

"I won't mind that. I really don't like him."

"Good. At least you're finally developing some judgment."

"I never did like Reardon," Iris said, firing up. "I just didn't have any choice."

"I don't want to argue today," Monty said. He got up and reached for his clothes. "If we don't get started, Madison is going to send Salty after us."

But the temptation to disagree was too strong. They were arguing when they reached the Circle-7.

"At it again," Fern said. She and Madison were sitting on the porch when they rode up. "Are you sure you two want to get married?"

"We've been arguing for so long, we hardly know how to do anything else," Iris said.

"You'd better find out," Madison advised. "Once you get married, you'll really have something to fight over."

Fern frowned at her husband. "Don't listen to him. He's just irritated I don't want to go back to Denver just yet."

"The first snow," Madison said. "And I'm coming after you."

"I'm glad you're staying," Monty said. "I've asked Iris to move here until we can get married."

"I knew it," Fern said, turning to her husband, delighted to have outguessed him. "Now I'll have somebody with me. And it will give me a chance to get to know Iris."

"The first snow," Madison repeated.

"You'd better hurry up if we're going to have more than a cup of coffee together," Fern said, glancing at the gray skies. "Winter seems to be coming early this year."

"I'd better be getting back," Iris said. "I promised my brother I'd be home by dark."

"I'll ride with you," Monty offered.

"You'd better not. Carlos isn't going to like this. I want to tell him myself."

"Why?"

"He knows you don't think much of him. He's always been afraid my husband would make me take back his half of the ranch."

"You can give him the whole thing for all I care," Monty said.

Iris jumped up and kissed him. "Thanks. I was hoping you'd say that."

"I think you've just lost your dowry," Madison said.

"It doesn't matter," Monty said with a slightly dazed look. "I got the prize."

"I still don't like it," Carlos said, facing Iris across the small table in their cabin. The empty bowls indicated they had made a meal of soup once again.

"But I do. I've been wanting to marry Monty practically my whole life. Please be happy for me."

"I'll try. After everything you've done for me, I'd be a heel if I didn't."

Iris reached out to lay a hand on his arm. "You did a lot for me, too. I can't tell you how much nicer it was all during that endless drive to know I had a brother with me."

Carlos sobered. "You realize I'm not really your brother, don't you?"

"Yes, but I hope you'll still think of me as your sister."

Carlos nodded.

"I'm glad. I never knew how terrible it was to be alone."

"You had Monty."

"That was different. There's something about family that isn't like anything else. I never understood that before. I guess it's why the Randolphs can fight like they do and still love each other."

"You sure Monty won't object to your giving me half of the herd?"

"He said I could give you the whole thing if I wanted."

"Well, if he really means it, the least I can do is try to learn to like him."

"You will," Iris said, giving Carlos a slightly self-conscious hug. "Now I've got to decide what to take. I want to leave first thing in the morning. Are you sure you and Joe will be okay by yourselves?"

"We've been by ourselves before. We'll do just fine."

"We're not doing it," Carlos shouted at Joe. "I never thought it was a good idea from the first. But after all she's done for me, I'd be a first-class heel to kidnap her."

He had waited for Joe in the bunkhouse. He knew there would be an argument, and he didn't want anybody to hear it.

"We wouldn't really be kidnapping her," Joe said, "just keeping her here until Randolph can deliver the gold. I like your sister. I wouldn't do anything to hurt her."

"Look, Joe, we got a good place. We got steady jobs, and I got nearly two thousand head of cattle. In a few years we can be sitting pretty."

"I don't have anything," Joe said.

"Yes, you do. You know I'll share everything with you. It's the way we've always done it."

Joe waved his hand toward the bunkhouse. "It doesn't stack up very well against the gold." The logs needed to be chinked, there was no heat, and the beds were nothing more than boards covered with a blanket.

"We don't have the gold. We don't even know the Randolphs have it—"

"I saw it. You saw it, too."

"—but we do have this place. It's ours, we're here, we can stay. I'm sorry she didn't want to marry you instead of Randolph, but we're not touching Iris."

"Okay," Joe said. "You'd better talk to her about some money before she leaves. We got the ranch, but we don't have money to buy nothing, not even coffee."

"I'll talk to her. You just forget about the gold or marrying Iris."

"I'm not forgetting about any gold," Joe said aloud after Carlos had left the bunkhouse. "You don't want any part of it. Fine, but I'm not settling for a few hundred cows in the coldest corner of the earth when I can have enough gold to live like a king anywhere I want."

"I still don't see why you insisted on giving everything back," Betty said. "He did give it to you, and Carlos could use the stove and beds just as well as you."

"I don't feel right leaving everything for Carlos and Joe when I know Monty dislikes them. I'll give Carlos half the money as soon as I can get to the bank in Laramie. That should be more than enough to buy what he needs. As for the furniture and stuff, Monty doesn't have anything for his own house. I think he ought to have it back."

"I suppose you're right, but it somehow seems rude to return a man's presents. It's like you don't want them."

"But I do." Iris laughed. "They're my dowry. Considering I've given half of everything I have to Carlos, I don't have much of one."

Betty drove the wagon, and Iris rode. At least she could bring her own horse and saddle with her. Their progress was slow. There was no trail between the two ranches. While the land was open, it wasn't easy to drive a wagon up and down hills and through streams, even though most of the streambeds were dry. Iris offered to drive for a while, but Betty declined.

"My family never could afford riding horses, but I've been driving a wagon since I was old enough to hold the reins. Oxen, mules, horses—it doesn't make any difference."

So they proceeded along their way. While Betty picked a careful path across the countryside, Iris tried to alleviate her boredom by identifying as many plants and grasses as she could and riding to every ridge to get a view of the land.

"If I'm going to live here, I ought to know everything I possibly can."

"I imagine you'll move to Laramie or Cheyenne before long."

"Maybe for the worst part of the winter, but I've made up my mind I'm not going to ask Monty to live anywhere he doesn't like. Madison took Fern to the city, and you can see she still longs for the freedom of the country. Monty would die without it."

"What about children? You can't bring them up out here."

"I'll worry about that when I get there. Right now I'm still not married."

"I wonder what we forgot."

"What do you mean?" Iris asked.

"Joe's coming after us. We must have forgotten something."

"I hope nothing's happened to Carlos," Iris said. She turned back to meet Joe.

"Is anything wrong?" she asked.

"Naw," Joe replied. He reached over and took hold of Iris's reins. Iris was so surprised, Joe easily jerked the reins from her slackened grip. Leading her horse, he headed toward the wagon. Iris made a grab for the reins and lost her balance. She had to hold tightly to the pommel to keep from falling.

"What on earth are you doing?" she asked.

"I've got a message I want Betty to take to Monty Randolph."

"I can take it," Iris said. "Now give me back my reins."

Joe drew alongside the wagon. Betty regarded him with a good deal of apprehension.

"You tell Monty Randolph I got his girlfriend," Joe told Betty. "You tell him if he wants to marry her, all he has to do is give me one hundred thousand dollars of that gold his pa stole. He don't have to worry she'll come to any harm. I'll take extra special care of her. Of course if he don't want her himself, I just might take a fancy to her."

"You're insane," Iris said. "There's nothing to that gold story. Everybody knows that."

"Everybody didn't see him passing out gold pieces to Frank and his bunch."

"That was my money," Iris said.

"Good try, but Carlos told me how the bank took everything you owned except the cows. You tell him to deliver the money to Carlos," Joe said. "Soon as he does, he'll get his little lady back."

"I can't tell him," Betty called out as Joe started to ride away. "I don't know the way to his ranch."

"Hell. Do I have to give him the message myself? Just keep going in that direction. If you don't get there soon, he'll send somebody out looking for you."

With that Joe galloped off with Iris doing her best to stay in the saddle.

Chapter Twenty-five

"I keep telling you that was my gold," Iris said.

"And I keep telling you I don't believe you," Joe replied.

Joe had brought her to a small, crude lean-to hidden in one of the timbered valleys that drained the Laramie Mountains and supplied Sybille Creek and Chugwater Creek. Iris figured it must have belonged to some trapper years ago before the beaver gave out. It looked as if it hadn't been occupied in years. She doubted Carlos knew the location of this cabin. She was certain no one at the Circle-7 did.

"Everybody knows those Randolphs got gold," Joe said. "How else could they get rich so fast?"

"Hard work, something you might try if you live long enough."

"Why should I when there's all that gold just for the asking?"

Iris brought her balled-up fist down on a rickety table. "There *is* no gold." She shook her head in total frustration. "Monty will kill you. And if he doesn't, Hen will."

"Hen doesn't like you worth a damn."

"Maybe not, but the Randolphs stand together. You should have realized that when they went after Frank and the rustlers. The whole bunch of them will be after you now."

Joe drew back his hand to strike her.

"If you touch me, if there's so much as a single mark on me, Monty will beat you to death."

She had the pleasure of seeing Joe recoil.

She wasn't really worried Joe would hurt her. His goal was the money. Monty would be angry if he hurt her, and an angry Monty would be less likely to give him gold.

Only there wasn't any gold, so Monty would have to do something else. It was that *something else* that had Iris worried. She had no doubt that either Monty or Hen would kill Joe. She had to stop them. She didn't care about Joe, but she did care about Monty. She didn't want to come this close to her dream only to have Monty end up in jail for murder. It would be almost as bad if it were Hen. It would always stand between her and Monty.

She had to find a way to get away from Joe. But how? He hadn't left her for even a moment. But he would have to leave her to go back to the ranch to see if Monty had delivered the money. That was when she would get away. She just hoped it wouldn't be too late.

Betty hadn't said more than three sentences before Monty was racing to the corral for his horse.

"Stop him," Fern said to Madison. "If he goes off like this, somebody's going to get hurt."

"This Joe fella is going to get hurt no matter what I do," Madison said, heading after his brother. "Wait up, I'm coming with you," he called to Monty.

"Then you'd better hurry. I'm not waiting."

"You've got to wait, dammit. I'm not as used to saddling a horse as you are."

Monty threw a blanket and a saddle on a complacent-looking buckskin. "Can you cinch it up?"

"I can," Madison said, jerking the blanket and saddle from the back of the buckskin. He eyed the horses in the corral and headed for a line-back dun. "And I might even manage to get in the saddle, but I'd never succeed in making that slug move fast enough to keep up with your mount."

Monty's short bark of laughter eased his worried look. "Watch out. He bites."

"So do I. Didn't you know?"

"I thought you just cut people up with your tongue."

"That, too. I don't want to be thought one dimensional."

"You haven't changed a bit."

"Neither have you. That's why I'm going with you."

"Well, you'd better bring a gun."

"Why? As you've just pointed out, my best weapon is my tongue. Yours is your fists."

"Well, we'd better get this over before Hen gets back. You know what weapon he prefers."

Madison looked grim. "Do you think he'd shoot to kill?"

"He wouldn't hesitate," Monty said. He swung into the saddle and rode through the gate, which one of the hands held open for him. Madison rode through on his heels.

"Will they bring her back?" Betty asked Fern.

"Yes. I just hope they don't kill anybody in the process."

"Do you think they would?"

"Oh, yes," Fern assured her. "They wouldn't hesitate."

Carlos stared at Monty, his face white. "I don't know where Joe is. I can't believe he would do anything like this. I told him—" Carlos's voice trailed off.

"You told him what?" Monty asked.

Carlos clamped his mouth shut.

"Tell me, or I'll beat it out of you."

Madison put a restraining hand on Monty's arm, but Monty shrugged it off. "Habit," he said.

"What did you tell Joe?" Monty asked again. "Considering everything Iris has done for you, the least you can do is help us find her."

"It's the gold," Carlos said. "Joe wants the gold."

"What gold?" Monty asked.

"The gold your father stole."

The number and variety of Monty's curses surprised even Madison.

"There is no gold," Madison said. "There never was any. Why won't you people let that rumor die?"

"But we saw it," Carlos said. "You paid Frank in gold."

"That was Iris's money," Monty explained. "She was afraid the bank might take it if she left it in Texas, so she converted everything into gold. She had three thousand dollars strapped around her waist half the way to Wyoming."

Carlos whistled. "But Joe thought—"

"It doesn't matter what he thought. He was wrong. Now what did you tell him?"

"I told him I wanted no part of it. I'd have been content to work for Iris as a regular hand. I never dreamed she'd make me foreman. When she said she was going to give me half the cattle as well, I told Joe he wasn't to touch her. I told him I'd share everything with him."

"That was mighty generous. The man is a cheater."

"I know he's not easy to like, but Joe has been a good friend." Carlos looked as though he was trying to decide whether to say something. "He helped me out of a bad scrape. I owe him my life."

"Fine, let him kidnap you. That has nothing to do with Iris. We've got to find her."

"He has to have her somewhere on the ranch," Carlos said. "We haven't been anywhere else."

"We can't do anything until the morning," Madison said.

"You can't think I mean to leave Iris in that man's hands all night?"

"I don't think you want to," Madison said, "but since you don't know the country and you soon won't be able to see where you're going, I don't see what you can do about it. The best thing is to have all the men here first thing in the morning and begin a systematic search."

Monty wasn't happy with the plan, but he didn't have anything better to propose. The idea of Iris spending the night at Joe's mercy made him almost too mad to think straight, but he told himself if he was ever going to learn to be cool and careful, now was the time. Iris wouldn't be helped if he went crashing into this thing.

"Okay, but be ready at dawn," Monty said and stomped out.

"If Joe should contact you during the night, be very careful what you say," Madison warned Carlos.

"What do you mean?"

"Don't tell him you haven't seen us. He might be watching now. Tell him you don't know what we're doing. You might even tell him you think we've gone away to get the money. After all, nobody would keep that much money in a ranch house. You can tell him the best thing for everyone would be for him to turn Iris loose. If he does, I promise we won't do anything to him."

"If he doesn't?"

"No man has ever touched a Randolph woman and lived to tell about it."

"Iris is still a Richmond," Carlos said, a bit defiant.

"She's as good as a Randolph. You tell your friend that. You might also want to whisper a word of warning in his ear."

"And what might that word be?"

"Hen."

"This tastes disgusting," Iris said. She pushed away the plate of greasy food Joe Reardon had given her.

"Then cook it yourself."

"I can't cook," Iris told him. Only when the words were out of her mouth did she realize that was no longer true. She couldn't cook much, but she could cook. "What have you got?" Iris asked, getting to her feet.

"Bacon, some flour, dried beef, beans. I don't know. Look."

As Iris looked through the food Joe had carried in the sack over the saddle, she tried to remember everything Betty had told her. She had never cooked a stew, but she had watched Betty.

Finding a pot and settling it over the fire turned out to be a bigger problem than cooking. When the water came to a boil, she dropped in pieces of dried beef and two sliced potatoes. She added salt and some dried tomatoes. She remembered things she had seen Tyler do, so she added a few spices. In about 20 minutes the aroma caused her mouth to water.

"This ain't bad," Joe said, going through his portion before Iris had hardly begun. "You can do all the cooking from now on."

Iris almost laughed at the irony. Never in her life had she been allowed to cook. Not even those who loved her risked eating what she prepared. Now that she was a prisoner of a man who really didn't care if she lived or died, only whether he could get money for her, she was ordered to cook.

"Can you find a turkey?"

"What the hell do you want with a turkey?"

"To cook. I've been hoping someone would shoot one."

"There ain't any turkeys in Wyoming."

"There weren't any cows either just a few years ago. There might be now."

"Are you crazy?" Joe asked. "I never heard anybody carry on about turkeys like that."

"Monty likes turkey. I mean to learn to cook it for him."

"Good. You tell him to hand over the gold, and you can cook all the turkeys you like."

"I keep telling you there isn't any gold."

"We'll see. Now you might as well get some sleep."

Joe showed every sign of settling into his bed right then.

"Aren't you going to see if there's any sign of Monty?"

"Naw. He won't come tonight even if he has the gold. He'll talk to Carlos to make sure we've got you."

"Carlos won't help you. He'll tell Monty where you are."

Iris could find nothing comforting in Joe's laugh. "Carlos and me, we planned this together. You don't think he was taken in by that long-lost-brother act, do you?"

"I don't believe you. He'll help Monty."

"He couldn't if he wanted to. He doesn't know about this place."

Iris could well believe Carlos didn't know about the cabin. Joe was just the kind of person not to trust his friends. But she couldn't believe Carlos would help Joe to kidnap her. Not even for 100,000 dollars in gold.

But what did she know about Carlos? Monty had told her to be careful, to get to know him before she started to depend on him, but she hadn't listened. She had been so happy to find Carlos again, so ready to believe he wanted to restore their relationship as much as she did, she had taken him into her confidence. But she couldn't be sure he would help her instead of Joe. Setting aside the question of 100,000 dollars in gold, Carlos and Joe had been friends for a long time. They had probably faced several life-and-death situations together. Wouldn't he have a greater loyalty to Joe than to her?

Maybe, but even though half of 100,000 dollars was more than she could offer him, she didn't believe Carlos would double-cross her. She believed he did want to settle down, to make something of his life. She remembered all the evenings they had sat talking through dinner, the times they had spent planning what they would do with the ranch, the things they wanted to do when the ranch had finally begun to pay its way.

No, Carlos might have been tempted by the idea at first, but she was certain Joe was acting alone. Carlos would help Monty.

Joe's snoring broke her train of thought. He was asleep, but she knew he'd wake instantly if she tried to slip out.

She was worried about Monty. He wasn't one to stop to consider a problem carefully, especially not when he got mad. He would act and worry about the consequences later. Maybe Madison could convince him it wasn't worth risking his future to shoot Joe Reardon. No, Madison didn't look like a forgiving man. It would have to be Fern. No woman who was a wife and mother would value revenge above the safety of her family.

She just hoped Monty would listen to her.

Carlos paced the tiny cabin. After using every oath he knew at least a half-a-dozen times each, he'd concentrated on calling Joe every epithet he could think of. Finally, having exhausted his vocabulary, he consulted his feelings.

He hadn't wanted Joe to kidnap Iris. He had grown genuinely fond of Iris. He liked having a sister. He liked *her*.

He had resented her during all those years Helena had kept him from his home, but he knew it hadn't been Iris's fault. She had welcomed him without a single question about where he had been or what he'd done. She'd shown faith in him from the very first, taken his part against Monty, then divided her inheritance with him. She hadn't had to do any of those things. She'd done it because he was her brother, because she wanted some family to love, because she was too decent to inherit from a man who wasn't her father while his real son went penniless. He wondered if he would have been as generous.

Carlos felt like a heel to have even considered Joe's scheme, but now he made up his mind to do something about it. Only he didn't know where Joe had taken Iris. And for the longest time he couldn't figure out where to start looking. Then he remembered Joe had mentioned seeing an abandoned cabin on his way back from selling the remuda. Carlos didn't know where the cabin was, but he knew the route Joe had taken. If Joe had taken Iris there, he would be bound to come across their trail.

Carlos saddled quickly and rode out. He wanted to get to Joe before Monty did. He didn't really trust Joe anymore, but he owed him the chance to change his mind before one of the Randolphs killed him.

"You ought to go to bed," Madison advised Monty. "You'll want to be fresh for the morning."

"I'll be fine. Staying up all night is nothing compared to twenty-hour days in the saddle."

"She'll be all right," Fern assured her brother-in-law. "Joe can't possibly gain anything by hurting her."

"If I didn't know that, I'd be out there this minute with every man on the place." Monty heaved himself out of the chair. "I'm going for a walk."

"Iris wouldn't want you to go after that man now, and she wouldn't want you to go after him alone."

"Why?"

"Because you'll mean to kill him."

"So?"

"You'll jeopardize your future. And Iris's as well. She'd give him the money herself before she'd let that happen."

"How do you know?"

"That's what any woman would do. Her kidnapper isn't important. Neither is revenge. All she's thinking about is you. Your future together. She's praying you won't do anything to jeopardize it."

Monty was quiet for a moment. "I suppose you're right. That sounds exactly like something Rose would say. But I can't stay here."

"Want some company?" Madison asked.

"No."

"Five minutes?"

"Okay."

"Do you think he'll go after her?" Betty asked when the door closed behind the brothers.

"Of course. He wouldn't be a Randolph if he didn't," Fern answered. "I was only trying to tell him what Iris would want him to do."

"Do you think he listened?"

"I doubt it. He wouldn't be a Randolph if he did."

Monty and Madison walked in silence for three minutes. The night was cold, the sky clear. The moon and stars bathed the landscape in a cold milky whiteness that made it seem otherworldly. The gravelly soil crunched under their feet, the sound loud in the night. A horse snorted; an owl floated by on silent wings.

"Does George know you bought that ranch?" Madison asked.

"Yes. I sent him a telegram when I asked for the money."

"You didn't have to do that."

"Yeah, I did."

"Why?"

"I was complaining to Salty once, saying I didn't know why everybody was so damned worried about my temper. I said Hen went about shooting people and nobody worried about that."

"What did Salty say?"

"He said they did; they worried a lot. He said the difference was Hen didn't care what people thought of him. Salty said I did, especially George. He said it was George's approval I was trying to win, that and my own."

"Seems you've got yourself a right smart foreman there."

"Yeah, but George is never going to give total approval to anyone. He can't. It's not in him. There'll always be something more I could have done, another way I could have done it better, something I said or did that didn't fit George's sense of what was right."

"So how's your own ranch going to change that?"

"It's not, at least not for George. I won't ever be like George, and it's time I stopped trying. I'll run this place, and I'll do everything I can to please George and the rest of you, but I'm going to do what I damned well please on my own place. I don't say it'll be better, but it'll be just as good. You wait and see."

"I'm sure it will, but that's not why you're walking about in the cold at midnight."

"No. I've been trying to convince myself to be sensible, to wait until the morning. That's what George would advise. It's not what he would do, mind you, but it's what he'd tell me I ought to do. Well, I'm not going to do it, dammit. I'm going to saddle Nightmare and take to those hills. I don't know what I can do tonight, but I do know I can't wait until tomorrow. If anything were to happen to Iris and I was lying in that bed, I'd never forgive myself."

"I can't say I blame you. I remember riding into the teeth of a tornado after Fern. Looking back it seems like pure insanity, but at the time it seemed the only thing to do. However, since I'm not used to riding in these, or any other, hills at night, I'll wait for daylight. I'll meet you at the ranch house in the morning."

Madison watched his brother saddle up and ride away. He almost felt guilty for not going with him, but he hadn't decided to remain at the ranch merely to take care of Fern or because he'd been living soft for too long. He was convinced Monty wouldn't find Iris in the dark. It would be tomorrow's search that would uncover the necessary information. With Monty gone, it would be up to Madison to organize the search.

It annoyed him. He hated things like that, but he didn't blame Monty. If it had been Fern, he would have been out there if he'd had to walk.

*   *   *

Iris woke with the feeling something wasn't right. Almost immediately she remembered Joe Reardon had kidnapped her and carried her off to a cabin somewhere in the foothills, but that wasn't the source of her uneasiness. Something else was wrong, but she couldn't figure out what it was.

The snoring. It had stopped. She listened, but she couldn't hear anything, not even the sound of soft breathing. Joe was gone! He had gone to see if Monty had delivered the gold to Carlos. Fool that she was, she had believed him and gone off to sleep. She didn't know what woke her, but she was grateful.

Iris fumbled around in the dark for her boots. She had slept in her clothes. Much to her surprise the door was unsecured. She had known there was no lock, but she had expected him to prop a log against it, something to make sure she didn't escape.

Her horse! He had taken her horse thinking she wouldn't leave. That was where Joe Reardon made a mistake.

The thought of wandering about in those hills at night, even on horseback, scared her badly. Going on foot was crazy, but she wasn't about to stay here. Monty was bound to come for her soon. She must find him before he found Joe. There must not be a fight. She didn't care if Joe got away. She only cared that Monty would be safe.

Monty sat his horse in the yard at Iris's ranch. Now that he was here, what was he going to do? Carlos wasn't at home, and there was no one in the bunkhouse to tell him where he had gone. Monty glanced down at the ground outside the corral. A light frost had begun to form on the ground. When the moonlight reflected off the crystals at just the right angle, he could see the faint outline of hoof prints. One horse. It had to be Carlos. No one else would have left so late at night.

Monty followed the hoofprints. They became clearer where Carlos's horse's hooves had knocked the frost off the grass. Monty didn't know whether Carlos was helping Joe, whether he was helping Iris, or whether he was in it entirely for himself. He didn't even know if Carlos knew where to find Iris. But this was his best chance to find Iris and he would take it.

He would decide what to do about Carlos when he found him.

Iris had never been so cold in her life. She remembered snow in St. Louis, but she didn't remember being cold through to the bone. Her teeth chattered uncontrollably. She had worn a coat when she left for the Circle-7, but the day had been sunny. The coat wasn't heavy enough for the late-fall nights in Wyoming.

She hurried on, hoping that moving about would keep her from being so cold. She followed a faint trail along the base of the foothills to the Laramie Mountains. She didn't know where it led, but she felt certain if she followed it she would come to some ranch. Besides, Monty was more likely to follow a trail than just head out across trackless hills. Wyoming wasn't nearly as flat as Kansas and Nebraska, but its wide open spaces seemed as limitless as Texas.

A heart-stopping roar stopped Iris dead in her tracks. Ahead of her, a grizzly bear stood atop its kill, its fur smeared with blood, its long gleaming fangs bared in a bone-chilling snarl. It didn't seem the least bit happy Iris had interrupted its meal.

Looking frantically around, Iris saw a small lodgepole pine less than five yards away. Its branches reached down to the ground. She ran to the tree, dived among the branches, and started climbing as quickly as she could. She had climbed about 12 feet when she heard the snarl directly beneath her. The bear had reared up against the tree, its fangs still bared in a vicious snarl.

The lodgepole pine had grown up into the branches of a towering Douglas fir. Afterward Iris was never able to explain how she had crossed from one tree to the next, but when she saw the bear begin to climb the pine, she knew it was her only escape. Hoisting herself onto the thick branch, Iris crawled along it until she reached the trunk of the fir. She quickly climbed higher.

The bear apparently decided it was too hungry to pursue Iris just now. It left the smaller tree and went back to its meal. But every now and then it would stop eating, look up at Iris, and snarl, as though in warning she should not come down.

It needn't have bothered. Iris had no intention of leaving her perch.

Chapter Twenty-six

Joe cursed aloud as he rode back to the cabin; he whipped his horse across the shoulders to wring every ounce of speed from the tired animal. Where the hell was Carlos? Why hadn't he been waiting for him at the ranch house? He had told Iris he wasn't going to the ranch tonight, but he had really expected Monty to bring the gold today. He had expected Carlos to be there waiting for him. Now, as he hurried back to the cabin, he thought about Carlos's change of heart. But he couldn't believe Carlos would side against him, not as long as Carlos knew Joe could send him back to New Mexico on a murder charge.

But where was he? Carlos didn't know the location of the cabin. Maybe he had gone with the Randolphs to fetch the gold. If so, he should have left a message. It occurred to Joe as an unpleasant afterthought that, if Carlos did get the gold, there was nothing to stop him from taking off with the whole amount. He had been ready to cheat Carlos. Why wouldn't Carlos be just as ready to cheat him?

Cursing anew, Joe turned onto the path leading to the cabin. He hadn't gone 50 yards before he saw the cabin door standing open. Iris had escaped. Joe threw himself from his horse, but he already knew what he would find. The cabin was empty. Racing back outside, Joe mounted up. She couldn't have gone very far on foot in the dark. He would find her and bring her back. Then he would figure out what to do about that stinking bastard Carlos.

He headed off, taking a well-marked trail that led across the foothills several hundred yards below the faint game trail farther up.

Monty heard the bear from a long distance away. The animal sounded enraged. That was what started Monty thinking. A bear might be doing any number of things, even stalking its dinner, but it wouldn't be snarling like that unless it was threatened. He listened carefully. He didn't hear a second bear, just one. Nothing else could cause a bear to roar like that.

Nothing except man.

Monty looked down the trail. Carlos's tracks still led ahead, but somebody must be up there. From the way the bear was snarling, whoever it was might be in need of help.

Monty listened, but he heard no further sounds. Whatever had disturbed the bear was gone. He started down the trail once more, but as he came closer to the part of the hill where he thought the sound had come from, he became more and more curious. Maybe Carlos had changed trails somewhere ahead and doubled back. If Monty changed trails now, he could catch up with him sooner.

Maybe the bear had been angered about something else and Carlos was still ahead on the lower trail. Monty decided to check out the upper trail. He could always come back to the first one. He hurried along until he found a place in the hillside that looked gradual enough for his horse to climb. Nightmare snorted his objection, but he went up the trail without any difficulty. By the time Monty reached the dim game trail, all was quiet.

Monty pulled his rifle from its scabbard and started back along the trail, his eyes alert, searching the night for hidden danger.

Almost immediately he came upon the remains of a mule deer. The bear was nowhere in sight. Apparently the animal had decided the carcass wasn't worth the chance of a further encounter with humans. Monty looked around to make certain the animal wasn't hiding in a thicket, but except for a lodgepole pine ahead, there was no growth at ground level capable of hiding a full-grown bear.

Nightmare was restless but not snorting and dancing nervously as he would if he smelled a bear nearby. Monty dismounted, but close inspection of the trail showed no tracks except those of the bear. Carlos hadn't come this way.

Monty climbed back into the saddle and turned Nightmare around.

"Monty!"

The sound riveted him in his tracks. Iris!

"Monty!"

Monty looked around, searching for Iris's hiding place, but he couldn't see anything. The sound seemed to come from the heavens, but he had to be imagining things. There was nothing angelic about that urgent cry for help. Maybe Madison was right. Maybe he was overly tired and in need of a good night's sleep.

"I'm up here in this tree!"

"Which tree?" Monty asked, looking around, certain he was becoming delirious.

"The one with all the branches."

They all seemed remarkably full of branches to Monty and equally empty of Iris.

"Here," she called.

Monty worked his way toward the voice, staring up into the treetops all the while. A dead limb hit the ground a little way in front of him. Looking up he thought he saw a scrap of dark blue cloth. He rode close to the tree. "Where are you?" he called.

"Up here."

Monty craned his neck until he could look straight up the tree. Then he saw her, holding to the trunk of the Douglas fir about 50 feet above the ground.

"How the hell did you get up there?"

"The bear."

"Where's your horse?"

"Joe took it with him. I came on foot."

Monty decided Iris was completely unsuited for life as a rancher's wife. Between her penchant for walking among longhorns and surprising grizzlies in the middle of their dinner, she would give him gray hair inside a year.

He couldn't wait to get her down from that tree and kiss away all her fears.

"You can come on down. The bear's gone."

"I can't."

"What do you mean, you can't?"

"I'm scared to let go."

Monty's instinctive response was to order Iris to come down immediately. Anyone who could climb up a tree could also climb down. But even as he opened his mouth to shout the order, it occurred to him Iris had been chased by a bear when she climbed that tree. Driven by fear, she probably had no idea what she was doing until she stopped and found herself 50 feet in the air. She probably didn't know how to climb down because she didn't know how she had managed to climb up. Now she was petrified.

Monty had never been 50 feet up a tree. He figured he might be scared, too. But unless he climbed up to get her, it looked as if Iris was going to grow old holding onto that tree trunk.

"How did you get up there?" Monty asked. "This tree doesn't have any lower branches."

"I climbed the one next to it and crossed over."

Monty whistled in awe. He wished Zac were here. Zac was the one who liked climbing trees. Monty didn't really feel comfortable on anything higher than a horse.

Monty climbed the lower branches of the lodgepole. The tree didn't seem so sturdy to him. It was one thing for Iris, who weighed barely more than 100 pounds, to climb this tree. It was quite different when he attempted it with his 220 pounds of bone and muscle. By the time he reached the lowest branch of the Douglas fir, he was getting shaky himself.

Monty managed to cross over to the fir. He looked up. Iris seemed just as far above him as when he was on the ground. "Can't you come down any?"

"No."

Monty could understand. The higher he climbed, the more uncomfortable he became. But Iris was above him. He had to get her down.

Iris looked down as Monty laboriously climbed toward her, and her heart overflowed with love for this man who would unhesitatingly climb a tree for her. She could tell he didn't like it a bit. He kept looking at the ground and then up at her as if he couldn't believe they were each so far from where he was. Yet he continued climbing, keeping up a steady stream of encouragement.

She wondered if she would ever be able to do the same thing for him. It seemed she could only cause trouble. That was all she'd ever been, from the day she fell in love with him at 14 until this very minute. That was all she was now, sitting up in this tree like a fool, so afraid she couldn't move. Yet he had unhesitatingly climbed up the lodgepole pine even though she wondered at times if it could hold his weight.

Monty didn't deserve a sniveling coward for a wife. She might be a foolish and useless female—though she intended to change that—but she wasn't going to be a coward. If she had climbed up this tree by herself, and her present position was ample proof that she had, she could get down. Monty might think it was heroic to rescue her this time, but he wasn't the type to be forever pulling somebody out of the soup. One day he just might decide to leave her be.

It took an act of faith for Iris to loosen her hold enough to allow her foot to slide down to the branch below. Nothing in her entire life had taken half as much courage as it took to dangle her foot in space until it finally came to rest on the branch below. Heaving a tremendous sigh of relief, Iris moved down the tree. Bark scraped her cheek, the smell of resin filled her nostrils, but she kept moving.

"Stay where you are," Monty called. "I'm coming to get you."

"I'm coming down," Iris called back. She kept moving. If she stopped, she doubted she would be able to start again.

They met 35 feet above the ground.

"Ouch!" Monty yelped when Iris put a foot down on his fingers. But Iris didn't slow down. Monty moved to the opposite side of the tree trunk, and Iris practically fell the rest of the way until she felt his arms close around her. It was the most awkward embrace of her life, each of them holding onto a limb, the trunk and branches between them, but Iris doubted any kiss would ever be more important to her than this one.

"If George could see me now, he'd swear I had lost my mind," Monty said.

Iris laughed, relief, joy, giddy happiness all mixed up in the sound. "We both are. There can't be two people in the whole world any more unsuited for each other."

"And trying to kiss up a tree."

Monty held her close with one arm and kissed her once more. "Now let's get down from here. I want to do this right."

Carlos and Joe spotted each other at the same time. Carlos spurred his horse forward; Joe pulled up.

"Where have you taken Iris?"

"What have you done with the gold?"

"There is no gold. Madison said it was just a rumor they've been trying to kill for years. Now tell me what you've done with Iris. If I can get her back before dawn, you may come out of this with a whole skin."

"How do I know you haven't made a deal of your own? How do I know you don't already have the gold?"

"If I had the gold, do you think I'd be wasting my time riding about in the woods at night?"

"You sure as hell would. If you took Randolph gold, they'd kill you unless you gave them Iris."

"I don't have any gold, and I haven't made any deal. Now show me where you hid Iris."

"No."

Carlos leveled a hard look at his friend. "I told you I'd share everything with you."

"I don't trust you anymore. You've gotten soft. You've gotten scared. You don't have the guts to go for the big score anymore. You're willing to settle for a piece of some two-bit ranch that'll keep you working your ass off for the rest of your life."

"I haven't gone yellow, Joe. I just don't want to live on the run anymore. You don't think anybody, much less the Randolphs, would give you a hundred thousand dollars and just forget about it, do you? You'd be a hunted man, Joe. With Hen Randolph on your trail, you'd be dead inside a month."

"I'll take my chances."

"It wouldn't be a chance. It would be a dead certainty. Come on, Joe, tell me where you took Iris. You know I won't forget what you did for me."

"It's too late now. Those Randolphs aren't going to let me turn over Iris and go on living here like we're the best of friends."

"You may have to go away for a while, but you can come back. I don't expect they'll stay here once they get that ranch going."

"You don't understand, Carlos. I don't want to be chasing after cows for the rest of my life, not for you, not for me, not when I can get enough money to live easy. It won't matter if there ain't no gold. Those Randolphs got enough money to pay plenty."

"I'm not going to let you do it, Joe. She's my sister." Carlos rode forward. He didn't know exactly what he was going to do, but he expected Joe would give in to a show of force. There was no point in going on. Joe's only hope was to give up Iris and hope the Randolphs wouldn't hold a grudge for very long.

Carlos couldn't believe it when Joe drew his gun. He couldn't believe it when he saw Joe point it at him. He still couldn't believe it when he felt the searing pain in his chest, felt himself falling from the saddle. The last thing he remembered was being facedown on a prickly carpet of needles as Joe took his horse and rode away.

Then he believed it.

Monty had just reached the ground when a gunshot nearby shattered the night. He grabbed Nightmare's reins to keep the skittish animal from running away. It wouldn't do for both Iris and him to be without a mount.

"What was that?" Iris asked, as she fell out of the lodgepole pine into Monty's arms.

"A gunshot," Monty said, setting her on her feet.

"I mean, who could it have been?"

"I don't know, but it must be Carlos or Joe. Carlos wasn't at the ranch when I got there. And Joe must have left you to go do something."

"Do you suppose they met each other?"

"I don't know, but we'd better find out."

Monty put his hands around Iris's waist and lifted her into the saddle. She didn't know how he could do it so effortlessly. Her shoulders and arms ached from holding onto the tree; the rough bark had rubbed her hands raw. Monty acted as though he hadn't done anything.

Monty vaulted into the saddle behind her. "Hang on. It's going to be a rough ride down the slope."

It turned out to be easier than she expected. They didn't have far to travel before they came to the spot where Carlos had fallen.

"Is he dead?" Iris asked.

Monty jumped down. He placed his hands on Carlos's neck. "He's still alive."

"We've got to get him to a doctor," Iris said. "This is all my fault. He would never have been hurt if he hadn't tried to help me. Will he be all right?"

"I can't say until I know how badly he's hurt." Monty turned him over. "He was shot in the chest. Do you see his horse? We've got to get him back to the ranch as soon as possible."

Iris looked around. "It must have run off."

"Or Reardon took it," Monty said. "Get down. You'll have to help me lift him into the saddle."

It took both their efforts and they still nearly didn't manage it.

"Now climb up behind him," Monty said. "You're going to have to hold him in the saddle while I lead Nightmare."

Iris did as Monty said, but she was scared it was going to be a useless effort. Carlos was unconscious. It was all she could do to keep him from falling out of the saddle. She could feel the warm, sticky blood where it had soaked through Carlos's shirt. Ignoring the sickly feeling in the pit of her stomach, she put pressure on the wound to slow the bleeding.

"This is going to be a long walk," Monty said. "I wish we could find his horse."

They hadn't gone very far when they saw a horse on the trail in front of them.

"There's Carlos's horse," Iris cried. "His reins got caught in that bush."

But even as Monty started forward he felt something was wrong. About 20 yards away he knew what it was. The horse's reins weren't caught in the bush. They were tied. Reardon had to be watching them this very minute.

"Reardon's here somewhere," Monty hissed. "He probably has a rifle on us this very minute. Don't move unless I tell you."

"How do you know?"

"The reins. They're tied, not caught."

Monty kept walking forward. He didn't know what Joe had in mind, but he needed that horse.

"Where's the gold, Randolph?"

The voice came out of the woods somewhere above them, but Monty didn't look for it. He kept walking toward the horse.

"There is no gold," Monty said. "There never was any."

"You're lying," Joe called as Monty reached for the reins of Carlos's horse. "I saw it."

"You saw a few hundred dollars, not the hundred thousand dollars you want."

"Don't touch that horse," Joe said, but he was too late. Monty had already untied the reins. "You're not leaving here until I get the gold."

"It wouldn't do you any good if I gave it to you," Monty said. "I'd just have to kill you. I can't let anybody steal anything from me, not gold, women, or cattle. If one man gets away with it, others will try. I wouldn't have any choice."

"Maybe you'd try, but maybe you wouldn't succeed." Joe didn't sound as confident as a minute ago.

Monty prepared to mount up. "You'd better forget about this whole thing, Reardon. If Carlos gets well, we might let you off." Monty swung into the saddle.

"Stop, or I'll shoot!" Joe stepped from behind a tree trunk about 100 feet up the slope. "You're not going anywhere. Now get down off that horse, or I'll blast you out of the saddle."

What would have happened next no one would ever know. A bloodcurdling roar shattered the night, and the grizzly bear erupted from a thicket just a few yards up the slope from Joe. Gripped by pure terror, Joe whirled and fired at the charging bear. He managed to get off a second shot before the great beast reached him.

Iris hid her face in Carlos's back. Monty walked the horses a short distance away.

"Wait here," he said after the woods were once again silent. He was gone only a few minutes. When he returned, he was leading Iris's horse as well as Joe's.

"What happened?" Iris asked.

"He got the grizzly, but the bear got him as well."

Chapter Twenty-seven

"We're not going to have the wedding until you're well," Iris told Carlos. "I want you to give me away." They had brought Carlos to the Circle-7 ranch. Fern was only too happy to give up her morning nap so he could have a bed.

"It'll also give George and Rose time to get here from Texas," Madison said, grinning at Fern. "You wouldn't want to tie the knot without the approval of the head of the clan."

"Stop it, you'll scare the poor girl to death," Fern told him. "He's really quite nice," she said to Iris. "If he can approve of me, you ought to pass with flying colors."

"It's Rose I'm afraid of," Iris confessed. "According to Monty, she never does anything wrong."

"Rose is the dearest person in the world," Fern assured Iris. "She was the first friend I ever had. I have to admit she is practically perfect, but you'll love her anyway."

"And if you don't, you'll be living two thousand miles away," Madison said, "so it won't matter."

Fern gouged her husband in the side. He responded by laughing and putting his arm around her.

"Rose thinks all the boys ought to be married, so she'll welcome you into the family with open arms," Fern told Iris. "Just remember one thing. George is the most important person in her world. Do anything to make him unhappy and she'll cut your heart out. Otherwise she'll love you with her whole heart."

"What a terrible thing to say," Madison told his wife.

"No, I understand," Iris said. "Nothing else you've said has made me like her so much. Except the story about losing that baby."

"Rose will never be happy until she has at least one more child," Fern said. "Maybe I'll give her my next one," she said, turning to her husband. "This monster told me I didn't have to have any children if I didn't want to. Before I could say *well, maybe*, I was expecting. You'd think two rambunctious boys would be enough, wouldn't you? It was easier to keep track of a whole herd of cows."

"They're too much like their mother," Madison said, giving Fern a squeeze. "They're never happy unless they're in the saddle."

"That's one problem I won't have," Iris said, looking a little wistfully at Monty. "Monty doesn't want children."

"We don't know that," Monty said. "Everything's happened so fast I don't know what I want. It might be children, but right now a purebred Angus bull would come in handy."

Iris pulled Monty outside to protect him from Fern's vigorous attack.

"I probably will want some boys to help with the ranch," Monty said. He sat down on the steps. Iris settled next to him, her arm in his, her shoulder leaning into his embrace, her red hair in stark contrast to his blond fairness. "It would be cheaper to hire four or five hands, but sons would make the relatives happy."

"I think Wyoming would be a great place to rear your sons," Iris said, an impish gleam in her green eyes. "They'll have plenty of natural playmates. There must be at least a hundred bears, panthers, and wild bulls on the place."

Monty bit Iris's ear.

"Of course they'll wear nothing but buckskins and moccasins. There're plenty of stones lying about to make weapons."

Monty nibbled her neck.

"There must be at least one cave in those hills where they can live. I wonder if they'll draw on the walls?"

Monty nibbled at Iris's lower lip.

"But I don't know what we'll do with them if Rose and George come to visit."

"Send them to Colorado," Monty muttered between nibbles on Iris's upper lip. "They've got even more caves and bears down there."

Iris laughed. "Be serious. Do you want a family?"

"Probably, but right now I'm content with you."

Iris shivered with pleasure. Monty was doing fantastic things to her ear. "Are you sure? I know I'm not the kind of wife you wanted."

"I didn't want a wife of any kind."

"I'll never learn to cook like Tyler, and I can't keep house like Betty."

"Then it's a good thing I don't expect it."

His kisses along her neck made her want to melt into his arms.

"And I'll probably disagree with you fairly often."

"I love a good fight."

He kissed the back of her neck. Iris had to push him away or disgrace herself right there on the steps.

"I'll want to go wherever you go. I don't want to stay home and make beds."

"I'll build you a new travel wagon. Then we won't have to make love in the brush."

Monty attempted to undo the top button on her shirt, but Iris removed his hand.

"We're not going to make love on the steps either, so you might as well sit up and behave yourself."

"Only if you tell me you don't love me."

"I could never tell you that."

Monty attacked Iris. She responded with a shriek.

Inside the cabin, Fern looked up. "Do you think I ought to go out there?"

"No."

Fern started to rise from her chair.

"Don't go near the window either."

"I don't trust Monty not to take advantage of her right there on the porch."

"There'll be nothing but cows to see if he does." Madison slipped his arm around his wife and scattered kisses on her cheek. "Besides, I think he's got a great idea. There's more than one bedroom in this house."

"You're hopeless," Fern said. "All of you Randolph men are hopeless."

"I know, but we're cute."

"But I'm pregnant," Fern protested.

Madison pulled his wife toward the bedroom. "Yes, but not very much."

They sat on the porch, their arms around each other, staring at the sunset. It wasn't anything spectacular, just an ordinary orange streaked with blue, but it seemed wonderful to Iris.

"Do you mind if I give Carlos the ranch?" she asked.

"I thought you had."

"Only half. I mean the whole thing."

"Sure. Why?"

"Robert Richmond wasn't my father, but he gave me a name. This is the only way I can pay him back."

Monty started to chuckle. "And after all the trouble it took to get that herd here."

"Hmmm, it was a lot of work wasn't it?"

"Never noticed it."

Iris punched Monty. He chuckled softly.

They sat quietly for a while. Then Iris started to laugh.

"Do you realize how desperate I was to hang on to that herd? Now I've gone and given it away. I'm penniless, the one thing I feared most in all the world." She laughed again. "I'm just as crazy as you Randolphs."

"Welcome home," Monty said and kissed her softly.

Author's Note
Cattle Trails

American farmers have been driving their cattle to market ever since Colonial days. That didn't change even when the cattle growing area moved to the Midwest. In 1845, young John T. Alexander trailed 250 Illinois cattle all the way to Boston. During the 1850s Isaac Funk bought cattle in Texas and trailed them to Illinois for fattening. During the same decade, Texans trailed herds east to New Orleans, north to Missouri, and west to the California gold fields. But it wasn't until after the Civil War practically made the millions of wild cattle in Texas a natural resource that trailing herds of longhorns to market became a phenomenon of national interest.

The first trail north from Texas was the Shawnee Trail. Following a route used by Indians and immigrants, it was in use as early as the 1840s. It passed through Austin, Waco, and Dallas and crossed the

Red River at Rock Bluff Crossing. It passed through eastern Oklahoma Territory, turned east at the junction of the Oklahoma, Kansas, and Missouri borders, and headed for St. Louis. The trail was effectively closed in 1866 by quarantine laws aimed at keeping tic fever out of Kansas and Missouri.

In 1866 Goodnight and Loving established a trail that went directly west from the headwaters of the Concho River through 80 miles of dry country until it hit the Pecos River. From there it trailed north through eastern New Mexico to Colorado and Wyoming.

Cattle drives up the Chisholm Trail, the most famous of all the cattle trails, began in 1867. The trail passed from Waco to Fort Worth through the center of the Oklahoma Territory to the cattle markets of Kansas. Half the cattle that left Texas during the years of 1867–85 followed this route. Estimates of the number of cattle passing over this trail exceed 500,000 in some years. At times as many as 15 herds could be seen at one time. Once 60 herds backed up waiting to cross a rain-swollen river.

The western trail opened around 1876 and trailed through Abilene, Texas, to Dodge, Kansas, and north to Ogallala, Nebraska. This trail was used by Western cattlemen with herds going to the new grazing lands in Wyoming and Montana.

The trails were closed in the 1880s by the westward movement of settlers and the spread of railroads.

LEIGH GREENWOOD

"Leigh Greenwood is a dynamo of a storyteller!"
—Los Angeles Times

Jefferson Randolph has never forgotten all he lost in the War Between The States—or forgiven those he has fought. Long after most of his six brothers find wedded bliss, the former Rebel soldier keeps himself buried in work, only dreaming of one day marrying a true daughter of the South. Then a run-in with a Yankee schoolteacher teaches him that he has a lot to learn about passion.

Violet Goodwin is too refined and genteel for an ornery bachelor like Jeff. Yet before he knows it, his disdain for Violet is blossoming into desire. But Jeff fears that love alone isn't enough to help him put his past behind him—or to convince a proper lady that she can find happiness as the newest bride in the rowdy Randolph clan.

_3995-8 $6.99 US/$8.99 CAN

LEIGH GREENWOOD'S

SEVEN BRIDES

Laurel

Although Hen Randolph is the perfect choice for a sheriff in the Arizona Territory, he is no one's idea of a model husband. After the trail-weary cowboy breaks free from his six rough-and-ready brothers, he isn't about to start a family of his own. Then a beauty with a tarnished reputation catches his eye and the thought of taking a wife arouses him as never before.

But Laurel Blackthorne has been hurt too often to trust any man—least of all one she considers a ruthless, coldhearted gunslinger. Not until Hen proves that drawing quickly and shooting true aren't his only assets will she give him her heart and take her place as the newest bride to tame a Randolph's heart.

_3744-0 $6.99 US/$8.99 CAN

SEVEN BRIDES:
DAISY

LEIGH GREENWOOD

The state of Texas isn't big enough for Tyler Randolph and his six rough-and-ready brothers. So the rugged loner sets off for New Mexico in search of a lost mine. He is out to find gold in them thar hills, but he strikes the real mother lode when he rescues a feisty and independent beauty from the wilderness. Attacked, shot, and left for dead, Daisy is horrified to wake up in Tyler's cabin. Then a blizzard traps them together, and she is convinced that the mountain man is a fourteen-carat cad—until his unpolished charm claims her love. Before long, Daisy is determined to do some digging of her own to unearth the treasures hidden in Tyler's heart.

___4742-X $6.99 US/$8.99 CAN

LEIGH GREENWOOD

The Reluctant Bride

Colorado Territory, 1872: A rough-and-tumble place and time almost as dangerous as the men who left civilization behind, driven by a desire for a new life. In a false-fronted town where the only way to find a decent woman is to send away for her, Tanzy first catches sight of the man she came west to marry galloping after a gang of bandits. Russ Tibbolt is a far cry from the husband she expected when she agreed to become a mail-order bride. He is much too compelling for any woman's peace of mind. With his cobalt-blue eyes and his body's magic, how can she hope to win the battle of wills between them?